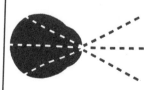

This Large Print Book carries the
Seal of Approval of N.A.V.H.

No Less Days

NO LESS DAYS

AMANDA G. STEVENS

THORNDIKE PRESS
A part of Gale, a Cengage Company

GALE
A Cengage Company

Farmington Hills, Mich • San Francisco • New York • Waterville, Maine
Meriden, Conn • Mason, Ohio • Chicago

Copyright © 2018 by Amanda G. Stevens.

Unless otherwise indicated, all scripture quotations are taken from The Holy Bible, English Standard Version®, copyright © 2001 by Crossway Bibles, a publishing ministry of Good News Publishers. Used by permission. All rights reserved.

Scripture quotations marked KJV are taken from the King James Version of the Bible.

Thorndike Press, a part of Gale, a Cengage Company.

Thorndike Press® Large Print Christian Mystery.

The text of this Large Print edition is unabridged.

Other aspects of the book may vary from the original edition.

Set in 16 pt. Plantin.

LIBRARY OF CONGRESS CIP DATA ON FILE.
CATALOGUING IN PUBLICATION FOR THIS BOOK
IS AVAILABLE FROM THE LIBRARY OF CONGRESS

ISBN-13: 978-1-4328-5287-0 (hardcover)

Published in 2018 by arrangement with Barbour Publishing, Inc.

Printed in the United States of America
1 2 3 4 5 6 7 22 21 20 19 18

*Now unto the King
eternal,
immortal,
invisible,
the only wise God,
be honour and glory for ever and ever.
Amen.*
1 TIMOTHY 1:17 KJV

est chair, a wobbly o
for a child's height. I
knees poking up, ar
chest. He could lectu
reaction or he coul
someday he'd believe
ous. Candles weren't
have to be followed
zling skin, where skir

A third option did
that a century of ov
strong indication he

However, he wasn'
man.

The bell chimed ov
stood. An apology r
had to think him ne

Tiana set the burr
lid off, cleaned out,
one hip against the
plaid work shirt. "Y
some incense as a ki

"Exactly that."

Her head tilt said
Good for her.

"And what tone di

"You know. The I
happy tone. You d
when you do, it thu

"I don't want fire

ONE

His books were burning.

He let the glass door slam behind him and charged into the shop. The smell of smoke wafted around him. Where was the fire? He turned a circle at the bookcases in the front. The new books, not burning. In the back then — old books there. Irreplaceable books. He barreled up the two steps to the main landing and darted down the nearest aisle, sci-fi on one side and Westerns on the other. Save them all, hundreds of them, open a window and pitch them outside if necessary, and it would be necessary. Fire didn't hesitate, didn't sate itself, didn't tire. His scalp prickled.

The smell was fainter back here. He headed along the back wall, boots tracking rain over the old green carpet. No flames. No visible smoke.

"I hope that's you, David." The voice drifted from the children's shelves.

7

"Tiana." He deto[...]
smell almost disa[...]
find it first. Strong[...]
that way and call[...]
thing's burning."

"Um, no?"

"Yes."

"I promise, there[...]
her head into the [...]
lowed him. "Are y[...]
cense?"

David halted [...]
"Your . . . what?"

"Behind the coun[...]

He stepped over [...]
and then behind it, [...]
him, infiltrated his [...]
The burner was a s[...]
the color of a robin[...]
through holes in th[...]
vid backed into the [...]

"Get rid of that t[...]

"It's perfectly safe[...]

"Tiana, get it out[...]

"Okay." She shuff[...]
edged over to give [...]
tone."

She grabbed a bl[...]
have brought from [...]
burner outside. Da[...]

"There was no actual fire in the burner."

"Smoke isn't good for them either."

A long look, and then she shrugged. "Jayde wanted to come by after classes tomorrow and start training, if you're good with that."

"Of course."

"She's like you about books. She'll want to touch all the first editions and have a moment of communing with literary history."

A laugh filled his chest. "Appropriate for a lit major. Is her track American?"

"Yeah. Mid-nineteenth century is her area of interest."

"Civil War?"

"The whole thing. Popular fiction of the time, slave narratives, Underground Railroad, Reconstruction. Apparently people made time to read even in conflict like that."

David leaned against the shelf behind him and crossed his arms. "It's only recently that people don't make time to read."

"Oh, here we go." She smirked.

"Digital distribution cheapens everything," he said. And reclaiming esteem for the written word would require something universal. A blackout, perhaps. Some days David enjoyed the possibility — the death of digital, the forced return to reading paper, no more screens.

10

"And while you rail against it, some of my friends who would never read a physical book are addicted to their Kindles."

That was always her argument. And she wasn't wrong. Still, he wished people valued books — paper, ink, effort, art, knowledge — the way they used to.

He pushed away from the bookcase. "So you want to give me another of your Sunday afternoons?"

"No other plans." Tiana shrugged. "Show me the haul."

He stepped outside and held the door for her, and she let him. She pointed to a patch of dirt to one side of the entrance, smudged with a dark-gray stain.

"Look at that. The big bad pile of ashes already got rained away."

David sighed. Tiana walked around the building to the rear parking lot where he kept his work van. He opened the doors, and she clasped her hands in front of her. Boxes of books filled the van all the way to the front seats. He'd long since removed the back ones.

"How many trips will you need?"

"This is the whole lot."

"It's a lot of a lot."

"And a steal of a lot. Five dollars per box."

They both leaned into the van, reached

11

for a box at the same time. Their arms could have brushed but didn't. He'd never know if she was deliberate about things like that. The way he was.

They kept the boxes shut and hunched over them to protect the books, but the rain had slowed to a light mist. They each made over a dozen trips from the van to the store and back again, quiet while they worked until David brought in the last box. Tiana had already opened several.

"Aw, look at all the children's books. Can I read some?"

"It's Sunday."

"But you're paying me."

"And I owe you two years of breaks."

She sat cross-legged on the floor and pulled one of the boxes to her side. "*Make Way for Ducklings.* Do you know this one?"

"It's a classic."

She didn't bother to throw sarcasm at him. The illustrations had already captivated her.

The afternoon passed like a few heartbeats. They unpacked and inventoried like treasure hunters, which they were, and the pleasure of discovery filled the air around them. Then Tiana glared over David's shoulder at the regulator clock on the wall, ticking all this time beneath their voices.

"I hate that it's already after five," she said.

Could it be? He turned. 5:37p.m. David rose and stretched. "Should I have been keeping track?"

"Of time? You? Right."

Tiana slid a nearly new illustrated children's edition of *The Red Pony* back into a beaten cardboard slipcase. A 1945 edition unless he missed his guess. Not a rarity, but not a common find either. David blinked. Right. Emerge from the books, give her his focus, try not to prove her crooked smile was justified.

"I do have to go," Tiana said, "but while I'm thinking about it, are you going on vacation next month?"

Caution settled on his shoulders. "Why do you ask?"

"Seems to be your habit."

"Two consecutive years doesn't make a habit."

"Three pretty much does." She pushed to her feet. "I noticed while I was looking at the inventory logs from three years back. You didn't acquire or sell anything the first two weeks of October."

He'd hired her for her attention to detail. He couldn't scowl at it now. He went to the coatrack behind the long counter and shrugged into his trench coat, dug his keys from a pocket. Time to lock up, eat, head home.

"I'd just like to know if I'll be off work a few weeks."

"I know," he said. "And yes, I'll probably be away next month, but I can't give you a date yet."

"September's almost over."

He forced a smile. "Call me spontaneous."

Tiana grabbed her purple peacoat and followed him outside, watched as he locked the store. The rain had stopped, but the clouds overhead guaranteed this was only a temporary reprieve.

She looked up at him, coat buttoned to her throat, breeze riffling her hair. "So you'll do what you did last year. No planning, just call me the day you leave and the day you're back."

"Most likely, yes."

"You're very frustrating sometimes."

No arguing that.

"And I'll see you tomorrow."

She rambled across the parking lot, crunching fallen leaves, zigzagging her stride to step on as many as possible. Her legs were long, lean muscle defined by the slim-fit jeans above her cowboy boots. Her two-inch-long hair flared out from her head in black coils. Her skin was deep umber and smooth. Two years of knowing her, and the sight of her only grew dearer to him. It could be a problem, if he were the kind of man to let it.

She saluted him before ducking inside her little khaki-colored Ford. He returned the gesture.

Then he walked. The wind still tasted like a storm, and the gray clouds overhead weren't empty yet, but his coat was resistant. Only two miles home, and he'd walked to the store early this morning. The damp promise of rain had blown through his hair and filled his nostrils, his mouth as he drank the air with his head back. He did it again now, his lungs glad for each deep breath. Satisfied. However long he lived in Michigan — ten years or less, of course — he'd enjoy each change of season.

Another block, and he stopped at the family-owned sandwich shop on the corner. He stepped in and scuffed puddles from the soles of his boots.

Bobby, the owner's youngest son, grinned at him from behind the counter. "The usual?"

"To go."

David had tasted every sandwich on their menu before settling into his rut. He waited only minutes for Bobby to hand over a white paper bag with the receipt stapled over the fold.

"North Atlantic cod on grilled ciabatta and cream of asparagus soup."

"Thanks, Bobby."

"Have a good night, Mr. Galloway."

The sky began to spit again, speckling the restaurant bag, as he traversed the last mile home. A few hundred feet from his door, the clouds gave in altogether. He tramped through the downpour, drew up his collar around his neck. He unlocked the door and squinted up at the heavens, let the drops fall through his hair, into his mouth and the creases around his eyes. He blinked the rain away. Water, one thing that was always older than he was.

He went inside and shut the door, shed his coat, had dinner sitting at the desk in his library. Shivered a few times, but he couldn't begrudge the rain when he'd chosen to walk in it.

He should catch up on news. He opened his computer and settled into his overstuffed chair, feet propped on the leather ottoman. At his favored news site, he clicked headlines. World. Local. National. He read the stories. Heaviness fell on his shoulders. Accidents and crimes. Terror and war. Suffering.

16

Nothing changed. Or rather, nothing improved.

He closed his eyes and leaned his head back.

One story of kindness. One, and he'd stop reading. He opened his eyes and searched.

Breaking story. Happened today around noon. DAREDEVIL ATTEMPTS TO CROSS GRAND CANYON, FALLS TO DEATH.

Don't go there. Don't.

He clicked the link.

A man's grinning face filled the top of the screen — white guy, blond, keen blue eyes, no older than thirty. Zachary Wilson. The article called him "popular," but David had never heard of him.

Then again, David ignored entertainment news.

A daring stunt. No net, no harness. Unexpected winds. The body hadn't been recovered yet.

David set the laptop aside and surged to his feet. He tried to work his jaw, but his teeth were locked. He stopped at his cherry-wood bookcase and braced his hands on a low shelf, let his shoulders cave under the weight of everything he'd just read, absorbed it, every life that had been ended today. He straightened and pressed his palm to the spines of his books. Ran a thumb over

17

his first editions of *Vanity Fair* and *War and Peace*.

He scrubbed one hand through black hair that gave no sign of thinning or graying, over a face he'd worn for two lifetimes — strong cheekbones, straight nose, no wrinkles. He sank back into his chair, using muscles and bones and joints that refused to wear out.

That man, Zachary Wilson. Such a long fall . . . it would be a kind of soaring, if he'd closed his eyes. No way to live through it, so nothing to dread really. Only open space and gravity, molecules of air rushing past faster than lungs could breathe them in. Maybe he had tucked his limbs in and rolled; maybe he held his arms tight against his body and dove as if he'd meant to do this thing. Or he'd flailed and screamed as if those actions would slow his descent.

David should go there. Should dive into the wind. Find a place with no witnesses, of course, but . . . he'd never fallen as far as this man had today. Why not discover how it felt?

He shook his head. Recovery wouldn't be worth it.

He stared at his books and tried not to let his imagination burn pictures into his brain. What his own body would look like after a crash like that. What Zachary Wilson's corpse looked like right now. He kneaded his jaw and sat forward, elbows on his knees.

Stupid, stupid children, believing they would never die.

He couldn't simmer here in his chair all night. A man had sacrificed himself in search of a rush. Men died worse deaths, though few for more pointless reasons. David stood and left his books behind. He stepped into the backyard barefoot. No point in soaking his shoes.

He'd sleep out here in the tent tonight, free of walls and processed air. Few things calmed him as well as rain pattering on canvas. He sat on the back steps, concrete chilling his thighs, and peered through the drizzling dusk toward the two-foot pen he'd built against the side of the house, a hexagon of stacked two-by-fours.

The smell of wet soil filled his senses, and drops pattered in his hair, on his shoulders. Inside the pen, dandelions, hostas, ferns, and strawberry plants bobbed in the soft impact of the rain. Nothing else moved.

"Fine, don't come out. Wait until the rain stops, though you've much sturdier protection than I."

He knew better than to believe in any attachment on the turtle's part. Half the time she never poked her head from where she hid. Tonight she eased into the open from under an old log he'd set in her pen years ago. She lumbered like a small dinosaur, craning her neck, blinking in the rain. David leaned forward.

"Good evening then."

She pushed up from all four legs, lifting her carapace off the ground, and lurched across the grass away from him. She spotted a surfaced earthworm, and her mouth gaped open and clamped down, ferocious and not in a bit of a hurry.

"Protein first," David said. "Now don't forget a strawberry. Dessert."

She clawed at the worm, swallowed it, and then sat there. The rain had nearly stopped, leaving a shine on her shell.

"Shall we delve into philosophy tonight? Why we're here, what we should be doing with our time? Or would you rather enjoy the rain?"

For an hour or more, he watched her. She prowled the pen for a while, found a strawberry to nibble, and then wandered into the concealment of the hostas.

"You're no help," he said to her retreating tail. "I don't know your purpose either, to be frank."

He stayed outside until the dark was thick

around him, until the rain had moved on and his bare feet had mostly dried, bits of grass sticking to them. Until he could sleep through the night and wake up in the morning trusting higher ways than his own.

Then he went inside for his sleeping bag and pillow. He hung his slicker in the closet, changed into pajamas, and padded out into the yard still barefoot. Wet grass tickled between his toes. He unzipped the tent door and ducked inside. It had been pitched so long in the middle of the yard the grass beneath it was dying. That didn't matter on nights like this, when rain and restlessness converged and would have kept him shut up inside, were the grass too wet to sleep on.

He laid out his thermal bag and pillow and crawled inside. The flannel lining was soft against his feet, his arms. Exponentially nicer than the heavy coarseness of a bedroll. He closed his eyes.

The last week of September. He might not get many more nights like this before winter, if most of October was lost to him again.

He folded his hands on his chest, the old ceremonial melancholy tugging at him. He would die in October, more than likely. No way of knowing if it would be this one or the hundredth from this one. Maybe he'd know when it was happening. If he did, if this was the year for it, he'd call Tiana and tell her about the turtle. Tiana would find a home for the old girl, maybe even keep her. The thought pulled another smile out of him — Tiana with a pet older than she was.

Enough. He wasn't going to die next month and had no reason to imagine otherwise. He tried to mute his thoughts and tune his senses to the rain, imagined every drop that hit his tent and slid down into the ground around it. Drops that joined creeks that joined rivers, drops that evaporated into new clouds to fall on the earth again and again.

Two

"I'm sorry."

Tiana stood on the customer side of the counter, feet apart, shoulders pulled back. She looked as if she expected a mountain to fall on her and planned to try her best to hold it up.

He wasn't that menacing. Or that heavy. "Why should you be sorry?"

"Jayde's my friend. I vouched for her."

"I interviewed her," David said. "I hired her."

"I hounded you into it."

Really? He cocked one eyebrow at her.

"David, the first four times I brought it up, you said we didn't need a third person and you had no intention of hiring one. Ever."

The one person alive whose opinion of him mattered, and she made him sound like an ogre.

Tiana paced over the wood floor as the

bell above the door jingled and a woman bustled into the store, leading a girl by each hand. Neither of them could be more than six years old, each wearing blond pigtails that curled at the ends.

"Hello," the woman said.

David nodded to her. "Morning."

"There aren't many children's books in the window. How's your selection?"

"Oh, we just got in a ton of them." Tiana led the woman to the first row of shelves. "These three shelves, and one more down at the end if you're looking for anything teen."

"Not yet." The woman smiled. "Thank you."

"Ask if you have any questions."

Tiana marched back to the counter and faced David again, her stance no less defensive. "This isn't like her, really it's not."

"When did you call her last?" he said.

"About ten minutes ago." She crossed behind the counter and snatched her phone up from its cubby, hidden from customers. "She didn't answer my texts either." She held the phone to her ear and waited.

A fortysomething man entered the store, nodded to them, and walked back to shop as if he'd been here before. Had he? David should remember. He tried to place the man, the black leather jacket with Western fringe that shouldn't be forgettable.

"Maybe he'll buy something this time," Tiana said.

"Oh?"

"Yeah, he was in here on Friday and browsed for like an hour and then left. Remember?"

"Right." No. David's hand clenched at his side, out of sight behind the counter. Normal for this time of year, but he hadn't expected it quite yet.

How he pitied old minds. So many experiences lost.

Tiana's phone burst into an Adele ringtone, and she snapped it up to her ear.

"Where in the world are you?" She paced again, listening, then pressed a hand to her forehead. "Well, I hope you called the cops on his useless butt."

His shoulders tensed, and Tiana made a palm-down gesture at him that had to mean, *Chill, David.* He nodded.

"What are you talking about? Jayde, that man never did a thing for you. You've got to stop — that's not going to work on me, and you know it."

A pause, and then Tiana lowered the phone to her side and stared at him.

"She's not coming to work," she said.

"On whom is she calling the cops?"

She walked behind the counter, slid her phone into its cubby, and released a sigh. "Nobody."

David motioned her to one of the foot-high children's chairs that had been left near the front. She gave a chipped laugh as she dropped into it. He stepped out from behind the counter and looked down the rows of shelves. No customers in sight. He turned back to Tiana and tipped his head. They both knew she had to tell him.

"That loser she's with."

David grabbed a second kid chair and sat next to her. "How many times, do you know?"

She blinked at him, something she always did when he skipped to the end of her story without waiting to hear the middle. "At least two other times I know about."

"Does she need medical treatment?"

"She won't be getting any, but she's not coming in, so . . ."

An icy needle punctured his chest and sent slow coldness outward into his limbs. "And she would if she were able."

Tiana ducked her head and hid her face behind her hands. "She isn't the type to call in."

The man in the leather jacket rounded the

corner. David stood and nudged his chair against the wall. Tiana sprang up and walked away, disappearing toward the non-fiction shelves.

David rang up the man's books. Nicholas Sparks and Ian Rankin? Okay then. As the bell above the door announced the customer's departure, Tiana reappeared. Her mouth pinched less, but she avoided David's eyes. More to the story. The part she least wanted to tell.

She would tell him, though. Silence wasn't in her.

She lifted her head. "Jayde always says, 'He puts up with a lot from me too, you know.'"

He nodded. Same old story.

"I want to go over there and yell at her. Or drag her out of his apartment and . . . and keep her away from him for good."

"How?"

"It wouldn't work. Nothing I do ever works."

When he nodded again, she looked ready to smack him. "Tiana, you know you're right. Otherwise you'd be over there now."

"She'd have to be locked in. It's the only thing that would stop her from going back."

"Exactly."

"Could we?" The tone was sardonic, but

the tilt of one eyebrow said she'd follow him to Jayde's boyfriend's apartment for a kidnapping team-up, if he'd lead the way.

"I don't lock people in," he said.

She rocked back on her boot heels. "Even for their own good?"

"Even then."

She volunteered to man the register, the job he'd hired Jayde for. Of course he let her. He'd hole up with his inventory and continue cataloging the haul from yesterday. But after three years, organizing their growing stock required two people. Despite his original refusal, he wouldn't have hired Jayde if he didn't need her.

He'd been working an hour when Tiana poked her head into the stockroom.

"Did you see the news yesterday, about Zachary Wilson?"

David fastened his focus to the box of books in front of him. *Boxcar Children,* maybe fifty of them. "The daredevil who fell."

"And everyone thought he was dead."

He shuffled the books into series order. "Not something people could be mistaken about."

"Except they were."

He marked a tally sheet on his clipboard — title, condition, location in the room for easy tracking later. "Tiana, the man fell thousands of feet."

"Except he didn't."

"What was it, a publicity stunt? He really did have a net?"

"He had an angel."

The scoffing sound bounced off the boxes surrounding him. She couldn't possibly be . . . He looked up. She raised her eyebrows, pure challenge. Yes, she was serious.

David set down the books and stood from his crouch beside the box. "He isn't dead."

"An angel caught him."

"You believe that?"

"How else could he be alive?"

Good question. Tiana held her phone out to him. He took it and tapped PLAY on the news video.

The anchorman spoke over a video of a helicopter search in the dark, then of a team on foot this morning, tromping around the bottom of the canyon lugging a rolled-up stretcher, water bottles, and more video cameras. Mist hovered around hiking boots. Sun slanted into the camera from the right. The recovery team's pace was unhurried, but no one seemed to notice the beauty around them. Resignation.

"Now watch this dramatic moment," the anchorman said, "as those who went into the heart of a tragedy, hoping to bring back whatever remained of this brave young man, come face-to-face with something beyond their wildest hopes."

David allowed his eyes to roll. Everyone was brave these days. No one was stupid.

"Shut up and watch," Tiana said.

In a cleft of the rock above the cameraman, no more than ten feet ahead, something moved. A few rocks slid down, plinked off each other. The man ducked a spray of pebbles, and the camera wobbled then steadied.

"Watch," Tiana whispered.

A blond head seemed to poke out of the rock itself — obviously an illusion caused by the flat lens, but it was an effective one. Zachary Wilson stepped forward and jumped down to the ground, grinning. The camera blurred from his waist down. He was naked.

"About time," he said.

Someone offscreen hollered, followed by a few bleeps from the news station. People surged into the camera's view, circled Wilson as though he might be an angel himself, and then the camera shut off and the anchorman's face filled the screen.

"We're taking you now to a live interview with Zachary Wilson, who —"

Tiana gave a small *oh* pitched an octave too high.

David cocked his head at her. "Fan?"

"Something like that."

"Fangirl then."

"Hush, the man is about to speak."

She tilted the phone toward her with one finger as the camera caught up with Wilson. He was sitting on the open tailgate of a black F-150 parked a few hundred yards from the edge of the canyon. The camera crew had jumped on the opportunity for drama, using an angle that set Wilson slightly off-center and included the cliff edge. He was wrapped in a coarse-looking blanket patterned in a Southwest checkering of brown and blue and yellow. His shoulders were bare.

"You've been checked out by the paramedics?" said the artificially red-haired woman holding the mic for him. They were going for urgent here, no small talk for the man who'd plunged to his death yet avoided it.

"Not a scratch." That stupid grin again.

"Mr. Wilson —"

"Oh, come on," he said. "Zac. Please."

The woman's smile bloomed. David glanced at Tiana. "So how many fans does this guy have?"

"Six hundred thousand followers on his social media accounts. *Before* this happened."

He'd have to process that in a minute. Something about this was wrong. Something other than the angel story.

"Zac," the interviewer said. "When you were first rescued, you said you were 'caught up.' Could you share that story for us?"

"Well, most of it's a blur." The smile held mischief, but something clouded his eyes for a moment. "Literally, of course. I can tell you I was falling for a long time, and then I wasn't. Something caught me and I sort of . . . bounced upward; that's the only way I can describe it. And a voice said, 'Not yet.' And then I was standing on a jutting rock a few feet above the ground, sort of hidden by the canyon on all sides. And I knew I wasn't dead, that I was safe."

Tiana's hands clasped in front of her. "Wow."

"Wow," the interviewer said.

David slanted a look.

"Shut up, David."

No cause for the bitter taste at the back of his throat. Overanalyzing, that's what this was. He should stop it. But Wilson's story was not true.

"Do you know how close you were, when

32

this happened?" the interviewer asked. "How close to . . . um, the end?"

Wilson's lip pulled. The movement was small, quick, but it wasn't a smile. More of a sneer. Then it was rinsed away by the warmth of his laugh, which sounded as joyful as it ought to, coming from a man who had escaped death. A chill washed down David's spine.

"Honestly, I'm just grateful not to have hit the ground."

Lying. And enjoying it.

"And do you have any explanation for your . . ." The interviewer blushed. "Um, state of dress when you were rescued?"

"No, I don't." The regret in his face — causing such a scene, having to answer this question — it looked real.

David could be wrong.

But if an angel did catch you midair, it wouldn't likely cause your clothes to vanish. Barring anyone else down in the canyon with him when he'd landed, that meant Zachary Wilson had stripped himself.

So he was an exhibitionist. All part of this act.

Or his clothes contradicted his story.

"What?" Tiana said when the interview ended.

"It's a stunt." There. Identified, boxed up,

put away.

"Angels rescued Peter from prison. Chains fell off, the cell door opened . . ."

"You're comparing Zachary Wilson to Simon Peter?"

"You know what I'm saying. Have you seen the — the other video?"

Of course there was footage of the fall.

"I watched it once, just now, because I knew he was fine. But I never want to see it again. Here." She took her phone, tapped the screen a few times, handed it to him again, and left the room.

David watched.

Wind, a tip, a moment Wilson seemed to regain his balance, and then a flailing plunge trailed by the phone-videographer's shrill teenage scream. As he disappeared into the canyon, the phone fell too, its owner still shrieking, and then the video stopped. A professional would have been recording the moment as well, but of course this was the version that went viral.

The fall truly didn't appear intentional.

David closed Tiana's browser and went to find her, keeping one eye on the checkout counter. She was among the teen books, head down, facing the corner.

"Hey," he said.

She swiped tears. "Sorry."

"You thought he was dead."

"I really did." She held out her hand for her phone, and he set it into her palm. "But that's what happens to dumb celebrities, right? They die on camera. Nothing to cry over."

"You really think I'd say that?"

"I didn't say *you* would say it."

"That was my voice."

"I don't . . ." She shoved her phone into her pocket. "Do I?"

A smile pulled his mouth. "You make the attempt."

"Not gruff enough? Or not Canadian enough?"

"I'm no more Canadian than you are."

"You sound like it, every once in a while."

"Interesting." He never expected his accent still to exist, but people occasionally commented on it. And of course, up here, everyone assumed they were hearing Canadian.

"Anyway," she said, "there's something else we need to discuss."

"Oh?"

"You used the term *fangirl*. Accurately."

He held in a smile. "I do live here."

"Harbor Vale? Michigan?"

"America. Planet Earth."

"Those lazy curls and those eyes of his,

35

just piercing, you know? And he's actually witty in addition to . . ." He must have made a face, because she laughed.

The woman and her pigtailed girls surfaced from the sea of books, each hefting armfuls. David tipped his chin in their direction.

"I'll go up," he said.

"Nah, I'm good. Zac's alive: I'm great." She swiped her cheeks dry and brushed past him.

Alone with his books, he couldn't shut out those videos or the question of what had happened after. The things he'd imagined last night. Wilson's body, his own body. Different outcomes. But what if their outcome was the same?

It was the most outlandish thought he'd had . . . perhaps in his lifetime. Another like him wouldn't be walking tightropes on live television.

But the clothes. There'd be no explaining that kind of blood loss, of total tissue and bone destruction. Not without a corpse.

He knew nothing. Even he might be dead after a physical devastation like that. The impact would be worse than full thickness burns — it would have to be. He shut his eyes. Pressed his thumbs into them. No, Zachary Wilson couldn't be like him. God wouldn't do this to anyone else.

But he had to go to that canyon and see for himself.

THREE

The only flight to Phoenix within the next twenty-four hours departed at eight in the morning. David called Tiana from his gate at seven.

"Hello?" Her voice dragged over the word.

"It's David."

"I know that. Why?"

He held in a chuckle. "Feel like running the store yourself for two days?"

A cupboard door shut. "About time you gave me the chance."

"Don't worry about restocking. Just ring up the sales. If Jayde comes in, put her to work."

"Is this day one of your spontaneous October vacation? I'd just like to point out that it's still September."

"I'm unavailable, that's all. Nothing to do with vacation."

Another cupboard door. "I'll sell so many books you'll promote me."

"To what? Owner?"

"Yeah, good point. See you Thursday."

"That's the plan."

He hung up before the boarding announcement could betray him. No one would ever know he'd gone to Arizona in search of . . . something.

The flight from Detroit to Phoenix was almost five hours and gave him plenty of time to think. To second-guess his impulsivity. To debate his first step. He could drive a rental car three hours to Grand Canyon National Park, trek to the bottom some way that didn't involve breaking his bones, and search for the clothes Zachary Wilson had disposed of. It seemed like madness. He wasn't a detective. Then again, it wouldn't take a detective to identify blood and other bodily materials. Even if Wilson had cleaned up the scene, even if he'd buried the clothes, something would be left behind.

His other option was to find Wilson and question the man.

Too risky. And he doubted Wilson was still in Arizona. News reports said he lived in Colorado when he wasn't traveling for stunt events — or for pleasure, which he seemed to do often.

By the time the plane touched down, David had resigned himself to three hours in a rental car. He'd figure out the rest when he got to the canyon. His return flight left close to midnight the next day. Should be plenty of time.

He drove two miles to the Hilton Phoenix Airport hotel, booked a room, but left his carry-on in the vehicle. Then he started driving. Desert highway. Windows down, soaking in the heat and the sun after so many rainy days. Northern Michigan was beautiful in the fall, but it could be cold. And wet.

He drove the first hour without music, letting the wind and the whir of passing traffic serenade him. Then he turned on the radio and found a crackling folk station. His fingers tapped the beat on the steering wheel, trying to anticipate the percussionist and grinning when he failed. At the first strains of "The Skye Boat Song," his hand hovered over the dial. He couldn't listen to anyone butcher this song, but the young duo made a fair attempt at it. David's hand resumed its rest on the wheel.

By the time he reached the canyon, it was almost four, and he needed food. He stopped at a tourist restaurant for a burger and then drove into the Grand Canyon Park.

More traffic than he expected on a weekday. In fact . . . no, surely not . . . He drove at the 25 mph limit, a winding blacktop road with signs. One of them directed him toward Marble Canyon and was decorated. With streamers. Hardly park ranger approved. He headed that way. Six hundred thousand fans — likely a few of them had shown up to commemorate the spot.

A mile later, traffic stood still. David braked, didn't move for six minutes, crept forward, stopped. He found a place to park as soon as he could. He'd walk faster than this, and he'd enjoy the time more anyway. He locked the car, pocketed the keys and his phone, and set out.

As he neared the canyon, the crowd around him grew, everyone surging in the same direction. Most of them were no older than thirty. And most of them were female. Conversations flitted around him.

". . . if it happened to me, I'd never walk a tightrope again."

"Me either, but that's what makes him Zac."

". . . don't think we're like actually going to see him . . ."

". . . right now if we can get close enough . . ."

"I made white chocolate chip!"

"Ohmygosh, that's his favorite!"

41

Two teenagers pushed past David, one carrying a lidded plastic container. Girls rushed around him like a herd of sheep dodging a rut in the ground. Several of them carried similar containers. Baskets. Gift bags, red and blue and green and purple, rustling tissue paper peeking out the top of each, swinging at their sides or held close to their bodies against the jostling crowd.

He followed them. Listened to them blather on about Zachary Wilson — his bravery, his hotness. His generosity in staying here to sign autographs when the sight of the canyon had to be "beyond traumatic."

It made sense now, Wilson's motivation. By the time David reached the end of the autograph line, his jaw felt as hard as the canyon walls.

How dare an adult man deceive not only the general public but also thousands of worshipping girls? What was wrong with this guy?

Forget finding the clothes. If he had to wait until the sun set and the autograph seekers departed, he would get a word with Wilson. And he'd ask his question. Whether he investigated the canyon itself would depend on Wilson's response and what David could read in the man. Liars always betrayed something.

First order of business: bypass the fan-girls. David prowled over the rocks and sand to approach Wilson's location from the right flank. Of course Wilson or his publicity team had positioned the canyon at his back.

As David neared the end of the line, the publicity team's existence became indisputable. Wilson had a trailer. He'd slept here, or he wanted to give the appearance he had. Communing with the angel that had caught him up. Reevaluating his life. David huffed and skirted a scorpion. He was safe in professional hiking boots, but there was no sense in crushing a living thing if he didn't have to.

Black-garbed security guards formed a perimeter around the trailer, which proved Wilson wasn't a delusional self-worshipper. Or an idiot. For the moment, the crowd was respecting the rope boundaries; but one of those cookie-baking fangirls was sure to rush him sooner or later, and the passion in the voices that had drifted around David suggested they weren't incapable of becoming a mob. If one of them got close enough to touch the idol, they'd all want to get that close.

The guards had been watching David's approach for the last five minutes. While he stayed a hundred yards away, they didn't call him off.

He gave up on the oblique approach as visibly as he could, lifted his hands to the nearest guard, lifted his eyebrows too. The guard nodded him closer. Yeah, they were armed. And David wasn't. That fact tasted like chalk, but he kept walking.

"Stop right there, sir," the guard said from about thirty feet away.

David halted. "I'd like to talk to Wilson."

"Get in line."

He smiled and let it twist with cynicism. Waited for the guard's measure of him.

"People have waited today for an average of six hours just to shake his hand or have him sign theirs. I let you line jump and we could have a riot."

"I'm not here for him to sign my hand," David said.

"For what then?"

"To ask a question."

"We've gotten a lot of those today too. Most commonly asked is how it feels to get caught by an angel."

"Caught up, you mean."

The guard's eyes never stopped roving the area, but his mouth twisted, and a gleam entered his eyes. Not a believer. Only an employee.

"I don't need much time."

"Really, man, you'll have to wait in line. That's just how it is."

Fine. It was irksome, but they had a job to do. He nodded. His eyes left the armed man nearest him and found Wilson himself a hundred feet away, lounging in a chair in front of the trailer, accepting a blanket-covered basket that could have come from the set of *Little Red Riding Hood*. Wilson grinned at the girl, signed a glossy photo, and glanced to the side. He'd been keeping track of his guard's movements.

The grin froze on his face. Then flattened into disbelief. His attention wasn't fixed on the guard who'd allowed David to get too close. It was fixed on David.

Wilson stood and crossed the sand toward David, ignoring whatever the nearest guard said to him. The line of fans leaned in his direction, straining eyes and ears and pressing against the ropes. Someone screamed — who did they think this guy was, John Lennon? — and Wilson turned to hold up a single finger. His smile was primed for every cell phone within a line of sight, and he held it for two whole seconds.

He didn't look away from David as he walked up to the guard David had been talking to.

45

"What's this guy want?"

"To ask you a question."

Wilson stepped past him.

"Sir, please don't —"

"Relax, Tommy."

They stood face-to-face now, David and the celebrity. Something skittered up David's spine. Wilson was staring. At him.

"Give us a minute," he said.

"Really, Mr. Wilson —"

"I said step off."

Tommy retreated several yards.

"I know the question." Wilson smirked. "But go ahead."

This man wasn't threatened. Wasn't offended. Wasn't even cautious. As if he knew not only David's question but David himself.

"Well?" Wilson said.

"I want to know if you hit the ground."

"Might as well cut to the chase." His smirk flattened, and a mask seemed to drop from his face and shatter between them. "Yes, John, I hit the ground."

Cold filled David from the inside out, an instant freeze, a sensation like cracking in his limbs.

"More than worth it, though, if it brought you here."

46

"John?" The only word David could manage.

"John Russell. It's about time. Well, about a hundred years past time, but there's no *too late* for us, is there?"

David kept his breathing level as the name pierced him. The name he never expected to hear again, the name he'd discarded in 1973.

FOUR

He should have denied it. Walked away too fast for Zachary Wilson, with his entourage of security and fangirls and white chocolate chip cookies, to follow. Reached the rental car long before anyone could track him. Driven away.

But hearing his name again — the name Ma and Da called him, the name Sarah called him — it paralyzed all caution and sense. He shook his head at Wilson, who stood there with something on his face David didn't want to see. Smug satisfaction he could have resisted, perhaps even walked away from. But this, the first genuine expression he'd glimpsed on Wilson's schooled face, was a blending of disbelief and veneration. Whoever Wilson thought he was, whatever Wilson thought David had done to deserve that fixed stare while a thousand-plus people stared at Wilson with the same expression . . .

David had to know what he knew.

"Don't go anywhere," Wilson said, as if he could see the danger he posed to David, the itch in David's spine to bolt and vanish in the distance.

If he knew who David was, then he knew the rest too. And if he was another like David, he should be taking the same precautions; yet he walked tightropes without nets. He survived the impossible and did it in a spotlight.

He measured David, and Tiana was right. The man's gaze was intense when he wasn't veiling it behind a smirk. He extended a hand, palm out, asking for a minute.

"Surely you don't expect to slip away unnoticed." David nodded to the fans that strained the ropes to get a better look . . .

At him. The man who had enticed their idol to abandon them. In one glance he counted seven cell phones tilting and clicking and capturing his picture. He stepped a foot closer to Tommy, cutting off their angles. The groans of frustration carried across the sand.

Wilson was watching him.

"I'm not interested in becoming a hashtag," David said.

"No?" His mouth tilted. "My old high

49

school buddy. My secret lover. Take your pick."

"Excuse me?"

"Let's see, distinguished height, dark hair, dark clothes. Vampire pallor. We could give you an angst-ridden backstory, something like . . . my brother who was lost at sea, lived on coconut milk and crabs, rescued in time to run to my side while I undergo this difficult emotional recovery."

David snorted. "Difficult, aye. Just look at you, sacrificing so much to the queue of autograph seekers."

"Did you just say *aye*?"

So many words, phrases, songs, meals — a whole life locked behind inner doors — and that name, John Russell, the key to all of them. "Strut on back to the teenagers, Wilson. You don't want to cause a stampede at the edge of a canyon."

He glanced back at the multitude, and then his eyes met David's without a hint of levity. "It's Zac."

"Your birth name?"

"Not even close."

He had no reason to believe this man other than the obvious one: it was the simplest explanation to everything that had happened in the last three days. The most impossible? Yes. And the simplest. Zac Wilson was unable to die. And Zac Wilson knew him. The only person left alive who knew John Russell.

How?

He would endure the man's company long enough to sort through what this meant.

He held out his hand. "David Galloway."

Zac shook it. "If you would, give me . . . oh, about an hour."

"Thirty autographs per second ought to manage that."

"My team is about to earn some bonus pay." He motioned Tommy over. "Get this guy back to his vehicle without being accosted. Prevent any pictures if possible."

Tommy cocked his head.

"I said *if possible.*" Zac clapped one hand on David's shoulder. "Please don't disappear on me."

His face held hope. For answers? The tightness around his mouth, the lift of his eyebrows — what did he expect David to know?

"I'm at the Hilton," David said. "At the airport." And not going to wait for this man to dispense with his groupies.

"Of course."

"I fly out tomorrow."

Zac nodded, acknowledging the lack of information — no time, no destination. "I'll

Dunn Public Library

be there tonight, then. We'll get late dinner, drinks, whatever."

"Fine."

The smirk surfaced as he reached into a jacket pocket and withdrew his phone. "Don't take this the wrong way, but can I have your number?"

They exchanged contacts, and then David set out. Tommy could follow or not. After a few strides, the man kept pace just behind his right shoulder, and then another guard joined at David's left.

David shot a glance at Tommy. "Is this really necessary?"

"Yes, sir."

He sighed, but . . . yes, all right, they were there to box him in. They couldn't prevent every picture, but they could prevent good ones. Maybe even usable ones.

He pointed out the rental car and thanked them for their escort. The youngest-looking one, a thick-chested guy with red hair, hesitated when his colleagues turned back.

"Where did you serve?" the guard said.

Ach, this lie. The one he hated most. "Iraq, three years."

The kid smiled. "Same. Army?"

"That's right."

And now the pause, the expectation of detail. Rank, a shared experience, solidarity, something. He couldn't do it, had nothing to offer. He held the man's gaze a moment, tried to convey his respect, then turned away and got into the car. The guard turned on his heel and walked away without looking back.

Better than weaving more lies. Accepting credit for a battlefield on which he hadn't served. He should be there now, maybe. Through five wars, he'd made a first-rate soldier. If he were stronger — but he pushed away the self-recrimination. He was strong, not impervious.

He turned the key in the ignition, and the flare of pain in his wrist made him wince.

No.

Too soon. He was supposed to have another week — a week to catalog that stock of books, buy enough canned soup to last him a month and enough night crawlers to last the turtle.

All right, calm down. He started driving. He'd rest at the hotel and be ready for a drink and a conversation with Zachary Wilson. He'd fly home tomorrow and order groceries online if he had to. He'd make it back in time.

He maintained a speed of 70 mph all the way back to the Hilton. He might be an old man, but he'd be hanged before he drove like one. Cruise control kept the car going more reliably than his foot on the accelerator. His ankles were aching like his wrists. Like his thumbs and knees and elbows — his first red flag. Forgetting that customer had been a yellow flag, and he'd ignored it. Been careless, preoccupied with the surviving daredevil and blind to anything but possible answers. So he might get his answers now. The cost might not be worth it.

No, that was anxiety talking. Not logic.

He pulled into the hotel lot and parked. If Zac Wilson provided answers, the trip was worth it.

He eased out of the car and almost dropped the keys. He curled stiff fingers around them. On the softest flesh of his hand, between his thumb and forefinger, an age spot had appeared in the last three hours. This wasn't a red flag. This was a BRIDGE OUT sign. He had to get to his room.

No one looked at him twice as he strode across the hotel lobby to the elevators, backpack and carry-on in tow. His knees tried to lock up, but he forced his feet not to shuffle. He stepped onto the elevator alone. Small favors. He stood in the middle and braced his feet as it rose to the fifth floor and opened. He stepped out and hauled his bags down the carpeted corridor to room 211. Swiped the card. Turned the handle. Went inside and hung the DO NOT DISTURB tag.

He kept up the firm strides all the way to the bed, but willpower would take him no farther. He lay down, flat on his back, and shut his eyes.

He was in trouble.

He wouldn't rise from this bed for days. When he could, he'd be weak from hunger and thirst, able to manage nothing more strenuous than feeding himself. He would pause to catch his breath after crossing to the bathroom. He would fight to hold on to memories he made in the next month, though all the others would remain sharp and bright as a cinema picture.

He set a hand on his chest, measuring the difficulty in each breath. Always, this was the hardest thing to bear. The thing that would probably kill him at last, some October. He'd discover his lungs weren't filling anymore and he'd suffocate in bed. Alone. The thought shouldn't scare him so much, but his heart raced even now.

Enough. Stop. Shut it down.

He didn't sleep. Couldn't. Hours ticked down. A maddening fog seeped into his mind. He was supposed to do something tonight. Go somewhere. He was going to find answers. To some question that mattered a great deal but now evaded him. Oh well. If he was finally to die, the question didn't matter so much after all.

Solitude throbbed in the room. David opened his eyes. The ceiling was a predictable eggshell color. The painting on the wall across from the bed consisted of only a few brushstrokes — an impression of red flowers in a white vase, set in the center of a green table.

He lifted his hand. Looked at it, fingers splayed against the ceiling. It trembled, a new age spot now marking the back of his hand, but no wrinkles. Never wrinkles nor gray hair. It didn't make much sense, but it was consistent every year. He curled his fingers, and the pain of movement crinkled his forehead. He let the hand fall back to his chest.

"Are You here?"

His voice rasped. Ancient and brittle, gruff and lilting with the Scottish brogue of his father. He couldn't remember at the moment how to speak like a modern American.

"If Thou hast cursed me, stay and speak Thy reasons. I'll not deny I deserve cursing as much as the next man."

He pressed his palm to his chest. Heart

rate slowing. To be expected in the first few hours of this process.

He drew a boggy breath and closed his eyes. "Please, Lord, if it's something I've done, be merciful and show me. Let me strive to right the wrong before Thee. Let me be Thy servant again. Or take me to Thy rest. Only . . ." A tear seeped from his eye and trickled down his temple into his ear. "Dear Lord, I pray don't make me bear agelessness forever."

He lay still as pains built in his body.

"Is Thy grace sufficient for me? Or is Thy grace withheld, therefore I linger here?"

He was silent an hour, perhaps two, perhaps longer. His mind drifted, yet he knew he was drifting. A white mist. A memory. His bonny dark-haired Sarah dancing in the wheat field while rain poured from a beautiful black sky and soaked the earth. John danced beside her, laughing, sweeping her into his arms and spinning her around, her boots off the ground and her green muslin skirt twirling above her ankles. He kissed her mouth and tasted honey. He set her down, pushed the bonnet off her head, and kissed her hair. Had to lean to do it, she so small and he towering over her.

He drifted again. He was standing outside

their tiny bedroom, waiting alone. Widow Kerrigan's voice was not muffled by the quilt hung for privacy.

"There, there, Sarah, that's it. Sure and you're doing well, so you are."

But Sarah wailed. She had to be dying. The babe they'd longed for, prayed for — the babe was killing her, surely it was. John knelt at the stove and bowed his head, gripped his thighs and rocked when she wailed again.

"Lord Almighty, I pray Thy mercy on her," he whispered. "On her and on the bairn. And on me — only don't take them from me, Lord, and I'll ask nothing else all my days."

So many days since that one. His Sarah. And Michael James Russell, their firstborn son. Gone now. Gone so many years.

"Lord," the voice of the old man whispered — his voice, so strange to hear it. "Forsake me not."

He drifted.

The buzzing sound was not a memory. He opened his eyes. That vibration near his head — on the nightstand, a phone, his phone — it was happening. Here. Now. Where and when were muddled, but he wasn't John, and Sarah was not here with him. Nor was Michael — not the infant Michael, nor the boy, nor the man.

Too tired to raise his arm that high, but someone was on the other end of that line. Even a wrong number would be a human voice. He dragged his hand over the phone, and it nearly fell between the nightstand and the bed. He dropped it onto his chest. It would go to voice mail any second. He swiped his finger over the screen.

Silence, then, "David?"

Ah, his name. He closed his eyes.

"You there or what?"

"Aye," he said.

"I'm in the lobby. Are you coming down?"

"No."

More silence. How to get the voice to continue? He blinked. He had to clear his head. "Are you okay, man?" the voice said. Zachary Wilson's voice.

"No," David said and then huffed. He deserved a kick for that. Not that he'd be kicking himself or anyone else today.

"Room number?"

"Two eleven." He shouldn't have said that either. But the room was too quiet, and Zachary Wilson knew John Russell.

A minute later, a knock came. Then a shaking of the door, and then Zac's voice from the phone. He hadn't hung up.

"Let me in."

The mist was falling too fast.

Something cracked. The lock? David opened his eyes as footsteps entered the room. Training, adrenaline, experience flooded in and pushed him up until he was sitting on the bed, legs lowered, feet on the floor, trying to stand.

Every joint, every muscle, every bone refused the orders of his mind. He fell back.

A face loomed over him. "You're rejuvenating now? Crap timing."

Did he look rejuvenated? He growled.

"There's an age spot in the middle of your forehead, and I'm not an idiot." Zac paced away from the bed and cracked his knuckles against his other hand. "Great. Now what?"

David tried to think. Tried to move.

"I have to move you, and you can't fight me. Because that will get us noticed, which could get me recognized. I don't want to think about the possible scandals." As he spoke, Zac pulled up a contact in his phone and raised it to his ear. "Wrinkle in the plan. Rejuvenation. Unexpected, given he got on a plane to find me."

Someone else knew. David rolled onto his side and sat up, all his muscles resisting the movement. He had to fight back. He couldn't allow himself to be taken. He couldn't fail the mission. He had to escape, get back to his troops.

No, that wasn't right. So much fog in his brain, he seemed to be feeling his way, hands outstretched, through his own thoughts. What was he trying to do? Why was his body so weakened, and why was that voice still speaking?

"He's John freaking Russell. I'm not leaving him here. And it's bad. That theory we had about stale blood? He can't move."

John Russell. Yes. He was. First Sergeant Russell of the United States Army, and if the enemy was going to try to kill him, he had to get away before they discovered they couldn't.

"Well, I guess it's a good thing you came to town for an intervention, isn't it? Meet at the RV as soon as you can get there."

The voice stopped. John braced up on his elbows and got no farther. It was true; he couldn't move. The Germans had done something to him. But this man spoke English. His face came into view above the bed, familiar. Zac. If they knew each other, he ought to feel safe.

"Okay, man, I think I can help you, but I need you to cooperate. Will you?"

No. Yes. "Am I . . . wounded?"

Something flickered in Zac's eyes. He

nodded. "Yeah. I'm getting you to a medic. Okay?"

"You aren't German."

"No, soldier. I'm an American like you."

Zac hefted him over his shoulders and carried him out of the . . . hotel room. A hallway, carpet, housekeeping cart draped in white towels. This wasn't 1917. His name was David Galloway, and he had hung the DO NOT DISTURB sign but not remembered to flip the bolt on the door. He was being hauled on the shoulders of a celebrity — down a stairwell, out a discreet exit into heat that parched his skin. Zac shuffled jingling keys and shifted David's weight, then lowered him across the back seat of the car.

"If you die before we can have a proper conversation, I'm going to be pissed."

"I won't," David whispered.

"I'm not convinced right now." He pushed David's feet out of the way and shut the door.

David never should have come to Arizona.

FIVE

He resolved not to close his eyes as the vehicle sped along, though staring at the ceiling helped him not a whit. It was beige. He was destined to stare at ceilings today. A car's ceiling might be called something else, though. . . . He battled away the fog. Zac had told someone about him.

The man might lie, but asking risked nothing. "Where are we going?"

"Hey back there," Zac said. "Name, rank, serial number?"

"David. Twenty-first century."

"Good. Keep that up."

Silence settled for a minute, lulling, tempting David to give in to the mist and the memories. No.

"We're en route to my RV," Zac said. "It's parked off the beaten path for some privacy. Probably another twenty minutes. Can you sit up?"

David tried, just for the sport of it. His

hand lifted an inch higher than he expected before dropping back to his side. "Not now."

"Is it this bad for you every year?"

"The last thirty or so."

Zac didn't answer.

He couldn't track the time. He lay still, weakness and aches weighing him down. If Zac and his cohort planned to eviscerate David for science, if they planned to sell him to a lab somewhere and let them do the eviscerating — whatever their plan was, they would go through with it. Perhaps they knew how to kill him. If all else failed, decapitation would do the trick, or so he'd always figured. His heartbeat stuttered, and his breath caught. Death might find him today. He would try to be ready.

Prayer would be prudent. A petition for mercy. If God had rejected him, yet these people forced David into His presence. . . . He stalled the thoughts. They made no sense and helped by no means.

After what felt like a long while, the vehicle slowed and stopped. He was jarred a bit as Zac shifted into park.

"Still here?" Zac said.

"Aye."

The driver's door opened, shut. Then the door behind David's head opened and Zac stood over him. His eyes seemed to hold concern, but that wasn't a difficult sentiment to feign. Attempting to get up would result in more collapsing and humiliation. David lay still, but adrenaline jolted his body when Zac picked him up under his arms and dragged him out of the car.

Footsteps over the gravel.

"Are you sure it's him?" A new voice.

David's heart pounded. They team-lifted him, and he turned his head as they passed desert-stunted brush and the car, a staid sedan in salsa red. At least the color fit the man.

"Not much of a car," David said.

"That's the point, man." Zac grinned down at him. "Nobody expects me to be driving it."

The mist was thickening in his mind again. Tugging at him with chilled tendrils. When he came back to himself, Zac and the stranger had lugged him through the door of an RV furnished in gleaming oak and granite. David's head drooped to one side, and linoleum the color of sandstone filled his vision. He lifted his head. He would not look the invalid in the midst of possible enemies.

Aye, he was doing a fine job at that as they carried him to the couch.

They laid him down. The gray leather

upholstery was chilled by the air-conditioning. Cold caught him, contrasting the heat he'd been carried through. His body gave a shiver.

The other man stood back, staring. He looked a little younger than Zac did, maybe twenty-five, his floppy hair a shade of red not much deeper than blond. Green eyes, a long mouth that pressed itself thin as he studied David.

"It is him."

"You don't say." Zac folded his arms.

To the left, outside David's vision, the door shut. Was locked. Another set of footsteps plodded nearer.

Three of them. David's eyes darted to Zac, who was watching him as astutely as he had at Marble Canyon.

Zac lifted his hands. "I can't say anything to persuade you right now. In your position, any one of us would be freaking out."

He didn't freak out, as a rule. This situation didn't follow the rules.

He shut his eyes, then opened them as the third pair of feet tromped closer. The third man, later thirties and not much taller than Zac, stood to one side. His hair was a flat brown, his face forgettable but for the ice-gray eyes.

Those eyes shot darts at the back of Zac's

head, but his words were for David. "Can you prove you're John Russell?"

"Not at the moment."

"But you can." He stepped around Zac to pin his glower on David.

"If I choose to, yes."

Zac gave a measured sigh. He jabbed a thumb at the gray-eyed man. "Simon." Then at the quieter one. "Colm."

"David," he said, though Zac might already have told them.

Zac glanced between his companions and then edged closer to the couch. "How educated are you about our physiology at the microscopic level?"

Too many syllables in those words. He gritted his teeth and shook his head, trying to make sense of the sentence, but one word stuck to his mind when the rest of them slipped away.

"Our."

Zac nodded at Simon and Colm. "They're like us."

He curled his hand, and the pain in each joint sharpened his thoughts. "How?"

"Great. We've gone to all this trouble for an imbecile," Simon said.

Colm watched them all, hands in the pockets of dark khakis, head tilted slightly, no judgment, merely curiosity. One of the track lights above the kitchen sink brightened the red tints in his hair.

Agelessness didn't perfect one's physique, but for David, it helped intentional fitness along. These three seemed to share that with him, though each had a different body type — Simon tough and compact, Colm stocky, Zac lean and nimble. On his feet, David's six-foot-two frame would be the tallest in the room. Instead, he stretched the full length of the couch, feet against the far armrest.

Zac turned to the others. "I vote we fix him first, explain later."

Colm nodded.

"If that's what you called me here for . . ." Simon took a step back.

"Well, I figured even you would want to meet him."

"We have no proof right now. We have nothing but a physical resemblance."

"He came to us."

"To you."

"He asked if I hit the ground. His skin was young this morning, and now look at him. I'm telling you, it's him."

Simon eyed David as if he were part of the furniture. Not an unfair assessment at the moment. An old fury rose in him, untouched since his final jungle skirmish,

68

rain and blood and bodies and the knowledge he'd live no matter which of the men beside him did not. He'd live now too, whatever they did to him. Simon glared at him, and he glared back.

"Even if he is Russell, we don't know him." Simon turned to Zac. "I won't do it."

Zac paced the floor in front of the couch, his eyes not breaking from Simon's. His was the walk of an athlete, not brute strength but controlled agility. No doubt he could perform a gymnastic routine as easily as a tightrope walk. Not that he'd succeeded at his last one of those.

If he was giving Simon a minute to reconsider whatever "it" was, he might be succeeding. Simon looked from Zac to David and back again.

"Colm, thoughts?" Simon said.

Colm shrugged and pushed away from the granite counter. "It's true, we don't know him."

Zac huffed.

"Chill a minute," Colm said. "We don't know him, but we can't leave him like this either. I say we keep him here, keep an eye on him while he's rejuvenating. In a few days he'll be recovered, and we can see where he stands on things. He's in no shape to talk now."

A few days? That was wrong. David tried to sit up, and Colm crossed to the couch.

"Hey, lie still."

No. Get up. He fell back, and his lungs strained for air. Grain formed in his vision, starting at the edges, creeping inward. The voices still came clearly.

"He's not good."

"That's what I said."

"Simon, come on, man. He needs blood now."

He . . . what? Blood? He wasn't bleeding. Perhaps the mist left him confused.

Or perhaps they weren't like him at all. Vampires. That's what they were. And they thought he was one. They'd turn him into a vampire and he wouldn't be able to —

Calm down. Think. Vampires were fiction.

As were men who couldn't die.

"What if he's just an old man? We'll be changing him forever, someone we don't know. He could end up a third-world dictator a hundred years from now, with my blood in his veins. Zac could be mistaken."

"I'm insulted," Zac said.

"Does he look like a normal old man to you?" Colm. "Not a wrinkle, not a gray hair. It's rejuvenation. He's one of us, and he's been alone. His cells probably look like raisins in the sun."

"Well, in a few days they'll be rejuvenated."

"So we let him go through this when we could help. That's wrong."

"Not like he's dying." Simon gave a dry laugh.

"You're outvoted," Zac said.

"It's my blood. My vote's the only one that counts."

In the silence, David's chest ached. He wished they'd talk again. Distract him. The words fell through his mind like drops of water through a cupped hand, but the sound of voices was something to focus on.

"Lord," he whispered.

The silence changed. They'd heard him. They were waiting for him to speak again.

He couldn't. His next breath wheezed.

"Simon." Colm's voice was barely more than a whisper. "Something's wrong. And if he dies, you're going to regret this."

"Why should I?"

"Because you know who he is."

A sigh. "I'll get the supplies."

Zac's face loomed over him again. "You can get through this faster if you'll give us permission to help."

Not a chance. David licked his lips, but they stayed dry. "How?"

"It's a transfusion, basically. First we'll

71

remove some of yours. Are you good with that?"

He tried to shake his head, but mist fell between him and Zac. He drifted for some time — minutes, an hour — and he was John again, perched on a joist of Abel McGinnis's barn, helping to hoist the supports for the roof. The sound of hammers ricocheted around him, including his own, nail after nail. Then he was back down the ladder, then sipping lemonade Sarah brought him. Sarah, his bride of only six weeks. So beautiful she was, pink ribbons of her bonnet dangling, a lock of dark hair loose from her bun. He tucked his hand into her bonnet, tucked the hair behind her ear.

Then he was standing on a knoll to one side of the grave, a hundred feet removed from the others. Everyone was gathered around, a knot of dark clothes and quiet tears. The casket was lowered. His children held each other, held their spouses, held his grandchildren. Talked about missing Grandmother and seeing her again. Some spoke of heaven. Some said she had become an angel and would hover always over their shoulders wearing white-feathered wings, and if only they could see her there sometime.

He watched his grandchildren, raised

believing him long dead, as they stood quietly for the graveside service: Frank, Thomas, Seth, Alice, Laura, Rachel, Susanna. There would be great-grandchildren in a few more years. He waited here, apart, eyes fixing on Michael and Kathleen as the service ended. They wouldn't speak to him, but they would meet his eyes. Once.

Their attention remained fixed on the manicured grass. They left their mother's grave without a glance back.

When they'd all gone, John went to the grave and brushed his palm over the flowers they had left. He would come back when the stone was in place and finger its smoothness, trace the letters and dates. *Sarah May Russell,* it would say. *December 1, 1852– August 20, 1910.* He knelt and bowed his head.

"I know it's selfish." His voice shook worse than his folded hands. "I know there was pain for you, at the end. And I'm sorry. But it was a comfort to me, knowing you breathed in the world somewhere, knowing I wasn't the only one who held our memories."

He reached for the flowers, rested his hand there, but couldn't lift his head. They hadn't looked for him. His children.

"I'm not remembered any longer," he said.

He covered his face to hide the tears, but no one was left to see them.

"David."

The mist cleared. Stucco ceiling. He was flat on his back. Blue eyes studied him. Zac again.

"Name and date?"

"You can end it sooner," David said.

"That's right."

A tear squeezed from his eye and trickled down his temple, fell onto the pillow with a soft sound.

"Are you giving permission?"

"Yes."

Zac's sigh was more of a gust. This mattered to him, though his motives were impossible to guess. David kept his eyes open, trying to ward off the memories, and watched while Zac and Simon and Colm worked around him, setting up an IV. He didn't flinch when the needle entered the vein in the crook of his elbow.

"Don't move," Zac said.

"Not likely."

He drifted again, came to with the needle gone from that arm but with a new pinching in his other hand. He looked down the length of his body to the hand resting at his side. They'd drawn blood from one arm, and now . . . In his other hand, another line.

74

A transfusion indeed.

His body jerked. Stiffened.

"Might have to hold him." That was Colm.

Zac's hands pressed David's shoulders. "Easy, buddy. We're helping you."

David's body jerked again, involuntary, arching his back, then tilting his head so he could see behind him. Simon sat in a chair, a red line running from his arm. The glare hadn't cooled, and he angled it now at Zac.

David's body went limp. Heat traveled up his arm, into his chest, where it exploded. It coursed down his limbs. Filled his belly. Pooled in his head, his face. Hotter. Fire.

He was burning again.

"Hold him."

"Trying to . . ."

He groaned. Not the mist, not the memory, it was happening now — burning. His flesh and his insides. The men yelled at each other, but he couldn't understand the words as the fire consumed him from the inside out.

Not right. Burns started on the outside.

He writhed, or tried to, pinned in place by hands he couldn't identify or even count. Time ground onward as he burned, and then, in the center of his chest, a drop of coolness rippled outward. Another drop fell in his forehead and another in the pit of his stomach. The coolness traveled his veins. He quieted. He lay still.

Somebody swore. "We killed him."

"No." That was Colm. A hand rested on David's chest. "Breathing, see. And easier than he was."

"I've never seen . . ." Zac's voice shook. "None of us ever . . ."

"It makes sense," Simon said.

"I know, but . . ."

When David forced his eyes open a few minutes later, the line was gone from his hand. Exhaustion laced his bones, but the mist had cleared. The bog in his chest had drained away. He made a fist, and his fingers curled with ease. He tightened a muscle in his leg then one in his shoulder. Nothing ached.

"There," Zac said. "Skin's always last."

David turned his head. The three of them stood in a row, watching him. Cotton was taped to the inside of Simon's elbow.

David lifted his left hand. The age spots had cleared.

"Any questions?" Zac barely smiled.

He pushed up from the couch. It was . . . over? He tried to stand.

Colm stepped forward. "Whoa. Not yet. You need a few hours' rest. And a lot of protein, as I'm sure you know."

Right, of course. They had somehow sped up the annual process. He had to treat his body as if it had just emerged from that pit. He felt as if he'd been taken apart and put back together. Perhaps he had, somehow. He tipped his head back against the couch.

"I need an explanation for this."

"Which part?" Zac said.

He angled a look without lifting his head. Not playing that game.

"Let's see." Zac's mouth twitched. "We can't die."

David waited for him to get over his sense of humor.

Zac nodded toward the front of the RV, then at Colm. "Want to drive? Find us a place with steak and eggs."

"It's five in the morning, man." But Colm headed up to the driver's seat.

Five in the morning? David shook his head, trying to piece events together. Everything was fragmented. He'd arrived back at his hotel room around twelve hours ago. He rubbed the lingering ache above his eyes and hunched forward on the couch.

Zac sank onto the leather couch across from David's. He gestured at the padded chairs around the table in the kitchenette, a few feet nearer the front. "Have a seat, Simon. You'll want to correct me as needed."

"Got that right, Fall Guy." Simon tugged a chair up and sat.

Zac sighed. "Could we address that topic later?"

"Definitely."

"Anyway." He shifted toward David, body language blocking Simon from the discussion to which he'd just invited him. Over Zac's shoulder, Simon watched David.

Distrust was only reasonable here. David nodded to him, and the tightness eased around Simon's mouth.

"I'll try the brief version, and you stop with questions if you want," Zac said. "Once a year your body has to essentially reboot itself. Or rather, the organisms in your blood have to, which leaves the rest of you — all the human cell components — without anything to fight off aging until those organisms are back in shape. Tends to wipe us out for a few days unless we have access to Simon's blood. He's type O negative, and for some reason his blood jump-starts the rejuvenation process. Instead of days, we can be on our feet again in hours."

Days. Hours. Organisms? David shook his head. "You said something before. On the phone at the hotel. Stale blood."

"Didn't think you were hearing me. But

yeah, it's a theory — that without Simon's blood once a year, ours would get stale. Might prolong the process even more, naturally, over time."

He couldn't find harm in telling them this. "Last year, I lost twenty-three days."

Simon's eyebrows shot up. Zac's face grew still as he leaned back and threaded his fingers over his waist.

"Twenty-three . . . days."

"I want to know how you knew me. How you found each other, how many of us there are."

Zac held up his hand, fingers spread. "Now that we know you're alive."

"Who's the fifth?"

"That would be Moira," Simon said. "She's in Europe at the moment."

David shut his eyes. How could there be five? If they'd found each other, why hadn't they found him? He lifted one hand to rake through his hair, but he was shaking. Even his breath shook as he exhaled.

"We've been up all night," Zac said. "And you'll be a wreck until you've eaten a few times. Speeding up rejuvenation is like notching up your metabolism to *burn, baby, burn.*"

"Burn is right," David said. The lack of filter between brain and mouth should disturb him, but he was too tired.

"Yeah, I'd have warned you, but it's not that extreme for us."

"Stale blood, as you said."

"It's the only explanation I have." He stretched out on the couch. "If you'll get some shut-eye while Colm drives, you'll wake up stronger."

His experience backed that up. Protein and sleep. He lay back against the pillow and let his body sink into the cushions. By now his body heat had bled into the couch, enough to warm it without chilling him. Besides, after that metabolic experience, he might not be cold for a while.

He closed his eyes. The sorrow of time had receded again, and his soul lightened at the mercy of that. The treasures of Sarah, of Michael and Kathleen, of all of them — they nestled against his heart, pieces of him that would be missing always. But he was no longer lost in the losses. Inside him were the two ages, not grating but fitting together, teeth in two gears that propelled each other. He was one hundred sixty-seven years old. And he would always be thirty-five.

He curled his fingers on his chest as exhaustion won. He held on to the ages that made him who he was.

Six

David woke first. He lay still a minute, breathing in and out, then tested his legs and arms. Physical movement remained an effort. He pushed to his feet and explored the RV, stealth a challenge when his feet insisted on shuffling.

Colm had parked behind a Denny's restaurant and was now asleep, sprawled on top of the bed at the back of the vehicle. Zac hadn't moved from the couch across from David's, and Simon slept in a recliner halfway between the couches and the kitchenette. Surprising that David came to on his own; he typically slept at least twelve hours the first day after . . . fine, rejuvenation. He might as well have a term for it.

His stomach growled, as hollow as if he hadn't eaten in a week. He flexed his hand and tested the memories that came with the soreness there. It all came to him, easy, vivid, but he stood in Zachary Wilson's RV with desert sun pouring through the east windows and didn't lose himself in recent or old history. If he'd needed a final confirmation, this was it. His mind, not only his body, was sound again.

Sound but not strong, not yet. His single pass up and down the vehicle left his legs shaking. He sank onto the couch and lay there, eyes closed, until the others stirred.

"Denny's?" Zac sighed. "Epic fail, Colm."

Footsteps approached from the bedroom. "They have great breakfast food."

"They're a chain."

"Guess you shouldn't have let me drive."

"Forget it. Let's wake the new guy. Oh, he's awake."

It wasn't quite nine in the morning, and most of the booths and tables stood empty. The hostess seated them at a table in one corner. David claimed the chair with its back to the wall and watched the others. Simon was the only one to glare at him. He wanted that seat.

David gave what he hoped was a look of acknowledgment, but in this condition he wasn't putting his back to a room. Simon sat to one side and angled his chair. The glare didn't cool.

"New guy's privilege," David said.

Simon made a scoffing sound.

82

Their waitress, a ponytailed blond whose name tag read BEKAH, brought waters and menus and perked up when they said they were ready to order — all of them but Zac, who claimed he had never been to Denny's. By the time the rest of the table had ordered, Zac was ready with a request for an ultimate breakfast skillet and a side order of chocolate chip pancakes. Colm gave him an eye roll as Bekah bustled off with their menus and orders.

"Chocolate chip pancakes," Colm said.

"Sweet follows savory, mate." Zac pushed up the baseball cap he'd tugged on before leaving the RV. He'd put his back to the restaurant as quickly as David had claimed the chair opposite. "So, questions. You seem up to asking them now."

"Here?" David said.

Zac shrugged. "Anyone overhearing us will think we're sci-fi TV writers or something."

True enough. Something he'd know if he'd ever talked about these things in a group before. The realization cracked something in his chest. He sipped his water, head ducked. When he set down his glass and lifted his head, the room spun around him. He gripped the edge of the table.

"Hey," Colm said. "Hang tough a few

more minutes."

He couldn't nod without spinning the room faster. A faint buzz filled his head as his body caved forward.

Beside him, Simon snaked an arm across David's chest, gripped his far shoulder, kept him upright. "He's going to pass out."

"Possibility," David said as his vision turned grainy.

"Excuse me." Zac was on his feet. "Could we get something, a bread basket, or anything? He's crashing. Hypoglycemia."

"Oh." Bekah's voice filled with concern. "Of course. I'll be right back."

Zac resumed his seat. Someone might have spoken, but David couldn't track the words. Then Zac was thanking Bekah while Colm plucked a slice of white bread from the basket now occupying the center of the table.

"This is crap," he said as he set it into David's hand. "But it might keep you conscious for another few minutes."

"Thank you." David's hand shook as he lifted it.

The silence around the table made him want to punch all of them in the face. Or that might be the hunger talking. Bleached flour shouldn't taste this good.

The others made small talk while they

waited for the real food. Not a mention of the latest box-office hit or sports news, no stories about coworkers or wives or kids. Simon recited an abstract of a scientific journal article about advances in artificial intelligence. They volleyed opinions back and forth — ethical and practical ramifications, predictions of how many years it would take for these things to become reality and common knowledge. They quoted da Vinci, Darwin, Turing, Asimov. Discussing AIs somehow turned into reminiscing about October 30, 1938, and the *War of the Worlds* radio drama. Among them, only Colm had caught it live.

"You don't play murder in soft words," Simon intoned, actually sounding like Orson Welles. Colm laughed.

David listened, too fuzzy to add anything to the conversation. He propped his elbow on the table and his head in his hand and closed his eyes, but he let their words, their thoughts, their memories keep soaking into him.

When Bekah brought their plates, the smells of food made him faintly nauseated, but he'd take this wallop of an aftermath over three bedridden weeks. He tested a bite of toast, nibbled until he finished it, let his stomach settle. Then he dug into his Philly cheesesteak omelet. After a few bites, he was able to broaden his focus from the food to the guys around him, the clinking of their forks, the ease of their quiet. He met Colm's eyes. The man had been watching David eat. He tilted an eyebrow, and David nodded. Colm returned the nod and started on his own breakfast.

David sipped his coffee and glanced around the table, stopping at Zac. "You said there are organisms in my — our — blood."

"Have you ever looked at your blood through a microscope?"

"Of course." Back before he'd given up solving the riddle of himself.

"I mean a high-powered one."

David salted his hash browns. "It's been awhile, maybe thirty years."

"Sometime we'll have to show you what you missed back then. For a long time technology wasn't advanced enough to see them."

"I'll look into that."

"Too bad I don't have a microscope in the RV." Zac paused with a forkful halfway to his mouth. "Should've planned ahead. Just in case I meet John Russell in Arizona, what'll I need to bring along? Then again, figured you knew this stuff."

That nettled. David didn't bother answering.

"Cut him some slack," Colm said. "How many decades did it take the four of us to figure it out? And we had the common denominator right in front of us."

Four, right. Moira in Europe.

Simon pushed aside his half-cleared plate and propped his elbows on the table, steepling his fingers. "You know the planarian."

David nodded.

"Well, in essence, we were gifted a mutated, microscopic version that gradually permeated our blood cells and became sort of a second nucleus in both platelets and hemoglobin. They are antiaging obviously, but that's not all. They have a hyperhealing ability that activates when they sense the host organism is near death."

They let him sit a minute, processing that, while he finished his omelet and slathered his other slice of toast with strawberry jam. The planarian he knew of could be up to an inch long. This must be an altogether different organism. Microscopic . . . worms. Undying worms. In his blood cells. He shook his head, and the room stayed put this time.

"Yes," Simon said. "You'll never see them

87

with a cheaper microscope, but they're there."

"Where did they come from?"

"Our theory is that they originated in a pond on the outskirts of our old town. No way of knowing if they exist in multiple places, but I keep track of the science journals, eyes open for a discovery of them. Nothing so far."

"Who discovered them, then? Who did this to us, who — who did this to — ?" He took in a silent breath and steadied himself. "Do you know who's responsible?"

"We do," Colm said.

From across the restaurant a new group arrived. Five college-aged girls, laughing and shoulder-bumping, escorted to a table across the aisle. Zac repositioned his chair, back to the girls, and Simon gave a loud sigh.

Zac smirked. "Someone's got to walk the rocky road of fame."

"Until your clumsiness, you were best known to females aged sixteen to thirty."

"Do you have fans, Simon?"

Simon leaned back in his chair, arms folded.

"Then don't dis mine."

"You did not just use that word."

"Haters gonna hate."

Colm laughed.

The ease among them pinched in David's chest. He cleared his throat.

Zac sobered. "Let's finish this away from here."

"Just tell me," David said.

"Really, man. The rest needs to be discussed in private."

They finished eating in relative silence and paid their checks. Bekah's face was flushed when she brought back the receipts. Zac had been the only one to pay with a card, and her hand might have trembled as she returned it.

"Here you are, Mr. Wilson."

The smile he gave her was less cocky than kind. "Thanks, Bekah."

"I can't believe it. I knew you looked like him under that hat, but I can't believe it."

"Not a word?" He gave a sidelong glance at the table across the aisle, where the girls still perused their menus.

Simon coughed.

Bekah didn't notice him or Colm or David as they all tossed cash tips onto the table, stood, and pushed in their chairs. She hardly blinked as long as Zac held her eyes. "Not a word."

"Thanks," Zac said.

She all but ran from their table. David

eyed Zac's pen as he scribbled down a 1,000 percent tip. The guy might be about 70 percent ego, but he wasn't a jerk. He straightened and grinned.

"Let's get out of here."

SEVEN

They'd barely stepped into the RV when Colm announced the discussion was on hold until he took a shower. He disappeared before anyone could protest.

Simon shook his head. "He's been like this since the invention of the shower."

"I'll take us back to the vehicles. It'll take him that long to come out of there." Zac went up to the front.

He was right. They didn't have far to drive, less than fifteen minutes, and the water was still running when Zac pulled off the highway and parked beside Simon's car and his own.

In a few minutes, Colm emerged from the shower. "Anyone else who cares about cleanliness." He gestured toward the bathroom.

David glanced down at himself. His blue crewneck shirt was rumpled enough to look slept in.

Zac flopped onto one of the couches. "If you want to clean up, your gear's in my car."

"What?"

"I went back for your bags. You probably don't remember." He stood and grabbed keys from the counter beside the stove, offered them to David.

"I'm fine. But thank you."

Zac shrugged and put back the keys.

David sat up straight in one of the padded kitchen chairs, resolve steeling his spine against the weariness. He'd clean up later today, after the answers had all been given. The others claimed seats as well, Simon last, perching on the edge of the couch where David had slept. He still watched David with something like disbelief. Hard to blame him.

"Tell me who did this," David said.

"Okay," Zac said and then didn't continue.

Simon steepled his fingers, elbows on knees. "You remember the town of Fisher Lake."

A name, like John Russell, he'd never thought to hear again. His heart rate increased. Their expressions shifted, all three of them watching him more closely. His face must be giving all of it away.

"I never saw the lake." His voice steadied

by the end of the sentence.

"Well, as previously described, it's more of a pond," Simon said.

"You're from Fisher Lake?" Nods around the circle. "All of you?"

"And Moira," Colm said.

The origin of his curse. Not a quid pro quo of the Almighty after all, healed for a cost: healed forever. So long he'd wondered, and now here the blame was placed not on God, not on David, but on . . .

"Dr. Leon." They didn't deny it. "He did something to me. And to you?"

"To save our lives," Zac said. "He didn't know the side effects of his project. He died not knowing. He believed he'd given us a one-time superhealing serum, but he never used it on himself."

"Why not?"

"He contracted TB. And he had no idea the serum would do something against disease. He used it on fatal injuries."

They'd experienced something, each of them. They'd been dying, and then not dying, perhaps as unaware as David had been of the consequences. What had happened to each of the men here with him? A tiny jolt traveled his limbs. No telling when he'd last been curious about someone else. Well, someone who wasn't Tiana.

He had to fly out tonight. Get back to the store, to his life, to Tiana, but these men, this knowledge, all of it . . .

They watched him, waiting for him to put something together. He shook his head, and the motion seemed to dislodge his thoughts from their tiredness.

"You knew my face," he said to Zac, who nodded. "You'd seen me before. You were there? In the road? You took me to the doctor."

"No," Zac said. "But we studied Leon's work for a long time, after he was gone, and . . . well, you were the first of us. The first to be given the serum. His notes on you are copious."

Notes . . . "And a photograph?"

Zac rose and disappeared into the bedroom, returned in seconds with a laptop he was already booting up. "Showing's better than telling in this case. Just give me a minute here."

Silence reigned while Zac tapped to open folders and files. David wasn't the only one affected by this moment. Anticipation warred against something else inside him, heavy on his shoulders and tight in his stomach.

Zac handed him the laptop. "This is how I knew you."

He'd opened a folder called *John Russell* within a folder called . . . "Longevite Data?"

"Zac's nickname for us." Colm tugged his hair. "We haven't broken him of it yet."

"As in longevity?"

A hint of smugness lifted the corners of Zac's mouth. "Less arrogant than 'immortal,' you know? And more accurate, we can assume."

Probably.

"If we're ever an acknowledged part of history," Zac said, "I hope no one has the audacity to coin something else."

David scanned the folder bearing his name. Scans saved as PDF files. He looked up.

"I was his patient for less than two days. Stayed in town until the wagon was repaired, but I didn't see him again."

"Take a look." Zac nodded to the laptop.

David opened a few of the document scans and found minute script over yellowed pages, a few of them cracked down the center or disintegrating from the corners inward. Scanning them had been wise, yet they were in better condition than he'd have expected from a medical journal kept in the 1880s. The pages had been preserved with great care. He reached out one finger to the laptop screen and touched his name, written in the careful, ink-blotted hand. His pulse thrummed as he read sections of the text.

17 March 1883, Patient brought to me before dawn this morning, gravely injured . . .

. . . crushed thorax region including left lung and all bones of the chest and rib cage, abdominal cavity distended with rapid bleeding, patient choking on blood, incoherent but conscious . . . death was imminent . . .

. . . administered serum and beg now Almighty God and His Son, for no other thing can be done. Though patient remains in dreadful pain, he yet breathes. I write these words at the bedside and shall not leave it until such time as he improve or pass on.

David looked away. This was history, old history, but he couldn't meet the eyes of men who had known since meeting him about this, the second most physically painful event of all his years. Dr. Leon had begged God for his life while David had begged for death.

He closed the document. Opened an image. Caught his breath.

Leon was a skilled sketch artist. The page's edges were a little tattered, a medium-distance rendering of him lying in the patient bed, his face smooth in sleep. The exact face he saw in the mirror today. Zac didn't work hard to recognize him, though David's eyes were closed in the picture.

He opened a second image — his bare torso and shoulders. The bruises covered him, starker in black and white, blackest at his abdomen and left ribs. Chest and sides sunken, crushed. Here, now, his lungs shut down. No one who looked at this image would see a patient. They would see a corpse. David fought a wave of memory. The moment he knew he couldn't correct the skid of the wagon. *Cut the horses loose, spare the horses* and then more urgently *jump, jump clear.* But there hadn't been time, everything moving so fast, rain dripping over the brim of his hat, driving at his usual speed though he should have slowed in that weather, on a road he didn't know well. Thrown and falling and the explosion of pain as the wagon crushed him. To death.

He spread his hand over his eyes, shut them tight.

"Yeah," Colm said quietly, but David couldn't focus on his voice.

A woman wept. The weight on him lifted. Hands raised him from the mud. Somewhere in the back of his darkening brain he wondered why no one helped the man who was screaming.

"Come back, man."

David shook his head, lowered his hand from his eyes. The picture still filled the screen — black hemorrhaging and smashed bones beneath the skin. He shut the laptop. Looked up. Simon had wandered to the kitchen, but Zac and Colm still sat with him.

"Happens to all of us sometimes," Colm said.

No. David shoved to his feet and pushed past Colm. He tugged open the door and stepped into the desert, into heat like a wall. He walked until sweat poured down his back and chest. Until weakness leached into him, the fuel of one meal and three hours' sleep used up. Full recovery would require more time. His legs folded, and he sat on the ground, knees bent, arms wrapped around them. He scuffed one shoe over the top of the sand, drawing a wide line. Moment of truth. Yes, there was a lure to all of it. For the first time since he'd been with Sarah, he wouldn't have to hide the dichotomy.

But he might not remember how to stop

hiding it. And he might not want to. The way things were now . . . solitary, sure, but safe too. Not that safety had ever been his final determiner before.

Or his excuse.

He sat awhile in the sand. A lizard skittered from behind a rock, leaving tiny footprints as it fled in an arc away from David. He squinted at the blue expanse above him. Halfway to the horizon, a hawk circled. Cars passed on a highway half a mile away.

He pushed to standing and spread his feet until his head cleared. He plodded back to the RV and made decisions. The cool air from inside hit him as he opened the door, habit keeping him to one side of the doorway, giving him a second's pause before he ducked inside.

"I think it was a chance for a ratings spike." Simon's words bit the air with a false calm that crackled.

"I'm not a TV show," Zac said.

"You're not a household name, either — or rather, you weren't until this week. It irked you and you decided to do something about it."

"By smashing every bone in my body? Do you think I'm pathological?"

"It's crossed my mind."

After the glare of the sun, David's eyes

had to adjust. He shut the door behind him as the sweat cooled and dried on the back of his neck. He shivered.

Colm lounged in the driver's seat, feet on the dash. He found David over his shoulder. "Ten more minutes and we were coming after you."

David leaned against the door. Zac's laptop sat beside him on one couch, and Simon paced in front of him.

"You have to stop," Simon said. "You're going to end up dead or, worse, in a hospital somewhere, and we'll have to steal your blood samples like sidekicks in a spy movie."

Zac leaned back against the couch and watched Simon's strides try to carve a rut in front of him. "And you call me dramatic."

"You know how it works, Zac."

"Whatever happens to me or Colm or Moira, you'll go on undetected and unaffected. Go to work in your lab, pick up your white coats from the cleaner's, monitor the science journals."

Simon halted in front of him, jaw clenched, fists looking as if they itched to deck Zac. A one-two punch would knock his head into the wall. Up front, Colm was reading Dashiell Hammett, so absorbed David almost believed he didn't know how the novel ended. The dog-eared pages throughout hinted otherwise.

Simon stalked to the pegboard over the kitchen counter, where several sets of keys hung. He snagged one and turned to face them all.

"My flight's leaving at six, and there's no point in continuing this." His gaze met Zac's.

Zac shrugged, the slant of his shoulders somehow indicating the door.

Simon jingled his keys. "David. It was good to meet you at last."

"Likewise. And thank you for your help."

"Seems to have turned out all right." The man's mouth tilted. Another nod, and he headed out the door.

"See you at Thanksgiving," Colm said as the door shut.

"Thanksgiving?" David said.

"You're invited, obviously. Tradition. We spend Christmas wherever we are, but Thanksgiving and Fourth of July are . . ." He shrugged.

"Are longevite holidays." Zac stood, smirking. "You'll meet Moira too."

It was too easy. The integration. The welcome. Perhaps it made sense, only five of them in the world, and their four a solid group. The disagreement just now had felt worn, old words like old clothes.

Colm swung his feet to the floor. "I guess rock climbing's out of the question."

"For the new guy? Yeah." Zac shut the laptop and tucked it under his arm.

"Figured you wouldn't go for it either, at least for a few weeks."

"Oh, that. I'm healed up. Hundred percent. Beat you to the top."

"If you'd return me to my hotel first?" David said.

Zac and Colm set a time and place to meet, and before Colm left he shook David's hand.

"Hope to see you around." Colm didn't wait for David to commit to anything, just smiled and went to his car. It was a bright green Honda that shouted his presence twice as loudly as he did himself. Dust trailed his departure, dissipated until the car turned onto the empty highway and vanished into the horizon.

Zac locked up the RV and left it. David got into the passenger seat of the red sedan. His bags were indeed on the back seat. Thoughtful. Zac stowed his laptop at David's feet, though there was room in the back for it.

They'd been driving in silence for two miles when Zac nodded at the laptop. "Reading material for you."

David turned his face to the passenger window. "Later."

"You're not taking it with you."

"You can email me."

"Listen, man. I want us to part ways on equal footing. This" — he gestured at the desert surrounding them — "isn't."

"Not sure what you mean."

But he was, and neither of them had to spell out who held the advantage. Zac's gaze didn't move from the road, but the knowledge held between them. It was obvious what Zac wanted him to read. If he read it, he'd be accepting something. He had to decide now if he wanted to.

He bent and picked up the laptop from the floor. Unzipped the case, pulled it out, woke it up. The folder was still open. *Longevite Data.* Named subfolders, five of them. Zac had closed *John Russell.* David scanned the names of the others: Joseph Wirth, Colm O'Carroll, Anders Eklund, Mary Whitefield.

"Well?" he said.

Zac cleared his throat. His gaze didn't waver from the highway, not even a glance toward David. "Open *Anders Eklund.*"

David looked at a few of Leon's sketches first. Zac's face had changed no more than David's had. But the bodily damage Dr.

103

Leon had captured of this patient was an entirely different sort. Blood, lots of it, not pooling inside body cavities but showing here in the pictures, staining the bedcovers and the bandages wrapped around Zac's arm and torso. David looked across the console again at the man who had survived this. Zac didn't meet his eyes.

David clicked on the document scans — the same minute script, the same fragile yellow pages that would smell like the first-edition case in his store. Musty but preserved. Irreplaceable. He focused on the words.

19 September 1887. Patient Anders Eklund. Brought to me last evening with two bullet wounds, left arm and abdomen. Great deal of bleeding from the latter. I was able to remove the bullet from the patient's stomach but could not stanch the bleeding.

. . . has lost much blood and suffered much, and his only chance now is that the serum which has healed others was given in time to heal him also. I pray God Almighty and His Son may grant Eklund mercy. None in town can tell who shot him or why. He was found in the road outside town. Sheriff Wirth has been to see him. I

informed him the patient is not yet conscious and death may yet come for him.

David closed the laptop. "Same road?"

"Same." Zac sat back a moment, spine
pressed into the seat, and then his shoulders
relaxed. "The town got rid of the bandits
within a week. Patrolled, shot one of them.
I was their only victim."

David nodded.

"Lay there over an hour before she found
me. Death takes time when you're gutshot."

"She?"

Zac met his eyes a long moment before
refocusing on the highway. "Moira. Mary
back then. It's how we met, but I've got no
memory of it. I don't know how she got me
into her buggy — she says I helped. She
held me all the way to the doc's. Reins in
one hand, pressure on my gut with the
other."

"Your file says 1887."

"I was the fourth. Simon was last, 1890.
So yeah, by the time Moira brought me to
Doc Leon, she knew he had a serum that
could save . . . well, a life that wasn't sav-
able. Told Simon the victim of the crime
would pull through despite the odds, which
is why he came to see me before I was even
conscious. Leon never was an optimist,

though. His notes are like that for each of us — 'patient has suffered untold agony, pray God they keep breathing through this day of agony, but probably they'll die in great agony.' "

"Simon was sheriff."

"Yep. And looking back on it, so stereotypical. Gruff and conscientious and carried a big stick. You didn't mess with the man. It was needed some of the time, but generally Fisher Lake made Walnut Grove look like the O.K. Corral."

"And now he works in a lab?"

"Worked law enforcement on and off until 1976. It got risky, the identity issue."

David sat quietly, letting the miles bring him closer to the plane that would take him home. Take him away from these people and their stories.

"If you want to know about the others, all you've got to do is ask," Zac said after a minute. "But you ask them."

"Of course," David said.

"Since you didn't get a choice in our knowledge of you, I figured . . ." He shrugged. "Now you know me equally."

"Thank you."

Zac shifted in his seat, and one hand flexed then resumed its grip. "So what were you doing, driving horses in that weather?

I've always wondered. I remember the wagon was barely salvageable."

So long ago. No, the memories hadn't dimmed, but they glittered from a faraway place inside he didn't visit anymore. He knew the way back to them, though. He let himself venture there.

With the recent upheaval of his mind and body, the memories weren't as distant as usual. He sat with them, acclimating, until Zac reached for the radio knob.

"I was going home," David said.

Zac's hand withdrew to his lap.

"I hadn't seen my wife in twelve days."

"And a flash flood wasn't about to slow you down."

"Certainly not."

Zac changed to the far left lane and passed a silver tour bus, the type to be filled with band equipment and instruments, perhaps even band members. David kept his eyes on the bus as it flashed past and faded behind them, then sat forward as Zac merged to the right again.

"In Michigan, you can stay over there." David nodded to the left lane. "They call it the fast lane."

"So that's where you live now?"

"The last three years."

"What took you away from home — back

then, I mean?"

"Buying seed for planting."

He could smell the dirt, feel it between his fingers. He flexed his hand at the memory of blisters that would turn to calluses, leather reins deftly handled to keep the horse plowing a straight line — a different skill than driving a wagon. Days he thought his back would break. Days he knelt in the dusty furrows of his fields and prayed for rain. One year he bowed to the earth in the middle of a cornfield destroyed by hail and begged his Lord for help to pay bills this crop would have covered.

"You were a farmer," Zac said.

David tilted his head back and closed his eyes, letting the past soak his heart. "That I was."

"You cared for it. For the work."

"For the land."

"What are you now?"

"I sell books."

Zac chuckled. "Of course you do."

David opened his eyes and sat up. "What's that?"

"Something literary about you, that's all."

"And what was Anders?"

"Ah." His mouth twitched. "Started as a freighter, back in my teens. Worked for a company until I could get enough stake to go out on my own. I loved the constant movement — actually I'd wondered if you were a freighter, the way you drove on through that storm, but if so you weren't a smart one."

David shook his head. "Freighting would have been too rootless for me."

"When I decided to settle, I opened a mercantile. If you bought seed in town, you bought it from me."

So strange. He tried to go back there, all the way back, standing at the counter of Fisher Lake's general store and counting over carefully saved bills and coins in exchange for the goods that would keep his farm going, the seed that would grow in his fields. But the man he'd paid, the man who would have smiled and bid him a good day . . . No, only a blur. He certainly didn't remember the name Eklund.

"You, a merchant," David said. "I can't see it. Ah, wait, yes I can. You could sell anything to anybody, Wilson."

Zac's laugh was unrestrained. "Including my autograph, it seems."

David darted a glare at him, and Zac laughed again.

They hit downtown Phoenix in a few hours. Zac looked across at him when they caught a red light.

"Food?"

"Good idea."

"Find somewhere that's not a chain," Zac said.

David used his phone to navigate them to a family-owned Italian grill. He ordered spaghetti, requested extra meatballs, and ignored the breadsticks. Right now, extra carbs would crash his system. He'd prefer not to sleep through the flight.

Conversation remained sparse as they ate, Zac digging into chicken marsala and both of them sipping coffee. Zac ordered tiramisu for dessert, so David sipped more slowly and let the man savor his sweets.

"A good tiramisu can't be outclassed," Zac said.

"I'm a chocolate cake guy myself."

"Not from a box, I hope."

David chuckled. "How about from a chain restaurant?"

Their words dwindled again, maybe a distaste for triviality after the revelations of the last day. David drained his mug and pushed it aside and watched the stranger in front of him who could never truly be a stranger. None of them could be, not even Moira, whether he met her or not. But a small nudge inside him knew he would. Wanted to. Thanksgiving. Maybe he'd do it.

"How's the arm?"

Zac looked up from his fixated enjoyment of the tiramisu. "Arm? Oh." He flexed the left one. "Serum took care of it."

David nodded.

"Secondary injuries are healed too. Or was it not that way for you?"

"It was, with the wagon accident." He paged through his memories. "You're saying anytime I'd have died, I've been left unscarred."

"Right. But anything that's non-life-threatening doesn't activate them, which is why we can scar from milder things."

His nod was slower now as he fit each major physical injury in his life into one of those two categories. "I hadn't thought of the distinction. Always puzzled me that I could heal sometimes but not others."

A chill zipped up his spine. The car accident, 1978, walking away from the paramedics and insisting he was fine, not telling them his head had hit the steering wheel, that he'd been unconscious at least a minute or two but woke before they arrived. He told Zac about it, about the blinding headache that assailed hours later. He'd curled into a ball on the floor of his apartment and hugged a pillow to his face. Sometime after dark the pain washed away in a soft coolness that spread from the center of his skull.

"I was dying?"

"Based on what I know, yeah," Zac said. "Sounds like a brain bleed or something."

"Why did the . . . organisms . . ." Still felt strange to say it. "The serum, why did it take so many hours to work?"

"It was working the whole time. Stanching bleeding, healing capillaries, whatever it does. But yeah, we've all noticed the pain relief is sudden when the healing completes. How should I say this? For one of us, you sound normal." He smiled.

For some reason, it was good to hear that.

EIGHT

"Anyone waiting for you back in Michigan?" Zac said as they left the restaurant a few minutes later.

"No." The turtle did not count.

"No one at all?"

The image flashed of Tiana in her cowboy boots and peacoat, stomping fallen leaves and turning back to smile at him.

"No," he said.

Zac nodded and slid behind the wheel.

David let him merge into traffic before speaking again. "You?"

"As far as the public's concerned, I'm happily unattached."

Not an answer. Before David could call him on it, Stevie Nicks began warbling from Zac's phone. *"Well, I've been afraid of changing 'cause I built my life around you . . ."*

"Huh," Zac said and brought the phone to his ear. "You're not on a plane over the Atlantic by any chance, are you? . . . Phoe-

113

nix, I told you. I'll be in Denver tomorrow morning. . . . Um, the Hilton at the airport. Wait, what?" After a few seconds, he shook his head and hung up.

David cocked an eyebrow at him.

"As you might have guessed, that's our wandering waif, but she must have grabbed an earlier flight . . . and, um, she's here. Meeting us at the Hilton."

"She flew into Phoenix?"

"Yep, called me on her way to the baggage claim."

David glanced down at his rumpled clothes. Well, nothing for it.

As they entered the hotel lobby, Zac slowed for half a stride, and David followed his gaze. Moira was seated on a black leather bench that backed up to a plant-and-stone arrangement in the center of the traffic. Around her, people checked in, checked out, milled about with luggage wheeling behind them. She had been watching the doors. She smiled and came to meet them.

Zac gave a sigh that seemed to come to rest. David edged aside as Moira neared, but she swerved to collide with him, not Zac. Her embrace was easy, warm, and brought the top of her head to his chest. She couldn't be taller than five foot two.

Her brown curls smelled like pomegranates. David's arms encased her, politeness evaporating as an ache filled his chest.

He was being hugged.

"Our long-lost longevite." Moira stepped back like a proud grandmother, *let me look at you* in the laughter around her eyes. "John Russell as I live and breathe."

The aging process had stopped in her early twenties. She was fine boned and brown eyed, and she had to be overheating in a burgundy blazer, skinny jeans, and knee-high oxblood boots. She grabbed David's hands and held on.

"You're tall," she said. "I know, an obvious statement, but for some reason I didn't expect that."

"My apologies?" He smiled.

"Not at all, be as tall as you like." She hugged him again, and he stood and let her, every cell of him soaking in the human touch and hoping she didn't notice. She stepped back after a few seconds. "If the boys forgot to invite you to Thanksgiving, consider yourself invited now. Even if you have previous commitments, you should join us for part of the day. Where are we this year, Zac?"

"Colm says Chicago."

"Of course he does. Where's your home,

David? Would Chicago be feasible for you?"

"I'm a few hours north of Detroit."

"Oh, perfect." As if it were settled, Moira turned to Zac. "So I'm told we're to call you Fall Guy."

Zac took a step back. "You talked to Simon?"

"Colm."

He shook his head with a sigh and included David in his smirk, but if David could see through the levity, surely Moira could. As if Zac knew his mask was porous, he let it slide from his face. His Adam's apple dipped.

Moira brushed her hand across the back of his head. "Skull intact?"

"It is now."

She closed her eyes for half a heartbeat and then tilted her head to look up at David, an exaggerated pose. "Have you been fed recently?"

"If you mean within the last hour."

"Colm told me about the rejuvenation."

David dipped a nod.

"If you'd let me know you were coming, we could have eaten here," Zac said.

"That would have been nice."

"Well . . ."

"I know, my own fault."

"We could get coffee," David said with a

116

nod toward the café tucked in a far corner of the lobby. "I have an hour or so."

He checked out of his room and met them at a table a few minutes later. Two servings of caffeine would wire him, might even put a tremor in his hands, but if it kept him awake until he made it home, that was a small price. He sipped and listened to Moira's stories of Italy and couldn't help adding to her descriptions of Rome.

"When were you there?" she said, lighting up.

"1981, '82."

"You don't know which?"

"Well, it was Christmas of '81 and New Year's Day of '82."

She smiled. "Your choice of timing is interesting."

"I'm never home for Christmas. I spent '79 and New Year's 1980 in Israel."

"That must have been a very spiritual experience." Her eyes lit with reverence.

"It was," he said.

Zac's gaze moved from her to David and back, but he didn't join in. The desire to know more about them tugged again at David, but he sipped his coffee and held his peace. Starting something like this . . . he had to get home and take stock of the situation. Or process it, anyway.

117

They chatted until forty minutes before David's boarding time, and then he and Moira exchanged contact information.

Moira hugged David again, and this one lingered. "See you soon."

Zac shook his hand. "Thanks for tracking me down."

"Thanks for falling to your death."

"I thought I had this time."

Something about the tone of that, the openness that dared David to ignore it.

"Go climb some rocks," David said.

"I intend to." Zac smiled. *"Bene vale."*

And he accused David of bookishness. "Godspeed."

The shuttle got him to the airport in six minutes, and for once TSA didn't make him step out of line. Nice of them, especially since the second dose of caffeine had socked his system and he now fought both fatigue and jitters. Couldn't the serum even that out, leave him awake and calm? He shook his head as he fast-walked to his gate. Minuscule unidentified cell components. In his blood.

He found his gate, sank into one of the deep-seated vinyl chairs, parked his luggage at his feet. He flexed the arm into which they'd injected Simon's blood. He couldn't discredit their claims, not with such clear physical proof.

Boarding went smoothly, and he hunkered down in his window seat. He buckled in, though if Zac could survive that fall, chances were David could survive a plane crash.

Too many new concepts. His brain, even on caffeine, felt pummeled. He had to finish recovering before he could process all of this. He tugged his battered travel copy of *Ben-Hur* from his backpack, switched on the reading light overhead, and settled in. Four hours to Detroit, nearly five hours driving. Then he could collapse into his own bed.

The flight was turbulent, the terminal was crowded, and his feet were heavy by the time he found his car in the airport lot. As he drove home, oncoming headlights smeared his vision. He left his luggage in his car and trudged up the garage steps into the house. Shower. He'd never gotten a shower.

First things first. He took a small plastic tub from a shelf in the refrigerator and opened the lid, which was dotted with tiny holes. He gathered up a handful of worms and went to the living room.

The box turtle wouldn't be in danger of starvation, not in a few days, but she'd be hungry. David lifted the mesh top from the terrarium, her winter home to which he'd transferred her while he was away. Cold enough outside now that he hadn't wanted to chance her freezing overnight. He dropped the worms into her food dish. She was hiding under her favorite log, half-burrowed into the cypress mulch, but she would smell the food. Normally he enjoyed watching her as she craned her neck, eyed her prey, chowed down in slow motion. Tonight he left her to a solitary meal and trudged to the shower.

Finally clean, he tugged on flannel pants and fell into bed. No reserves of energy left. He'd stay holed up here tomorrow. One more day needed to refuel with protein, to rest . . . A smile found his mouth. To rejuvenate.

He set no alarm and didn't stir until after three the next afternoon. No surprise that Tiana had left him two voice mails. He dragged himself upright and shuffled to the living room. The turtle was burrowed with her head visible, and the worms were gone. He smiled.

The sleep portion of his recovery seemed accomplished. His mind was functioning, and recent memories were sharp — bidding goodbye to Moira and Zac, the flight to Detroit, the drive home. Physically, though, some weakness lingered. He went to the kitchen, grilled chicken and asparagus, and devoured both. Still hungry. He opened the refrigerator and gazed into it without inspiration. Maybe he'd go up to the corner and get a sandwich. He'd not be walking that far today, though. Have to drive. He sighed.

Someone knocked on his door. Strange. He was expecting no packages. He crossed the living room to open the door.

Tiana. One hand held a white paper bag from the corner diner, and her eyes were beyond sparking — more like hurling napalm.

"You're here."

"I am."

"And you couldn't answer your phone? Or better yet, call in to say, 'Hey, you'll be manning things one more day, and thanks for bringing in six hundred fifty-three dollars and eighty-nine cents yesterday on your own —' "

"Tiana," he said.

She clasped the restaurant bag in front of her. Her eyebrows arched almost to her hairline.

"I apologize."

"I closed up the store to come over here."

Mouthwatering scents were seeping through that bag. "You brought lunch?"

"In case you were sick." Her gaze took in

the neighbors on either side of him, bunga-lows not unlike his own, cars in the drive-ways but no one outside. "I can go if this is . . . inappropriate?"

"That's up to you."

"Small towns talk."

"Because a female entered my house in broad daylight?"

"The female who works for you. Not like I can be mistaken for any other woman in Harbor Vale, even at a distance." She ges-tured to her hair.

He couldn't care less about the sort of people who would jump to a critical conclu-sion, but women were different. "If you prefer, we'll eat on the porch."

Tiana looked past him into the foyer, seemed to weigh something in her mind, then stepped inside. David shut the door, locked it out of habit, and led her to his kitchen.

She stood a moment, taking in his living space. He let himself see it through new eyes, but nothing was remarkable. Nothing in the kitchen, anyway. Slate-blue walls, black granite counter, faux stone floor, stainless steel appliances. The room had just enough square footage for a small table in the corner across from the fridge and stove.

"It's so neat," Tiana said. "Way to defy

bachelor stereotypes."

He laughed. "I don't eat in here."

"You cook, though." She nodded to the skillet in the sink.

"Only the basics."

"And the way you are about your books, I'm really not buying it if you tell me the rest of the house is a mess." She set the take-out bag on the counter, lifted out two Styrofoam bowls of soup and packaged oyster crackers.

"Mm." His stomach seemed to hollow at the promise of more food. His metabolism must still be amped up.

"I thought asparagus soup might make you gag if you were feeling queasy, but it smells like you've been cooking some anyway. Did you just eat?"

"Not long ago, but I could again."

They sat at the table. Tiana handed him one of the soups without checking the flavor. "They're both chicken noodle."

"You didn't want cream of broccoli?"

"Well, if I thought asparagus might make you gag, I wasn't going to force you to smell broccoli."

Neither of them spoke again until they'd opened the bowls, stirred them, taken test bites, and warned each other it was still hot. Tiana stirred in a whole package of crackers and offered him the other one.

A food he wouldn't eat on its own. For most of his life, a food he wouldn't eat at all, convinced any hardened white-flour product would taste like hardtack. He used half the package and gave the rest to Tiana.

"So," she said, munching them straight out of the little bag. "Have you been sick?"

Close enough. He nodded.

"For two days? You didn't mention it before."

"It knocked me down fast."

"But it's not why you were gone the first day."

A sigh. "No. Something had come up. Something personal."

She studied him and ignored her soup.

David paused, a bite half raised to his lips. "What?"

"Thanks for not lying to me."

When they finished, his stomach was warm and full, and he could have slept again. He blinked away the drowsiness and threw away their trash as Tiana wandered from kitchen to living room. Nothing there but a couch and love seat, the TV, his movie collection . . . oh, and —

"You have a turtle," she called.

He joined her. Tiana crouched at the glass and tapped the pad of her finger against the glass without making a sound.

While the turtle craned her neck toward the movement, David stared too, no longer seeing his place through Tiana's eyes. Instead, he was now seeing her in it. He shouldn't. Couldn't. But the glimpse was captivating.

"You," Tiana said. "A pet."

"Not exactly. That is, petting isn't required."

"What's its name?" She didn't stand up, didn't look away, as if she'd never seen a live reptile before. Well, maybe she hadn't.

"Mostly I call her Turtle."

"How do you know she's a female?"

"Eye color."

Now she did look up, mouth open. "For real?"

"Males have a bright red eye."

"David Galloway, zoologist."

His laugh caught on something, but she didn't seem to notice. She straightened and crossed the room to the entrance of his library. David followed.

"Oh . . ." Tiana stepped into the room and turned a full circle, head tilting to see the top shelves near the ten-foot ceiling. "How many?"

"A few thousand."

"Come on, I know you. Exact count."

She didn't know him. But she could —
could truly know him. All he had to do was
tell her everything. Even now she knew him
better than they did, Wilson and the others
— she knew David would have an answer
for her question, knew he favored cream of
asparagus soup, knew he'd rather be digging through a box of old books than serv-
ing customers or balancing accounts. This
was true knowledge of a person. Personal,
not scientific.

No one person knew all of it. For the first
time since Ginny left him, he wished someone did.

Tiana was frowning at him.

"Three thousand, eight hundred, forty-
two."

Her lips parted. She looked around the
room again. "Including the antiques?" She
motioned to the slim bookcase set apart in
one corner.

Right. Antique. That's what he was. What
he would be to her if she knew.

"No," David said. "There are one hundred
sixty-seven of those."

She opened the glass door and bent to
read the lower titles. "Oh, these last ones
aren't old at all. So they're in chronological
order?"

"I buy a first edition every year. Whatever

new release I enjoy the most."

"Going all the way back to the eighteen hundreds?"

A cold finger traced his spine, but she'd never figure it out.

"Wow. Some of these must be worth a lot of money."

"Quite a lot."

"They're insured?"

"Yes, but I doubt I'd be able to replace them all."

"Yeah," Tiana said. She shut the door and walked the perimeter of the room, an Austen heroine putting herself to best advantage, except Tiana didn't know she was doing it. The wonder in her eyes, the appreciation for his most prized possession, attracted him as much as the lithe movement of her jean-clad legs.

He didn't want just any person to know him. He wanted it to be her. The awareness of that wasn't new, but it had never before made his heart pound or his voice fail.

"You don't have any children's books." Disappointment lilted in her voice.

He wished he had a whole case of Caldecott winners so he could watch her plop down cross-legged on the floor and flip their glossy, colorful pages.

She pulled a few books out randomly, old

and new blended on his shelves, hardcovers and paperbacks. "They're not from library sales. They're in perfect condition, every single one of them. Even the antiques."

He nodded.

"Did you inherit them or something? Or do you go into debt to collect books?"

Perhaps not a lie to say he'd inherited them. From one generation to another, lifetimes passing. His own, that's all.

It hung in the air around him like an aura — the choice. But he'd already made it.

She stood in front of him, waiting, one hand hooked on a back pocket of her jeans.

"I've been collecting books a long time," he said.

She cocked one eyebrow at him, waiting for more.

"A . . . a long time."

"Thirty years? You started in kindergarten?"

"There's something I need to tell you."

Don't do this. The voice screamed in his head. Experience. Common sense.

Fear.

He wouldn't give in to it.

NINE

"David." Tiana crossed the room and stood before him. Close enough to smell her freesia body splash. "It's okay. Whatever it is."

Because she didn't know what it was. His chest heaved.

Remember Ginny. Don't ruin this too.

No. Ginny was proof he had to do this. Now.

He motioned with one hand, and Tiana followed him. Halted at the doorway of his bedroom.

"Um . . . ," she said.

"Wait here."

She stood in the doorway while he crouched in front of the cedar chest at the foot of the bed. He unlatched it, lifted the lid, and picked out his proofs. Hands full, he nodded her out of the way, and she trailed him back to the library. Yes. Do this in the company of his books. Their collective age calmed him as he knelt in the center of the room and set everything out on the carpet. Tiana knelt beside him. Silent.

He held out a handwritten receipt for his first edition of *The Silmarillion.* Nodded to the first editions case. Tiana took the slip of paper and crouched at the case until she found the book, then looked back at him.

"So you keep receipts. . . ."

"Look at the date." His stomach tensed.

Tiana looked down. "September 20, 1977. So . . . ?"

"Look at the purchaser's signature, Tiana." She knew his handwriting as well as her own, especially the sweep of the *D* she teased him about. *"People must think your name is O-avid."*

Her fingers crinkled the edge of the paper. "You bought this book in — wait, that would make you — well, over forty — no, you obviously didn't buy it the year you were born, so that would make you . . ." She shook her head. "I give up. This is your adult signature. But you're not sixty."

"No. I'm not."

"You're a time traveler?" Her mouth tilted up.

"I'm . . ." His every muscle tightened. Resolve didn't make the words come easier. "I'm older than sixty."

Her face flattened. She shook her head. "Your sense of humor needs more work than I thought."

"It isn't a joke."

"You're thirty-five."

He reached for another artifact. Handed it over. A bent sepia photograph not much later than the ones scanned into Zac's hard drive. David and Sarah, and wee Michael perched on her arm. All her lovely hair pinned up, David's hat in his hand at his side — he'd forgotten to remove it until the last moment.

Tiana's hand trembled once. "Who are these people?"

"My wife, Sarah. My son, Michael, when he was three."

She turned over the picture and read the penned date. 1884. She looked up at him, lips parted, eyes too wide.

"I was thirty-five when I stopped aging. I was badly hurt that year, and a doctor tried to save my life by putting something experimental into my blood. This" — he motioned to his face — "is the result."

"You stopped aging. Like Dorian Gray," Tiana said.

Ah, how many times he'd read that one. Imagined a painting of himself, of a man stooped and wrinkled with grieving eyes.

"You believe this," she said, handing the photograph back to him. "You believe the man in this picture is you."

"It is."

She scooted closer to the items spread on the floor. "What in the world . . . ?"

He let her examine each piece. His driver's license from 1975, a theater ticket from the first time he saw *Gone with the Wind*. He'd chosen nothing with John Russell's name on it — no sense now in complicating the explanation. She paused finally at the frayed blue uniform jacket.

"This is . . . a Union soldier's uniform. But it looks too small."

"I was a drummer. Only a boy, you see — thirteen." By the end of the fighting, the cuffs had ended four inches above his wrists and the seams strained at his shoulders.

"David, where did you get this, really? It should be in a museum."

"My ma kept the uniform. When she passed on, I found it and couldn't make myself discard it."

She folded her hands in her lap, studying him. "Why would you discard it?"

"When I look at it, I . . ." He shook his head. He'd keep talking as long as she kept listening. Something he said would be the right thing. "I taste hardtack and muddy

132

water and smoke and blood. That iron taste blood leaves in the air. I — I've many memories, Tiana, decades of them. Many of them good and pure and right, but many of them . . ."

She gathered the things in her hands and set them atop the uniform, then knelt in front of him. "Have you talked to someone about this?"

An ache filled his chest. "A psychiatrist, you mean?"

"There are . . . you know . . . medications."

He stood. "What about the photograph? It's me, isn't it?"

"The resemblance is crazy. I'm sure you're related."

"There's one man represented by these artifacts, and it's myself. That's my signature on the receipts, on the driver's license. And though I can't prove it, I wore that uniform when I was a lad and the beat of my drums told our troops the speed of our march."

"Okay, listen to me, okay?" Her voice shook. "Given this person is clearly an ancestor of yours, I'm going to trust you didn't rip off any of this stuff from a museum or . . . or anywhere else. I think these are heirlooms, and somehow you've, you know, internalized them or something."

So blind he'd been to try this. All of it could be explained away. He did a quick inventory of the contents of the cedar chest — documents, mostly, photographs she'd say were of this same ancestor. If these things hadn't convinced her, those wouldn't either. And call him a coward, he wasn't going to bring out a gun from the bedroom cabinet and put a bullet through his heart. Likely he'd pass out and she'd call an ambulance.

"I have a favor to ask," he said.

"I'm not going to tell anyone about this."

"That's not my concern." Not with her.

"What then?"

"Would you stay on, please, until I can find someone to replace you?"

She blinked. Cocked her head. "Did I say I was quitting?"

"You said I'm delusional."

Tiana pushed up from the floor and stood in front of him, head slightly tilted to meet his gaze. She was sizing him up in a way she'd never done before, but something else lingered behind that look.

"I need to know something," she said after a moment.

"Of course." Whatever it was, she deserved an answer after this.

"Why did you tell me this now?"

"I wanted you to know."

"Why?"

If only he could include the others in his explanation, but that wouldn't be right; and why should she believe that five people on the earth couldn't die if she refused to believe in one? David scooped up the things she'd piled and took them back to his room. She didn't follow this time. He packed them into the chest, ran his palm down the front of his uniform a final time before closing the lid. When he returned to the library, Tiana was sitting in his chair, legs drawn up to one side, scanning his books again from ceiling to floor. David turned the desk chair to face her and took a seat.

"You thanked me earlier," he said. "For not lying to you."

She met his eyes, pulled her knees up, and nodded.

"This had been a lie of omission."

"Okay. Is there . . . anything else?"

She called his whole life a delusion and then asked for more pieces of him. He shook his head.

"It must have been hard to tell me."

He looked around at his books, their patient welcome emanating from the shelves. Something literary about him; yes, Zac was right. He could stay here among the pages for months before he missed the company of people. People who fought and fretted and aged and died. Yet this woman before him — he'd miss her soonest.

He'd been unguarded once. Long ago now, but he remembered what it was not only to miss people after absence but to crave closeness every day, to live without a mask, to know folk who saw his true face and allowed him to see theirs. For a moment he'd wanted that again enough to take a risk.

A mistake.

He cleared his throat, set his hands on his knees. Tiana watched him.

"My wife, Sarah — she and I discovered this thing together, as she grew old and I didn't. She never questioned if it were true because she witnessed it."

And Ginny . . . aye, she'd witnessed it too, but bloodier and in the space of hours, not years. Nothing for her to doubt either.

"I should have realized the difficulty of proving myself," he said.

Tiana studied him a long moment.

"What?"

"I've worked for you for two years, David. It feels like we've talked about everything by now, and I just never . . . you've always been . . ."

"Sane?" His lips twitched.

"I've been waiting for you to get agitated or something, you know, the way schizoids do when they're challenged, when their beliefs are challenged."

"Ah." Smart woman.

"But that doesn't mean I can accept something like this. It violates the order of creation. We're born, we live, we die, and to be absent from the body is to be present with the Lord. Does that . . . scare you, maybe? That we're going to die someday?"

If she only knew.

He shook his head, all words spent for now. He tried not to let it matter, but it did.

Tiana closed her eyes a moment then opened them to study him. "Coming back to work with me?"

"Tomorrow."

"Once you've found somebody else, will you be letting me go?"

"I won't look for someone else unless you want me to. Whether you continue at the store is up to you."

"Oh." She gave a long sigh. "Thanks. I mean . . . I want to stay."

He saw her to the door, shut and locked it, watched her little Ford back out of his driveway and disappear past the view of his window. He shuffled to the terrarium and crouched at the glass.

"She doesn't believe me," he said to the turtle. "Shall I give up, then? Never mention it again?"

The turtle gave him a slow blink and pulled herself an inch toward him, then stopped.

"Aye, you're right of course. One step at a time."

He had to be ready for a full day tomorrow — customers, cataloging, and stocking. He took stock of his physical condition from the inside out and knew what he had to do whether he wanted to or not. He trudged to his room, set an alarm to go off in three hours, and climbed back into bed. In his dream, he wore the Union blue and beat his drum and stared across a dirty creek at a black woman washing clothes, her hair too short for propriety. She looked up and met his eyes, and while he searched his memory for her name, she pointed at him as if she knew him.

He found her name in his mouth, familiar, three delicate syllables that together held strength. As he drew breath to say it, Tiana shouted across the water, "Now I know you, Dorian Gray."

TEN

A fine tension hung like smoke between him and Tiana the next day, but somehow there was no awkwardness. They didn't avoid each other, didn't blunder into each other's sentences. Several times David looked up to find her studying him, and she didn't look away even when he shrugged and resumed whatever task he'd been about. She asked questions as she always did — why he stocked those books there, why he priced one edition of the same book ten dollars higher than another. She didn't mention yesterday. Neither did he.

Jayde showed up to her afternoon shift five minutes early, shaking David's hand in a professional grip and apologizing for her poor first impression. She stood a little shorter than Tiana and wore her copper hair long and loose. As for the business-casual dress code, where Tiana emphasized *casual,* Jayde emphasized *business.* David clarified that a skirt and heels weren't required every day, and she nodded toward Tiana's boot-cut pants and the strappy flats David would always think of as Mary Janes.

"Tiana told me. But I like to work in good clothes." She said it with a quick glance downward.

"Nothing wrong with that," he said, and her shoulders relaxed a bit.

In an hour she more than demonstrated her ease with the customers. She'd be a fine addition to his little place, if she could learn that ease with him as well. David ground his teeth against the knowledge that, hidden under her classic wardrobe, bruises marred her skin.

Over the next week he was able to achieve almost a complete inventory of the backlog in the stockroom. Books in his hands: the most excellent of tactile pleasures. Varying cover stock, textured pages, deckle edges, and laminated dust jackets. He burrowed into his work the way his turtle burrowed into her favorite corner of the terrarium, thinking of human beings as little as possible until he got the first text.

NEW THREAD, ADDING DAVID.

It was Moira.

Yo. An unidentified number.

HOPE YOU ASKED HIS PERMISSION. BE-

WARE, DAVID, WE TAKE FREQUENT ADVAN-
TAGE OF THIS TECHNOLOGY. Another unidentified number.

COOL. HEY DAVID. His phone recognized
that one. Zac.

He texted back. HELLO. THANKS FOR THE
ADD.

He quickly determined the first unknown
had been Colm and the second, Simon. As
he created the new contacts, his phone
continued to vibrate with new messages. At
first he thought they were making Thanksgiving plans, but the thread continued ping-
ing his phone once or twice a day, random
thoughts from any one of them.

He spent the weekend at a campground
twenty miles north, bundled against the
chill, fishing on an open, empty lake and
drinking up the beauty around him. Out on
the lake with no cell service, their absence
was glaring. Strange that they'd fit into his
thoughts so easily in only a week.

Monday found him back in his store,
enjoying the new freedom to sequester in
his stockroom. Tiana poked her head in long
enough to let him know the coffee was·
ready. Otherwise, she and Jayde had left him
alone. The hushed tones from the front
counter hinted at a somber if not heated
conversation.

David flicked out his pocketknife and opened a box that had been sealed with packing tape. He was nearing the most recent acquisitions now. He'd bought these books only last week. He sighed, and a settled feeling formed around him and the stock shelves. He could ask for no better work than this.

He closed the blade, shoved it back into the pocket of his khakis, and pulled open the flaps of the box. His thumb raked across one of the flaps, and he jerked his hand back. The slice in the pad of his finger gaped for a moment, raw pink tissue on each side before blood filled it. He suppressed the reflex to shake the sting away, instead clamped his other hand around his thumb and headed for the first-aid kit in the bathroom. Halfway across the store, his path intersected with Tiana's.

"What're you doing?"

"Box cut."

"Is it really bad?"

"Nah. Need to keep blood off the books, though."

Blood altered by a serum. If it dried, would its potency be destroyed, or . . . not?

"Maybe I should look at it," she said.

"I'll be fine." His voice clipped, and she hesitated, brown eyes wide, measuring him.

"Truly."

"Is it bleeding that much?"

He removed his other hand, and only a drop ran down the inside of his thumb. "See, nothing."

She sighed. "You were holding it above your heart, like you'd amputated your finger or something."

"Reflex."

A minute later, he stood in front of the bathroom sink wrapping a Band-Aid around his thumb. Tonight he'd call Zac and interrogate the man — what his blood could do to someone else, whether any of the others had had to deal with this. He'd have asked before if his thoughts had been sharper then.

In the narrow hall outside the bathroom, Tiana waited for him. He cocked an eyebrow at her as he shut off the light.

"You really did need a Band-Aid." Her mouth puckered as she studied his finger.

"You saw the cut."

"But I thought by now . . ."

He showed her the stain through the bandage. "Bled but good."

"Right."

"What is it?"

"Nothing, only . . . I almost for a minute expected you to . . . heal." A glance toward the front confirmed Jayde stood behind the counter, ringing up a customer. David motioned Tiana down an empty aisle and lowered his voice as she had with that last sentence.

"Only mortal injuries."

She blinked. "Right."

"Forget it." He tried to smile, then turned back toward the stockroom.

"Actually, I . . . I want to hear you out, if you don't mind."

To what end? He glanced up and down the aisle again and ran his palm over the book spines nearest him. Then he faced her. "I don't age, and injuries don't kill me."

"That's it?"

"That's it. I get as tired, hungry, thirsty as anyone else, and I can be hurt."

"Okay."

The moment she believed him, he would know. He had to stop wishing for that moment. "Okay."

"And back to work we go." Her smile held warmth. She headed for the front of the store.

Somehow she both disbelieved and trusted him. He ambled back to the stockroom the long way, cutting down one of the children's aisles and standing still a moment, taking in their thin glossy spines and the cluster of colorful chairs. Maybe the piece of Tiana that trusted him was the piece that still loved children's fairy tales. Maybe that piece wanted him to be telling the truth.

"Manager to the front, please," came Jayde's brisk voice over the PA.

David headed there, checking his surroundings as he went. They didn't page each other in a store so small, and her formality might mean an unruly customer.

No raised voices as he neared. Jayde was speaking casually. A man answered.

David rounded the corner and halted to keep from crashing into Tiana's back. She stood in the middle of the main aisle, clutching a stack of books to her chest, staring, mouth open. David looked toward the counter.

Zac and Moira. Standing in his little shop, smiling and chatting with Jayde, who must not know who Zac was. Jayde shot a smug glance over her shoulder — no, that was full knowledge. Tiana's fangirl gushing likely reached a higher pitch of enthusiasm when shared with a female friend.

Zac followed Jayde's look, and his mouth tipped between a smirk and a smile as he spotted David. "Hey."

David stepped sideways past Tiana, up to the counter, and shook his hand. "How did you find me?"

"You named your store Galloway Books."
David laughed. "That I did."

"It's delightful." Moira pushed her hands into her jeans pockets and turned a full circle on the braided rug in front of the checkout counter. "So vintage. I could curl up in a corner and sleep."

"That's a compliment?" Zac said, and she shoulder-bumped him.

"We're being tourists for the week," she said. "I want to see the dunes way up north, and the trees, if we're not too late to catch their color."

"I was just telling them, early October is best," Jayde said. "But the little towns are still worth a look, if they dress warm."

She was hardly keeping the grin off her face as Tiana stood frozen behind their group. Maybe normalizing Zac's presence would encourage her to approach. She'd be mortified later if she didn't.

"I've camped up there in the fall," David said. "It's good land."

"We hoped you could help us plan an itinerary." Mischief lilted in Moira's tone. She'd guessed the source of Tiana's petrifaction.

"How long are you here?"

"A week, ten days." She fluttered her hand.

He had no idea what she did for a living, if she did anything. They'd all had over a century to buy, sell, and save through the ups and downs of the market, the end of the gold standard, rising inflation. Unless they spent stupidly, they should all be as well off as David was.

"We're ready for lunch," Moira said, "but we wanted to track you down first. Join us?"

"Sure." He glanced over his shoulder.

Tiana had revived. She carried her stack of books behind the counter and stood sorting them, head ducked. If she had some reason to speak to Zac, she'd pop out of her shell in a moment, articulate again if not at ease.

David cleared his throat. "While I grab my coat, maybe Tiana wouldn't mind showing you around the store."

Her head whipped up at the sound of her name. "What?"

"You're not busy, are you?"

"No, I mean, I was just . . ." She stepped forward, and her smile outshone the stuttering. "I'd love to show you around."

"Good then. Moira, Zac, meet my store manager, Tiana Burton. Tiana, Zac and Moira are friends from out of town."

"Nice to meet you." She was already leading them down the first aisle of shelves.

When they disappeared around the corner, Jayde leaned over the counter toward him. "David!"

"Yes?"

"You know Zac Wilson, and you never told her?"

"Not until very recently, and I didn't know they were in the state, much less coming here. There's no setup, Jayde."

"Well, good luck." She shook her head, but a grin split her face. "She's going to lose her mind the second you all walk out of here."

"Then good luck to you." He winked.

It was the most relaxed conversation she'd had with him since he met her.

He grabbed his coat and keys and stood waiting at the door until Tiana finished her tour. She brought them up to the front, laughing at something Zac had said.

"Thanks for the tour," he said.

"Anytime." Definitely a blush there.

"You have a beautiful place," Moira said to all three of them.

David opened the door for her then held it for Zac, because why not? — but Tiana said, "Um, Zac?"

He turned and put his hand out to keep the door open. "Yeah?"

"I believe in angels. And I'm glad one was

sent to you."

The smile he gave her was the one he'd given the waitress at Denny's. He recognized devotion and didn't scoff at it — truly didn't, or David would have seen it in him after the waitress walked away.

"Thank you," he said.

Tiana nodded. Zac walked outside, and her gaze found David's.

"Are you going to explain any of this?"

If he could find a way that didn't reveal Zac and Moira, though she wouldn't believe him if he told her. Then again, Zac had survived a fall into Marble Canyon. Tiana might hold enough pieces of the puzzle to solve it on her own.

"Later. I'll be back in an hour, maybe two."

"We're fine," Jayde said. "We'll close up if you decide to hang out with them longer."

He left them to retell each other what had just happened.

He offered his Jeep Cherokee rather than use Zac's rental car. Moira rode shotgun and Zac hopped into the back. David pulled around to exit the little parking lot and caught Zac's gaze in the rearview mirror.

"Did you choose a restaurant yet?"

"We thought we'd ask the local," he said. "What's the quirkiest place around?"

Moira was sitting forward in her seat, eyes trained out the windshield. "What a sweet little town, David. I see why you settled here."

"Settled being a relative term." He turned left. Quirky . . . hm.

"How long have you been here?"

"Three years. The store does quite well, for its size."

"It's a delightful setup, and so organized. I've been in used-book stores where I couldn't find a thing. Books stacked everywhere, I wanted to pull my hair out."

David chuckled. "I pledged never to allow Galloway's to devolve into chaos. Tiana says I'm orderly enough to be a drill sergeant."

"Or at least a soldier."

He glanced away from the road to meet Moira's eyes. "Zac told you?"

"We don't tell each other's stories," she said. "But it's in your bearing. Your posture, your watchfulness."

Not the first person who'd noticed, of course, though usually those who pointed it out were soldiers themselves, like the red-headed bodyguard at Marble Canyon. David nodded.

"How many wars?"

"Five," he said, flexing his hands on the wheel.

"Ending with?"

"Vietnam."

Moira's hand brushed his arm then drew back to her lap. "That's a long record of service."

A frown tightened his mouth as he tried to decide what to do with her words, with . . . her respect. It filled something deep in his core, a hidden well he hadn't known was empty. He cleared a lump of gravel from his throat.

"Thank you," he said.

"I'm grateful you made it home every time."

He brushed a hand under his eyes. "I —" His voice broke. Curse it. He cleared his throat again. "If you don't want classic diner fare, I'll take us to a Mongolian grill. Assemble your bowl and they grill it in front of you, hit the gong if you approve of the service — that type of place. About as quirky as we get around this town."

"Sounds perfect," Moira said.

"Sounds like a chain," Zac said.

"Oh, go to Paris, Zachary."

Over lunch, David talked more about himself in an hour and a half than he had in four decades. Zac and Moira's questions seemed endless, but he held up until Moira asked if he had any living family.

His voice failed. Moira turned a page of the dessert menu before registering the silence, though Zac was already watching him.

She looked up and nudged aside her iced tea to touch David's arm. "Sorry, I guess I'm prying now."

He shook his head. "I'm not accustomed to it, that's all."

"Being interrogated?" She smiled.

"Speaking freely."

"I can't imagine living the way you have."

The words stung, though she clearly hadn't meant them to. "There's a bakery four doors down, if you'd like to try some Michigan cherries. They put them in everything, even ice cream."

Her slow blink acknowledged the boundary he'd just set up. Good. He wouldn't deny the group texts were a comfortable addition to his days, and Zac and Moira's unexpected presence in his shop had felt like a gift. But he had to maintain boundaries, or . . . well, he had to, that's all.

They ambled down the wooden walk in peeking sunshine that glistened on puddles collected during yesterday's rain. A brisk wind would help dry things out, but the stillness today meant more warmth. At the dessert shop, Moira tried one of the cherry-

152

laden ice cream flavors, and Zac tried everything in sight.

"If you get high on sugar, I'm leaving you at the bookstore," Moira said. "And the resident fangirl will never fawn over you again once she's heard you talking at the speed of light."

"Whatever, woman."

"David, what else is there to see in your town?"

Hours passed as he gave them a tour with stops at almost every store, Zac munching a cherry-almond-white-chocolate-chip cookie as they walked. They stayed longest among local artisan shops, and Moira gazed at the wares with an eye both enthusiastic and expert.

"You're an artist," David finally said.

She grinned. "I paint."

"For how long?"

"Oh . . ." She shrugged. "I sold my first work in 1904."

"And how do you manage that?"

"Well, my name changes, of course. My body of work is attributed to six different women, each of whom was reclusive and didn't allow photographs taken. Other than that first one, Mary Whitefield. She's known to a very select group of connoisseurs."

A grin pushed onto his face. "You have fans."

Her giggle was that of a twenty-year-old girl, pleased at the recognition. Maybe the dichotomy lingered in all of them — the dual ages, informing who they were inside and out.

"Zac's fans are teens and twentysomethings. Mine are elderly museum patrons. I feel my legacy is preferable, but he refuses to agree with that."

From the other end of the aisle, Zac looked up from a framed photograph of the Mackinac Bridge. "Pretty sure your patrons don't bring you cookies."

"Pretty sure your fangirls don't analyze your work in guided tours."

"I'm not a relic."

Moira choked down a laugh. Triumph formed his smirk as he turned to walk down a neighboring aisle.

"Do you always let him have the last word?" David asked, a smile tugging at him too.

"Well, he's so fond of it." She was still grinning.

By the time they drove back to the store, the sun had set. David parked beside the rental car, and they all got out, Moira's arms weighted with packages — carefully wrapped and bagged glasswork, hand-beaded earrings, some six-inch copper sculpture of a seagull that all but choked her up. David had lost count of her purchases halfway through the day.

"Let me." He took a few of them as Zac jingled the car keys and walked around to the driver's side.

And jolted to a stop. Zac's right arm came up, a blocking motion, and something else moved on that side of the car — a man. Springing upward, head just clearing the car windows. A red hoodie, pulled low to hide his face. David dropped the bags, and something shattered at his feet. He surged around the car as Zac made a sound that was both gasp and groan, then blocked again. Metal glinted in the streetlight. The man crashed into Zac, thrust the knife center mass, yanked it back, said, "Zachary Wilson."

And stood there, staring, while Zac doubled over with one hand braced on the car roof. Blood fell, shiny on the ground under the floodlight.

David charged. The man startled and ran, and David sprinted after him.

ELEVEN

What he'd do with the man — he shoved
that thought aside as he drew deep breaths,
legs pumping. David ran down dark side-
walks along the empty streets. The man
dashed without discretion, under streetlights
and past shoppers who wandered toward
their cars as the last restaurants closed. He
must have hidden the knife in the hoodie's
front pocket. David watched as he ran. In
front of an abandoned house with a brow-
ning untrimmed yard, the man pitched the
knife into a patch of weeds, a flash of white
hand and silver blade. He didn't miss a step.
  David didn't either, until the man crossed
the road at a DO NOT WALK. Headlights
slashed across his form, a full-size van that
would have killed him if the speed limit had
been faster. A horn beeped, then another as
the van skidded and swerved, but the man
kept going. David took a few strides off the
curb and tried to weave around the cars,

but the timing wasn't on his side. One vehicle nearly hit another trying to avoid him. He backed up, looked to the other side of the street.

The man was gone.

David punched one hand into the other then gripped the back of his neck with both as his gaze scoured up and down. Only a few seconds he'd looked away. He crossed when the sign turned. He searched for ten minutes, but the man could have ducked behind any building, any bush. Could be watching David now from inside a car parallel parked at the curb; stupidly, people left them unlocked all the time in a town this small. He glanced into each windshield as he backtracked to the light where he'd crossed. No sign of anyone.

Go back. He had no trail to follow. The pounding in his pulse slowed as he processed events past the adrenaline rush of *Mission* and *Go go go* and *Target, take him down, whatever it takes.* The man had spoken Zac's name. A personal hit. And he'd thrown away his weapon. He wasn't out in the dark now, ranging for his next victim. Or probably wasn't.

On his way back to the store, David retrieved the knife. Crouched to hide his actions in case someone should pass by, then wiped Zac's blood on the grass and hid the blade along the inside of his coat, keeping one hand tucked there as if he were cold.

The rental car still sat in the back lot beside his Jeep, Moira's packages abandoned beside it. She and Zac had moved to the grass island that separated the bookstore's parking from the massage therapist next door. Zac crouched on elbows and knees in the grass, curled small, head bent. Moira sat on the cement curb, talking quietly to him, her hand on his shoulder.

David stopped in front of them. "I got the knife."

"Good," Zac said without lifting his head, but Moira's words covered his.

"It's bad, David; two wounds and he's bleeding everywhere."

Before she finished the sentence, Zac pushed to his feet, shrugging off help. He took two steps, and then his legs buckled. David scooped him up, made his arms a cradle rather than hoisting Zac over his shoulder with those wounds. Zac stiffened. He tried to shove David away, but his arm flopped out from his body, uncoordinated. Shock setting in.

"Relax, man," David said.

He did. "Tables turned, huh. Didn't take long."

Moira followed as David carried Zac across the lot, leaving all her bags, including whatever David had dropped and broken. He showed her which key would unlock the door and pointed out light switches along their path to the break room.

"We need plastic," she said. "Garbage bags or something."

"In the cubby behind the front counter, under the cash register."

She hurried back the way they'd come, then joined him in time to flip the break room's light switch.

Tiana had left a copy of *The Giver* on the little break room table. A half-full bag of blue corn tortilla chips sat on the counter, and he'd find hummus in the refrigerator if he looked. Across from the fridge, a low tweed sofa stood against one wall. Moira spread the garbage bags over every square inch of the plaid cushions, arms, and back, and then David eased Zac down.

"This had better be mortal." Zac groaned. "Moira?"

She grasped the hand that hung off the couch. "Right here."

David removed the attempted-murder weapon from inside his coat and wrapped it in a garbage bag. Then he unzipped and opened Zac's jacket. His mouth dried. Blood was soaking Zac's T-shirt, the jacket liner, even the waistband of his jeans. The shirt was sliced in two places, one just below the left ribs and one lower, the right side of his gut. The bloodstains were spreading every second, had already merged into one.

David fetched the first-aid kit from the bathroom while Moira retrieved her shopping bags from the parking lot. She deposited everything on the floor in the entryway, not bothering even to set them on the counter. David turned out lights in the entryway and front room, and they retraced their path to the back. Zac lay motionless other than the shallow rise and fall of his chest.

"Zachary," Moira whispered, and he opened his eyes. "I'm here. I'll be with you the whole time."

"I know. It's okay." Zac coughed, and blood frothed in his mouth.

Then he was choking. His eyes sought Moira's, wide and pleading. Fear, the only response to an inability to breathe, regardless of one's age or experiences. Moira leaned over him and fit her arm under his back, holding him half upright. David reached to the other end of the couch for a pillow and propped it behind him.

After a few moments he drew a breath. "Better get me something to vomit in."

David reached for the lined wastebasket and set it beside the couch. He knelt and opened the first-aid case.

He used the small scissors to cut away Zac's shirt. A full-color tattoo spread over the top half of his left pectoral, below the collarbone — a ship, sails unfurled, buoyed on cresting blue waves. The two stab wounds were deep, made with a blade the width of a butcher knife. Blood flowed, slicking and warming David's hands. His mouth remained too dry to swallow, as if only he stood in the gap between Zac and death.

"He got an upward angle here," he said as he pressed gauze over the higher wound.

"Yeah." Zac shut his eyes. "Lung, breathing's not . . . right."

David covered both wounds as best he could, exhausting the supply of gauze in the little case. Zac maintained such silence, David looked up several times to see if he'd passed out. He remained conscious, staring at the ceiling. Moira gripped his left hand between both of hers and kept her eyes shut the whole time.

"Done," David said at last, and Moira opened her eyes. "Anything else you need besides hard liquor?"

"You could knock me out," Zac said.

Yes, he could. Wouldn't harm Zac further. But he had no way to do it other than brute force, his fist cracking into Zac's temple or snapping his head back hard enough to sever him from consciousness. A man already weak and in pain. A man willing to let David render him defenseless. The idea of physically attacking him caved David's chest in.

Zac's eyes were closed again, but Moira was watching.

David looked away. "I'd prefer not to do that."

"Change your mind, I start rambling in Swedish." He was starting to slur.

"Whatever you say, I'll be none the wiser."

"No English till my teens. Worked hard for a real American accent." His smirk at David seemed to use all his energy. "Unlike that brogue of yours."

Tears stood in Moira's eyes. She was watching David, not Zac, a plea behind the tears. Keep him talking? David could do that.

He tilted his head at Zac. "The brogue emerges only in extremis."

"Aye, that it does." The attempt at a Scottish burr was atrocious. Zac grinned, blood on his teeth, then shut his eyes and kept a groan behind tight lips.

"Enough," David said. "Shut up and lie there. Pass out if you can."

Zac hunched forward, away from the pillow, and began to choke. David grabbed the wastebasket, and Moira held Zac up for a long minute as he vomited blood. When he finished, she eased him back against the cushions, and he reached out to grip her hand. A single tear slipped down her cheek.

Zac tugged her hand. "Memories, eh?"

At his smile, Moira gave a quiet sob. She ducked her head, and Zac met David's eyes. The mask was crumbling; pain pinched around his eyes and mouth, and he'd begun to shiver. David shuddered at the memory of going into shock — weakness, nausea, feeling so cold.

Maybe he should drive them all to his place. At least Zac could recover in a bed. But moving him probably wouldn't be worth it.

"I'll be gone only a few minutes," David said. "Be back with whiskey. And the pharmacy might have suture thread —"

"No need."

"Won't it hasten recovery to seal the wound properly?"

"Not enough to let you poke and tug

and . . ." Zac's struggle for air was becoming audible. The lung filling with blood.

David glanced at Moira, and she shook her head. Well, fine then. Zac's call.

"In the meantime," Moira said, "where's your computer? I need to set up an anonymous call to the police."

David cocked an eyebrow at her. "The longevites involve police?"

"I'll simply say I witnessed a stabbing and can't identify anyone," she said. "I'll give a basic description of the man. They're on their own after that, but they have to be alerted."

She was right, and no risk was involved if she knew what she was doing. "You've done this before?"

"I have."

Zac's eyes opened, and his head turned to catch her gaze, but she didn't notice.

"And you got a look at him?"

She shrugged. "Height between you and Zac. Average build. White, though that won't help them. It seems to be the default in this town."

"Quite so," he said, his mind straying to Tiana's words to him while standing on his porch. "I'll bring my laptop in a minute."

In the bathroom he scrubbed Zac's blood from his hands, gritting his teeth against the whole situation. Could Zac bleed out enough to negate the serum? No, if that were possible, the wounds David suffered in 1916 would have killed him. He had to remember to compare all things to that. And to Zac's fall. This was nothing.

Someone had to find the man who'd done this. If not the police, then David would do it himself. Zac's inability to be murdered didn't erase the crime. He wished the others were here to help him create a perimeter, Simon especially. David was a soldier, not a detective, but if he had to be —

A doorknob jiggled.

He stiffened. Listened. The back door. Only one person other than David had a key.

"David?" Moira called.

"Stay there."

He dried his hands and headed for the door, reached it as Tiana opened it and stepped inside, eyes bright.

"I saw your cars in the back. I won't stay, but if they're heading somewhere else tomorrow, I'd like to say goodbye."

David tried not to frown at her and probably failed.

Hurt flashed in her eyes then was shielded behind the arching of one eyebrow. "Don't worry. I'm resolved not to say anything stupid in front of him."

"It's not that, it's —"

"Wait, why are the lights off?"

From the break room came the noise of coughing, then choking, then vomiting, and then a groan that tried and failed to mute itself. Tiana stood frozen, staring toward the sound.

"David?" Her voice tiptoed.

"Tiana." He set his damp hands on her shoulders and waited for her to meet his eyes. "You need to go."

"That's Zac. He's sick? What did you guys do, get drunk or something?"

"I need you to go."

"But you're not drunk at all." She pulled away from him. "What's going on?"

If only she hadn't heard that sound. She eased back from his hold on her shoulders and marched toward the break room.

David cursed necessity and blocked her way.

She stared at him. Eyes wide. Mouth parting.

She tried to see past him, and he braced his arm against the doorframe, his elbow a right angle, obscuring her line of sight. But she'd seen something, because she ducked his arm and burst into the room. She went still when she saw Zac lying half propped on the couch. Both his wounds had bled through the gauze already, bright red on white. What had soaked into the waist of his jeans was still wet, obvious.

"Oh," Tiana said.

Zac struggled to sit up but fell back, one hand pressing the gauze below his ribs. "David, take her out of here."

Tiana approached, firm strides, a tightness to her mouth. Moira stepped up to block her way, several inches shorter, and Tiana ignored her, kept staring at Zac over Moira's head.

"Did anybody call an ambulance?"

"No," David said, his voice overlaid with the same word from Zac and from Moira.

She was a different woman than the one who'd blushed and stammered in front of Zac eight hours ago. This was the Tiana David knew. The Tiana who was already pulling out her phone and pressing the nine.

"No!" Moira slapped her hand, and the phone flew halfway across the room to skitter over the counter against the fridge and fall into the sink.

Tiana lunged for the phone, and Moira lunged for Tiana, and David placed his body between them in time to catch Moira's nails across his throat. Adrenaline kicked in. He blocked her hand but restrained himself from further defensive reflexes. He stepped around both of them and scooped up the phone.

Moira was all but baring her teeth. "Is something wrong with you, girl?"

"He's dying, that's what's wrong with me, you stupid —"

"Okay." David shoved the phone into his jeans pocket and nudged Tiana toward the door. "Come on."

"He is bleeding to death!"

"Tiana. Come on. Please."

She preceded him from the room, face scrunched up and fingers clenching, and stared as he fetched his laptop from behind the counter.

"*What* are you doing?"

"Hold on."

"Give me my phone back."

He held up an open hand, hoped his face conveyed more plea than order, and took the laptop to Moira, who said nothing as she moved from Zac's side to take it. Tiana still stood in the middle of the room when he returned, and he motioned her to follow him. Of all wonders, she did. Wordless until she and David were in his Jeep, en route to the party store three blocks over.

"Tell me why."

"Because Zac wants it this way."

"You're letting him die, David. He's going to die."

No, he isn't. If only he could say that. Tiana covered her face with her hands. David drove on the lookout for a man in a red hoodie, but the streets were emptying by this hour. Another minute passed before she spoke again.

"Was he attacked? Someone tried to kill him?"

"Yes."

"Shot?"

"Stabbed."

"David, why the — ?" She stopped, drew a shaky breath. "Why can't we call an ambulance?"

"Moira's calling in an anonymous tip to the police. But Zac cannot be identified as the victim."

"I'm not talking about the police. I'm talking about paramedics. To save his life."

"Which you know would result in a police report." And a blood draw. And a medical chart detailing anomalous results.

"But he's *dying.*" Shrillness crept into her voice. "And where are we going?"

"I'm getting him something for the pain."

"What, alcohol? He needs morphine or something. And surgery. And antibiotics."

He turned into the five-space store lot and

169

parked. "Come inside with me."

"So I can't call 911 while you're gone?" But she was getting out of the Jeep, following him as she said it.

Inside, David kept his voice low while he headed for the liquor. "All I can say right now is that things aren't what they appear to be, and I need your trust."

"That's not fair," she whispered.

"Not at all, but I have to ask it of you."

She didn't answer.

Given what Zac faced in the next twenty-four hours, he deserved the highest proof in the store. Given Moira had just tried to claw Tiana's face off . . . . In addition to the whiskey, David bought a bottle of red wine. The thin graybeard behind the counter grunted at the two beverage choices set beside each other on the counter, but he rang them up without comment. David and Tiana ran out to the Jeep under a fresh downpour.

She set the bag at her feet with a quiet clanking of glass on glass. "You never would have told me about any of this."

"No."

"He's going to die, and I'd never have known it happened here if I hadn't come back."

"Why did you?"

"To read. You know, in a bookstore." The bristle in her tone fell away as she covered her face again. "Oh, Lord. Zac. Dear Jesus, save Zac somehow. Heal him somehow. Please let him live."

Nothing David could say was safe, not without Zac's permission. He crushed the impulse to gather Tiana in his arms as she continued praying aloud the whole way back. When they got there, she climbed woodenly out of the Jeep and started to follow him inside.

By tomorrow she'd know Zac wasn't going to die. David wouldn't subject her to a night of distress for no reason. He carried the bag of bottles in one hand and tucked Tiana close with his free arm. She fit bonnily, just the height to rest her head at the crook of his shoulder. When they reached the door, he nodded for her to open it. They stepped in together.

"Come on," he said.

She drew a deep breath before they entered the room, and whispered, "Please, Jesus."

When they entered, Moira released Zac's hand and stood to face Tiana. "Get out."

David pitched his voice low, gentle. "Moira, is that for the best right now?"

Her lip wobbled as she considered the options, as she must be imagining Tiana sans supervision, going to the police anyway. She sank down onto the couch and took Zac's hand again as if she could pour protection through the contact.

If anything, Zac looked grayer, sweat on his forehead, his breathing more shallow. He didn't open his eyes. Moira had draped the leather jacket over his chest, bloody liner facing up, but he shivered every few seconds.

David set the bag on the table. "Is he conscious?"

Zac's eyes opened. "Liquor. Now."

David went to the cupboard over the sink and fetched one of the white mugs. He opened the bottle of whiskey and, as he poured half a glass, Zac saw Tiana.

His growl was weak. "Who let the mortal back in?"

"What?" Tiana said.

Without answering, David held Zac upright while Moira tilted the mug to his lips. Zac scrunched his eyes tight at the first swallow, then finished it all, about three shots. Should help, especially if his resistance wasn't too built up — though a century and a half built up some degree even when consumed in moderation. David lowered him to the pillow.

Zac sighed. "Thanks, John."

Tension rippled through the room. Moira stepped closer and set her hand on Zac's head, and he opened his eyes, looked from her to David.

"It's getting . . ." He coughed. "I can't think."

"You don't have to," Moira said.

Tiana crept around David to stand at the couch.

"I guess David told you." Moira's tone had flattened. Resigned, maybe.

"I didn't call an ambulance, if that's what you mean."

Moira looked back and forth between them, attention coming to rest on David. "You didn't . . . ?"

"Not mine to tell, but she's going to know before long." Surely Moira saw that.

"Then please just tell me." Tiana wrapped her arms around herself, still watching Zac. "Tell me why he wants you to let him die, and tell me why you're listening to him."

Moira measured her with a long, calm stare and then sighed. "He isn't dying."

"Wh–what?"

Again she took Zac's hand. "Zachary? I want your agreement."

He said nothing, but his fingers tightened around hers.

Moira nodded and kept his hand in her lap. "I . . . I haven't explained this in so long. I don't know where to begin."

David did. And now he could. He cleared his throat. "She already knows."

"What?" Moira said.

"She knows about me. Well, she doesn't believe me. Didn't believe me. Likely will after tonight."

He glanced at Tiana, but she continued to stare at Zac. David scrubbed a hand upward through the back of his hair and perched on the edge of the table. He waited, but none of them spoke, and then Zac was choking. David held the wastebasket while he vomited, and when Moira lowered him to the pillow this time, his mouth stayed open in an effort to breathe.

"No." The word seemed to burst from Tiana. "It's not possible."

David gave her a moment to sort it out for herself. She was more likely to believe it that way.

"He called me the mortal." She turned on David and jabbed a finger at his chest. "You went to Arizona."

"I did."

"To find him after he fell."

He nodded.

174

"You believed he was . . . You believe he . . ."

"Because it's true."

"He's like you." Her voice had flattened, disbelief morphing into a dread that couldn't keep doubting him, though she wanted to. "He's . . . old. And he can't die." She stared at Moira. "You too?"

"Yes," Moira said.

"But he's still bleeding. There's — there's more — red."

"It takes time."

Tiana took a step nearer. "Zac?"

His eyelids flickered before opening.

"Was there an angel?"

He grasped a deeper breath. "No."

"You fell into the canyon."

"Yeah."

"But you can't die. This, now, you won't die from this either."

"I won't."

She turned away from him. "How long will it take for him to heal?"

"About twelve hours," Moira said.

"And no scars, or anything?"

"No scars."

She sank into a chair. "How many of you are there?"

When Moira hesitated, David shrugged.

"Better for her to know than to overestimate."

"Five," Moira said.

Tiana's eyebrows arched. "In the US?"

"In the world, we think."

"They've known I existed from the beginning," David said, "but they could never find me."

"So you found them, on a hunch. Had you believed you were the only one?"

"Until I saw the news story. In my experience, angels don't deliver us from earthly consequences of behavior — ours or anyone else's."

Zac let out a hard breath, responding either to David's words or to fresh pain.

Tiana sat twisting one of her thumb rings. The skepticism in her eyes had brightened into amazement, and David had to punch down a fierce hope in the center of his chest. That her opinion mattered so much — it wasn't sensible, and it could be dangerous.

Yet he had to know. "Do you believe us?"

"I guess I will if he's alive in the morning." But the edge in her voice wasn't defending against them. The foreignness of this reality had to feel threatening. "And . . ." She stood. "I guess I should . . . go."

Moira still appeared to be gritting her teeth, but she gave a nod, and after a moment a long sigh caved the tension from her shoulders. "Thank you."

Tiana hurried from the room, and David followed her to the door. On the slab porch, she turned.

"Your name was John?"

"Years ago."

"How many years?"

The questions he'd wished she would ask, yet saying the answers aloud felt rusty and wrong. He leaned in the doorframe. "I took this name in 1973."

She stood looking at him for a moment, unreadable. "And they've lived the same way. Not choice but necessity."

"They have."

"I won't intrude, David, but I want to see him tomorrow. Just see him and then go, if that's what they want."

"I don't think they'll have a problem with it, now that you know." Moira might, but he'd talk to her.

"I'll call Jayde in the morning and let her know the store's closed."

"Consider it a paid holiday."

"You can't afford to keep doing that."

"I can, actually."

"It doesn't feel right to me, but thank

you." She twisted her thumb ring. "I don't know how to get my head around this, any of this. But I'm glad you found them. Even though you didn't know to look for them."

He watched her walk to her car, get inside, start it up. When her taillights disappeared, he remembered what he'd meant to fetch from the Jeep. He pulled from the hatchback two emergency items he'd never expected to use — a sleeping bag and a thick afghan, woven in brown and green and gold and transferred from one vehicle to another for the last fifty years. Not until he was striding back to the store did he process what she'd said. A stranger to her would not have picked up on the allusion at all.

He had found kin without knowing to look for them. She had looked for hers, inquired across the world to Burundi, and found nothing.

He brought the items inside and set the rolled sleeping bag in front of the refrigerator. The conversation with Tiana was pushed aside as he focused on immediate concerns. "I should go into town again. Try to hunt him down."

"And do what?" Zac slurred, eyes closed.

"I don't know."

"He's long gone, David." Moira's voice was quiet. "Don't go."

David folded his arms and rubbed them to generate warmth, though the room wasn't cold. "We have a responsibility to do something about this."

"Simon would tell you crime fighting is not a hobby."

"Would he call in a vague tip and let it go at that?"

"I believe he would," she said.

She folded Zac's jacket and set it aside. David handed her the blanket, and she draped it over Zac instead.

Her face crumpled. "Thank you."

"Of course." Didn't she expect the best care he could offer?

"And thank you . . . that she's gone."

"That was all Tiana. She understands now."

Moira threaded her fingers with Zac's, and a few tears fell. "I don't mean to be watery. But what he said earlier, about memories . . ."

"He told me how you met." David moved one of the chairs out from the table and dropped into it.

"Did he?" She nodded. "He would. Fairness, of course, but also . . . well, all of us have wanted to find you, but I think it's mattered most to him."

"Why?" Simon was right — for all they

knew, David was a rotten person.

"If you hadn't noticed, he's the gregarious one." She smiled.

David nodded.

"Whatever else it may be, we haven't discussed."

"Do you have bags with you, a change of clothes? Or is everything in your hotel room?"

"Rooms." She said it automatically then looked up to meet his eyes. "But no, we hadn't booked anything yet. It's all in the car."

"In the morning, if he can move, I'll take you to my place for showers and such."

"That would be appreciated." She waited for him to ask, but that wasn't going to happen. At last she sighed. "We maintain a semi-platonic relationship."

He laughed. "Now there's a creative term."

"Perhaps a better description would be . . . platonic more often than not."

"It's not my business unless you want it to be."

"You're right. And I don't."

"Well then."

They sat awhile. David sent a prayer that Zac would sleep through the worst, but in about fifteen minutes, he lurched up on the couch with a strangled sound and vomited again. It appeared to be more blood than whiskey; he fell asleep as soon as he lay back down.

David and Moira sipped wine and talked quietly into the night, stories of their travels, their occupations, nothing about anyone loved and lost. Moira had seen more of the world than he had, and she described Spain, Belgium, Japan, Brazil, Norway, and Sweden — she'd been there though Zac had not — with affection and an artist's eye. When he mentioned his long-ago pilgrimage to Scotland, she probed with questions that understood things he didn't say. It had been good to explore the land of his father, and he'd thought before the journey that he might stay forever; but he'd found himself ready, seven months later, to return to America. Home, for better and worse. Moira nodded, though he wondered if she considered any place home.

Their conversation sometimes paused but never ceased. He couldn't blame the wine for his loose tongue, given he'd had only two mugfuls. But when the brogue crept into his speech, it took him an hour to notice.

Before David bought the place, someone had installed a dimmer switch on every light, and around ten he lowered the break room's to half brightness, then lowered it again a little past midnight when Moira's eyelids drooped and she listed in her chair.

"Hey there." David nudged her upright with a hand on her shoulder. "Roll out the bag and get some sleep."

"But Zac."

The man hadn't stirred in two hours. "I'll watch him."

In the dimness she rolled out the sleeping bag on the floor in front of the fridge, tugged off her knee-high boots, and crawled inside. "By the way, you ought not squelch that burr, David. It's pleasant."

He gave a low laugh.

Five minutes of silence, and then she whispered, "David?"

"Hmm?"

"My near-death. It wasn't in any way remarkable. Many women died the same way I was supposed to."

He clasped his hands between his knees and sat forward in the chair. The ticking of the regulator, hung on a wall halfway to the front of the store, seemed louder while he waited.

"My second child," Moira said. "A breech birth, and Dr. Leon couldn't turn him. In the last hours, the child was still, and I told the doctor he was dead. I . . ." The sleeping bag rustled as she turned onto her side, finding his gaze in the near dark. "I was weak when he finally came, and then the bleeding was very bad. Dr. Leon asked both of us, me and my husband, if he might try to save my life. He didn't know if the serum would work on a case like mine, but we agreed to let him try it. He might have given it to the child too, but I was right. He had been dead some time."

So many children lost in those days — at birth, in the weeks and months after. Sarah had lost two pregnancies after she had Kathleen. Early on, before she was showing, no one but the two of them knew their loss. David had held her through nights of keening grief each time. To carry a child to term, to labor for its birth, and then to feel its death only hours before it came . . .

"I'm sorry," he said.

"I didn't become pregnant again," Moira said. "When I understood what had happened to me, I counted it a boon. It's different for all of you — you could be fathers, probably. But a child of mine would receive nourishment from my blood, and there's no way to know . . . the consequences."

He'd never considered it. A chill traced his spine at the image of an infant that couldn't grow up.

Moira rolled onto her back again and nestled deeper into the sleeping bag until the top of it reached her chin. "Thank you for all of this. Letting us stay here, taking care of Zac . . ."

"A wee bit of alcohol." He smiled and hoped she saw it in the dark.

"That too." She smiled back. "Don't let me sleep all night. You need rest too."

"All right."

For the next four hours, David didn't stray from his charges. Zac would scoff at being called such, but the man needed care, undying or not. Twice David put a hand on his shoulder when he woke moaning, and each time he gave Zac a few swallows of whiskey. When Zac drifted off again, David paced the open path in the middle of the room, between the sleeping bag and the couch.

As the sky outside crept toward an overcast dawn, Moira stirred in the sleeping bag and sat up.

"Zac?"

"Shh," David said. "He's sleeping."

"What time is it?"

"Around five."

"Why didn't you wake me?"

She'd been wrung out. She'd needed the sleep more than David did. He shrugged.

"Stubborn." She scooted her legs out of the bag and stood. "Here, at least lie down an hour or two."

He took off his shoes and his button-down shirt. The sleeping bag was one for outdoor use, and he was hot-blooded, generally. In his khakis and undershirt, he slid into the bag and closed his eyes. The floor was harder than earth but not intolerable. If Zac and Moira hadn't come, he could have gone home and read a novel this evening with his turtle for company, then slept in the comfort of his bed.

Mortal wounds aside, this was better.

TWELVE

He awoke when the sunrise poured orange beams through the clouds, in the window, into his eyes. Voices brought him awake the rest of the way — Moira's hushed, Zac's too weak for much volume.

"Bleeding's stopped."

"And the pain?"

"Shouldn't be much longer."

A quiet sigh.

"Hey. You know I'll be fine."

"I'm sure you'll tell yourself that if I'm ever stabbed and spend hours drowning in my own blood. I'm sure you'll maintain perfect calm about it."

After a silence Zac drew a long breath. "I think I told David to knock me out."

"You did. He didn't."

"That woman, Tiana . . . Did I say anything?"

"You called David 'John,' and you called her 'the mortal.' "

Zac's voice rose, spitting expletives.

"Even if you'd been unconscious, we'd have a problem. She saw the damage."

"She didn't have to know about all of us."

"David had already told her about himself. Do you remember?"

Time to join the discussion. David sat up. Zac tried to do the same, got about halfway forward from the pillow before falling back. He found David in the gray light. "You . . . what?"

"She didn't believe it, but I told her a few days ago. Well . . . I don't know, maybe she did believe it."

"What else does she know?"

"Only that there are, to our knowledge, a total of five of us. But Moira told her that one."

Zac's attempt at a glare was blunted by fatigue.

"Think about it." David freed his legs from the sleeping bag, stood up, and buttoned his shirt back on. "It wouldn't do for her to be looking for immortals around every bush. This is better for her and for us."

"You trust her," Zac said.

"She's a good woman, and safe."

After a moment Zac nodded. He stretched his legs from under the blanket and tried again to leverage himself up. Moira helped, repositioning the pillow at his back.

"Showers?" David said.

"That should be doable," Zac said.

He couldn't get to his feet yet; David supported him to the Jeep and then tucked him into the back seat before Zac could protest being picked up. Convenient that he wasn't taller. Did he mean for Moira to help him shower? David truncated the thought and got behind the wheel. They didn't converse on the five-minute drive to his house. Tired, all of them.

They settled Zac on the sofa in the den, across from the terrarium. He peeled the gauze, stiff with dried blood, away from the wound below his ribs. It had sealed overnight into a bright pink scar, fresh and delicate but without a seam. Whatever still reknit inside him, the outside wound would not reopen. Exposing the gut wound revealed a similar line of healing there.

David shook his head. His own body would have taken three days to reach this point. "This is a typical recovery speed?"

"For all of us? Not quite." Moira gathered up the soiled gauze and tape. "Zac's always been the fastest healer. The rest of us would take about eight more hours for this."

"Do you know why he's different?"

"Only guesses," she said. "Blood type maybe, since Simon has a similar uniqueness with the whole aiding-rejuvenation thing."

Ah, that. And with David's blood refreshed, he might be like them, might never take days to heal again. He told Zac and Moira he'd make coffee and fled with casual steps to the kitchen. Every time he thought he'd processed all of it, something new presented itself. They had shaken his life up and set it right in ways he'd never known to wish for. He set the coffeemaker to brew a full pot.

It was the first time he'd done this in decades — made coffee, in his home, for someone other than himself. He leaned one arm on the counter, bent under the sudden weight of the moment. Their voices came to him from the other room, at ease here. David's chin dipped to his chest. A need filled him, a sense of the Presence that sometimes felt distant but right now stood beside him, waiting for David to approach.

"Lord," he said. "These people — are they gifts? Did You bring them? Dare I hold on to them?"

Too soon to say.

He straightened as the scent of coffee permeated the kitchen. The pot began to gurgle. He set out not one mug but three.

"Your ways, not mine," he whispered. "Higher, I know. That these people should come to me now . . . You know I've forgotten how to do any of this."

"Promise me you won't retreat." Sarah's voice, rasping with age. Her hand, soft as the page of an old book flipped too many times, cradled in his own — smooth and hard and ageless. *"Promise me, John. Don't retreat from them. Keep your heart engaged with them, though they age like me, though they die. Like me."*

He had tried to honor her last wish for him. Succeeded for decades that eroded a hole in his spirit. And then there'd been Ginny, and after her, nothing left to give.

What was there now?

He poured two mugs and carried them to the den.

Moira wrapped her hands around her mug and lifted it to inhale the fragrant steam. "Mm, thank you, David."

David lifted the second mug toward Zac, eyebrows up.

Zac winced. "Still too many holes inside. I might have dinner tonight, though."

With Zac occupying the couch and Moira the only stuffed chair, David brought in a kitchen chair and sat. He sipped from his mug and listened to their silence, which wasn't quite: Zac's breath tightening for a few seconds, Moira sighing into her coffee.

"About Tiana," David said.

They both looked up.

"She'll be coming by whenever I give her the all clear. She left last night only half convinced of all this."

Zac was nodding against the back of the couch even as Moira's mouth turned down. "She's welcome." He gestured to his blood-stiffened jeans and bare chest with a smirk. "Shower first, though, yeah?"

He let David carry his bag and help him walk to the bathroom. Then he shut the door in David's face. Around random conversation with Moira, David kept his hearing tuned for the thump of a falling body; but in a while Zac emerged with damp hair, wearing fresh jeans and carrying a red knit shirt. His legs shook as he sank down on the couch, hunched forward, and handed the shirt to Moira. Together they worked it over his head, his arms into the sleeves. All bravado had leaked out of him by the time Moira pulled the shirt down over his torso and helped him lie back on the couch. He closed his eyes, sweat on his forehead.

"Go away," he whispered.

"You've overtaxed yourself."

"And take your obvious statements with you."

She sighed and motioned David to follow her into the kitchen. She drained the last of her coffee and deposited her mug in the dishwasher.

"If Tiana doesn't want to be cursed at," she said, "she should give him half an hour."

Tiana answered her phone on the third ring. She asked if they'd like her to bring breakfast, took orders from David and Moira, and showed up twenty minutes later at his door. The smells of the bag she carried made his stomach rumble. A sense of déjà vu flooded him; she'd come here with food three days ago. This wasn't their new normal, was it?

Tiana had included a blueberry muffin for herself. The three of them ate and threw away the take-out boxes while she continued to dart looks toward the den.

At last Moira's face softened. "Go ahead. If he's sleeping, please don't wake him."

"Of course not," Tiana said, but no edge resided there now, with morning broken bright outside and Zac alive one room away. She paused before stepping into the room, anticipation in her smile. David turned away, poured another cup of coffee, and ignored Moira's eyes on him as they entered

192

the den.

Tiana was sitting in the kitchen chair, pulled closer to the couch. Showing both scars but not the tattoo, Zac's shirt was pushed halfway up his torso. No doubt he'd have stripped it off, were he in less pain.

"I can't believe it," Tiana said, clearly not for the first time.

"Convenient, eh?" Zac grinned and tugged the shirt back down.

"It's all true."

"Yep."

"How old are you?"

"One hundred fifty-nine in January."

"How old when you stopped getting older?"

"Thirty-two."

"Your online bio says you're twenty-nine."

"Gives me a few years to grow into." The grin again, but it fell as his eyes shut tight and he drew a sharp breath.

Tiana jumped to her feet. "Zac?"

"Give him a moment," Moira said.

Zac's body seemed to cave deeper into the couch.

"Is he . . . ?" Tiana's voice trembled.

"He's nearly healed," Moira said, "but this last bit is draining."

Tiana took a step back. "I'll leave him alone then."

Zac's eyes opened with effort. "Am . . . 'kay, just have . . . to rest now."

"Sure, of course." Her eyes grew shiny. "Rest well."

A small smile, and then his eyes closed.

Tiana watched him a moment, then turned to David, voice hushed. "I was hoping we could talk. You and me."

David nodded, and she went to the library without hesitation. This conversation would be nothing like their last one in this room. A smile pulled inside him but didn't make it onto his face. Not with a would-be celebrity killer somewhere, maybe in town. Not with wounds knitting in Zac's body that would have killed someone else.

Tiana shut the french doors and sat on the library floor with her back to the only open wall, an unsure expectance in her eyes. Rather than sit above her in the sole chair, he sank down across from her and let the chair support his back. Bookshelves filled every other wall.

Tiana watched him with a half-squinting fixation as he folded his legs, set his hands on his knees. Her gaze rose to his chest, his shoulders, then his eyes.

"Tiana," he said. "I . . ." He let the put-on accent, natural as it was after so long, fall away. She would hear truth from his true voice. He sighed. "I'm only a man. I'm unchanged from yesterday, from last month. You know more of me, that's all."

She jolted upon first hearing the brogue, but by the time he stopped speaking, she was nodding, as if somehow all he said made sense to her — no, fit with something she'd been trying to understand.

"So go ahead. Say what you will."

She fidgeted on the floor, folded her hands in her lap. "It feels odd to talk about this with them in the house. But I guess it shouldn't."

"They can't hear us."

"So you don't have any other . . . special powers?"

"What I described to you before is the extent of my — our — abilities. Nothing that can compromise your privacy."

"Okay." She scrubbed both hands through her hair and continued to stare at him. "I . . . I didn't really sleep last night. Too much thinking. There's so much I want to ask."

He nodded her on.

"No, it's not that easy. I was writing them down, like I was going to interview you or something. Like you were one of Jayde's research topics and I was going to barge in and pry into all the secrets of this historical figure . . . but you're here, and you're alive, and you're . . ." She shook her head. "You're *David.*"

That statement still meant nothing to him, but he offered a smile. "Aye, I still am."

She jabbed a finger at him. "Your words, your accent, what . . . ? Are you — were you — Irish?"

"I was born in Scotland. My parents immigrated here and formed a community with many other Scots. Other nationalities too — everyone in that time was from somewhere else — but you learn to speak what you hear at home. And my father was a proud Scotsman, never would curb his accent. It was many years before I was willing to alter mine."

"Why did you?"

"Because of the questions. Was I English, Australian, Canadian, Irish . . . then how long had I lived here, what brought me to the States, was my family still in Scotland or had some of them come with me . . . ? Whole conversations of one lie after another, you see?"

"I hadn't thought of it like that."

"Easier to blend. Constant lies weary a soul, even lies to strangers you never see again."

"How old were you when you came . . .

196

to America?" She shook her head. "That was the nineteenth century. You were alive in the nineteenth century. I know we established this part, but I . . . believing it is . . . I have to say it myself."

She laced her fingers under her chin, propped her elbows on her knees, and waited. She was hearing him. Believing him. Accepting him. He couldn't speak for a moment. He held her eyes, and she seemed to see the barrier within that he had to push past. The moment of patience was her gift to him.

"I came here at nine years old," he said. "1857."

"Four years before the Civil War."

"Aye."

"And at thirteen you wore that uniform and went to battle."

"That's how it was." A drummer boy didn't often fire his weapon, but he marched with war around him every day. Saw war. Heard it. Tasted and smelled and touched it.

"What were you fighting for? You personally."

"Ach, I was thirteen. A man's age at that time, but too young to understand all the intricacies of life. My parents were in favor of abolition, of preserving the Union. I thought it would be an adventure."

"They gave you permission to go?"

"Not at first. I wore them down. But no one expected four years of war, of . . ."

He looked away from her for a moment. Some of those images remained with him to this day. Some of the scars that foolish boy gained had only faded, not disappeared. That war had made him aware that adventure was no worthy goal.

"You . . . you're . . . an old man," she said.

He laughed away the heaviness. "Indeed I am."

"It's just — you don't seem like one."

"Glad to hear it."

So tempting to put the walls back up. But what Tiana had seen last night, this morning — circumstances had catapulted her over his walls. She was left feeling her way through the labyrinth that was John Russell and David Galloway, both. Too bad for her.

Yet she was pressing forward. Fighting to understand . . . him, of all things.

"Not your looks," she said. "I mean — obviously, your looks are . . . um . . . not old . . ."

The blush spread over her curved nose and cheekbones.

"But I mean, you don't act old. Well, maybe occasionally." A smile tugged her mouth. "Actually, I can see you telling kids to stay off your lawn."

"I'd never." His turn for a reddened face.

"You have! You so have!"

Her laughter chimed around the room. She took a few seconds to sober. When she did, David squashed the desire to sit beside her and reach for her hands, which she tucked under her thighs.

"Do people frustrate you?" Her voice dropped nearly to a whisper. "Are we like a giant cloud of gnats you want to swat away all the time? Do you hate it here, do you wish . . . ?"

He closed his eyes. "Yes. No. No. And no, never for long, only the days . . ."

Fabric ground lightly against the carpet. The sound came again, to his right, close. Very close. Her hand alighted on his arm. David didn't move, and neither did she. She wasn't going to ask more questions. Not if he left this answer unfinished.

"The days pass," he said. "Yet ahead of me I see no less than there were before."

"I can't imagine that."

No, she could not. He waited for her to say more — a platitude, a verse from scripture, a promise she couldn't keep. Tiana was silent. Her hand didn't move away.

"Remember what you said before about

the created order of things? It isn't dying I want, Tiana. Only to see . . . the purpose in the fact that I can't. Only to see His hand in it. But I don't." He drew up one knee and rested his forehead, kept his eyes shut.

The soft weight of her hand lifted from his arm. Settled between his shoulder blades. "I'm sorry."

He lifted his head, opened his eyes. "You owe me no apology."

"It finally hit me last night, what this really means. How many people you've known and loved, and grieved. How much you've seen. And no one to know."

He couldn't move.

She set her hand over his that rested on his knee. Still he was motionless, as pressure built in his chest and behind his eyes.

"So if it's okay with you, I'd like to know you."

Dangerous, wasn't it? Hadn't it always been? But he gripped her hand. "It's okay with me."

"I'll do my best not to treat you like a historical figure."

A chuckle eased his chest. "There's a fair amount to know."

"I think we should begin with the important things."

He swallowed a lump of gravel and misgiving, but then her eyes twinkled. "Go on then."

"The best movie you've ever seen in theater."

David chuckled. "For entertainment?"

She cocked her head. "Is there another purpose to see a movie?"

"Well, not all movies are entertaining. Some of the greatest aren't, in fact."

"Just answer the question."

"*The Best Years of Our Lives.*"

"What's that?"

He shook his head, stood, and pulled her to her feet beside him. "You've never even heard of it?"

"What year was it?"

"November 1946."

She stared at him a long moment. "Black and white, then."

"Aye. And a great film."

In the theater's darkness as the film reached its close, something that had been balled up inside for two years, something muddy and gritty, washed clean out of him while his tears fell between his knees, soft drops onto the hardwood floor. The power of a story — of truth in a story. He sat for long minutes after the film ended, and half the theater had sat there too. A man no older than twenty-one, seated two rows in front of David, leaned his head on folded arms and sobbed loud enough for the whole theater to hear.

"Let's watch it," Tiana said.

He took the weight and measure of that idea, letting her into something so personal. Aye, he wanted this, but . . .

"Or we don't have to." Her fingers ghosted over his arm then withdrew. Without their noticing, some walls had risen between them again.

He needed some of them back up, for now.

"We can watch it," he said. "I'm still . . . acclimating. To all this."

"And you think I'm not? My boss and my celebrity crush are both immortal."

Her boss. Right. Good reminder. Sure, she wanted to know him; to work with him and not know him would be disconcerting now. The warmth in her — it might not be personal, not from someone like Tiana who held kindness out to everyone.

"What about illnesses?" she said as they left the library. "Do you get sick at all?"

"I catch something — cold, flu, normal things — every few years, about as often as I did before. My guess is as long as it's not a terminal disease, I can be affected by it."

Tiana paused before the threshold of the den, out of sight. Her voice lowered. "I told you, I don't want to intrude on them. I'm a stranger. Worse — a fan."

He chuckled. "Now that he's healed up, Moira's glare has defrosted some."

"She acts like his bodyguard. He's an adult. A very capable adult. For the love — an immortal adult."

He let her huff then cocked his head.

Tiana sighed. "And he was pretty much incoherent last night, and he's a public figure, and this is sensitive information, and I'm a fan who for all she knows . . ."

"Indeed."

"I want to earn their trust, David."

"Don't you think you're on your way to that?"

"I hope so." She looked up into his eyes in a way that made him want to pull her close. "Do you see it? The bond you'll have with them? It's . . . well, in a way, it's biological."

Not the way he'd have phrased it, but she wasn't wrong. "I see it. It's new, though. Unexpected."

"Fair enough. But don't underestimate it, David. If you have questions about — well, who you are — they might have answers."

"I know."

Before he could decide if he should say more, verbalize the thing she hadn't, Tiana sighed. "I love my parents, and they love me."

He knew that. He also knew they were white. And their relationship today wasn't everything Tiana wanted it to be.

"We're slowly getting back what we had when I was growing up. Before."

Before she'd tried to trace her African heritage. David nodded.

"But, David, it's always going to be a fact that I don't share blood with anyone born on this continent."

He nodded again when she paused. She had more to say. He waited.

"This — the history you lived through, they did too. And no one else alive can say that. It's worth finding out if you can trust them — I mean, really trust them. As family."

Most days, he didn't come face-to-face with how well she understood him. She knew the lone wolf in his spirit that could walk away from all of them rather than give them time and space to earn trust. He grazed his palm over her shoulder, and she didn't step back, so he let it rest there a moment.

"I plan to do just that," he said. "But I might need reminding at some point."

She smiled. "I can do that."

THIRTEEN

David emerged from the shower to voices drifting from the den. Raised voices. He towel-dried his hair, dressed, wandered out to track down the bickering. Tiana's soothing alto was silent. Perhaps she'd left by now. Noon had come and gone.

Zac and Moira faced each other across the low table in the center of the room, both standing with feet apart and arms folded, seeming oblivious to the mirroring of each other's pose.

"The man shoved a butcher knife into your stomach."

"David's got the knife."

"And knives are so hard to come by."

"Moira, this guy doesn't control where I go or what I do."

She cast her gaze around the room as if searching for something to throw at Zac's head. "This isn't about holding on to normalcy. This is about luring him into the open so you can knock his teeth out."

"So what if it is?"

"It's a stupid risk."

"I'm not the one who could end up dead."

"It isn't worth it, Zachary. We can drive up to the" — she raised her hand in a mitten shape, imitating the Michigander-speak Tiana had shown her at breakfast — "the top of the fingers or whatever they're called, and we can sightsee up there."

"No," Zac said.

Moira pivoted away from him to face the window, leaned her forehead against the glass.

David stepped into the room. "You want to catch him?"

"I checked the local news," Zac said. "If the cops got him, they didn't tell the media, which seems odd for a town this small."

"Last night you called me off." And hadn't been wrong to do so, though a pull to action still tugged in David's brain. "This morning you want him dead?"

Zac pressed a hand below his ribs. "Well, it was a long night."

"Not funny," Moira said.

He raised his hands. "Okay. Look, we need to know what this is about. If he's hunting me or just random guys. Maybe he recognized me after he stabbed me."

As a plan, it wasn't unwise. Or if it was, David had participated in more foolish ones. He gave Zac a single nod. Moira gave a whimper.

A sense of purpose rose in David, creaking with disuse, a lever that could swing the whole of him — mind, soul, body — if he gave it control. Awareness rose to a higher level than what he lived with daily — sitting with his back to every wall, seeing exits in public wherever he went, taking stock of the guy in line behind him at the grocery store. This other awareness was the heightened sense of his body, the space around him, the walls, the couch, how many strides he stood from Zac, how difficult or easy it would be to pitch Zac over the couch and land on top of him in such a way as to break bones and neutralize him.

"David?"

He blinked. He'd been staring out the window at the sunshine. At the oak tree's orange leaves, vibrant in their seasonal death.

Moira's eyes were hazel, not far in brightness from those leaves. In them David found curiosity mingled with something like affection.

He looked from her to Zac. "Let's try to find him."

Zac smiled.

"Has Tiana gone then?"

"A little bit ago," Moira said. "Which is for the best, I suppose, if we're going to hunt a madman."

"We're not hunting," Zac said. "We're exploring town the way we would have done anyway. More prepared, is all."

David had told them yesterday, driving back to the store, that his town was easily viewed in an afternoon and evening, that they'd seen everything of consequence. But something in Zac's expression kept him from repeating the words. This was the face Zac had worn at the canyon's edge, signing autographs. He was donning the mask again, becoming the daredevil, stating as fact the persona everyone who bumped into him in town would believe. Including the attacker.

Moira swept past David into the hallway, ignoring the false smoothness of Zac's features. She must be used to it.

David pulled him aside as Moira went out to the Jeep. "Do you have a weapon with you?"

"No."

"This guy might attack someone else." Someone who could end up dead. "At least one of us ought to be armed."

208

Zac studied him a moment. "I appreciate that."

"Tell her I'll be out in a minute."

David went to the bedroom for his favored sidearm. He put on a light jacket to cover the shoulder holster and joined the others.

Yesterday's cloud cover had offered the sun an unconditional surrender, and its warmth and light were reclaiming every inch of ground. Even the shade seemed brighter today. Zac grumbled that they shouldn't have left the rental car at the bookstore, that David should stop and switch vehicles, until Moira snapped at him. But he wasn't wrong, from a mission standpoint. The attacker was more likely to recognize the rental. David caught his eye in the rearview mirror and gave him a nod.

David parked at the library on the north end of town, and they set out to walk the two miles of State Street, the main stretch of downtown. For three hours they retread the walkways, revisited the shops. Zac was recognized twice by teen girls with whom he paused for a picture.

"You want to be mobbed?" David said after the second girl fast-walked away already texting someone.

"Whatever it takes." His smirk was the daredevil variation. "But seriously, you're overestimating my fame. And the belligerence of a small town."

All right, well . . . Zac would know.

The shops that had stalled Moira yesterday still held her enchanted. She studied paintings, repurchased the ceramic candle warmer David had broken, and tried on necklaces made of beach glass and Petoskey stone and Leland bluestone. David wandered the aisles, enjoying the handmade creativity but not understanding why some people chose to buy items like these. He rounded a corner and met Moira . . . and Tiana.

"Oh, David." Moira smiled. "Tiana's going to join us."

"No," he said.

Tiana folded her arms. "She filled me in. If daggers start flying, I'll get out of the way."

"Tiana."

"You've been roaming for hours, and you haven't seen him. Also, I'm not a blond male, so if he's targeting a specific image, I'll be fine."

Zac had no problem with her presence either, smiling warmly when he saw her. He and Tiana left the store first, already chatting, and David pulled Moira to one side behind them.

"You didn't even want to come back here. What's this about?" It couldn't be a craving for Tiana's company.

They fell into step behind Zac and Tiana, allowing enough distance to speak privately.

"We didn't detour to northern Michigan on a lark, David. We came to know you better."

"Moira." David lowered his voice. "She works for me. That's all."

"So you go around telling your true age to everyone you meet?"

She waited for him to answer. He huffed. "Obviously not."

"Simon's wife died eleven years ago. She was the last mortal to know."

He slowed his pace, absorbing that. Eleven years that none of them had allowed a mortal into their lives as deeply as Tiana was part of his. Well, before her, he hadn't allowed one either. Not since . . . He couldn't place even Ginny in the category of intimacy Tiana now occupied, marriage notwithstanding.

"So as far as getting to know Tiana" — Moira shrugged — "a bit of self-preservation might be involved too."

"I see now," he said.

Moira smiled.

At first Tiana shot regular glances of

211

concern in Zac's direction, but soon she seemed assured that he'd made a full recovery. Then she drifted to David's side and walked with him, and Zac and Moira followed.

"Let's hit the Natural Art Gallery," Tiana said the next time they crossed the street.

They'd been there yesterday, but it was David's favorite place in Harbor Vale, other than his own store. Most tourists strolled past without noticing. On the outside it was a narrow rectangle of a house, vinyl sided with flat windows. Inside, the owners sold botanical and natural history illustrations from the nineteenth century. Everything in the place was original. Yesterday Zac and Moira had stood a long time, whispering, in the aisle of framed Audubon owls and hawks.

"I should have bought something," Moira said as they entered the store, with more hush to her voice than when she'd said the same about the ice cream shop.

That Zac and Moira would grow quiet within the place was expected. That Tiana would do the same . . . David watched her pad up and down the aisle of botanical prints, as if any noise from her might disturb them. He stood in front of the plastic-protected color plates and waited for Tiana to reach him.

She picked one up and turned it over. "This was made in 1879. Some of those ones over there are from before the Civil War."

"Haven't you been in here before?" He was sure of the answer.

"Yeah. But . . . These things — they used to just be — old things to me. I figured it was nice that someone decided to preserve them. . . . But when this was made, you were almost forty."

"Yes."

She pressed the matted art to her chest. "Back then, did you have books like the ones these came from? Naturalist drawings — plates?"

"Only one, given the cost of them, but yes."

"You loved books even then, didn't you?"

The dark depths of her eyes held some feeling he couldn't name. He nodded, and she squeezed his hand before walking away.

They stayed another half hour and left without buying anything.

"I couldn't choose," Moira said, and behind her, at David's side, Tiana whispered, "Me either."

Tiana had had her apartment here for a year and a half. In a town so snug, that was long enough to be able to find one's way blindfolded. The few shops David had overlooked yesterday, Tiana led them into today — jewelry and clothing stores, and a bakery that Zac declared the best yet.

"You failed us yesterday, man, forgetting this place," he said around a mouthful of cupcake.

"What flavor is that?" Tiana reached for it.

He held it over her head. "Mint-chip bumpy cake. Get your own."

She scurried to the glass case beside the checkout counter.

"The first thing on your stomach in eighteen hours is mint-chip bumpy cake." Moira shook her head and took a bite of her apple fritter.

"Oh, right." He stuffed the rest into his mouth and shrugged. "Guess I'm fine."

He meandered after Tiana, and David tried not to frown at his retreating back. Moira stood eating her fritter, watching the other customers but darting a look or two at David. Inviting comment? Very well then. He motioned toward Zac.

"Seems he's forgotten the potential threat."

"Not at all," Moira said and took another bite.

"He's more concerned with desserts, at any rate."

She turned from her people watching to study him. "You seem to be someone who can be taken at face value."

He shrugged. He did try to be, perhaps to make up for the necessary secrets.

"Well, Zac usually isn't."

David looked across the shop. Zac and Tiana were laughing as she took a giant bite of cupcake, smearing mint frosting over her thumb. If any part of him remained on alert, David couldn't see it.

They left with a variety twelve-pack of mini-cupcakes for Tiana and Zac to duel over later. Tiana was already gushing to Moira over a store called Appleseed Apparel.

"I don't know that store," David said.

"Of course not," Tiana said. "It's female apparel."

Zac groaned. "How many chick stores does this town have?"

"This is the last one." Tiana grinned. "I swear on the cupcakes."

Five minutes inside were four too many. The very smell of the place — no doubt the product of an essential oil diffuser containing lavender and geranium and something else David couldn't identify — seemed created to repel him. Or he'd spent too much time in clothing shops today. In unspoken solidarity, he and Zac left to stand outside on the plank walkway and watch passersby.

"I'll need to get back to the store tomorrow," David said after a few minutes.

"Of course."

"I don't think he's going to show."

"Doesn't look that way."

David paced a few steps one way, a few steps another, as Zac's phone began playing "Landslide."

Zac tugged it out of his back pocket. "Aren't you supposed to ask women for wardrobe advice . . . ?" He reached out and gripped David's arm.

David halted. "What?"

Zac was darting looks up and down the street. He pulled David around the side of the store. Under a spreading maple tree, they stood between Appleseed and the jewelry shop next door. Out of sight. Zac hit the SPEAKER button on his phone.

". . . come around the back to the empty lot, and leave your cop friend out of it." The voice wasn't unique. This man might be Zac's attacker. Or he might not.

"I don't have a cop friend," Zac said.

"That guy who chased me."

"He's not a cop."

"On second thought, bring him. I'd rather keep him in sight, and he's standing next to you anyway."

David's mouth dried, but no, the man couldn't see them. It was a reasonable guess.

"So yeah, that's the deal. I'll let these chicks go once you show up." The call ended.

The two of them barreled back inside and swept the little store in a few seconds. Tiana and Moira were gone.

Zac shoved his phone into his pocket as they met at the back door, where their caller must have entered and left. "Empty lot?"

"Other side of this wall. I should stay out of sight."

"He's been watching us all day."

"Maybe not."

Not that it mattered at this point. David had lowered his guard for the first time all afternoon, and Tiana might pay for it. Tiana, whose days could end. His stomach became a burning knot.

He shook his head. Clear thoughts. Clear objective. He motioned Zac to follow him outside and halted when they stood more or less where they'd been standing before. "Walk past this copse of trees, veer left. You'll be standing directly behind Appleseed, where there are no windows. Unless someone blunders onto us, we'll have privacy to deal with him."

"Where'll you be?"

"I'll have your back, but he won't see me."

Zac nodded. "I'll let him know."

Wise? Yes. David nodded back, and Zac stole away through the trees. David drew his weapon, held it down at his side, skirted to the right, and crept toward the clearing. And began to pray.

FOURTEEN

"The Lord, my rock, who trains my hands for war . . ."

The mission's grip on David's mind was twice as strong now as it had been when he pursued this man the first time. And yes, it was the same man — no hoodie today, green T-shirt and blue rain jacket, jeans, black trainers, a leather-banded watch on his left wrist and what might or might not be a gun in his right hand, pressed into the center of Moira's back. Brown hair, pale blue eyes, clean shaven, straight nose, eyebrows thick enough to make up for the receding hairline. David cataloged every feature as if he would be helping a sketch artist later. He might be. This store had only one security camera, pointed at the check-out counter. Maybe a coincidence, or maybe the man knew it.

"Zachary Wilson," he said. "Can I call you Zac?"

"Not while you're threatening innocent people," Zac said.

"Where's your buddy?"

"Keeping an eye on you."

The man shuddered then drew back his shoulders, though it made him no taller. "Pull up your shirt."

Zac lifted the hem and turned a full circle, then let it fall. Over the course of the afternoon, the scars had vanished. "See, no gun. Now what's this about?"

His tone was a balance of bored and put out. His posture was relaxed, his mouth at ease, no tension in his jaw or his eyes.

The man spluttered, and the barrel of his gun wobbled against Moira's back. In contrast to Moira's blank expression, Tiana was biting her lip and staring at Zac as if the sight of him kept her composed. David slunk nearer under cover of a brush heap, mowed down weeks ago and left to dry out. He hunkered twenty feet behind Zac, to the left of everyone, not as near as he wanted but unable to close any distance across the clearing without showing himself. That didn't make him useless, unless the other man pulled the trigger first.

"It's about — I stabbed you last night, man; that's what it's about."

"Obviously you missed. Let the chicks go

so we can talk."

"I did not miss!" The wobbling arm again. Not a killing machine. In fact, this man might never have perpetrated violence before last night. The bravado of his phone call had dissolved. "The knife went right into you, twice. I made sure. And here you are anyway, which makes me right about everything."

A chill raced over David's arms. He strengthened his grip on the gun.

"See, I know what you are, Zac." The man's eyes sparked with excitement. Anticipation. He nodded toward Tiana and Moira. "I think they do too."

Zac took one step closer, blocking half the line of sight. David ground his teeth.

"You're a god."

"I'm . . . what?"

"I've always believed in you. That you visit us. But which one? Who are you?"

In the pause, the whisper of breeze through dry leaves was too loud. Civilians crossed not far away, laughing, the sound cutting off as they entered a store and let the door shut behind them.

"Come on, after everything I've risked, you have to tell me. Who are you really?"

"Thor," Zac said.

The man's mouth opened. After a moment he blinked and nodded. "You're shorter than I would've guessed, but that's just your human form, right? To help you blend in? You still look Norse."

"Yep." Zac shifted from one foot to the other. "And these are my servants, kept in thrall. So let them go."

"They're just human, right? They can get hurt."

David's jaw felt ready to crack. Be careful, Zac. Might not be in the man's skill set.

"This conversation goes no further until you let them go," Zac said.

"Compromise. Pick which one you want." The man nodded from one woman to the other.

"No compromise."

"I've got the gun."

"And I'm Thor."

"Yeah. Sorry. You're right. Okay, you go on." He motioned Tiana toward Zac.

Tiana took a few wobbling steps across the clearing, steadying with every step, lips pressed into a controlled line. David aimed past her and Zac but still had no clear shot.

The man kept the gun trained on Moira. "When she's gone, you can go."

Moira nodded, submissive as any compelled servant of a god.

Tiana neared him. Almost safe. It was

almost over. David strove to keep praying, but the only words in his vocabulary were *innocents* and *save them* and *center mass.* He hurled them toward heaven and grasped for others — *Lord God* and *please.*

She passed a yard from him. He should spring to his feet, gun raised, aimed at the man. He should move to shield Tiana.

No. Stay down.

Moira took a step away from the gun, and there it was, the open shot at last. The kill shot. No commander in his ear whispering *green,* but he didn't need permission for this.

"Go to the car," Zac said, and Moira followed Tiana around the store.

Safe.

David's finger withdrew from the trigger well.

"I let them go," the man said as if he'd done something uncommonly noble. He lowered the gun to his side, a blurred sweep of motion. "Now we talk. Just you and me."

"Hey, buddy," Zac called. "Come on out."

David stood as he'd wanted to do moments ago, gun held at chest level, pointed at the man. With a yelp the man dropped the gun. As David strode toward him, he scrambled back.

"I wasn't going to shoot anybody." His

glance bounced between David and Zac, face flushing red. "It's not even loaded."

David lowered his weapon and snatched up the one in the grass. The man shrank from him. Good. He checked the chamber — empty.

"You're an idiot," David said, "and you're going to get yourself killed."

"It's not loaded."

"You deliberately made us believe otherwise!"

"Hey," Zac said.

Right. Thor's servant. David turned his back on the cowering simpleton and offered the empty gun to Zac.

"Take it with you," Zac said.

"I have a license for that," the man said.

"Do you have a license to terrorize women with it?" David didn't try to tame the growl behind his words.

"I'm sorry." He seemed to believe the two words pardoned him.

David dropped the empty gun, holstered his own, then headed back to the Jeep as adrenaline continued to pummel him.

Tiana.

She'd never been in danger. But his pulse didn't believe that yet. Neither did the constricting muscles in his chest. Someone had held a gun on her. Seconds in the past.

He drew as deep a breath as he could. Past. It was past. He couldn't let it dig a groove into the record of his brain. That record already had a few places that tended to skip, get stuck.

Motion helped him work it through. He skirted the populated pathways, hugging corners of buildings, angling through maple and oak copses whenever possible. He wasn't in the mood to be observed by strangers.

He'd parked in one of the gravel lots behind the library, bordered by a tiny park-like area. Thick wooden posts had been laid along the ground to separate grass from gravel — a casual space and mostly empty. Picnic tables stood at intervals in the grass, and Moira and Tiana sat side by side at the one closest to the Jeep. Tiana's shoulders were hunched.

He strode toward them, both of them alive — Tiana alive. The last of the fight-or-flight response, preferably fight, drained from his system.

He stopped in front of them, and Tiana stood.

"You're all right?" he said.

She nodded. Trembled less than he did at the moment. "I might have some terrifying dreams for a while, though."

225

"The gun wasn't loaded."

"What?"

"Where's Zac?" Moira said.

"Talking, I imagine. He seemed in no hurry. Ordered me to go, which I had to do, as Thor's bodyguard."

"If he doesn't contain this . . ."

"I assume that's what he's about now. I doubt the man will talk if a god tells him to shut up."

Tiana set a hand on his arm. "What about you, are you okay?"

His chest heaved. He sank onto the picnic bench as she rubbed warmth into his arm.

"David?"

"You're — you're fine?"

If that gun had held bullets and if one of them had pierced Tiana's body — a dozen images, jerking bodies of men, impact of bullets, blood spray, arms and legs left on the battlefield, open unfocused eyes — he shook his head.

"Completely fine," Tiana said.

"Then so am I." The women's expressions didn't buy it.

Zac, feel free to show up anytime now.

Thor must have telepathic powers. The man strode into view a minute later, ease in his step that bespoke success. Their assailant didn't follow him.

Moira stood. "Where is he?"

Zac shrugged. "Wherever he wants. I swore him into the Friends of Gods and Demigods Society."

"You're not serious," Moira said.

"His name is Paul Tait, and he's thrilled to be trusted by Thor. I don't know if he'll break the pledge of secrecy or not, but it was all I could do aside from locking him in David's house for the next fifty years."

"And if he does tell the media?" Tiana said.

"He'll look mighty stupid, eh?"

Moira shut her eyes and pressed her thumbs into the sockets. "Does he live here?"

"No. That chick who took my picture two days ago? She posted it everywhere, and he saw it. When I left, he said he'd stay a little while and commune with my spirit."

"He's beyond obsessed," Tiana said. "He's unstable."

Flippancy left his face, if only for a moment. "I'm not arguing that."

"What if he decides some other guy is Thor too? What if he decides there are demigods all around us, and he should stab a few to prove it?"

"As long as they didn't fall from a tight-rope recently, they should be safe," Zac said.

"You can't know that."

"I told him I'm the only one of my kind on earth and any further violence from him would hurt a mortal person like himself. He believed that. He said he would never hurt a human. If he'd thought he could kill me, he wouldn't have attacked me."

"Unstable people aren't always predictable."

"I know that." He touched her shoulder. "But I've been reading people for a long time now, and I'm telling you, he's not going to hurt anybody else now that he's fulfilled his quest."

Tiana crossed her arms. "It's not a guarantee."

"Do you want to call a mental hospital and try to commit him? You're a stranger; you don't have anything like guardianship over him, and he's competent enough to drive here from Indiana."

She twisted her thumb ring. "A hospital wouldn't keep him."

"No, they wouldn't."

"Then you call the police and give them the knife. It'll have his fingerprints on it, and you can say you found this weapon and don't know who the blood —"

"No," Zac and Moira said together.

David pushed to his feet as he echoed

them. She didn't know what she was saying.

Tiana threw her hands out, palms up. "It's the only evidence we —"

"A forensic lab is not getting a look at Zac's blood," Moira said.

"They won't know it's his."

"They'll know it's nothing they've ever seen before." A blaze lit behind Zac's eyes. "One person will show another until the right person starts a true investigation."

Moira chimed in as though the conversation were a baton they passed along. "They identify us, they come for us, and they take us."

Tiana looked to David — for the voice of reason, she probably thought, for backup — but this same knowledge had lived in him as long as he'd known what he was. His voice came out dry and strained.

"That's what happens to oddities, Tiana. Since the beginning of history."

"You're not specially gifted heroes," she said.

"Exactly," Moira said. "If a group of people — the government or somebody else — comes to take me, I won't be breaking handcuffs and walls. I won't be running in a blur to escape them. I won't even hear or smell or sense them coming."

"All we'll manage to do is keep breathing

while they vivisect us," Zac said quietly.

Tiana shuddered and ducked her head to stare at the ground. She wouldn't argue further, at least not this point. She knew history too well to say it could never happen again.

David paced away from the others. They had put into words things he tried not to imagine. He made a fist and pushed it against his other hand.

"I hate this," Tiana whispered.

"This is how it is," Zac said.

She closed her eyes and nodded. "Yeah, okay."

"If I thought he was going to hurt mortals, Tiana, this would be a different conversation. He was after me. It's over."

Moira stood. "We should go."

As they drove away from downtown, they passed two cop cars. Maybe Moira's call from the night before had caused increased patrols. Maybe somehow it would be of use. They remained quiet as David drove back to his place, until Tiana met Zac's eyes in the rearview mirror.

"You think he believed you, really? That you're Thor?"

"He believed."

A tremor ran through her.

David gripped the wheel tighter. Alive.

Never in danger. Soon he'd be able to rest in that.

Zac turned to Moira with a feeble smirk. "Simon's going to love this."

The moment they got back to the house, Zac went to the living room and asked permission to bring the turtle out. David nodded. Zac opened the lid of the terrarium and lifted her and set her on the carpet. He watched as she craned her neck in his direction, the rest of her motionless.

"I have never owned a turtle," he said.

"Me either." Tiana crouched beside her, and the creature withdrew halfway into her shell. "She's so interesting."

"She?"

David left them to bond over his pet. In the kitchen he made coffee only to do something with his hands. Moira stood in the doorway between the rooms and watched not Zac and Tiana, but David.

"Thank you for doing that before Zac had the idea," she said as David poured in the water.

"Oh?"

"He can't make a drinkable pot to save anyone's life."

David chuckled.

She leaned on the doorframe. "You're not fine."

"What?"

"You've been quiet since the encounter with the numbskull."

He poured grounds into the filter, pushed it into place, hit the button, and a green light promised coffee in minutes. He pulled down four mugs and tried to decipher the question behind her remarks.

"Sometimes panic isn't obvious," she said.

"I'm not panicked."

"Not now, of course."

He set one finger against one of the mug handles and turned the mug in place. He looked up at her. "I know this is well meant, but it's not necessary. I've been fine the whole time. Besides, I've never had a panic attack."

"Never?"

The way she said it, he would bet one or more of them had. Two lifetimes were enough to accumulate a cause or two. He shrugged. "A few tough memories made in my time, sure. Sometimes they hit hard. That's all."

"Do you have triggers?"

"What's this third degree now?" He went to the carafe and filled the mug, sipped the coffee black. Mm, just right.

Moira's face held no apology. "Letting someone know about triggers is simple

common sense. Suppose we're all out camp-
ing and a beehive falls on your head and
oh, look, David's phobic about bees?"

"You'd be informed at that point, no
doubt."

"David."

Another sip. He held the bitterness in his
mouth a moment before swallowing. "I
simply prefer weapons not be aimed at innocent people."

She leaned her elbows on the counter and
studied him. "Especially Tiana."

The truth of it clamped a fist around his
gut.

She rounded the counter to stand near
him, picked up the carafe, and poured her
own coffee. "Sugar?"

"That ceramic jar beside the stove."

Tiana's laughter rang from the living
room. David looked toward the sound, and
Moira smiled. His face flamed.

"You blush adorably," Moira said.

"She's thirty-one."

"And she wandered town with us most of
the day, and I never wanted to slap her
unconscious, which shouldn't have surprised me. You wouldn't be attracted to a
bimbo."

"Perceptive."

She gave a soft laugh as she spooned sugar

into her coffee. "You're fighting it as hard as you know how."

"She's . . ." He shook his head. Leaned into the counter and closed his eyes. This conversation had to stop; he should want to stop it.

"I know." Moira set her hand in the crook of his elbow, and he opened his eyes to find warmth brimming in hers. "She's dying."

His chest squeezed. He nodded.

"I'm sorry for it. Truly."

Nod again. No words for the images in his head now — age and time, personified as some wrinkled microscopic monster that lurked in Tiana's bloodstream the way the serum lurked in his, sipping her youth this very minute, while she laughed at his turtle and probably flirted with Zac.

Moira set her mug on the counter and wrapped him in a hug, and this time his arms didn't hesitate to return the embrace.

FIFTEEN

"It's not like that," Tiana was saying as David stepped from the back storeroom.

Jayde laughed. "Sorry if I'm a little skeptical."

"I know him as a person now."

"So you don't think he's hot anymore?"

David's feet slowed. Whomever they were talking about, he ought to have this information. But if he had to skulk on the other side of the wall while they discussed male physique . . . not worth it. He stepped into view.

Tiana's back was to him as she dusted the shelving unit behind the checkout counter. Jayde gave him a wink and cleared her throat, but Tiana kept dusting.

"I didn't go blind this week, woman. I'm just saying . . . a celebrity crush can't really stay in that category after spending a day being touristy and — and normal. He's really . . . well, nice. More than you'd think, the way he struts anytime a camera shows up. Which for some reason makes me even madder at the chicks who talk about him like he's the property of the fandom."

Celebrity crush, fandom, right. David crossed the floor to lean his elbows on the counter and place himself into her vision.

"Oh, hi," she said. "What's up?"

They were somehow both more and less at ease with one another today. He should try to figure out why. He shrugged.

"I finished inventory on all the books from our latest acquisition. Want to help me price?"

Tiana finished with the feather duster and stowed it behind the counter. "You always price the books."

"Thought you might want the experience."

"Well, of course."

"If it gets busy up here, let us know," he said to Jayde.

Zac and Moira had waited until Tiana left last night before calling the others to inform them about the last twenty-four hours. Moira called Colm after Zac volunteered to wrangle Simon. Neither conversation had lasted long, and they'd seemed unperturbed afterward. They'd driven up to the dunes early this morning, before David had left for the store, and would probably get a hotel up there.

In their absence, normalcy settled. Routine. A needed thing, at least for a day.

For half an hour David and Tiana discussed nothing but books. Their worth based on age, edition, condition. Tiana's numbers were as uniform and legible as his own, and they penciled dollar signs and digits and decimals in the upper righthand corner of every book's first page. They worked easily together, as they always did, but she might want to tell him something.

Or he wanted to tell her something.

"These Bradburys can go out," he said, hefting a pile he'd just finished. "Someone cleaned us out of him last week."

"Okay." Tiana kept marking, didn't look up.

As he was sorting the children's books from the rest, Jayde's voice found them — words undecipherable, tone shaking.

Tiana looked up from the hardcover Elmore Leonard story collection in her lap, pencil poised. A wrinkle formed between her eyes.

"Does she sound scared to you?"

David stood. Yes, she did.

A male voice joined Jayde's, volume rising, and Tiana leaped up, catching the book and guiding it to a gentle landing on the floor. "He found out where she works."

"Will he do anything in public?"

"I don't think so, but I didn't think he'd come here either."

David strode out into the aisle and turned right toward the front of the store. The man facing Jayde across the counter was an inch or two shorter than David but probably outweighed him. Hard to tell how much of that bulk was muscle beneath a shirt and loose jacket.

"We don't do this kind of thing without talking first."

"I know," Jayde said. "But I want to work. I want to work here. Just go, and we can talk about it later."

"Just go? You hear yourself?"

David stepped up to the counter. "What's the problem?"

Jayde bit her lip but held his eyes. "No problem, boss."

"Boss, huh?" The man pinned his glare on David and took a step toward him. "Hi, boss. I'm the fiancé."

Jayde had never mentioned an engagement. No way David could say *congratulations* without irony.

"Jayde's coming with me until we can sort out some things."

David looked to her, arching an eyebrow. "Oh?"

She took a step back from the counter. "Chris, please. We'll sort it out when I get home tonight."

Chris shook his head, and his next step took him closer both to the counter and to David.

Physical force would be the last resort. As always. But he'd haul the man out of his store if necessary. David's shoulders drew back, feet spread, muscles tensed; he let the man see his stance and hoped it would be deterrent enough.

"Chris," Jayde said, quietly, a plea.

A presence hovered behind David, bristling the hair on the back of his neck. He shifted to one side. Tiana, of course.

Chris spotted her too. "You put her up to this."

"I did no such thing," Tiana said.

The bell above the door jingled, four college-age kids bustling through it — three girls and a boy. The boy shot a glance toward them, but the girls were focused on the books before they reached the shelves. After a moment's pause, he followed.

The only thing to Chris's credit so far was his pause until the four kids were out of sight. Then again, it proved he was in control of this persona that threatened to storm all over them if denied his way.

"I'm not leaving here without you, babe."

"Please, Chris."

"This conversation appears to be over," David said.

The air around the four of them charged with something Chris must want to be danger. "Oh, really?" He stepped forward one step, two, three.

Close enough to deck. Good thing David wasn't tempted. "This is my store, and Jayde is on my time right now. If she chooses not to go with you, then you're going to leave and let her get back to work."

"And if I don't, you'll call the cops? I haven't done anything."

"I'm not one for calling the cops."

"Oh yeah?"

"Chris, don't be stupid." Jayde lurched around the counter. "I'll come with you. Just stop making a scene, okay?"

A glint in the dark eyes. The left side of his mouth tipping upward. Conquest.

She turned from him to David. "I'm sorry. I'm so sorry. I promise we'll sort this out."

He softened his tone. "This is what you want?"

"Enough, Jayde. Come on," Chris said over his shoulder, already moving toward the door.

Jayde ignored him, looked up into David's face as her eyes filled. "Are you going to fire me?"

"No," David said.

The tears brimmed over. "Thank you," she whispered.

She bustled after Chris with her head down, suppressed sobs in the shaking of her shoulders. The bell jingled over the door as Chris held it open for her. Irony caught in David's throat.

The door shut, and a silent sigh leaked out of him. He ran a hand over his face. Same old story.

"Why didn't you do something?" Behind him, Tiana's voice shook.

He turned to her, his bones feeling heavy. "She didn't ask me to."

Tiana paced up and down in front of the aisles, looking for their customers, then returned to his side, hands on her hips. "What were you waiting for, magic words? 'Hey, boss, I'm afraid of this man'? Does this not bother you at all? Or just not enough to take action?"

She knew better than that. He'd let her spout everything she needed to. She stood glaring at him. He cocked one eyebrow. *Finished?*

Her lips tightened. "He intimidated her and made demands, and you just stood there."

David motioned around the counter to the stool Jayde sometimes perched on while she rang up customers. It swiveled as Tiana scooted onto it, and she held it still with her feet.

"Jayde heard me offer help, did she not?"

"She couldn't take you up on it with him standing right there."

"Couldn't she?"

"He might've broken up with her on the spot."

"Her fiancé."

A storm gathered in Tiana's face, mouth turning down, eyebrows drawing together. "He's never proposed to her."

"So she let him claim a relationship he doesn't have a right to. She let him talk her into walking out on her job. She didn't know I wouldn't fire her for that. Another employer might have."

"But she . . . but you could have . . ."

"You've told me yourself a forced intervention won't work. She had a choice, and she chose him."

Tiana hunched on the stool and gripped the edge of the seat with both hands. "I know."

He rested his hand on her shoulder, and she looked up, eyes searching his, lower lip jutting.

"I'm sorry," he said.

The lip wobbled. "She's the one who'll probably get hit tonight."

"And she'll tell you about it. She'll let you see."

She shrugged.

"That's hard to carry."

A slow nod, teeth worrying her lip, and then she lowered her head.

"But listen now. She's not putting on a face for you."

"It wouldn't do any good at this point. I know too much."

"She trusts you," he said. He tipped up her chin, withdrew his hand as the simple touch sent a longing through him to cup her face, kiss her cheeks where tears wanted to fall, seize that lovely lip between his own and . . .

Focus, you clod. Of all the times. "When Jayde's ready, we'll be here."

"I will."

"And so will I."

"Really?" The whisper was as hopeful as a child's. David nodded.

Tiana slid off the stool to stand in front of him. Close. Whatever had betrayed his straying thoughts, she'd seen it. It was reflecting back to him in her eyes.

"David . . ." The hoarseness under her voice pushed heat into his veins.

Customers in the store. Work to do. Not to mention the old vow to himself. He took a step back, and Tiana watched him too closely, cradling a new awareness. A lift to the right side of her mouth, which he also wanted to kiss.

Her hand reached out. Didn't rest on his arm, only brushed fingertips over his shirt-sleeve, then withdrew as his own hand had done. He strove to fasten his gaze some-where other than her — slender hand, curve of mouth, warm eyes. So full of light, she was. So young and so good. To hold her — the thought of that privilege robbed his breath.

"After closing," she said, a gentleness in her now that seemed to think he was some frightened wildlife specimen, "could we . . . talk?"

Walls — build them back up now, before the breach was permanent, before desire and admiration joined forces to flank him. Before feelings of the moment dragged him into an atrocious decision.

"Aye, we can talk."

A brighter light beamed from her now.

"Good."

"If you hear from Jayde, let me know."

She nodded. "I'll stay up front while you work on pricing the rest."

"Thank you."

Making distance between them was a sound plan. David worked in the back until ten to six then came out to help Tiana with the closing routine. A final customer came to the counter at 5:57 p.m. with at least a dozen books. While Tiana rang him up, David did a full sweep of the store. The man left, and David turned the sign to CLOSED and locked the door.

And faced her.

She was running the tape on the register, brow puckered, fingers flashing. He left her to finish; as much as she hated numbers, she wouldn't appreciate an interruption. He returned to the storeroom and continued pricing until Tiana appeared in the doorway.

"Finished?" he said, setting aside a book.

"Yeah."

He stood. "Good then."

They got their coats from the rack. Tiana hung her orange purse over her shoulder and watched him set the alarm code. They stepped onto the porch together. A soft evening, breezeless and dry and almost warm. The floodlight reflected in her eyes.

Tiana's hand reached out again, and this time her fingers seemed more delicate as they rested on his arm and stayed there.

"For a while now," she said, as if it were a full sentence. A full paragraph. A short novel.

This. This was why he couldn't prevent the crumbling of the walls. A few days of knowing, and she understood. Chose to stay. Touched him. He let his thumb graze her knuckles, and the touch was far from enough.

"Yes," he said.

"But you haven't asked me."

"No."

"Not because I work for you. Not because you don't find me attractive. Not because I'm black."

"Tiana."

She set two fingertips of her free hand on his lips. "I admit, the age gap was never a reason I came up with before. But you're such a convincing thirty-five."

Thirty-five and not a day older. Thirty-five and alone for fifty years. Her cool fingers branded heat onto his lips.

"Anyway, it's not that either."

He shook his head.

"Sarah, your wife? You can't love someone else? Or is it because she died, and you won't risk that again?"

Words rose in him, a flash flood splintering inner dams he'd neglected over the last few weeks. No one was to know these things; no one would ever have asked.

Her hand cupped the nape of his neck. Her thumb nestled in his hair. "You were so closed off. Kind and fair to work for, even someone I could call a friend, but always behind these sky-high fences with KEEP OUT signs all over them. It didn't matter what I wanted; there was never any possibility."

"There isn't," he whispered.

"Then tell me why." Her other hand left his arm and settled an inch higher on his neck, fingers in his hair, poised to pull his lips down to hers.

He wrapped her in his arms. Held her to his chest. Not a hug. David held her. She molded to him, close. He breathed her in. His body gave a long shudder as he splintered inside.

All the nights. All the days. Never to have this again.

She pulled back by inches, lifted her face, lips parted, and he kissed her. Gentle. Slow. She made a sound into his mouth, and the kiss went on, and she clung to the front of his shirt until they parted for breath.

She traced his cheekbones with her thumbs. "David."

He kissed her temple, her ear, her mouth again. She was sweet and salty and pure. He eased back. The side porch wasn't visible from the street, but pedestrians venturing off the walkway could spot them if they were looking. He would always be too old-fashioned to kiss a woman in public.

"Dinner," he said. "And then wherever you want to go."

"Let's walk through town and just talk."

He led her to his Jeep, shut her door, and walked around to the driver side. He began to drive with an instinctive direction, both of them silent until he parallel parked in front of the crepe place. It was the only elite restaurant to be found in Harbor Vale, but the food was worth waiting for. More the size of a café, seating only two dozen or so at a time, but David hoped it wouldn't be too crowded.

They were shown a table immediately. They were quiet again while they looked over the menu, and remained so after ordering. Tiana spread the cloth napkin over her lap and looked out the wide window at the traffic, the pedestrians . . . looked at everything but David.

He had to tell her things. He stared down

at the white tablecloth and pressed his thumb to his eyebrow as an ache formed. Perhaps he didn't have to display the deepest core of him now. No hurry, was there?

Yes, there was. He'd told Tiana this wasn't possible, and then he'd contradicted his own words. Nothing honorable in that. He had to make it right.

"Second thoughts?" Tiana said, her voice barely reaching him over the background drone of voices from the other tables, of clinking dishes from the kitchen.

"Not that."

"Then what?"

"This isn't the place to discuss it."

She frowned.

Unfair of him. He fought the old edge reforming inside, blunt and shielding. A fence, as she'd called it, to crouch behind. A place to nail KEEP OUT signs. He'd nearly forgotten how hard a grip this instinct had when it latched on.

"I don't want tonight to be about me," he said. "This last week's been composed of outlandish revelations. You must be sick of them."

"Not yet." Her mouth turned up.

He huffed a laugh and shook his head. "Well, I am. I want to hear about you. Can we do that?"

"Sure. After we sort out what we're doing here."

"I want that too. Truly." Only . . . He shook his head. He had to tell her his thoughts, not keep them from her. "I might need a bit of time, to be able to get some things out. Things you need to know."

She sat back in her seat. "How much time are we talking about?"

"An hour or two?" Heat rose in his face. This open-book practice certainly humbled a man who didn't know how to crack the pages of himself anymore.

But a slow smile lifted her mouth. "I think I can handle that."

Relief poured from him in a long breath, and she gave a soft laugh.

"Oh, David."

"What?"

"You're doing fine."

They ate quietly, remarking on the food and the ambience and the unexpected pleasantness of the night, that even as near to the door as they sat, no autumn wind gusted in on them when people entered and left. David asked if she wanted dessert, and they split a chocolate éclair crepe with vanilla-bean pudding in the center. Tiana ate two-thirds of it.

They left the restaurant, and David fed

the parking meter a few more quarters. Then they set out.

For the first block they said nothing. The crisp air filled David's lungs, and the soft tap of Tiana's boots was a comfortable sound. She kept pace beside him, her long legs unhurried. They didn't touch.

"You know that lone picnic table at the end of Valerian Boulevard, just this side of the private beach, before the lake?" he said as they reached the third intersection.

"Past the COUNTY ROAD ENDS AT WATER sign."

"Aye, that one. We could talk there."

"Works for me."

"Or we could keep walking."

"We can do that after."

He led them one more block, and then they turned down Valerian. Passed a few houses, including one that had been for sale when David moved here. He'd favored the house but couldn't have tolerated tourists parking in front of his home for minutes or an hour, walking down to the water, walking back, leaving to make room for the next influx. During the summer he sometimes wondered what he was doing in a tourist town at all.

As they reached the dead end, the rhythm of the waves washed over them. Poplar trees rustled in chorus. He and Tiana were the only people there for now. The weathered wooden picnic table sat perhaps fifty feet to the right, its legs sunk a few inches into the sand. For a moment David floundered as he tried to find some way not to leave his back open to the dark beach that stretched perpendicular to Valerian. But that meant facing away from the street, the way they'd come. He opted for the former, and Tiana sat beside him.

Now to say what needed saying.

Sixteen

"It's not a risk. What you said before, about not doing this again, it's . . ."

In the dark Tiana watched him.

"It's a certainty, do you see? Unless somehow something changes for me, physically."

"I'll die," she said.

He saw it. All of it. Her hair lightening to gray, fine lines around her mouth, her posture stooping, limber legs stiffening and slowing. Her body hollowed out by cancer, or her mind hollowed out by dementia. Or tomorrow or a year from now — a car accident, a mugging, a fall, an undiagnosed heart condition, a brain tumor — so many ways to die. He covered his eyes.

Her arm slipped around his back. "Am I worth saying goodbye to?"

"What?" He lowered his hand.

"I mean, assuming for a minute this goes . . . well, where we think it might. I know it's not a fair question, because I don't know what I'm asking, not really. But I've been thinking about this a lot. Since Zac got stabbed, actually — since I knew it was true. And that's the only way I can find to sort this. Either I'm worth it or I'm not. And it's really okay if you say I'm not."

They sat for long minutes that eroded the thickest wall he had left.

"I've been married twice," he said.

Tiana edged closer to him on the bench. "Go on."

"I married Virginia — everyone called her Ginny — in 1966. That love was different than the love for Sarah. Ginny was . . . She woke me up. I'd gone through the motions of living for a few decades by then. Ginny made me really live. And laugh. We laughed a lot."

"How did she die?"

He bowed his head as the wall crumbled for good. "She didn't."

Tiana's hand rubbed a slow circle over his chest. He had to shut down now, before he said too much. But Tiana. She had to know. Or he had to walk away.

Should he?

"Tell me, David."

He pressed her hand against his chest. "We owned a farm. I'd been a farmer

254

before, and I missed it. Ginny was a self-proclaimed hippie, and I didn't even have to persuade her. She loved the idea of living off the land. It wasn't much of a working farm really, not large anyway, but we . . . It was home. Life."

For a few minutes he couldn't speak. Nothing left to tell but the pieces he should hide. Tiana didn't prod again, stayed close and quiet. The waves swished against the shore, gentle in the still night.

"A farm needs machinery," he said.

Her breathing stilled against him. Aye, she could guess.

"There was an accident. She found me. It was —" He coughed, a reflex from the surging memory. "No cell phones then. To phone for help, she'd have to leave me on the barn floor, bleeding out. And they'd never get there in time. So Ginny, she . . . she held me."

He kept his footing against the wave of the past. It was all still there — blood pulsing from the wound carved in his chest, Ginny's screaming and then her sobs, her arms rocking him, waiting for him to stop breathing — but he held his own, and it didn't blur the present.

"She didn't realize what was happening. Not for an hour. Or more. I don't know how long. But she never left me. The bleeding slowed after a time, and . . . Well, when I didn't die, she watched over me, still thinking every minute that I would."

"Hold on. She didn't know?"

"No."

"But you married her."

"I did."

"You let her think she knew you. You let her pledge herself to — to less than half of you."

"I did."

He waited for condemnation, but she was quiet, open to the rest of the story.

"I don't know why she didn't put me in the car and take me to the hospital. Shock, fear I'd die in the back seat while she drove — I don't know. But in a day I woke up. Two days after that . . ."

"No scar," Tiana whispered. "What did she do?"

"She . . ." Ach, he'd thought he was past this, but his eyes were burning.

"She left you, didn't she?"

"Packed her things while I slept. Left a note."

"That day? After you should have died?"

"She was terrified. I ought to be glad she didn't try to burn me for a demon while I was unconscious. She believed in them, but her ideas were rather outside biblical doctrine."

"You were the same person as before. And you were her husband."

David hunched a little on the bench, head bowing. "I reaped what I'd sown, nothing less than that."

Tiana closed the gap between them and wrapped her arm around his back. He leaned into her as she placed her other hand on his chest.

"You woke up all alone." Her hand fisted his shirt.

"I did," he said, uncurling her fingers. "But it's years in the past. Many years."

"I'm sorry."

"I'm telling you because, if we're going to attempt this . . . well, a second wife would be a bit of an unfair omission."

Tiana sat back but stayed within the circle of his arms. "Did the two of you have any children?"

"No."

"Did you ever see her again? Hear from her?"

"Divorce papers, of course. But not face-to-face."

"How long were you married?"

"Six years."

"And she didn't notice" — she trailed her

fingers down the side of his face — "this?"

"She groused about it sometimes, especially when her hair began to look salted. I was supposed to be midforties by then." He held her gaze, a tightness in his chest. She had to understand. "Tiana, I wanted her to know. From the first. But I never knew how to tell her, and then it rooted so deep, the secret. I couldn't find the way to dig it up."

"You should have. Before you married her."

"You think she'd have believed me? If Zac hadn't been stabbed, would you believe I've seen the turn of two centuries? However sane I appear, without proof the commonsense explanation is that I'm mad."

Tiana looked away, shaking her head.

"I'm not making an excuse for myself. Only trying to show you what was in my head at the time. It was wrong, I know that — I knew it then."

"Yeah, it was." She met his eyes. "Listen to me now, okay?"

When she didn't continue, he nodded.

"What she saw — her fear wasn't unreasonable. Maybe even her leaving wasn't unreasonable. But that doesn't mean I can't be sad for you — for the day you woke up to that note."

He cleared his throat, but the constriction

stayed. He tightened his arm around her, and she took his other hand and seemed to study it.

"Your hands were the first thing," she said. "So . . . guy. I told Jayde the first week I worked for you, 'My new boss has such masculine hand gestures,' and she was like, 'You're crazy, woman.' "

A soft laugh, and then her eyes welled up.

"She never even texted me after she left. Anything could be happening to her right now."

No words would assuage the truth.

"I don't know why I get blessed with a good man and she gets trapped with a guy like Chris."

A good man. Even after what he'd just told her? He fidgeted on the bench, looking out over the street.

"David, I want to pray for her."

"We can do that."

"You first?" Tiana bowed her head.

A lump filled his throat as he bowed his head over hers. She knew who he was, so yes, he could pray with her. With a fellow believer, interacting in sacred community. One more thing he'd never thought to have again.

"Father," he said, the words falling quiet but easy, without forethought, "we're two gathered in prayer to ask Your protection over Jayde this night. Grant her wisdom and courage. Surround her in safety. Hold her heart. If she be not Yours, pursue her with truth. In the name of Your only begotten Son."

A tear fell on his hand. He looked up, but Tiana kept her head bowed.

"Jesus, wake her up. Open her eyes to the harm that man's doing to her. Please keep his hands off her tonight. Thank You for loving Jayde, and I hope she knows I love her too. Give me the words to say to her, and help me not to get angry and push her away. Amen."

"Amen," he said.

Tiana swiped at her cheeks. "Thank you."

"Of course."

"You pray like . . . like a hymn."

A chuckle filled his chest and banished the last old ache of Ginny's memory. A lightness filled him too. Spoken prayer in the presence of another follower of his Lord, and of all people, it was this woman who mattered more to him than he'd known before tonight. Before this minute.

Her importance to him did not feel dangerous. Strange, that. He leaned close and kissed her forehead.

"We should walk," he said. This dead-end

260

street was too dark. Too secluded. Too easy to court dishonor. "And it's now your turn to talk."

"What do you want to know?"

"Everything, eventually."

She laughed. He tugged her to her feet. This time, as they set out, their hands remained linked.

Two hours of talk followed, and none of it about him. He asked few questions, instead let Tiana tell him whatever came to her. At first she kept mostly to her college years — the books she'd read, the classes she'd taken, how she missed it and hoped to go to grad school at some point, though she hadn't decided on a degree program. She trailed off several times, shrugging and asking what more there was to know about her. Those times, he ventured questions.

"I think I'm avoiding a topic," she finally said. "Namely, my family."

"We don't have to talk about it now."

"I guess you know most of it."

For a long time, she was quiet. David kept his fingers laced through hers as they walked. He saw the infant Tiana, his imagination placing her in a rough crib, wrapping her in rags that she kicked aside to scream out her hunger, her loneliness. He gripped her hand hard.

"I'm not going to drag you through my adolescent identity crisis." She stopped walking, turned to face him. The streetlight above them reflected in her eyes. "Summary, I grew up hearing that I 'talk white' and 'walk white' and . . . you know. All of that. It's confusing for a kid. And you know about the falling out with my parents. I think they're coming around, though. Slowly."

"Surely they can see now," he said, "it didn't mean you loved them less."

"But what if I *had* found relatives in Burundi? What if the orphanage had had records of some kind, something more than Baby Girl, date of birth unknown? I don't know if they would forgive me for that."

His jaw tightened. He rubbed at the tension there and sighed. "They're wrong."

"I've tried putting myself in their place. Sometimes I can."

David could not. If one of his children had not been born to him, had desired to know . . . He shook his head. Even that was too far for him to imagine.

"Anyway." She looked away from him, across the street at the emptying shops. "Yeah, we can move on."

"In a moment." He pulled her hand to his side. "Tell me about adolescence."

"Oh, really, it's not worth listening to."

"*You* are worth listening to."

Her eyes welled up. "Most of the time it was good. Sometimes it wasn't."

He squeezed her hand.

"Okay. The fact is — and you need to think about this if you're serious about dating me — the fact is I'm a black woman in a white town, David. The fact is everyone is color-blind until the black woman is manning the cash register unsupervised."

It had happened three times in the two years she'd worked for him. Always a tourist, two female customers and one male, pointing out to David the risk he took in his hiring choices. He'd asked them to leave his store, not out of a conscious desire to combat racism, but because he'd glimpsed the pain in Tiana's eyes and had wanted to cause those people physical harm.

"You have to think about it," Tiana said quietly.

"I know."

"I'm not saying you're naive."

"I know. Go on."

She tilted her head. "Go on?"

"You evaded the past by bringing up the present."

She was quiet a long time. They walked. David kept her hand in his.

"Seventh grade was the first time a class-mate called me . . . you know, the *N*-word. We were arguing about something stupid. We usually got along. And I guess she didn't know how else to win the fight, so . . . well, she won, because I was speechless. I didn't do the sobbing-my-teenage-heart-out thing until I went to bed that night."

He kept his grip tight and kept walking. He thought about manacles on black wrists and ankles, about ropes around black necks, about marches and fire hoses and police dogs and hopelessness and courage. He thought about all the ways humans ripped each other apart. About the casual stupid cruelty of the white seventh grader who left Tiana's heart with a hole in it.

"Basically," she said, "I knew nothing about blackness but what I learned from the people around me: you ignore it, or you degrade it. So I ignored it. Until I was in college."

He knew the next part. College was when she had sought her roots. And crushed her parents.

"There are transracial adoptees whose parents bring them up totally differently. Teach them their heritage and make it something important. I don't blame my parents for not doing that. But . . . well, the

264

way it all worked out, I'm pretty much culturally estranged. I've pieced 'me' together on my own. I'm just myself."

"Just yourself?"

"Yeah. The best self I can be, the self that God created . . . you know, all the clichés." She smiled.

He didn't know how to say what he felt without adding to the clichés, but that risk was worth it. He stopped walking, and Tiana stopped too, her eyebrows arched in question. David lifted her hand to his lips and kissed it.

" 'Tis a beautiful self," he said.

Her smile grew. "I'll take that."

"And thank you."

She tugged his hand, and they resumed walking. "It's sort of the journey that never ends, but I know who I am now."

"I've never doubted that. I see it daily."

"Do you?"

He nodded. It had been the first thing about her, beyond the physical, that attracted him.

"If my identity hadn't come from Jesus, from who He says I am in Him, I don't know what I would have done, David. Who I would have tried to become."

"That's true of all of us."

"Yeah."

They walked quietly for a time. It seemed she had finished the subject, but he would wait for her to change it.

"Did you know I play piano?"

He turned toward her in the dark between streetlights. "What's this now?"

"Lessons for five years, and I can also play by ear."

"I want to hear you."

"What about you, any musical skill?"

"Piano as well, but it's been years since I touched the keys."

"Sometime we should try a duet."

Yes, they should. "Tell me more."

"Like what?"

"Everything, as I said."

She grinned. "Let's see. My favorite form of exercise is kickboxing."

"I know that one already."

"Hmmm. I keep saying I'm going to buy a real camera, but I just keep using my phone . . . which you also know."

"Aye."

"You know I love children's books. . . . You know I love chips and hummus."

Laughter shook his chest. "Quite the summary."

"It's only the first date. I have to leave you in suspense about some things. Besides, I'll run out of life experiences long before you will."

"Still, not one new thing?"

"My favorite color is orange."

He stopped walking. "That I did not know."

"Not garish Halloween orange. All the other variations, though — peach, coral, Tuscan orange . . . I think pumpkin pie is a cool color." She poked her finger at him. "Do not mock me."

He would never mock her. Nor would he tell her tonight that he was ever more fascinated with the self she had discovered and molded. Ten o'clock came and went as they tramped over blocks they'd already covered, still chatting, telling light stories — David of his travels, Tiana of adventures with her adopted cousins. She'd been a sober kid, not unexpectedly, but she'd never been timid. As they walked, her thumb massaged the back of his hand, and she didn't seem to know she was doing it. David said nothing but couldn't keep from smiling.

At last he turned to her. "Ought to say good night."

"I guess."

They headed back toward the Jeep, this time walking on the side of the street that included Appleseed Apparel. A few paces from the store, Tiana slowed.

"This is going to sound stupid," she said.
"Doubtful."

"I know that gun wasn't loaded, but it really freaked me out."

"Not stupid." He wrapped one arm around her.

"No, not that part." Her smile didn't reach her eyes. "I love that store. I don't want to shy away from it in the future. So . . . could we go back there, reclaim it in my head? I think it'll help to be with you."

The store was closed, like every other on this street. She must mean the clearing in back. "Of course we can. It's a good idea. But are you sure now's the time?"

"I don't think night will matter."

They walked over the grass, around the corner of the building. Tiana stood a long moment at the edge of the brush where David had hidden trying to get a clear shot. His mouth dried. If he'd killed an unarmed civilian . . . Well, he could only thank God he hadn't.

Security lights on the back of the store illuminated the area, discouraging midnight loiterers. They stepped through the weeds to the center of the field. Here Zac had stood. Tiana kept walking to the place she'd stood beside Paul Tait. She planted her feet and looked around.

"Okay," she said. "Okay."

David stayed in the middle, silent. He pivoted slowly to watch the perimeter of the field, but they were alone. Safe.

"Thanks," Tiana said after a minute. "I think I'm ready."

"We can stay a bit longer if you need to."

"I thought I would, but it's just a place. You know? Maybe it'd be different if something awful had happened."

It would be. His gaze swept the area a final time. Tiana approached, crossing in the open, as a tingle lifted the hairs on the back of his neck.

He thrust an open hand at her. "Stop."

The bark froze her. She stared at him.

Move. He rushed her, wrapped his body around hers, and all but carried her to the edge of the clearing, to the cover of the trees.

"David?"

"Something's wrong."

She didn't ask questions. She didn't grab hold of him and refuse to let go. She stood still and nodded, *okay,* and watched while he ventured to the far side of the clearing, the source of the tug in his gut. A brush pile had been dragged over a few feet.

Overreaction. He huffed. Anyone could have moved the cut branches and debris, for any reason.

269

So why the full alert still clanging in his head?

He paced the periphery and came back to the branches. Long, some of them, well over six feet. They smelled of decomposing grass and . . . something else. Was it the smell that had made him react? Another visual sweep, but nothing moved, nothing threatened. David kicked the branches, and they rattled, dry.

He bent over them, and the stench grew.

His heart thudded. As many times as he'd smelled this before, no doubt what it was.

"David," Tiana called.

"Stay back."

"What is it?"

He kicked the pile again, tried to move branches with his feet, but the length and the tangle of them made it impossible. He pulled his gloves from his coat pockets and put them on, swallowed hard, and hauled the top branches off the pile. A few more and then, through the spaces, there. Open mouth. Clouded eyes.

"I'm coming over there," Tiana said.

"It's Paul Tait."

SEVENTEEN

Tiana's boots rustled the dry grass behind him. She halted a foot back then inched closer.

"Oh, Lord," she said. David drew her back from the sight, and she didn't resist. "He's dead."

"Yes."

"He's dead. There's . . . a . . . dead person . . ."

Her legs buckled, and David caught her against his chest. "Easy now. Try to breathe easy."

"I can smell him. Is he dead? Are you sure he's dead?"

Her alto was rising fast. David gripped her shoulders and held her at arm's length, ready to catch her, but her legs remained firm this time. "Tiana. Look at me."

Her gaze dragged from the brush pile to David's face. Her breathing was even, but her pupils were dilated. She was straddling the line between stress and shock. David cupped her face between his gloved hands.

"You're safe. You're all right. You need to take deep breaths and stay calm. Can you do that?"

"He died."

"That's right."

"Somebody killed him? Why would somebody kill him?"

He shook his head, thoughts grappling. He could let the store employees find this themselves. Disturb the brush enough to be sure they did. Land them in counseling for months. A sour option.

He could make an anonymous call, but that was more likely to arouse suspicion than if he identified himself and talked straight to the cops.

The man was dead. Appropriate dealings with him could wait a few minutes, or however long Tiana needed to recover. She was shaking now, staring at the branches. "I feel sick."

With an arm around her shoulders, he supported her to the edge of the clearing, but she didn't throw up. She leaned into him and wrapped her arms around his back.

"I'm trying to stay calm."

"You're doing fine. Keep breathing through your mouth. If your vision gets

272

spotty or your hands start tingling, tell me."

"David."

"Right here."

"What happened to him?"

"I don't know."

He held her a long minute, until she stopped shaking. Until she leaned her head on his shoulder and looked toward the body again, this time with a firmness to her mouth, her eyes no longer too wide. She was blinking at normal intervals again. David cupped her shoulder.

"I'm sorry." Her voice was small.

"Don't be."

"You're fine. You're not overreacting at all."

He drew her close. "It's not overreacting. You've just seen death."

"I was with my grandma in the hospital. When they turned off the machines."

"It's not the same, Tiana. Violent death isn't natural. It's supposed to sicken us."

"But you . . ."

"I'm too well acquainted with it. Your reaction is the wholesome one."

"What do we do for him now?"

The quaver in her voice kept his arm around her a moment longer. "He'll be turned over to the authorities."

"Do you think he tried to threaten some-

273

one else, but the person saw the gun wasn't loaded and attacked him?"

"No."

The reply came from instinct, but he was sure of it the moment it left his mouth. Perhaps there had been a mistake, a mugging gone bad. Tait out here meditating on Thor, a thug or two prowling away from the streetlights and the walkways, spotting the man and deciding to take his wallet, only he put up a fight . . .

It could have happened. Yet it hadn't, he knew.

Tiana's hand rested on his arm. "Time to call the police?"

He looked from her to the brush pile. Trudged back to it and looked into the dead face, as if its vacuity could somehow provide clues. David pulled away more of the brush and looked over the corpse. No blood, no bruising to the face, no scuffing of knuckles. Fully clothed. Had his wallet been left here? That would seal it.

Another branch lifted, and he could see the lower torso, the hips and legs. Both front pockets turned out. Any halfway intelligent killer would rob a body whether he cared about robbery or not. David drew a long breath through his mouth, and now, with Tiana recovered, his brain registered the racing of his pulse, the tightness in his muscles, the heat that coursed down his arms into fingers that remained slack only with effort. He drew the branches back over the body. She stood a few feet off, watching him.

"Let's go," he said.

"Okay." She reached for his hand and gripped hard, but her eyes trailed again to the brush. "He was supposed to have more days left, and somebody took them."

"Yes."

"Why?"

His jaw was killing him. He took out his phone and shepherded Tiana back to the side of the building, out of sight of both late-night pedestrians and the clearing. He removed his gloves and dialed.

"Hey," Zac said.

"You'd best tell me now."

"Uh . . . tell you what?"

The man did sound clueless. But he wasn't to be taken at face value. "What you've done, Wilson. Didn't leave town as early as you said?"

"David." Zac's voice held a hard gravity. "I don't know what you're talking about."

"You left with Moira this morning?"

"Yeah, we're driving back to the hotel now. Spending the night here by the dunes."

Lying over a phone line was easy. David shook his head, paced under the trees, stopped to brace his hand on a trunk. He breathed long and slow, trying to cool the seething in his blood.

"What's going on?" Zac said.

"Paul Tait is dead."

The silence wasn't long, but it held plenty of comprehension. "You're sure?"

"He's in the clearing behind Appleseed under a pile of cut brush."

When Zac's voice came again, the edge had been replaced with a hush David had never heard from him before. "And you think I'm a murderer."

"Who else would know to come here to his sanctuary?"

"Why would I kill the man?"

"The man who knew too much? Fairly classic scenario." He bent at the waist, clubbed by nausea. All that swagger about the Demigods Society — such a simple cover.

"Nothing he knew would have made a viable story. But even if he'd had something — David, I wouldn't do this."

"Would Moira?"

"She's been with me. And no."

He had to believe Zac or not. The depth of his wanting to almost shocked the breath

276

out of him. This man who'd known him for a hundred years and waited to meet him — these people who wanted to treat David like family — he couldn't allow that to cloud his view. Not with a man murdered.

"It can't be a coincidence."

"What do you think it is?"

Not a challenge. A question. "I don't know. When are you coming back here?"

"Well, we were planning on tomorrow, or the day after. The plan was whenever we got bored. But that's off now, obviously. We need to talk this through. Tonight."

"Aye, we do." In person, he'd see the truth of their involvement or their innocence.

"I should make it back to your place by midnight."

He hung up. Tiana had edged away from the clearing, stood beneath the shelter of a rustling oak tree and watched him cradle his phone in his hand while danger hummed in his veins like an electrical current. He put the phone away.

"No call to the police?" she said.

"No."

David took her hand and led her away, a brisk pace that didn't quite resort to jogging. She asked no questions, made no protests, said nothing all the way back to the Jeep.

When he stopped to unlock the vehicle, she clenched her hands together in front of her. "We would have to lie to them at some point in our story."

"Possibly. It would have become quite a labyrinth, at any rate — what to say and what not to."

"That doesn't mean we don't call at all."

"We can't, Tiana."

Yet a sense of impropriety dogged his choice. By now a police car should be pulling behind the building, no lights or siren. An officer should be getting out of his car, going to investigate. Maybe it would have been Jacob Greene, the cop who sometimes brought his two girls into the bookstore for more installments of The Boxcar Children and Nancy Drew.

By now the authorities should know that Paul Tait was dead. They should be marking off the scene with yellow tape, calling what had been done there a crime. David imagined the number of officers, the forensic team, the photographer and the incessant flash of his camera in the dark.

Instead, Paul Tait still lay there, his death unseen, unknown.

"If we're not going to call them, can we go?"

Her voice brought him back from his

reverie. David set his hand on her shoulder, drew a slow breath, and prayed he hadn't made any mistakes tonight.

They drove back to the store in silence. David parked beside her car, but she didn't get out.

"You really thought Zac did it."

He nodded. No sense in telling her he was far from convinced Zac had not.

"I've had my eye on social media for the last twenty-four hours. Paul Tait never posted a word suggesting Zac Wilson is Thor. That kind of thing would have gone viral in ten minutes."

"You think Zac's monitoring too?"

She shrugged. "I'm just saying, if he'd killed him, it would have been gratuitous."

"It *was* gratuitous." He rubbed his face. "I'm sorry for what you saw."

"I can't get it out of my head."

"You won't. But it will fade some."

"Guess I'd better head home." But she didn't move.

She wasn't waiting for an invitation, but she needed to understand.

"I'd tell you to follow me back to my place," he said. "Not to be alone, not yet. But I have to speak to them. I have to get them to tell me things they won't if you're there."

Her lips parted. "You think they're guilty."

"I think they know something."

"Oh, David, no."

"I need to be sure."

"Not Zac."

"I don't know." But it was connected. All of it. Too great a coincidence otherwise.

"This is why you didn't call the police. Not what you might have to lie about — what you might have to tell the truth about."

He nodded. Then he walked her to her car. "Will you be all right?"

"I think so."

"If you need anything, you call me."

"I will."

He went back to the Jeep and drove home, watching her headlights in the rearview mirror until her car turned while his continued straight. Toward home and a man who might have lied to him.

EIGHTEEN

A rare clear night for Michigan fall, stars poking holes in the fabric of the void, Orion's belt always a bit brighter than Ursa Major. David stood in his driveway for a moment, absorbing the old age of the heavens. They would be there after he was gone, after all of them were. Their courses were unchanged by the violence people inflicted on each other, by the crime against Paul Tait as well, but somehow this violence felt different, inflicted on one so young by one as old as David.

Was that what had happened?

He'd know shortly. He went inside, sat at the table, and waited. He tried not to try to solve the puzzle. He tried not to think at all.

Ten minutes past midnight, a soft knock came. David opened the door to both of them, somber and pale under the white porch light.

"May we come in?" Moira said, in a tone

unsure of the answer.

David made a sweeping gesture, and they stepped past him into the kitchen. They settled right there, sitting in the chairs, again seeming to believe they weren't invited farther inside than necessary. Guilt, perhaps. Or the ability to read their host's face. David paced the rug in front of the sink and ordered his pulse to normal speed. He didn't know anything yet.

Yes, he did. He knew a man had been killed, that justice must be done, and that as long as he withheld the outlandish truth, the police were working with a handicap. Then again, if Zac was the killer, the police couldn't be involved at all. David leaned into the counter and folded his arms and measured the two strangers sitting at his table.

"What do they know?" Moira's mouth crimped.

"Not who killed him," David said.

"Of course not." She leaned forward, long fingers curling on her knees. "But what do they know?"

"I didn't speak to them."

Her eyes widened a quick moment. "At all?"

"He's lying there still. Until some mortal

282

finds him who can be forthcoming with them."

She and Zac straightened in their chairs, watched him.

"Well?" Moira said.

"Well, I've protected both of ye as well as myself from discovery without knowing what might be discovered. Whatever that is, I'll not turn a blind eye."

The tension in the room tore down the middle like a spiderweb. Zac stood, and David planted his feet, an instinct though Zac made no move toward him. Moira looked back and forth between them.

Zac stood still, a quiver in his shoulders. His eyes were like ice. "I told you where we were."

"And admitted this isn't a coincidence."

Zac pressed his palms to his face, breathed deep, and rubbed his hands outward as if to wipe his expression. His eyes remained closed a moment, and then he looked out the window over the kitchen sink, into the night.

"No," he said quietly. "I don't see how it could be."

"Zachary," Moira said.

"And the cops wouldn't see it that way either." His gaze met David's again, frank. Guiltless? "They'd see a harassment and stalking case that got out of hand. That's motive enough to pursue me as a suspect."

"I expect so."

"Besides, I'm a narcissist. Ask anyone." Zac choked on a laugh. Pushed one hand through his hair, walked to the sink.

If he'd killed the man, he was the greatest actor David had met — including James Cagney. But Hollywood professionals didn't have a century to hone their craft.

There had to be some way to be sure.

David needed space away from both of them. Solitude to think. To pray. He went out into the backyard, left them to their strained silence. No, they'd have plenty to say the moment he was out of earshot.

He paced from porch to tent and back again. Had God brought him to these people now because of Paul Tait? Was David meant to find the truth? And if they were guilty, how was he to bring them to justice? It all felt backward, though. Paul Tait would still be alive if Zac hadn't fallen off that tightrope — of this much, the certainty ran deep in David's bones. Simpler for the Almighty to leave things alone. Unless . . . this was more than a mission. Maybe achieving justice for a mentally broken victim was *the* mission, the thing David had to complete. Maybe if he did that, his Lord would accept him home.

Or maybe he was doing this all wrong, and God would have preferred he call the police and leave it with them. He trudged to the porch and sat on a lower step.

The door opened, and he looked up. Moira, her dark hair glinting in the porch light, her eyes shadowed. "I have to say all of this in the time it takes a male of the species to use the bathroom."

David motioned to the space beside him, and she sat, feet resting on the step above his.

"You're not like him. You're men of action, both of you, but it's a different sort. There are truths that paralyze him, that I think put you in motion."

"You're not speaking very plainly for someone with only a minute to talk," David said.

Moira leaned forward and to one side, peering at what was once a flower bed. "What's the chicken wire for?"

"Turtle. She lives outdoors in the summer and about half the spring or fall when weather permits."

"I see." A smile found her lips but not her eyes. She turned to face David. "He wants to go after this. To make himself into a detective or something, I don't know, but you've got to refuse him. Let it go, and get him to do the same."

"Why?"

A muscle pulled in her neck as she swallowed. She laced her fingers on her knees. The silence thickened.

"Moira," he said.

"Because doing otherwise will hurt him."

He dangled his hands between his knees and breathed the crisp air. "I don't see how, if the evidence will prove him innocent."

"Leave it to the police. Please, David." The last words were nearly lost to the night, despite the lack of breeze.

"Because they'll solve it? Or because they never will, and you know it?"

Tension drew her knees up to her chest.

"You know something. Tell me what it is."

"What I know is that Zac did not do this. Now please leave it be."

She didn't know him at all if she expected to persuade him now. He let the silence strangle around them, the way hands might have done to Paul Tait's neck.

"Moira, there's a man dead." The words fell from David like stones that, though fallen, didn't lessen the weight of responsibility on him. "A man murdered, who couldn't harm Zac or any of us."

"He *did* harm us." Moira curled tightly

beside him. "Caused Zac a night and a morning of pain, and might have undone us all with his brash mortal theories."

The door behind them opened. Zac's footsteps joined them.

David angled his head to watch Moira. Her teeth clamped onto her lip.

"We could be out on a manhunt right now," Zac said over her shoulder, eyes locked on David. "You don't want this to end up some cold case in a filing cabinet."

"I don't," David said, and Moira shuddered.

"And if we work it together, at some point we'll get you proof of my innocence."

The more Zac talked, the more certain David was of that much.

"We've got to have some decent instincts honed by now. Ever try to solve a homicide before?"

"Not yet."

Moira sprang to her feet on the porch step and planted her hands on her hips. She faced Zac down with a tremble in her voice. "Don't, Zachary. This isn't our place."

"If the man's dead because of me, then it is my place."

"How could it be because of you? How does that make any sense?"

He sighed and rubbed his face. "I don't know."

"So give up this childishness. Stick to baring your body and falling from impressive heights and signing autographs for teenagers."

The attack was transparent, shouldn't have done more than bounce off the surface of Zac. Yet his face blanked as he took a step back into the door.

Something in the words Moira had chosen was a bullet to pierce Zac's armor, and Moira had used it. After asking David not to hurt him. It meant only one thing, and in a heartbeat's time, Zac had retreated too far to see it — which she'd counted on. David stood and stepped up to her, crowding the little porch.

"Did you kill him, or do you merely know who did?"

"I don't know what you're —"

"He was six inches taller, quite a bit heavier. You couldn't have physically overcome him, not on your own."

"I didn't do anything to Paul Tait, David."

And if Zac hadn't either . . . The way she'd cried and cared for him after the stabbing, the way she looked at him, touched him, spoke of him — these things weighed more than the words she'd just used to attack him. She was being a woman, wounding to protect, or so she thought.

But she wasn't protecting only Zac.

With a fifty-fifty shot, he might as well guess. He looked into her eyes.

"Simon?" he said.

"No, of course not." The words were simple, easy. They held a hint of surprise that he would be David's guess and not . . .

The other option.

Muscles in her face tightened. Her eyes darted to Zac.

"What?" Zac's voice broke. He'd seen too. "What?"

She shrank against the wrought-iron rail. The poise of years, the hardness of necessity, the supplication from a few minutes ago — all fallen off her. She was porcelain now. And young.

"Oh no." Zac clamped his fists in his hair and pulled. "Colm?"

"No." The porcelain was cracking. "No, it wasn't Colm."

Contrasted with the truth spoken a moment before, desperation in her words now marked them a lie. Zac's hands fell to his sides, and he stared at her. As if she were a ghost, translucent while claiming to be the woman herself. She reached for him, and he pushed past her and David, down the steps into the yard, stood past the floodlight with his feet spread, his back to them.

Moira had begun to tremble. "It isn't Colm. It isn't."

"You're the one that talked to him on the phone," David said. "You told him about the clearing. Paul Tait was a trespasser, and you sicced the longevite dog on him."

"The — what?"

"Colm should have taken him somewhere else. The place of the killing gave too much away."

She closed her eyes, and twin tears dropped to her feet. Not an act. No point in that now. She opened her eyes and stared past David into the yard. Zac hadn't moved. Silent tears dripped down her face.

"Is he the only victim? Have others gotten too close to your secrets and had to be dealt with in kind?"

The blade of David's words sliced all of them, but someone here had to be willing to wield truth, to lance the infection that might be as old as Fisher Lake. Zac stayed motionless in the yard.

Moira's small frame shook. She gripped the railing and bent toward it, her breathing sharp. "Please, David, stop this. You don't know what you're doing."

"I know I'm seeking justice for a man no

one else will speak for."

"There'll be no justice. Colm won't allow it."

She was a few shallow breaths from hyperventilating. David's own pulse quickened with concern, and he wrapped both arms around her and guided her to sit on the step. She was cold beside him.

"Peace now," he said. "Calm down, and tell us how you know these things."

Zac turned toward them, his mouth pulled into a grimace. Still he didn't move toward her, but she kept her eyes on him as she spoke.

"Colm told me. I never would have known. He came to me . . . to confess, though he'd never call it that."

"So you kept his secret," David said.

"I had to."

He looked away from Zac to find her caught on a quiet sob. "How's that?"

"It was best for everyone, David, and I don't regret it."

Silence pummeled them as if complete. As if no bare trees across the yard rubbed their branches. As if no far-off traffic passed on a road they couldn't see. Zac folded over, a slow collapse to his knees, hands braced on them and shoulders bowed.

Moira dried her eyes and stood, solid now.

She'd needed less than a minute to compose herself. She marched out into the yard. "Look at me, Zachary."

He did. Head lifting as if it weighed too much for his neck.

"I knew what you'd say, you and Simon. That he had to be stopped, whatever it took. And I couldn't do it, not to Colm."

His voice came firm and flat. "How many?"

"What?"

"David asked if Tait was the only victim, and you didn't say yes."

She shuddered.

Zac's voice came with a lethal hush. "How. Many?"

"I — I don't —"

"He's had a hundred years!"

"Paul Tait makes eleven."

"Dear God." Zac's arms came up to cover his head, face in the crook of his elbows as he bowed, face nearly to the ground. "Dear God, forgive us. Jehovah Elohim, forgive us."

Moira backed away as if a tongue of righteous fire might lash him out of existence. David stepped off the porch, but he was only halfway to them when something in the deepest center of his being flickered a warning. *Be still.* He halted.

Long minutes, and Moira didn't move either. Zac's arms lowered, and his palms pressed into the grass. He straightened slowly, seeming bent under the weight of all his years.

"I always wished for him to join us." He kept his back to them, facing the dark beyond the reach of the porch light. "John — David. As if he needed us. And all this time we've carried this . . . this rotten burden around like Bunyan's pilgrim and I never suspected it, I never sensed it. . . ." He covered his face. "Dear God."

"Zac," Moira said.

"I've celebrated a hundred Thanksgivings with him."

Moira knelt at his side and touched his shoulder. He didn't move toward her but didn't pull away. "I'm sorry."

"For lying to me?"

She flinched. Nodded.

"Only for that?"

"We protect each other, Zachary. I would have done the same for you."

"If I were a serial killer."

"You know I would."

He stood, looked down at her, his face drawn tight and gray, then turned and studied David as if measuring him for the first time against the sketches he'd memorized. "He won't stop. Even if he did — eleven people slain."

Moira looked past him only at David. "It's a sickness in him, a compulsion; if you knew —"

"Eleven souls," Zac shouted.

The release in David's spirit was like the squeeze of a father's hand followed by a nudge to the son's shoulder. *Walk on. Speak.*

"Moira. See those souls." The brogue thickened with every word he spoke, betraying the quake inside him. "How old might they have been — twenty, thirty, forty, fifty? Young ones, remaining meager years stolen. He cannot be allowed to rob another life, not one more."

She shook her head, kept shaking it as if she could undo the truth.

Zac lurched forward a step then bent with his hands on his knees. Before Moira could touch him, he straightened again and traipsed across the yard, feet dragging over the grass, up the steps and into the house.

NINETEEN

Moira was a marionette, and Zac's exit cut the strings. She slumped to the ground, knees folded under her, staring at the door. David took a step toward her, but she thrust an open hand in his face.

"I'd like a minute, please."

Even huddled on the ground, she appeared steadier than Zac had. David went inside.

Five paces from the door, Zac knelt at the edge of the rug, hands over his face. David looked toward the ceiling, cut off from the sky, filled with the irrational sense that the plaster and beams overhead had cut him off from the sky's Creator as well. He drew in the heated air and breathed out a prayer along with it. Whatever happened now . . . *Make my path straight.*

David dropped down to sit cross-legged on the floor several feet away from Zac. The man didn't heed him, but David stayed beside him. Motionless. Wordless.

In a minute Zac lifted his head and found David. The blue eyes were glazed. Zac shivered.

David went to the living room and got the brown blanket from the back of the couch. Chenille, good and heavy. Weight on Zac's body would anchor him. David draped the blanket around Zac's shoulders and tucked it over his hands. They were cold. He sat again to stay at eye level.

Zac blinked for the first time. "David."

"Aye."

"Eleven." Another shiver. Another minute of quiet, and then Zac said, "How does he kill them? All the same way or . . . experimenting?"

David maintained eye contact, tried to let Zac know each shaky word mattered to him though he had no answer.

"Has he killed women too? Children?" Zac pulled the blanket tighter around him. A good sign. "I'm trying to make myself believe it. Colm. I — I'm trying to . . ."

More silence. How long would Moira stay out there? Had she gone for a walk? A drive?

Zac's hands stirred, and he looked down at himself. He flipped a corner of the blanket toward David.

"So you're also a nurse."

A chuckle eased David's chest. "Just a man who knows shell shock when he sees it."

Zac scoffed, shed the blanket, and stood up, firm on his feet. He strode to the window and gave a slow nod.

"Where is she?" David said.

"On her way to the airport, I'm sure."

David's throat closed. He went to the front of the house, looked in the driveway. The rental car was gone.

Zac followed him, stood over his shoulder, and looked outside with a shrug. "Like I said."

"Zac, if I'd thought she would disappear . . ."

"She's Moira. Our nomad, our illusionist who vanishes and pops up months later and doesn't allow questions. She might do the same now."

"Will she warn him?"

Zac turned away, cursing. He beat his fist on the wall once and then stood with his back to David.

"We have to stop him," David said.

Zac gave a barking laugh. "What do you propose?"

"First we find him. Then we take him into custody. Then we decide the rest."

A slow nod. A hard swallow. "Would you

go quietly?"

A flash of smoke, dirt trench in front of him, bodies on either side, rain and filth, blood and knowing he must never surrender. He shook his head.

"Me neither," Zac said. "And Colm . . . he's as stubborn as Simon; he's just quieter about it."

"This thing will take both of us. We'll need your knowledge of him."

Another short bark. "We shouldn't count on my knowledge of any of them, eh?"

Not the point. "Can you do this to Colm?"

The bitter glint faded from his eyes and left them almost as empty as before. "Eleven ghosts to put to rest. I'll see it through."

"All right then."

Zac braced one hand on the wall and ducked his head. When he turned back, his eyes held a sheen. "Who were they? Where are the bodies? Why did he . . . why?"

"We need to talk to Moira again," David said.

"She won't tell us anything."

"She was about to. She wanted us to understand him. It's with her we've got to begin. She's listened to him explain his motives."

"Who gives a crap about his motives?"

"Any insight could help us stop him."

A long sigh poured out of him. "Did she ask you not to investigate, before I came out on the porch?"

"Aye."

"What reason did she give?"

"You."

"You mean the police?"

"Not only that."

Zac's mouth firmed. "What did she say?"

"That some things paralyze you."

Anger flashed behind his eyes. He cupped his fist in his other hand and paced. "And it's a pitiful weakness to the woman who prefers flight to the far corners of the earth. Yeah, Moira can always move, if the direction is away from you."

"She's not moving away from Colm," David said.

"She's never slept with Colm."

Ah, well then.

Zac cupped his fist again, pressing knuckles to palm. "Listen. We all would have stayed in contact, sure, but it would have been more peripheral without Colm. He's been . . . the glue, keeping us together. Setting our meetings in stone, dates and places. I don't know if there's anyone on the planet I have less in common with than Simon. And Moira — she's hard to get, David. She's the one who'll disappear, but she's also the one who wants peace. Always, whatever the cost. Half the time she disappears, it's because of some conflict. Usually between Simon and me."

David crossed away from the window, sank onto a stuffed chair. Zac perched on the edge of a couch cushion, hands still clasped, one in the other.

"Moira . . ." He seemed to search for words then shook his head and leaned forward. "She's protected a murderer and lied to me about it. What am I trying to do, justify her?"

"You love her," David said.

Zac shook his head again, but it wasn't a denial.

"I had it backward. I thought she was waiting for you to settle down."

This time the bark of a laugh came quietly, almost softly. "She does hate the fangirls. She hates every time I do a photo shoot, says I'm objectifying myself."

"And yet?"

"It's not just that. We . . . we don't really work anymore. I respect the lines she's drawn and don't inconvenience her." He swallowed hard. Something darkened behind his eyes, perhaps an old pain. "But I can't be both. So we're . . . this, now. Leftover care and jagged edges."

Compared to the simplicity David had shared with Sarah until her death, with Ginny until her leaving, Zac and Moira's dance felt like a soap opera. He shook his head.

"I'm just telling you how it is," Zac said. "How she is. You have to pay attention if you hope to predict her."

"Right now, I only want information from her."

"And she may or may not give it to you. It depends on the buttons you push."

"What buttons?" Sudden fatigue made the last word sound like nonsense. It was nearly two in the morning. Eight hours ago, he and Tiana had been closing the store, and his greatest concern had been whether the crepe restaurant would have a long wait.

Was she asleep? Had nightmares awakened her?

"Moira wants us reconciled, all of us," Zac said. "Anything that would prevent that, she'll try to prevent. Anything that will make it happen? She'll help you."

"How do I convince her I'm after reconciling?"

"Maybe I should call her." Zac stood to pace.

"All right," David said.

Zac stood still, studying the painting on

the wall as if for answers or guarantees this would work. He shook his head. "If I call her, she'll know we're teaming up against him. If you call her, maybe you can convince her I don't want anything to do with it."

David dug his phone from his pocket and pulled up her number. He tapped CALL and raised the phone, holding Zac's gaze as the phone rang. And rang.

"You have reached the voice mail of Moira Smith. If you'll leave me a message, I'll probably call you back."

He hung up. "Smith?"

Zac's quiet laugh splintered, the warmth in it seeping away. "That's some joke with herself. Her last identity was Jones."

Still in his hand, David's phone began to ring. "It's her." He accepted the call. "We need to talk, Moira."

"I don't agree."

"Then why call me back?"

Silence.

David paced, all his limbs craving motion, some task, any task. Perhaps it was the conversation with Tiana tonight that made his fingers twitch for piano keys to pound out everything inside him in minor block chords. Moira let him wait almost a full minute before she answered him.

"How is he?"

David glanced at Zac. "I have no idea."

"You're with him, aren't you?"

"Of course."

"Well?" An edge formed in her voice. "What's he said?"

It was the slightest hunch, but . . . "Not a word, so far."

Her breath caught. "Nothing?"

"I sat on the floor with him for a bit."

Zac glared and mouthed something. David shrugged. It was working.

"Moira, listen." He had to hit now, hard, while she was stunned and worried. It had worked before. "We need to talk about Colm. I'm ready to hear you out, but not over the phone."

"I . . . I'll meet you somewhere."

"I'm not leaving Zac like this."

Zac threw up his arms and glared, but then he huffed out a quiet breath and stood watching, understanding the play. He nodded, and David nodded back.

"No," Moira said, "stay with him. I–I'll come back to talk. But if you still aim to hurt Colm after that, I won't help you."

"I take it you've warned him?"

"I've spoken to Simon."

Interesting. "And?"

"I wanted him to hear it from me. He said what I've done is unforgivable."

303

In the silence, maybe Moira would read sympathy. Or whatever else she needed to read to step out from her defenses.

"I've turned the car around. I'll be there in a few minutes."

"Good," he said.

She hung up. As he lowered the phone and took a seat on the couch, Zac burst into a fury of pacing. His strides lengthened, up and down the room, until he seemed about to vault the couch. He was probably limber enough to do it. David leaned back and let weariness hold his limbs in place.

"She was afraid," he said.

Zac stood still.

"For a few moments, and then she put it away. But it was there. You saw it."

"Yeah. I did."

"She could have warned Colm, but instead she called Simon. Instead, she's coming back to you because she thinks something's wrong."

Zac held his eyes but offered no challenge. Let David pry. Maybe he shouldn't. But something was going on here.

"Look," David said. "You don't owe me personal information."

Zac looked up and down the length of the room, the path he'd just been pacing. He pushed a knuckle against his mouth then walked over and sat on the couch, settling this time, elbows on knees as he leaned forward.

"War broke me," Zac said as if commenting on the weather. "The First War. You know how it was. When we came home."

David nodded.

"I was one of those guys who looked fine on the outside. No war wounds. And I acted fine. A lot of the time, I *was* fine."

The quiet remained until David gave him another nod. He seemed to need acknowledgment, despite the small-talk tone.

"We lived together for a while, after the war. So Moira knew."

Nod.

"Well." Zac shrugged. "A hundred years later, I'm still claustrophobic, and sometimes — I mean, every twenty years or so — something'll happen, you know, something intense. Some sort of stressor kicks in, and I spend a few hours . . . blanked out. Never happened before that war."

"That's not what happened tonight."

"Pretty sure anyone with a moral compass would be upset tonight."

"But Moira thinks this is . . . that."

"Good instincts, letting it play out like you did." But his jaw was clenched hard.

"What now?"

"It'll throw her to see me lucid. Which is what we want, I guess." He rubbed his eyes. "I joined the air force in the second one. No more trenches for me."

Images came to David, mutually held memories that needed no explanation. He had seen it in other men, but Zac had experienced it. Experienced something that could leave a man with claustrophobia and acute stress reaction one hundred years later.

"Colm went into the navy." Zac shut his eyes a moment then focused on David. "What about you?"

"Army."

"Every time?"

"Both World Wars, Korea, Vietnam."

Zac shook his head. "I haven't served since World War II. I . . . ." He gave a long sigh. "I don't know if I'd be fit, but I didn't try."

"I'm not," David said. "Not anymore."

"Vietnam?"

A nod.

"Broke you," Zac said, again without gravity.

"No." He'd processed through this enough to know that answer. "But another war would."

"Stern stuff, man." Zac grinned, but it

faded. "I guess you might as well know. Don't try to get me on an elevator or public transportation."

"Planes?" Seemed no less confining, as a passenger.

"I do all right," he said.

David swallowed what felt like a whole yard of concrete. "Fire." He cleared his throat. "I don't do fire."

Zac studied David with the kind of understanding that wouldn't invade with words. They shared a nod, and then Zac stood.

"Wine?"

David cocked his head. "Whose house is this?"

"I was making a request."

"Coffee would be smarter."

"You be smart, then."

They went to the kitchen. David brought out a bottle of red and went to start the coffeemaker, then shook his head and poured a second glass of the wine. Zac tried to smirk at him, but the expression twisted and fell away.

They sat at the table, and Zac nodded his approval at his first taste. Then a shroud of trouble fell over him, over the room, along with silence that was broken only by the clinking of empty glasses set aside.

They didn't talk about Colm or Moira or

anything else. Twenty minutes later, a knock came at the back door, where he'd let them in a few hours ago without an idea of what kind of news was entering his house. David rose and let her in.

Mascara smudged at the corners of her eyes; she'd rubbed them if not cried. David led her to the kitchen.

He poured a third glass of wine and handed it to her as she sat across from Zac, eyes fixed on him. Zac folded his arms on the table and stared back, and Moira drew a long breath.

"You're . . . better?"

"I'm fine." He bit the words. "I never wasn't."

"But David said . . ." She looked from one of them to the other, and then her voice grew small. "Oh."

"If you're planning to feign moral outrage over being lied to, just skip that part."

"Zachary," she whispered.

She seemed genuine. Maybe she was. Didn't matter at this point. She was talking to Zac; his was the opinion that mattered to her. David stayed quiet and watched her face.

"Instead," Zac said, "try explaining yourself."

"I have nothing to say."

"Nothing?" Zac's knee started jumping under the table. "Eleven human beings. Dead. And you have nothing to say."

Her face crumpled like paper crushed in a fist. "That's right."

Zac pushed to his feet. His whole body seemed to vibrate with pent energy as he paced to the fridge and back, then stood next to his chair. Moira's eyes didn't stray from him. David might as well not have been in the room.

"If you need to do a few handsprings or something, go on, get it out," she said.

Zac slammed his palm on the table and leaned over her. She didn't cringe back an inch. "Stop it. Stop knowing me like that when — when —"

The light dimmed in his eyes. He sank into the chair.

"Moira," David said. She didn't seem to hear him. He shifted his chair into her line of vision, closer to Zac. "Moira."

She found David as if she'd forgotten him. "It was necessary."

"Their deaths were necessary?"

She flinched.

"Two hours ago you said you regretted nothing. Is that really true?"

She nodded. Her mouth firmed, but her gaze kept darting to Zac, who stared into the living room.

"Fine then. I don't care about your remorse," David said.

Her eyes widened for half a moment, a genuine start.

"You just tell me now, is he going to kill again tonight? Tomorrow? When did this start?"

Zac shifted in his chair and met her eyes. She spoke to him, not David. "In 1907."

A furrow dug between Zac's eyebrows. He nodded her on.

"Do you remember — of course you do — Rose Bennett, and . . ."

Zac covered his face with one hand.

She pushed her glass away, still half full, and addressed David now. "He's always lived in Chicago. Rose was a neighbor, and he was . . . I think they would have married, in time. There was a . . . traffic accident, one night, two carriages collided against a curb. He and Rose were walking home from the theater. Colm was walking nearer the street, but he thinks she saw it coming. She tried to warn him, pull him out of the way."

She looked away from both of them, a muscle pulling in her neck as she swallowed. She laced her fingers together on the table.

"She slipped and fell into the street." Zac's

voice had flatlined. "Was run over by the horses."

Moira addressed both of them now, voice steadying. "She died trying to save someone who couldn't die."

The weight of Colm's burden constricted David's chest. That level of guilt could warp the mind, no doubt. Moira watched him now as if waiting for his judgment of Colm — guilty or not guilty.

"Go on," David said.

"It's twisted inside him. He speaks of it rarely, but when he does now, it's something that was unavoidable, even right. He says she had to die that night, and he was the appointed vehicle of her death."

"And the others?" Zac's voice rasped.

"He says his role as death's instrument began the night she was killed because of him. Killed because she didn't know what he is."

"That doesn't add up."

"Of course it doesn't." She twisted her hands in her lap. "It's twisted, I told you."

They were straying from the mission parameters. David cleared his throat. "When will he do this again?"

"He . . . takes . . . one every ten years."

"You're sure about this?" If she was wrong, and he took another life tonight, wherever he was . . .

"It's what he's told me."

"What he's told you." Zac curled his fist in his hair. "You said he confessed, but why would he, if he feels no remorse?"

"I don't know."

"Who were they? How does he choose?"

"I don't know."

"You don't know any of those ten other victims?"

"Please, Zac, I don't." Her shoulders heaved. "I only know it's spring of the tenth year. Spring for when Rose died."

"It's October."

"I don't know why it's different this time."

"And is this the tenth year?"

"It's the ninth. But if he decided Paul Tait was the best . . . target, then . . . then in the spring he won't . . ."

"Or maybe he will," David said, and she looked away.

"He could be killing someone every year," Zac said. "Every month. Every week."

Moira hunched in the chair, shoulders caving in, head bent, chin to her chest. She closed her eyes tight and clenched her folded hands in her lap.

Zac studied her then stood and went to her side. "Moira."

She drew a sharp breath.

"When did he tell you?"

"In . . . in . . ." Her voice fell to a whisper. "In 1957."

"And you just kept this for him. Without conscience. Mortals, why weep for them? They're such brief sparks. We're the fire."

A strangled sound broke from her.

"Yeah." He cupped the back of her head, and his thumb stroked her hair.

She drew a breath and looked up at him, her voice firm again. "I've told you all I know."

"Except what he used to threaten you."

"Wh—what?"

"Tell me how he threatened you."

"He didn't."

"Moira. Tell me." His voice lowered. "I know you too. Remember?"

She jerked away from his touch and jolted to her feet. "You know what I show you. You see what you want to see, and I let you, because that's easier than disillusioning your ego."

He blinked. "That's not true."

"He did nothing to me. Absolutely nothing."

"You're lying."

Was she? David hardly knew her, but if this wasn't the truth, she had mastered her tells to a disturbing degree, especially given three seconds ago she'd been curled into herself, quietly fragile. He didn't know which woman was Moira, but they couldn't both be.

"I would never harm another immortal, one of our family. Stop trying to come up with an answer that doesn't fracture your idealized little worldview."

Zac stood staring at her. She didn't look away. Her lips were pressed into a firm line of anger and conviction. At last Zac nodded.

"You know what? Your reasons don't matter. If we hadn't found out, you'd still be protecting a murderer. That's what matters." He turned to David. "So now we stop him."

"You mean turn him over to the police?" Moira asked. "You can't do that."

"This isn't about us, any of us. It's about the lives of those victims, the lives of his future victims that can still be saved."

Her lips pressed thin with determination.

"You have to help us stop him," Zac said.

"Would you find a way to kill him?"

"Not if we don't have to," he said then scrubbed at his face.

Moira dropped into her chair as if her legs had been knocked from under her.

"Where is he?" Zac said.

She shook her head.

"Have you spoken to him? Is he still in town?"

She flinched. "Of course not."

Zac's sigh was ragged. He looked to David as if for guidance to their next step. He hadn't seen the flinch. Or he had and not interpreted it right, thought she was affronted by the question. He couldn't see straight while the shock and betrayal still sat on him with the weight of eleven gravestones.

"Moira," David said.

She looked up at him, unsuspecting.

"You have spoken to him. And he is here. In town somewhere."

Color bled from her cheeks. Zac swore.

No more time for talk, and no more need for it. Colm was miles away, in a hotel somewhere. He might be a block from the bookstore, in that little family-run place with the in-ground pool that never got filled. He might be across town at the Best Western. Only two options in Harbor Vale.

Time to move. To act. To execute a mission. David went to the mudroom for shoes, keys, jacket.

"Give me your phone," Zac said from the kitchen, his voice like shuffled shards of glass.

"Zac, please."

"It's that or you come with us."

David zipped his jacket and sorted through the possibilities. Even if they took her phone . . . He called into the kitchen. "She has to come anyway. There are two hotels."

"Where is he?" Zac asked.

The automatic ice maker dropped cubes with a clank, and David jolted. He tromped back to the kitchen, where Zac was tugging his coat from a chair and shrugging into it without taking his eyes off Moira.

"We're always going to know now," Zac said, "and we're not going to give this up. Tell us where he is."

She shook her head, a bit of the spark returning to her eyes.

"Fine." He motioned her toward the back door.

David armed himself, though Moira said Colm hadn't. Zac declined to carry any of David's other weapons. If his mental scars were deep enough, he might not be able to handle firearms anymore. That, or he couldn't fathom putting a bullet into Colm.

David drove them into town in more silence. Nothing to plan. They'd find him or they wouldn't. They'd be able to restrain him or they wouldn't. In twelve minutes he parked at the dark edge of the lot behind the Harbor Vale Family Inn.

Fewer witnesses here than at the big chain hotel. Fewer places to hide too. But if Colm didn't know they were coming, this might be his preference. It was the shy cousin of the Best Western — no continental breakfast or usable pool, but no hundred rooms either. It was a two-story building with ten rooms per floor, noise restrictions enforced by the owner himself.

Zac would have stayed somewhere glitzier. Colm might be quiet enough to crash here.

"Take care," Moira whispered.

Of themselves? Of a killer? The ugliest edge in David's gut could gag her and leave her zip-tied to the steering wheel. He couldn't gauge when she would shift again, from fear and remorse to defiance and detachment. He got out of the Jeep and opened the passenger door for her.

"Are you going to start yelling for help?"

She glared at him. Defiance was back.

"It'll do him no good. Any witnesses will be more likely to notice him if he makes a dash."

Still not a word. David held her elbow in a grip he had to check. He looked across the top of the Jeep. Zac stood on the other side, watching him, eyes bright in the flood-light.

"I want to talk to him," Zac said. "First."

"Zac . . ." Sentimentalism might not be the best plan.

"David, I'm going in there to talk to him. You can come if you want to."

"No, go on. I'll guard the perimeter."

More sensible anyway than the three of them getting turned around in a corridor while Colm made it outside and vanished. Zac nodded.

"Take me in with you," Moira said.

"Not a chance."

"It's important that I speak to him — immediately. Please, Zachary."

He didn't bother to answer her.

The building was old, but the management was modern and conscientious about identity protection. Tony Grissom knew David the way David knew him — the bookstore guy, the little hotel guy — and that knowledge would by no means earn an affirmative that Colm was here. Better to rely on the vulnerabilities of the structure itself. The staff entrance at the back was often unlocked for late-night arrivals to bring in their luggage without disturbing the rest of the floor.

For a silent hour they waited for someone

to come to that door — a family hauling four kids and more bags than seemed necessary. The youngest child looked no older than three, and she whimpered in her father's arms as they all plodded around the building to the back. The hotel clerk escorted them, pointed out their room from the outside, and disappeared back to his desk. Amid their coming and going, Zac sauntered up to the door and walked through it as if he owned the business. The worn travelers didn't look at him twice.

From David's vantage point behind the building, both side entrances as well as the back door were visible. The front was only windows, balconies on the second floor. A brisk wind kicked up in his face as he and Moira stood against the Jeep.

Zac couldn't make inquiries door to door. He might spend the night in some corner waiting for Colm to show himself. David and Moira might spend the night out here judging each other.

At least the sun would be up in a few hours. David loosened his grip on Moira's arm, and she leaned against the passenger door and huddled into her coat.

This was the woman who'd hugged him in the Phoenix airport with a beaming smile. The woman who'd spoken with understanding about the future facing him and Tiana. She resembled herself but little now, a distance in her eyes that David couldn't bridge. As if she could have carried this secret forever and its uncovering, not its keeping, had broken her.

If that was true, though . . . "Why aren't you running?" David said. "Why did you come back at all?"

She stared across the blacktop lot and folded her arms.

"If you believe we're right, you believed it long before now. If you knew Zac would do what you couldn't, you'd have told him."

"No," she whispered. "I wouldn't have told Zac. Ever."

"He's not as broken as you think he is."

"That's not what I'm talking about."

Ten minutes later, the back door opened.

TWENTY

Zac stepped outside first. Colm came close behind him, and David surged forward a few steps before he got a glimpse of the man's hands. No gun. He wasn't prodding Zac forward. He was following him.

David spared a look for Moira. She was watching the approaching pair like a white-eyed hare in a trap. "Surrender?"

"No," she said.

Nothing made sense. "You're not afraid we'll kill him. Are you?"

She was trembling. She bit her bottom lip and didn't look away from Zac and Colm.

"Moira, I need to know. Do you fear Colm? Has he made you fear him?"

She didn't blink. Didn't move. Then she shook her head.

He couldn't decide whether to believe her.

Zac and Colm reached them, and Colm held up his hands.

"Thank you," he said, maybe to all of

them. "I've waited a long time for this."

More words that made no sense. David slid behind the wheel and curled numb hands around it. Zac got in beside him and met his eyes, a long empty look.

Not a word was spoken as David drove. Back to his place — nowhere else to go — but bringing that calm, quiet man sitting behind him inside his home, letting Colm know where he lived, rubbed against the grain of David's instincts. He drove with palms sweating on the steering wheel, his mouth dry. The race of his pulse felt like more than adrenaline. And all the while, watching Colm in the mirror, he tried to see a true killer. And failed.

Dawn was creeping around the silhouettes of trees when he reached home. The moment the Jeep was fully stopped, Zac flung the passenger door wide and got out. He stayed in the yard as David led Colm and Moira inside.

Not enough beds or couches. But no one was ready to sleep yet.

"Have you discussed it?" Colm said when they reached the living room. "You know. What's to be done with me."

"Suggestions?" David bit the word.

"Execution wouldn't be out of the question."

"Of course it is," Moira said. "No one wants that, Colm."

"Hold on. Zac should hear this." Colm walked out into the yard.

They should restrain him. Lock him in a room somewhere. Something. Instead, they were following him, David and Moira both. The surreal had taken over.

"You could exsanguinate me." Colm spoke to Zac. "Put a little suction behind it, and I'm sure it's possible to drain our blood before the serum can replenish it."

"Shut up." Zac seemed to choke on the words.

"I'm not going to stop being what I am."

"Which is what?"

"Immortal, mate. Displaced from the cycle of life and death."

"Colm, it was an accident. That's all it was."

"I thought you believed in God." Colm advanced on him, halted just outside Zac's personal space. "No accidents. We have a purpose. It's just you three — four, judging from David's scowl — are hell-bent on denying it."

"Then why did you pick up your phone at the hotel? Why did you come out of that room and follow me outside?"

Colm's gaze darted around to all of them,

came to rest on Moira. "I guess I owe you one."

She ducked her head.

"Decided to bring the real me into the light?"

"David found the body. Put it together. I had no part in it."

"Hmmm," he said.

He might bolt any moment. David's muscles tensed. Preparing. He might have to tackle the man. At least his privacy fence meant only one direction Colm could flee — through the gate to the front yard. The wind kicked up, stinging David's eyes.

"I'm not going to stop," Colm said. "And I don't want to keep going."

The chill on his skin wasn't from the wind now. "Speak plainly."

"I'm asking you to put an end to me. I can't be other than what I am, so it's time for me to stop being. I'm ready." He looked to Zac. "Really, I am."

"No," Zac said.

"You were never supposed to know, but you do now, so that's no accident either, mate. I don't want to end myself. I want to be ended by all of you."

Zac backed away.

"Colm," Moira whispered.

He swiveled toward her, and she stepped

back. "Hush, pet." He turned back to Zac. "Together you'll find some way to do it. Call up Simon. He'll have theories."

Zac grabbed Colm by the arms and shook him. "I said no."

Colm returned the grip. "Don't make me bear it forever."

David's breath scraped his lungs. Such familiar words. From him, a prayer. Almost a psalm.

"Do their loved ones still bear it?" Zac shoved him away, and Colm staggered.

"I should have come to you years ago." Colm's breaths seemed to come as difficult as David's. "But you've just made that point for me, Zac. It's mine to bear. And besides, it was you."

Zac braced his hands on his hips and clenched his jaw.

"I knew you wouldn't embrace our purpose. Of all of us, you never would. And it helped, seeing myself the way you saw me. I didn't want to lose that."

"Solution: stop murdering people."

"That option isn't open to me."

"Do you enjoy it?" Zac spat the words at him.

"I'm performing a predetermined task. Enjoyment isn't required."

"Answer me straight."

Colm gave a slow blink. "No."

It was the last thing anyone said. Zac tramped back into the house, and after a moment they followed him. Once inside, David expected the deliberations to continue, but everyone remained quiet, exhausted more from the ordeal than the night without sleep.

He offered Moira the only bed. Colm stretched out on the couch, and David tied his hands and feet with coarse twine from a catch-all drawer. Zac motioned David out of the room, all the way to the end of the hall.

"Your home's been seized and occupied," Zac said.

David opened the linen closet and scrounged for the sleeping bag he'd months ago shoved onto a shelf somewhere. He offered it to Zac.

"If you want to sleep, I'll take first watch over him."

Zac shook his head. "You go ahead. I'll stay up."

"All night?"

"What's left of it."

No explanation needed. Zac wouldn't sleep whether he was guarding Colm or not. David nodded. "I'll sleep in the tent."

"Tent?"

"In the backyard. I sleep outside by choice often enough."

"I'll wait a few hours and let Simon know we have Colm . . . in custody." Zac looked away. "This isn't your catastrophe."

"If that were true, I'd never bring you all back here."

"Chances are good you'll live to regret it."

David gripped the man's shoulder, and Zac looked at him, eyes bleak but steady. "You're my people now. I'll not desert ye."

A corner of Zac's mouth tried to smile. They exchanged a nod, and David went outside.

He shuffled into the yard on old feet. Raked old hands through old hair. His bones didn't creak and grate with arthritis. But the spirit housed by this ageless frame was convulsed with Colm's words.

David knelt in the grass at the door of the tent. "Lord . . ."

His voice broke something. He fought for words beyond that one, but Colm's blotted them out.

It's mine to bear. . . . Don't make me bear it forever.

"Lord." He had to pray. But that awareness was guttering toward darkness, and the words didn't come. Couldn't.

He lay for an hour with the canvas roof

above him, eyes open, unblinking until they dried out. The prayer would not come — not a word of it. At last he sat up, groped for the door zipper, and emerged into the damp new day. He slipped into the house. All was dark, quiet. David took his keys from the rack by the landline phone and crept to the living room.

Colm lay asleep, and Zac sat in a chair across from him, head in his hands.

"Hey," David whispered.

Zac jerked up straight in the chair. He hadn't been asleep, but his thoughts had been elsewhere.

"I'm driving for a bit."

Zac nodded and made a gesture of dismissal without meeting David's eyes.

He trudged to the Jeep, got in, and turned the key. He drove until he realized where he was going, then kept driving until he got there.

His shaking hand bounced the keys around until he caught the right one. He let himself into the bookstore and flipped on the light. Quiet enfolded him in an embrace that should have softened his edges, calmed his heartbeat, opened his lungs. Sometimes the books seemed to breathe on the shelves, to add their personalities to the store's old soul. But tonight it was a building. The books were lifeless, paper and ink. No comfort while he fought whatever it was, this squeezing distress that stopped his tongue from forming needed words.

He needed . . .

Habit tried to push the thought away, but the moment it formed, it burned away all other thoughts.

He needed someone here to pray. For him.

No. Praying aloud with Tiana yesterday — it had been the first time he'd done so in many years. Someone here with him, praying *for* him? He couldn't.

"I can't be other than what I am, so it's time for me to stop being."

Skeletons. A row of them. Eleven. Soil caking them, deep underground, worms crawling between ribs and phalanges.

"God," David said. Loneliness opened like a grave before him, and headlong he toppled into it.

He pulled his phone from his pocket.

Her phone rang a long time, but he couldn't focus to count the rings. Then her voice came slow, husky. Sweet.

"David?"

He looked across the foyer at the old regulator clock between the windows. Five ten in the morning. He tried to speak.

"David, are you there?"

"Tiana."

"What's wrong?"

"I . . . I . . ."

"Are you home?"

"No."

Fabric rustled over the line, and then her voice came sharper, awake. "Where are you? What's going on?"

"I needed to hear a voice." The absurdity of the words didn't strike him until they were out in the air, irretrievable. "I'm sorry. Go back to sleep, please."

"I will not. Talk to me, tell me what's wrong."

"It's . . ."

"Did something happen with Zac and Moira?"

He propped his throbbing head in his hand. "Aye."

"Where are you?"

"The store."

"So I'm not the only one who hides away there." A smile lifted the words.

He couldn't speak.

"David?"

"It's . . . worse than . . . Tiana, I . . ." *Yours to bear now. Forever.* He let the nearest bookcase take his weight.

"Can I help?" Her voice was quiet now.

"Would you pray?"

A surprised pause. "You mean after we hang up?"

"No, now, for me, for . . ." He sat in a corner, knees up. "For strength."

The next twenty minutes blurred. Tiana's voice anchored him, first a prayer, then a quiet monologue. She should have been a lifeline. Knowing she was there on the other end of the line, knowing she knew his true self, should have been enough. But some darkness still lurked nearby.

He jolted as a key rattled in the back-door lock. On his feet by reflex, so fast his weary head grew light for a moment, but then the room steadied. He was staring at the door when it opened and Tiana stepped through the doorway.

She wore a purple zip hoodie and heather-gray lounge pants and neon-green tennis shoes. Her hair was wrapped beneath a red silk scarf. Not a bit of makeup touched her face. She went to him in a few strides, dropping her keys on the front counter as she passed, halting before him and taking both his cold hands in hers.

"Now," she said, "we can talk."

"Why . . . ?"

She squeezed his hands. "It felt important for me to come. Like talking on the phone wasn't enough right now."

He pulled her into his arms and clung to her. Surely this would dispel the shroud around him. Tiana held him in return, and they stood a long minute. But the quaking in David's core didn't stop. Soon the outer shell would be trembling too.

"You haven't slept at all," she said.

"No."

"Can you tell me about whatever it is?"

"No." His arms tightened around her. "You were right about Zac. He's an innocent party."

"And . . . Moira isn't?"

"I hope she is. I can't figure her. But it's . . ." He had to say it. "I think the thing is too great for me. I don't think I'm strong enough to bear it."

"Don't make me bear it forever."

He shuddered.

Tiana rubbed a circle over his back. "Maybe you're not."

Ice trickled into his bloodstream to join the cursed serum. If even Tiana thought he wasn't able to do this . . . His voice shook. "Years I've asked Him to make me able to carry it, what He's given me to carry. But now it's . . ."

Tiana pressed her cheek to his chest then stepped back and led him to the break room. She tugged him down to sit beside her on the couch but didn't let go of his hand. She looked into his eyes, and hers were clear and sure. The contrast to him right now.

"Okay," she said. "Tell me."

"It's . . ." He held her gaze, and the gentleness in her drew the words from the deep well in him that had never been heard before by anyone but God. "It's like a flattening. Like I'm finally too old, Tiana. Spent."

Her thumb massaged his knuckles. "I don't believe that."

"It's a feeling." He tried to smile. "Maybe not a fact."

"And you've prayed that you'll be able to keep carrying everything?"

He nodded. "You know Psalm 32, David's bones wasting away through groaning. The sin I've learned about tonight, it's not mine. But the man who's done this — he's not so different from me. He's felt the same things. The years, the . . ."

"The losses," Tiana said.

"Aye, the losses, they twisted his soul as I've felt mine twist at times, and who can say I won't become . . . ?"

The exposed root of it all — he caught his breath as his own fear became known to him only now, upon speaking the words. He ducked his head, chin hitting his chest.

"What if someday I do what he's done?"

"You will never do what he's done," she said with such conviction David nearly believed her.

"The death of the body is a mercy of God, Tiana. The soul can't bear endless years in this realm. In this evil." His body rocked, and his soul seemed to do the same. "Make me strong enough, Lord God."

"No," Tiana whispered.

From his lips came a groan like that of the king of Israel, the psalmist after God's own heart, a David who poured out deepest groanings and was heard.

"Listen to me, David." Tiana pressed her arm against his. "You don't have to be strong enough."

Surely he did. He couldn't set the burden down, that was clear enough. God Himself had placed it on his back.

"Have you lived all your life carrying all of it alone?"

"With the strength I ask Him for," David said. "Not my own, I know."

"It's time to let Him take it."

David shook his head. That couldn't be true, not for him. Not for one from whom the mercies of age and death had been removed.

"Unique circumstances don't change that you're His."

"I know."

"Doesn't sound that way."

"What would you have me do?" The clip in his voice wasn't only tiredness. She needed to back off.

Instead, she pulled his hand into her lap. "I would 'have you' cast your cares on Him and let Him care for you."

The words were like a blow to thin ice, sending cracks throughout with a deafening sound. He shut his eyes. He held on to her hand.

"Lord Jesus," Tiana whispered. "Take this burden."

His throat closed. His shoulders heaved. His eyes burned. She wrapped her arms around him, and the tears took him.

"Jesus," she said, while he tried and failed to silence his sobs. "You're good and kind. Be kind to David today, and give him rest. He hasn't rested in more years than I can imagine. Please help him. Please show his heart that it's okay to give his heaviest burden to You, that it's what You've wanted for him all along."

The darkness fled. He was laid open before his God, and light poured into his soul, and its writhing grew still. David wept aloud.

Tiana's arms remained around him. He let himself lean into her, and she settled on the couch in a position to hold him up. Tiana whispered things he caught and things he didn't, prayers for him. For his heart. For his peace. A long time later, he came to himself, no longer crushed. All the fragments inside were raw and new, but clean. He stirred.

"Shh," she whispered, but he had to speak.

"Lord." His voice reflected the hoarseness in his throat. Modern vernacular deserted him. His thoughts crossed into old Gaelic, but he kept to English in Tiana's hearing. "Lord, Father, I confess to Thee . . . I have striven to be the strongest man alive, to carry the weightiest load, and in Thy mercy Thou hast led me to fail. I ask now for Thy forgiveness, for holding this distance between Thee and me. And I ask . . ."

Tears surged into his throat. How could he have any left? Tiana moved her hand up and down his side, sweet gentleness in the touch. He cleared his throat. "I ask that in Thy mercy, I would become more truly Thine, nearer to Thee as long as I'm bound to these old bones on this old earth. Amen."

Wet warmth seeped into his shirt, the

shoulder where Tiana had rested her head.

"There now," he said. "No tears for a blind man who's clung to an error too long."

"We all do that." She sniffed, and a smile touched her voice. "I want to talk to you about something, but now's not the time."

"Fine a time as any."

Her hand moved to rub a slow circle on his chest. "I think you're more tired than you realize. You probably shouldn't be driving, even just home to bed."

Bed. The very word drew his eyelids down. He sighed.

"Do you think you could sleep right here once the store opens? I don't think you'd hear much if I shut the door."

"I've slept behind an artillery line firing mortars all night."

"Well then."

As if he were a child already asleep, Tiana eased off his shoes and lifted his legs to the cushion, then eased his head back to the pillow.

"Are you awake enough to listen to me?"

The soft quiet of her voice was enough to lull him the final steps to slumber, but he nodded against the pillow.

"I'm going home to eat and make myself presentable, and then I'll come back. That should be enough time to open at nine like usual. I'll lock the doors when I go, and turn out the lights."

"Fine," he said, or thought he said.

From somewhere she produced that old blanket from his Jeep, the one that had covered Zac three nights ago, smelling fresh and airy. She must have taken it home and laundered it. She tucked it up to his chin, leaned down, and kissed him. David let his eyes close. He should text Zac so he wasn't expected, but the effort seemed too much.

"Rest," Tiana said. "Rest your heart."

"Aye."

The light tread of her feet moved to the door.

"Tiana?"

"Hmmm?"

"Is it six now?"

"About a quarter to seven."

"Wake me at ten. Things at the house . . . to deal with."

"Eleven?"

"Fine."

"Will do. Now rest."

Darkness came from the other side of his eyelids as she shut off the light. Her steps faded, the break room's door shut. David surrendered to rest.

Twenty-One

He woke on his own at ten, as he'd ordered himself to do. It was a handy skill, honed by necessity over a long time of training his subconscious. Nightmares lingered like tattered veils at the edges of his mind. Colm's voice. Rows of corpses. Paul Tait's open eyes, and Colm's hands around his throat, around the throats of people David didn't know. He shuddered and sat up on the couch. Sunlight peeped around the edges of the shut window blind. David bunched the blanket in his hands for a moment and then stood.

He smoothed his hand down his shirt and was jolted to another recent time he'd slept in his clothes. The night of his rejuvenation. Colm's quiet ease, even with David, held a different cast now but felt no less genuine to David's memory. No clues lingered in his subconscious, nothing wrong about the persona of the man.

There'd be a great deal to face today. Time to do so.

No helping his appearance. He hoped no customers were checking out as he headed to the front. Tiana manned the counter. Alone.

"Jayde?"

"Nothing," she said. "Not a word. Not even an 'I'm still alive' text."

A cold finger ran down his back at the last words. Events of last night, even the dreams perhaps, still gripped him hard. Tiana had come to work in a pale pink top and her most casual black dress pants, flatteringly cut but widening at the ankles in a way that seemed more bell-bottom than business casual. Her hair and makeup looked impeccable as always, so that he probably wouldn't have noticed if he hadn't last seen her with clean face and hair scarf. No one would guess that a half-coherent man had woken her up at five in the morning, that she'd been present at a crime scene hours before that.

"How're you doing?" he said.

"Honestly, I think I'm putting off processing it."

He nodded. "Don't do that too long. Talk to me if you need to."

"Yeah, I guess you're my only option." She

looked around the store. "I can handle things. Go deal with . . . the other things."

"Are you sure?" It tasted bitter, the thought of deserting her again. "I'm sorry."

"David, seriously, don't worry about it." But her pause held its own worry. "Okay, I'm just going to say this. I need to know something."

"Go on."

"When you said, about Moira . . . is it possible she killed him? Or was it one of the others?"

With all the rambling he'd done in the wee hours of the morning, of course she had plenty of pieces to solve the puzzle. He leaned a hip on the counter. "It wasn't Moira."

Tiana's sigh was more of a gust. She studied him a long moment. "What're you going to do?"

"I don't know."

"In the light of day, it's always tempting to take it back."

"What's that?"

"Your burden."

A lump filled his throat. He crossed behind the counter and gripped her hand. "I'll keep that in mind."

"Good."

She tugged him closer for a hug, and he

held on a moment. So lovely she was. He linked his hands at her back and inhaled the sharp pleasantness of her scent, citrus and sage, shampoo and lotion and whatever else. Tiana tipped her face up, an invitation, and he kissed her. Soft, sweet, not needing to last. He pulled back, and she rested her hand on his chest.

"Something to take with you on a tough day," she said. "You know I'll come if you want me to."

"Aye, I know it. Thank you." He lifted her hand to his lips and kissed its soft palm. "If you need anything at all."

"Same to you."

Before he could leave, the Lambert family came in, greeting him the same way they always did, not seeming to notice the creases in his shirt or the shadows he knew left half circles under his eyes. Scottish complexion hid nothing, pasty as paper.

"You're leaving, Mr. Galloway?" the youngest girl said.

"Briefly, I hope." He smiled and prepared for a minute or two of polite small talk, but the vibration of his phone against his thigh rescued him. He pulled it from his pocket.

Colm.

"Excuse me, I've got to take this." He nodded to the Lamberts and left out the back door, the entrance that remained locked from the outside and bore a sign NO ADMITTANCE. Tiana once chided him for the choice of words, suggested something to encourage customers — PLEASE ENTER AT FRONT OF BUILDING. He had huffed and left the sign as it was.

The heavy door thudded shut behind him, and he swiped the face of his phone before the call could go to voice mail.

"Colm."

"Yeah. Hey."

"Should I assume you ditched them?"

"I left Zac asleep in the chair, poor guy. He lasted longer than I thought he would."

A sense of the surreal dripped down David's spine. He glanced back at the store. "Where are you?"

"Been walking your town. I was starting to think there's a shop on every corner, but you know the Lutheran church across from the yarn shop? It's quiet here."

"True, it is."

"We need to talk."

He'd turned himself over to them. Surely he didn't now want to speak in his own defense. Or perhaps he did. For all David knew of the man, he might have a second identity that wanted pardon. Only one thing mattered. Colm couldn't be allowed to disappear.

"On my way."

"I appreciate that," Colm said then hung up.

David texted Zac. COLM'S IN TOWN AND ASKED ME TO TALK. I'LL BRING HIM BACK. YOU TWO ALL RIGHT?

The drive was about five miles, nearer the edge of town. David drove with one hand and held his phone in the other, waiting for it to vibrate with a response, his mouth drying as minutes ticked by. Colm had left Zac asleep in the chair . . . unharmed? Or . . . ?

When he passed the yarn shop on his right, he almost missed the rental car Colm had parked there. David pulled in and parked beside it as his phone buzzed.

YES AND BE CAREFUL, Zac had texted back.

He sighed, pocketed the phone, and walked across the street toward the church. A company of pine trees stood guard along either side of the entrance, all of them close to a hundred years old, maybe older, so tall one could stand under their branches without ducking. Colm stood beneath one and watched David's approach. He looked as weathered as David felt, pale red stubble on his chin and a slight droop to one eyelid. His gaze roved past David to a boisterous

344

group of teenagers who passed behind him.

Colm had been people watching.

David did the same sometimes. Not frequently, but when necessity forced him to a mall, he might as well sit a minute and look around at the generations as they flowed past in individuals. He halted beside Colm, stood with his back to the trunk of the old pine.

"What do you see?"

Colm turned his head only briefly toward David before looking back out at the passing groups, couples, families, loners. "Trees. Everywhere. I'm used to concrete and towering buildings, or tamed suburbia when I go to Denver for Zac. I haven't embraced the quaint village effect in years, but it's pleasant."

Let him dissemble, then. Made no difference now that Colm wouldn't be leaving his sight. But he should have made a full escape, not called for an in-person chat. And David's confusion gave Colm the upper hand.

A minute later Colm's eyebrows drew together, a slow crinkle knitting between them. "You expect me to call them insects or something. Flies for swatting."

Oh, honesty? Good then. "It's a fair question."

"Sure. It is."

Time passed. They stood under the tree, side by side but no acknowledgment of each other, until Colm sighed.

"They're people. Senses, emotions, language, physical processes. Irreducible complexity."

"However?"

"There's no however. They're souls. And they belong to the cycle of life, unlike us."

"Seems you're finding your own way to fit into the cycle."

"Don't kid yourself, David." He stepped away from the tree and followed ten feet behind the latest group, a lagging pace that let others pass them on the sidewalk without overhearing too much. "I know she told you about Rose. Well, she told me about you too. All your wars. Distinguished service, no doubt. What's your tally of kills?"

David shook his head.

"What, you stopped counting?"

He'd had to. His fingers curled toward his palms. Not fists, cups of self-control.

"You think it's not the same," Colm said as he looked both ways and then stepped into the street.

They crossed but kept walking past the yarn shop, past their vehicles. "You don't believe in just war?"

"I'm not talking about war and murder. I'm talking about you and me."

Murder. He said it without hesitation. He knew what he was. Hair prickled on David's arms.

"You shouldn't have killed those enemy combatants because you shouldn't have been alive to do it. Outside the cycle yet interfering with it, see?"

"Are you attempting to justify yourself somehow?"

"Of course not."

"Then what is this?"

"Perspective, that's all."

For the coming debate. "Or persuasion."

Colm stopped walking. Stood in the middle of the sidewalk and forced other pedestrians to walk over the grass to get around him. He jerked his chin toward an easement between the yarn shop and its neighbor, a beauty parlor that never held more than one patron at a time. Pine trees stood watch there too. David stepped off the walkway and led him between the shops. Traffic sounds, voices, shop doors opening and closing all faded as they continued farther into the trees, as the carpet of needles over grass muted their footsteps. Anything could be said here. Colm stopped, stood facing David, arms at his sides, mouth tight.

"Suppose I asked you to do it," he said.

The air charged. David tilted his head. Make Colm say what he meant.

"Win for everybody — Moira and the guys won't have to deal with me, mortals won't have to deal with me, even I won't have to deal with me anymore. And you've known me a week; it's not like you'll lose sleep."

Nothing in his expression, his tone, his body language betrayed insincerity. Adrenaline began feeding into David's system. Tingled in his fingers. He shook his head.

"Come on," Colm said. "Think this through. Simon will want me dead, but he'll be outvoted. Zac and Moira's solution will be to buy some island and maroon me there for the next century. You think I'll let them?"

This — this was what God had purposed for David to do? Define justice and execute it? Be their vigilante? If this was the only way to prevent more murders, then he couldn't cower from the duty. He had to carry it out. He had to carry the weight. For all of them.

He turned away, braced his hand on the nearest pine, pressed his palm into the bark until it bit his skin.

It's why you found them. One more burden. Be strong now and bear up the weight.

"What do you say?"

A flame licked to life in David's hollowed core. His jaw clenched. He turned his head. "If I did agree, it would not be for you."

His Adam's apple dipped. He took one step back. Something far behind his eyes cooled. "It's for Zac and Moira. Spare them the decision."

"For your victims, Colm. No one else."

No.

It wasn't a voice in David's head, but the sense of something wrong was nearly as strong as that word. He tried to find the source of it. He tried to see what to do.

Colm was nodding. Unperturbed by David contradicting him. Any reason of David's would work for Colm if it achieved his purpose.

David's right hand twitched as he quashed a reflex to press it against the growing pressure in his chest. No sign of weakness. His stomach roiled. Danger was sparking in the air now, not for him, but for the civilians who passed them no more than fifty feet away. For anyone in the future who crossed paths with Colm if David didn't do this. Aye, Colm was manipulating him and likely knew David knew it. But what did that matter if this was the path God meant for him to walk anyway? Still, some muted warning was trying to get through to him. He trudged deeper into the trees. Grass rustled behind him as Colm followed, and he angled his body to keep Colm in his peripheral vision. At last David halted. Drew a tight breath.

Lord, help.

It was a flailing reach, but it was met with a Hand that would never slip. The nausea eased. David wasn't alone. And the weight of this decision — not his to carry.

He faced Colm. "No."

The man grew still. "I thought . . . if anyone would . . ."

"Maybe you thought right, if anyone would. But I won't."

A slow smile spread over Colm's face. "You won't."

"No."

"Well, I'm not surprised."

"Oh?"

"Not really. I had to present it to you just to see. To see, you know?"

Calm, assured. No concern in the green eyes. David shook his head. Colm didn't make sense.

"So this is what you do, David. Go back to them in a few hours; tell them I asked you to and you agreed. Tell them you drained me and cremated me. The problem's taken care of. They'll believe it because they'll want to believe it."

As long as he'd known them, as long as he'd been their touchstone if Zac were to be believed — Colm would deceive them without flinching. It wasn't only mortals he considered himself above.

"No," David said.

"You still don't get it."

"I'm not convinced there's anything to get here."

His eyes glinted. "No one who values humanity spends a century at arm's length from them. Don't try to tell me we have nothing in common."

Cold enveloped David from the inside out. "How do you know . . . ?"

"You told Zac you had no one waiting for you here. He's glad to have found you. Says you need us more than he expected."

"And?"

"And I want to know if you'll join me. I think it would be interesting."

This, finally, was why Colm had come. Not to offer himself up. Not to beg an alibi. This.

"Join you." The words choked in David's throat.

"If you want to be the cautious one, the principled one, cool with me. You won't have to take anyone you don't want."

David tried to respond. Couldn't. No words for the skewed vision through which he suddenly saw himself. A broken voice inside asked if Colm was so far off, really; hadn't David done as Colm accused, and didn't it prove how little he valued the crown of God's creation?

Oh, Lord.

But no.

A blaze kindled in him. He had failed in many ways, but he was not what Colm said. He would take Colm back to the others. To justice. In the silence that truth became plain between them, a final understanding that scorched the friendliness from Colm's face.

A sizing up of the other man. A stepping to one side, each of them circling toward each other. Colm shaking his head — *You don't want to do this, David,* and he was right; but David would do it anyway, for it had to be done.

They surged into motion at the same moment. Their bodies collided, locked hold of one another. Hands gripping the other's arms, restraining, grappling. They both skidded as Colm shoved David, tried to knock him off his feet. He dug his heels into the grass and leveraged Colm toward the ground and ducked one punch, but the second snapped his head back and he tasted blood. He knocked Colm's head into a tree trunk and the man staggered, dazed for only a moment, not time enough for David to put him down.

He punched Colm's ribs, stomach — fall, why wouldn't the guy fall? — Colm's knee came up, the target obvious, and David dodged that blow only so Colm could land one to his chest. His lungs tried to spasm with the impact and the memories — weapon lost, combat up close, hand to hand and head to head, teeth and nails and boots, mud and rain and blood. Fight. Not kill or be killed. Worse. Kill or be taken. History for David, present reality for Colm.

The past was choking him. Kill or be vivisected, discovered, used. He bent the terror to his will and held nothing back. Knuckles throbbed as he hit again and again, took hits himself rather than let go. The man fought not with trained finesse, not with brute strength, but with resourceful desperation, every possible strike attempted, any soft area of David's body attacked — belly, kidneys, throat — and then Colm kept trying for his eyes. If he escaped, if he murdered again because David lost this fight —

Sweat and blood in his mouth. The reek of both in his nostrils. Colm's fists and knees and booted feet. The blows and the shoves sent both of them staggering, tipping over to the ground. There was a near scent of grass and pine needles, a scramble up again, and then finally David's arm dropping over Colm's head, Colm's neck in the crook of his elbow. David squeezed. Colm's blunt fingernails tore his forearm. He kicked the ground and arched his back, trying to leverage David off balance. At last he went limp. David kept the pressure on his windpipe another thirty seconds and then let go. Colm flopped to the ground at his feet.

David dropped to a crouch. The shortness of breath came only half from bruised ribs and fight-or-flight. He fell forward to his hands and knees. Beside him Colm lay on his back, eyes closed, one cheekbone swelling and faintly purple, blood on his lower lip. His chest rose and fell.

Finish it.

David shut his eyes against the animal inside, but it was roused now from a sleep of decades. Awake and shaking.

He'll come to in a minute. He'll attack. He'll drag you to the Germans. To the Koreans. To the Viet Cong. You'll be an experiment. A dismembered mess that just keeps on breathing.

"No." David lowered his face to the ground. American pine trees. Soft Michigan grass. Crisp northern air. His lungs filled. His voice shook, but he had to speak aloud. Regain his reason, shut down the violence that fed on the fear. "It isn't real. It's the twenty-first century, and I'm no soldier anymore."

Tiana. The soothing smokiness of her voice and the acceptance in her eyes as she spoke words of correction, words of kindness. How he wished her here now.

"Lord," he whispered. "Take care of her. And please help me."

Beside him Colm stirred. David hauled him to his feet and decked him as hard as he could. Colm sagged to the ground again.

David hoisted him over his shoulders and peered out from the shelter of the pines. No one around. He carried Colm to the Jeep, laid him down on the back seat, and bound his hands behind his back with a discarded plastic grocery bag rolled lengthwise and knotted at the handles. Hardly secure, but Colm couldn't get free without a lot of rustling. At his wrists, especially the right one, the skin had been chafed and torn in his work to get free of the twine. He must have worked heedless of pain once Zac had fallen asleep. Well, that opportunity would not come to him again.

David nearly ran the stop sign in front of the little hotel. He passed the bookstore and turned his face from it, shame burning his gut at what he'd considered doing, what he'd wanted to do, under the pine trees scant minutes before. Colm would face a jury of his peers — essentially a legal trial. The closest they could get, anyway.

His hands squeezed the wheel until he pulled into his driveway. Moira burst out of the house, worry creasing her face. David parked and got out, and she froze halfway to him.

"David, what happened?"

"See for yourself."

He opened the Jeep, grabbed Colm under the arms, and hauled him out. Colm's feet bounced off the door and flopped to the ground as David dragged him from the vehicle and up the porch. Silent and pale, wearing a hoodie and lounge pants she must have slept in, Moira held the door open and followed him into the living room. Zac strode in from the kitchen and stood still in the entryway. Both of them watched David lower Colm's body and lift his legs to the couch.

They didn't say anything, do anything, offer anything, which was fine. Not much they could contribute at the moment. David straightened and blinked hard against the stabbing in his side. One thing he'd say for Colm, the man knew how to hit.

He went to the kitchen and rummaged through the catch-all drawer beside the stove. Black nylon zip ties. He knew he'd bought a package sometime, though he couldn't remember the reason. Aha, here they were. He shoved the drawer closed a bit harder than he'd meant to and returned to the living room.

Moira stood over Colm, her hazel eyes glossy. She stepped back as David turned him onto his side and nodded at Zac. "Come here."

Zac crossed the room to him. "Yeah?"

"Hold him."

"Is this really necessary?" Moira's voice quavered.

"I hit him hard," David said, "but I'm not Muhammad Ali. No way he's still unconscious. He's waiting for me to untie him."

Zac took hold of Colm's arms. One of the bound hands twitched. Zac met David's eyes, nodded.

Moira hid her hands in the pockets of her hoodie. "Waiting for what? To run away?"

"What else?" Zac said and shook the still body. "It won't work, mate. Give up."

Colm's eyes snapped open, glaring, and he gave a thrash like a fish just landed on a boat deck. While Zac held him down, David loosened and removed the plastic bag from his wrists and snapped the zip tie around them instead, just above the raw twine burn.

"David?" Moira said quietly.

"It's necessary." With Colm on his back again, David used the other tie on his ankles. Colm didn't bother to kick him.

"You could have spared all of us this next part," Colm said, his face flat. "Just keep that in mind."

David tested the zip tie around his feet with a tug. Good and secure.

Colm was restrained. No threat to anyone at the moment. Strength poured out of David's limbs, seeming to drain into the floor and away from him. He crossed to the chair and sank into it, hunching a little though he tried not to.

Across the room Colm watched him. "So that was interesting."

"Aye."

Moira looked from one of them to the other. She shook her head. The agelessness

358

of the gesture, a little girl baffled by the boys scuffling in the dirt, brought the ache back to David's chest. This day was going to break her heart.

Zac was standing in one corner. His gaze held David's, and David got the surreal sense that their thoughts had just mirrored each other's. Zac's silence was more somber than that of guys who didn't talk much. He glanced to Moira, but Moira was looking at Colm.

"This can be made right," she said quietly.

"I don't see how."

"You know what my role was."

"Moira." Colm's voice softened. "Do you think that's going to matter?"

She closed her eyes, turned away from him. Looked to David. "We need to call Simon."

They had to talk away from Colm. In the absence of a proper cell, David removed the bathroom doorknob and reinstalled it on the door of the guest bedroom closet, reversing it so it locked from the outside. Then he and Zac hauled Colm to the bedroom. David emptied the closet of boxes, and Zac unscrewed the lightbulb. They turned to find Moira standing in the doorway.

"Any reason he can't be in the dark?" David asked. Half sarcasm, but if Colm was going to panic as soon as they shut the door, Moira would be the one to know.

She shook her head.

Zac tossed the lightbulb a foot into the air and caught it. "Not sturdy enough to cut zip ties, but could be used as a weapon."

Her nod was stiff.

"How long do you think this will take, your deliberation?" Colm said. "More than thirteen hours?"

Moira left the room.

David and Zac didn't bother to answer him. Colm lay on the floor while they finished preparing his makeshift cell, watching everything, but he said no more. When the closet was safely bare, David dragged him inside then shut and locked the door.

He and Zac joined Moira in the kitchen, and for the first time, the house seemed to have shrunk. Too many people wasn't the real problem. It was too much strain, too much history, and a fierce need welled up in David to have his space back, his solitude. Loneliness with peace or companionship with turmoil? He was too wrung out to choose the latter, but the choice had been made already.

The growing hurt in his body didn't help. He dropped onto a kitchen stool and propped his elbows on the counter. Moira leaned into the right angle between the sink and the stove.

"How much does Simon know?" David said.

Zac paced the length of the island. "I called him."

"Is he coming?" Moira's whisper might have held hope.

"He's available for a conference call."

"Now?"

"Whenever we are." Zac was already pulling his phone from the pocket of his jeans. He dialed Simon, put the phone on speaker at full volume, and set it on the table.

David positioned his stool in a corner of the kitchen that faced the hallway to the guest bedroom and gave him line of sight to the front door. If Colm somehow got loose, doubtless he'd try to escape through the bedroom window rather than the front door, but David should hear that given Colm's zip-tied hands were likely to be clumsy. Right. Zip-tied hands. Locked in. The man wasn't going to escape.

The ringing line was cut off by Simon's snapping voice. "Now what?"

"We're all here," Zac said. "Me, Moira, David."

"I told you what needs to happen. There's

nothing left to say on the subject."

"We need to hear it from you, Simon. All of us." Moira twisted a dark curl around her index finger.

"He's not the person you think you know, Moira. He's a monster, and we need to kill him."

She pushed away from the counter and approached the phone. "What happened to 'crime fighting isn't a hobby' and 'leave it to the authorities' and — ?"

"Oh, come on, honey." Simon huffed. "This is the one thing we can't leave to them, and you know it. Any outcome is a disaster for Colm, not to mention us. Life in prison. Lethal injection. Think what happens to him in either scenario. Detectives would dig into similar cold cases and might very well find links to Colm, maybe even links between him and us, not only in this decade but all the way back before we should have been born."

"So we kill him because he can't serve a life sentence." She stared out the window as if Zac and David weren't in the room.

"No, Moira, we kill him because more innocent mortals will die if we don't."

"He says it's what he wants," Zac said, still in motion, his strides eating the length of the room again and again. "He doesn't want to live with it anymore."

"So?" Simon said.

"So the last thing he should get is what he wants."

"We do this because it's right. What Colm wants isn't a factor either way."

"Simon." Moira's voice shook. "We could buy a house — a fortified house. With a panic room. We could lock him in."

"For a hundred years?" Simon had to be shaking his head.

Moira still hadn't looked away from her fixed gaze out the window. "Rotating guard duty. A few months a year for each of us. I'm willing to do it."

"I'm not. It's too risky."

"Prison is risky?"

"When the inmate is one of us, yes. He'd have lifetimes to find a weakness, create a way out. Escape would be inevitable even if you put him in a straitjacket. It might take him seventy years, but he'd get out, Moira, and by then he might be driven to make up for lost time. He could kill a dozen people or a hundred people before we were able to stop him."

As he spoke, Moira's head bent lower and lower. By the time he was quiet, her forehead rested against the window. Her breathing grew sharp.

"I'm sorry," Simon said, and he seemed to mean it.

"We're voting, aren't we," she said in a tone barely loud enough for the phone to pick up. "We're his jury."

"That's the point of your call, isn't it? To get my vote?"

"And to hear your reasons," Zac said.

"Well, you've heard them."

"Don't you want to hear ours?" Moira said.

"You mean things I already know about you two? No, thanks. But I'd like David's vote before I hang up."

Zac didn't stop pacing. Moira didn't lift her head. The silence lasted.

David leaned into the corner and folded his arms across his bruised chest. "One thing we need to determine now, before we continue. How many votes are needed for a decision? And if we're two and two, what happens to him? I think we can all agree now that releasing him isn't one of the options."

He hadn't meant to glance at Moira, but she wasn't looking at him anyway. She stood bent with her forehead against the window.

"So there are two possible outcomes for him," David said, looking from her to Zac. "Imprisonment by us. Or execution by us."

"Yes," Zac said.

Moira was silent.

"For execution, we need a majority," Simon said, and Zac nodded.

Moira swiveled back to face them in time to see the nod. "In a murder trial the jury has to be unanimous for a guilty verdict."

"Guilt isn't in question here," Zac said.

"Nor is any possibility for rehabilitation. He's been clear on that." Clearer than they knew.

"But a tied vote means confinement," Moira said.

"Aye."

Zac nodded again.

David couldn't relax. His every muscle was coiled for action, even with Colm confined. They were in accord now, but they might not be in a minute. He tried to envision a few decades as an alternating prison guard. If it were only impractical, he'd do it. He closed his eyes and drew a long breath, sending a twinge to each bruise on his torso. He'd fought this man in the most desperate of scenarios, for Colm at least. If he'd gotten the upper hand and David were able to die, Colm could have killed him and would have needed no weapon to do it.

"He's dangerous," David said.

"That's not in question, either." Zac glared.

"I mean he's too dangerous. Simon's right. A prison wouldn't hold any of us forever." The words tasted like bile. David's stomach clenched. *Lord, if I'm thinking wrongly, show me.* "Even if he never killed again, he ought to pay for the lives he took. But he will. We all know he will."

Moira bowed her head, covered her face. A crinkle formed between Zac's eyes, but he didn't move toward her.

"Moira, you know we speak the truth." David tried to lower his voice, to make it gentle, but the edge inside surfaced in his tone.

"No, I don't," she said through her fingers.

"Finish your deliberating." Simon's voice cut between them, and Moira lowered her hands. "Call me when you know what's to be done." He hung up.

"I don't know why he said that," Moira said as Zac shoved his phone back into his pocket. "It's three for the death penalty and one against."

"I heard no fourth vote," David said.

Her eyes lifted to Zac with a sudden, stunning hope. Zac held her gaze as he pulled out a chair across from the one she'd vacated. She didn't move away from the window, instead leaned into the wall beside it.

Half of David expected Moira to pounce with demands, but she stood silently for the few seconds it took Zac to clear his throat, sit forward, and spread his hands open on the table.

"I might not have the right to vote."

Moira's mouth pursed, but she remained quiet.

"I know what has to be done." Zac held up one hand when she drew a breath to argue, and she seemed to shrink against the wall. "But I don't know if I can carry it out myself. And . . ." He looked up at David. "Asking you or Simon to do what I can't would be wrong."

"We'll sedate him," David said.

"It isn't that."

"What then?"

"You're all picturing exsanguination. Colm's picturing it too. Run a line into his arm, keep drawing blood until he flatlines. If he's already asleep, it's a serene death. Easy on us too. A body that looks asleep."

He stopped talking. David nodded him on.

"But I'm not sure . . ." Zac closed his eyes. "I'm not sure he would die."

David had much to learn, but this seemed

straightforward. "No blood, no serum. No serum, no healing."

"Yeah, we've always thought that. But if one of us is to be executed, we can't use trial and error on the method."

"And you have reason to believe Colm could survive without — ?"

Zac pushed to his feet and nearly tipped his chair. His gaze darted around the room, stopping at each of the four corners. "Sorry, I . . . Could we talk outside?"

Without another look at David or Moira, he left the room. The sliding door onto the deck opened and shut.

"Come on," Moira said and went after him.

First David went to the bedroom, his footsteps soundless on the carpet. He stood in the doorway and listened. Breathing. Slow, easy exhalations. Colm might have fallen asleep there in the dark. He had to be as weary as the rest of them.

David left him to it and went out into the yard, where Zac and Moira sat in the grass, their backs against the wooden privacy fence, their legs stretched in front of them. Zac was staring up at the sky, Moira's hand on his knee. They weren't talking. David approached and sat on Moira's other side.

His arrival seemed to focus Zac. The man

sighed and drew his knees up, and Moira removed her hand. He turned his head toward them.

"It's time to talk about Marble Canyon."

TWENTY-TWO

They moved from the yard to sit on David's porch, single file, feet on the step. Patio furniture would be a welcome addition to his place. David grabbed the thought as it flitted through his mind, glared at its flippancy, then realized it wasn't flippant. If these people were going to remain in his life, his home should accommodate their presence.

Zac gave a quiet half laugh and spoke to Moira. "I know you wondered."

"About the canyon?"

"About why I'm alive after falling eight thousand feet."

She shrugged, but her mouth turned down. "I did. I thought it had to be the serum."

"Moira, think what you're saying. The serum requires blood to work. Blood requires blood vessels. I fell. Eight. Thousand. Feet."

Moira rested her hand on him again, this time on his thigh. The gesture somehow spoke of layers of embroidered history, days or nights she'd sat with him exactly like this.

"I fell," Zac whispered.

"I'm so sorry." Moira leaned her head on his shoulder.

He cleared his throat. "When I came to, I was lying in . . . I don't know how to describe it. My own remains. There should have been nothing left. Of me."

"Why you disposed of the clothing," David said.

"Shreds, David. The physical . . . like the clothes had burst. Like a body had burst from inside them. But still on me. My arms in the armholes of the shirt. The waist of the jeans around my waist."

His eyes were losing their focus. Moira rubbed her thumb in a slow circle above his knee. Aye, they'd done this before.

Zac met David's eyes again. "So you see?"

Colm. David nodded. "I do."

"I won't experiment on him. If he has to die, you know how we have to do it."

The one thing David had always figured would be enough to end him: separating the brain that could die from the body that couldn't. Another nod, while acid rose in his throat.

Moira shook her head. "No. Zac, no."

"It's the only way to be sure."

"It doesn't make sense. It's not scientific."

David would defer to them in this if they agreed. They had more information than he. But if their conclusions were different, he had to weigh in. He tried to sort it all as both of them fell silent. Colm's body continuing to function without blood, managing to wake up when the drugs were drained away as well . . . . David shook his head.

"She's right, Zac. It doesn't make sense."

"Neither does my survival." He lifted a hand and turned it over as if his palm and fingers fascinated him, but his face was tight. His jaw clenched. "I will not take the chance of accidentally torturing him. We do it clean, or we don't do it."

Clean. All right. "But didn't you also survive . . . ?" He couldn't find a wholesome way to phrase it.

"Brain death?" Zac said. "Not that, I didn't."

"No," Moira whispered.

"He'll go to sleep first. He'll never know."

"Confinement. We'll be careful. He'll stay locked up as long as we live."

Zac shut his eyes.

"Zac," she whispered. "Please."

It wasn't that one death was more final,

more wrenching than another. But the reality of it had at last sunk into them both. So Zac's vote was cast. David stood unnoticed and slipped back into the house. He padded back to the bedroom and inspected the closet door again, listened to Colm's unbothered breathing and fought down a boiling desire to kill the man here and now. Kill him for the sorrow he was causing those who loved him with greater love than he knew.

Or perhaps he did know.

"You could have spared all of us this next part."

David turned from the room and went to his own and knelt in front of the cedar trunk. He lowered himself until he was prostrate, carpet fibers scratching his forehead, nose, chin. He spread his hands outward.

"Lord God," he said. "Is there no other way?"

Eleven souls. At least. Few serial killers confessed to all.

"If it's a righteous cause, if You wish the man's life ended, then I'll do it. Our duty to bear the sword against one of ours, against evil when the mortals cannot defend themselves. But, Lord, this weight is heavier than years."

He stayed on his face a long time, wrestling himself, giving the burden up. The others left him alone. At last he rose, opened the trunk, dug to the bottom, and lifted his saber. Untouched for so long but not rusted. He drew it from its sheath, and the steel gleamed. Sharp. Ready.

He set it on the lid of the trunk and went out to the others.

Seated on the living room couch, they were huddled together, feet drawn up under them, arms around each other. Moira seemed to be asleep. Her eyes were swollen, but Zac's held steel, saber strong.

"I called Simon."

David nodded. Sat in the chair and turned to watch the turtle. She was active at the moment, clawing a burrow into the one corner she hadn't dug up lately.

"He was at the gate for his flight. He knew what we would decide, and he said . . . well, he said he'll be a witness."

"From where is he flying?" Odd, David had never asked that before. Knew nothing at all about Simon, really.

"Florida." A smile tried to find Zac's mouth but failed. "We call him the old codger."

"Tiana's called me the same. I cannot fathom why."

Now the smile surfaced, though only for a moment. Zac cupped his hand over Moira's head and sighed.

"Have you spoken to Colm?" David said.

"No." The word was flat. Final.

"Seems someone should inform him of his verdict."

"Go right ahead."

"Zac . . ." David scrubbed at his face. The words wouldn't come. Zac said nothing, and at last David cleared his throat. "I've a saber in the house."

Zac stopped breathing.

"It ought to be tonight. Once Simon's with us."

"I know," Zac said quietly. He cleared his throat. "There's a bottle of sleeping pills in my luggage."

"All right."

"When I fly, one keeps me chill, but it doesn't knock me out. He'll probably need two or three, to be sure."

"Good to know."

"Okay." He drew a ragged breath.

"Will Moira be all right?"

Zac nestled her closer to him. She stirred but didn't awake. "She cares a lot. Even about him, I guess. She fell asleep still asking me to change my vote."

"I know it isn't your custom, but I'd like

to hear his story."

A little time passed in silence. David turned again to watch the turtle, but she was still now, facing the corner, half burrowed into the mulch.

"Colm was our smithy," Zac said, and David kept his face toward the terrarium. "He could make just about anything. He and his wife never had any children. When she died, he didn't marry again. Showed no interest in it, ever, until he met Rose. And after Rose he . . . well, he changed. Closed himself off to some degree, though I never . . ."

David faced him. "You couldn't have."

"Anyway, about Fisher Lake. He got sick, and Doc Leon decided it had to be appendicitis, and if it wasn't, maybe he could find what it was before Colm died. So he operated.

Come to find out there was some tumor on Colm's stomach, but when Doc tried to remove it, it ruptured and Colm started bleeding out. Like one of his organs burst or something. The notes are vague; Doc never knew what happened. But he figured if your internal injuries had healed, maybe Colm's would too, and nothing to lose, so . . ." Zac shrugged. "He was right, of course; Colm made a full recovery, and . . ."

Zac turned his face to the wall. Sighed

with something like a groan and then tried to laugh away the sound. "Yeah, uh, so that's the story. Of Colm."

"This isn't the way you thought his story would end."

Zac met his eyes with a hollow gaze. "I thought the serum would run out one day. And we'd become old men."

Together. David nodded.

"But he's cut other stories short, David. I know that. Men, women. With loved ones, families, lives left to live. He chose that. So he's written his own end."

"I'm sorry."

"I'll see it through."

Nothing more to say. David nodded.

After a while Zac eased Moira down to the couch and slid a pillow under her head. It was barely afternoon, but Zac said she had been up most of the night as David had, tossing and turning until the bed creaked. He set a kiss on her forehead and then followed David to the library.

Zac turned a circle, taking in the full bookshelves, before settling on the floor against the wall. David got them both coffee and they drank it in silence, but a nettle of a question had been pricking at him since last night.

"You called Him Jehovah," David said.

Zac's brow furrowed.

"Last night. You bowed and called on Him by name."

"I guess I did." Zac held eye contact, and his mouth remained flat. No smirk, no slipping on a mask.

"Do you know Him truly, then?"

He gazed out into the dark again. "I used to say I knew Him like Jacob did, before he was Israel."

"What of Christ?"

Zac rubbed the back of his neck. "I don't lack belief, if that's what concerns you."

"Belief is only one piece of knowing Him."

"Leave it be, David."

It was answer enough. He nodded acquiescence.

A minute passed, and then Zac shook his head. "What's between you and God is something I can't have."

David tilted his head. Let the man say more if he chose to.

"I wrestle. All the time. Never any peace." Zac clenched his eyes shut. "He gives me no peace."

"Then why do you wrestle?"

"It's that or submit."

Danger crept over David's soul. "Zac."

"Don't. It is what it is. I'm not built for surrender."

"Zac —"

"And no need to quote Philippians chapter two at me. I've tried to bow my knee. I can't do it."

"Why not?"

"I don't know."

Yes, he did. His expression told that much. "A century of wrestling?"

"It's exhausting, I can tell you."

Dear Lord. He would pray for this man's soul a hundred more years if needed.

When Zac stood and chose a book, David did the same, and he stayed to read while Zac went back to the living room.

Interminable time passed. Hours. They should eat, but it was safe to say no one felt hungry. Moira woke and asked after Colm. At some point, numb and idle, the three of them tried to make small talk, but it didn't feel right. David grilled Swiss cheese on wheat bread, and like children they each took a triangle sandwich slice from the plate and nibbled it. He got out an old checkerboard, and this didn't feel right, either, but he and Zac played ten games. David won eight of them because Zac's eyes kept losing their focus and straying toward the hallway to the bedroom.

David tried to remember a longer day in his life. There were a few, but they were draped in cobwebs, pushed to the back of his memory, not the kind he wanted to relive. This one would be joining them.

In the late afternoon, Simon came by taxi, no luggage but a backpack. He rang the front doorbell and entered David's house with heavy steps. Moira rushed to him and hugged him.

"There," he said, stroking her hair.

"Simon," she said.

"Where is he?"

"Nearest thing I have to a jail cell," David said. "Closet in the back bedroom."

They went to the back of the house, the four of them, led by David. He motioned them back as he unlocked the closet door. Colm might jump him. They had to be ready to restrain him if he got free.

The man was slumped in a corner. His eyes were bright in the dark, reflecting the sunlight from the window as he took them in.

"Simon," Colm said, as if the man's presence alone answered all questions.

"Colm."

"I've been sentenced to death for my crimes."

Simon stepped up to David's side. "You have."

Colm's mouth twitched upward. "So

you'll execute an immortal for behaving like an immortal. One of your own is worth less to you than a motley assortment of human souls."

"We're human too," Moira whispered.

"We were human, but it's been a long time since then."

"You said this is what you want."

Something flickered behind his eyes. He looked past the three of them at Zac, who stood back and to one side.

"You won't give me what I want," Colm said to him. "I deserve to live with myself."

"Yeah," Zac said. "But that's not relevant."

David hauled him from the closet and pushed him down in a corner of the room. He didn't resist, sat with his knees splayed out and his ankles bound.

"Tonight," Colm said. "You're going through with it tonight."

"Delay won't change anything," Simon said.

The expression in Colm's eyes became shuttered. He leveled a vacant look at Moira. Tilted his head. She stared back. Before David could understand what had passed between them, Simon turned to him.

"You and Zac figure out where. I'll stand guard for now."

The subtext was clear. Simon had things

to say to Colm. He nodded Moira out of the room as well, and she followed David and Zac to the kitchen.

"Listen to me." Her voice was shaking.

David faced her, and his breath caught. Her body quivered like a sapling in a storm. She was wide-eyed, as she'd been yesterday when he first guessed the truth.

Zac stepped close to her. "Moira?"

She rushed from the room. Zac pursued, and David trailed him down the hallway, stopping outside the bathroom. Moira fell to her knees in front of the toilet and threw up.

Zac crouched beside her, brushed back her hair with his hands, and held it. When she was finished, she stayed there, on her knees on the floor.

David grabbed the hand towel from its wall fixture, dampened it under the faucet, and offered it to her. She gripped it in both hands and began to twist it.

Zac eased her fingers from around the cloth and cleaned her face. Then he pushed a lock of her hair behind her ear.

"We can't kill him," she said.

"Why not?"

She cringed away from him until her back pressed against the wall. Her knees folded into her chest. "He's one of us."

The words she'd hammered at them before held no conviction now. David knelt outside the doorway, not wanting to crowd her, and she jolted as if he'd materialized from the air.

He tried to speak gently. "Moira, tell us."

"No." The word shrilled. "You — you want to take his life when there's another way."

David could have shaken her to get the truth if she weren't balled up in front of him, unblinking and heaving every breath. "Ach, please, Moira."

"He's one of us."

He stood and left the room. Zac could deal with her. David could not.

Simon was in the kitchen. Pacing. He looked up, concern lining around his eyes. "She's made herself sick?"

"You heard." David sank into a chair and watched the man's restless motion. One thing Simon and Zac had in common.

"Grief can do that to a body. And dread."

"And there could be something else."

The lines in his face deepened. "Go on."

"I think she fears him. Possibly has for a long time."

"We would have seen."

"I think she hid it deep."

The man's jaw hardened. He gazed past

David, toward the bathroom, which was silent now. In a minute both of them emerged, Moira's small frame tucked into Zac's arm. He set her in a chair at the table, and she curled forward with one arm around her middle.

"Moira," Simon said, utterly gentle.

She turned her face away. "He's one of us."

She was silent while Zac, Simon, and David worked out a plan.

It was the kind of planning that ought to take place after midnight, with hushed darkness pressing at the windows. Reality, though, was barely five o'clock. In Michigan this time of year, the sun wouldn't set for another hour. The village park would close then, but the maintenance crew would shut the parking lot gate and leave. Anyone who lived in Harbor Vale knew the park had no fences; the sign on the gate that said TRESPASSERS WILL BE PROSECUTED existed to deter tourists, and the one that said SECURITY SYSTEM was an outright lie. They could get to park property from the back lot of David's store, walking a more or less straight line for about a tenth of a mile. The woods would be ideal.

As they talked logistics that left David's stomach sour, his phone vibrated. He reached for it. Tiana. She'd have closed the store a few minutes ago.

DINNER? OR SOMETHING, WHEN YOU'RE FREE? YOU DON'T HAVE TO TELL ME DE-TAILS.

He wouldn't try to convey his thoughts in a text message. He walked out onto the deck and shut the door as he called her.

"David," she said on a breath. "I've been worrying for the last seven hours."

Only seven hours since he'd seen her? He closed his eyes and leaned his arm on the deck railing. "Tiana, I . . . I can't get din-ner."

A pause, but not a long one. "It's not over yet."

"No."

She'd put it together, what he had to do. She said nothing, probably because there was nothing to say. His stomach tensed. Two years of knowing her didn't mean she trusted him this far. This kind of trust went beyond what most people earned in a life-time.

"Will you call the police?" He hoped she'd at least tell him. Let him get ahead of them.

"Whoever killed that man should be tried and sentenced. Prison, or legal execution."

"He can't be imprisoned or legally exe-cuted. Not humanely. Not safely. And he will kill again."

Silence.

"Do you believe me?"

"I . . ." Tiana's voice shook. "Yeah, I do."

"Thank you." *For everything.* She might believe him, but that didn't mean she'd want anything to do with him after this.

"David, this . . . this is . . ."

He closed his eyes and tried to picture her expression. Her voice had gone soft, cautious.

"There aren't words for this."

"No," he said quietly. "There aren't words."

"Call me when . . . when you can." She hung up.

When he returned to the house, the others were in the back room with Colm, who held a glass of water in one hand and three Ambien in the other. They'd cut the zip tie on his hands but left his ankles tethered.

He looked up at David's entrance. "They tell me this is it." He lifted the glass in a toast.

"Aye."

"I'm surprised you got this far." He spoke to all of them this time. "Impressed, even. Strong traditional morality."

"Shut up." Simon's words came with a growl.

386

"I might be worried if I thought you'd go through with it. Just don't let Simon over-rule you when the rest of you come to your senses."

"You said . . ." Zac shook his head.

"An experiment." Colm's hand closed around the pills. "Reverse psychology."

"It's still a game to you."

"Maybe." As if to prove a point, he put all three pills in his mouth and downed the water and set it on the floor.

Moira looked away.

"Why don't you tell them, pet? About the game I've played on you for five decades and change. Tell them you believed it and see what they say."

She shut her eyes then opened them and stepped out of the corner, closer to him. "Tell them . . . I . . . believed it?"

"Without proof. Slinking along, my dog on a leash. Tell her it's a shock collar and she never tests it."

She pressed her hands to her stomach, and her voice was a husk of itself. "Colm?"

"Check your email again, pet. There's nothing there."

Her legs buckled. David surged forward, planted himself between her and Colm. Not physical protection. Something else. Colm was watching her with a lustful fascination that turned David's stomach. Zac's instincts had propelled him to a position beside David, but he didn't stop there. He charged Colm and fisted the man's shirt and yanked him forward.

"What did you do to her?" The words gritted between Zac's teeth.

Colm's composure didn't flicker. "Lied to her. That's all. I didn't have to do anything else."

Behind David, a gagging sound broke into a cry. He turned. Moira was still on her knees, curled forward now into the fetal position, arms drawn in, hair fanned on the floor around her. Simon crossed the room and hunkered beside her. When he touched her back, she gave another retching sob.

Simon fit his arms around and under her. Drew her close and scooped her up as he stood. Moira wrapped her arms around his neck, sharp breaths coming with whimpers. Simon didn't look at David before he carried her out of the room.

Thunk. Fist against flesh. David swiveled. Zac had knocked Colm senseless with a single punch. Tears and fury shone in his eyes.

"He never wakes up again," Zac said and left the room.

David re-bound Colm's arms to the chair.

Stared a moment, hackles standing up on his neck, at Colm's face smooth and harmless in sleep. David shuddered. His place was with the others, not here.

He went to them.

Moira wouldn't release her hold around Simon's neck. Her trembling earlier was like a quick chill compared to the now bone-deep, uncontrollable quake of her body. She tried to speak, but nothing was intelligible. Her fingers were locked around handfuls of the back of Simon's shirt.

"How do we help her?" Simon asked. He cupped his hand around the back of her neck and tipped his mouth closer to her ear. "Moira, honey, it's over. Whatever it was, it's over."

"Can't be." The words came past her sharp breaths.

"He was lying, Moira. You heard him say it."

"Lying about lying," she said.

"No." Zac crouched behind Simon, made Moira look at him. "No, he wasn't. Your email is going to prove it to you." He held up her phone.

She didn't answer, didn't move to take it. He woke it and typed in her passcode, and in a few seconds, he held up the email screen.

"No new messages," he said. "That's good, isn't it?"

She gave a small nod.

"So now you need to breathe easy. We know this drill. Remember? Slow, deep, three, four, five. Slow, deep, three, four, five. You've done it for me; now I do it for you. Slow, deep, three, four, five."

While Simon cradled her and Zac thumbed her tears and breathed with her, David stood apart and watched. Listened. For Colm's final escape attempt, he told himself first, but no. He watched and listened to these people care for one of theirs. His own people.

Whom Colm had hurt. For pleasure.

Calming Moira took a long time. Once she seemed to gain control then began to shake and gasp again when Zac asked her a question. David abandoned his sentry position, came near to them as she found composure and was this time able to keep it.

At last her arms loosened around Simon's neck, and he set her, limp as a sleeping baby, in a corner of the couch. She picked up a pillow in a feeble grip and hugged it to her stomach.

"Okay?" Zac said, and she nodded. "Can you talk to us?"

Another nod.

"Then you need to tell us how he silenced you, Moira. Why you don't want him dead."

She lifted her head, and in her eyes blazed a wild loathing. "I do want him dead. I've never wanted anything more in my life."

"What — ?" Simon's voice broke. "What has he done to you?"

Tears fell in the tracks of those that had fallen minutes ago, but this time her breathing remained easy and her words remained clear. She looked from Zac to Simon. She bent over the pillow, arms tightening.

"He said he had set Zac up for the murders. All of them. Meticulously. He said it was a dead-man switch. Once every twenty-four hours, he postponed it. If I ever crossed him — if I told you, if I told police, if I tried in any way to bring him to justice — I would get an email confirming the evidence had been sent. Zac would — would go to prison — a tiny cell without a window. Simon would — would find out. Would always believe Zac had done it."

She swiped at her tears, uncurled enough to look them in the eyes again.

"But he never . . . he never hurt you?" Zac said.

"Zachary, he said he'd hurt *you*." A sob broke her open again. "He said he'd hurt my boys."

Twenty-Three

They left the house at half past six, the four of them seated in the Jeep, Colm asleep on the floor behind the front seats. The silence tonight was like crashing surf on a beach. David had the impulse to hold his ears against it.

Everything needed for an execution was stowed in the hatchback.

When they reached the bookstore lot, Zac hoisted Colm over his shoulders. The others gathered shovels and tarps from the back. David took a shovel and the saber.

He led the trek to the park. They trailed him single file — Zac with Colm, Moira, Simon. Around them night seeped into the cracks between tree branches, between blades of grass, between each of the people who trudged over uneven ground, through uncut grass and weeds that grew taller as they approached the village property line. Cold wrapped around their shoulders. A wind kicked up, slapped their hands and sent Moira's hair into her mouth. None of it caused Colm to stir.

Five hundred yards into the woods, David stopped. No clearing here, only more trees — a grave in a clearing would be stupid — but they thinned a bit here. He turned to the others, gestured around him, and they nodded. Zac lowered Colm to the ground, in the shelter of an old log.

They dug six feet down and were finished more quickly than David expected.

They laid the tarp beside the trench in the ground. Simon set Colm on it then slid the second tarp under his head and shoulders. He pushed to his feet and nodded at David.

Ready.

Moira bowed her head. Her shoulders shook.

"You don't have to stay, honey," Simon said.

"Yes, I do."

While they each wielded a shovel, David had laid the saber on a broken tree trunk. He turned to retrieve it, but Zac stood beside the fallen tree, the saber in his right hand. He drew it from its sheath, and the metallic ring echoed off the trees.

"Zac," David said.

"It has to be me."

"It doesn't have to be," Simon said, a growl beneath the words.

"He was my —" Zac's voice broke. "He was a brother to me. Not to you."

Zac knelt beside Colm and lifted the saber. He stayed motionless until his arms began to tremble. David waited, but there was no question what he had to do. What all of them needed him to do. He stepped over the soft grass and knelt at Zac's side. He set his hand on Zac's arm and with the other cupped Zac's clenching hands and the saber's hilt and pried his fingers away.

Zac held on tighter. "It has to be me."

"No, my friend," David said. This was a burden he could carry.

After a moment Zac released his grip. His shoulders sagged. He moved aside but remained on his knees.

David wrapped both hands around the hilt and looked up, met first Simon's eyes and then Moira's. "It's time."

Simon nodded. After a moment Moira did too. David looked to Zac, and he gave the third nod.

"The Lord, my rock, who trains my hands for war."

David raised the blade and brought it down.

TWENTY-FOUR

They buried Colm together. Even Moira took up her shovel again. In the glaring beams of the flashlights, Zac was gray-faced. Simon's cheeks were wet with tears, but his mouth was a firm line.

None of them spoke as Zac turned over the final shovelful of soil. As David took up the saber and looked around at them. He would let them decide how long to remain here. What words to say over the grave.

Simon nodded to him, an acknowledgment, and wrapped an arm around Moira's shoulders. "Colm O'Carroll will become dust. He'll bring no more harm to us. He'll bring no more death and pain to the mortals. What was done here was rightly done."

Moira turned her face into his arm.

David waited for her or Zac to speak, but the silence stretched on. At last Simon wiped his face and motioned to David. "Lead us back."

Back. To the Jeep, aye, not a problem. To yesterday, when Colm had yet been alive, when all his memories had still been remembered, here in the world. To a week ago, before that idiot Paul Tait had stabbed Zac. But if David could lead them back in time, he would only be causing a different harm, a greater evil. Colm still murdering, Moira still mute in her terror, Zac and Simon still unaware he had to be stopped.

The three of them got into the back seat this time, leaving the passenger seat empty. They were nearly back at the house when Moira said quietly, "Zac?"

He gave no response.

Moira sniffed back tears. "Zachary. I need you to talk to me, please."

Nothing.

Simon huffed. "Zac, you thin-skinned, senseless, egotistical —" His voice broke. "Come on, Zac. Come on, you bighearted braggart. Talk to us."

"He'll be all right, Simon," Moira whispered. "He just needs a little time."

"I know."

"He needs patience, okay?"

"Don't I know that too."

She gave a soft, broken laugh. "David?"

"Aye, you can stay at my place. As long as he needs."

"Oh. P–perhaps one more day?"

"Of course."

She quietly broke into tears.

"Thank you," Simon said.

"You're welcome to stay as well." David pulled into the driveway and shut off the Jeep and swiveled toward his passengers in the back.

Zac was staring straight ahead. The glaze David had seen come over his eyes before was nothing in comparison. Zac had shut down. He'd seen it through, the worst of everything, as he'd promised he would do. Now it was over. If David had anyone left who knew him so well, any friendship that had lasted so long and then been so betrayed, his own devastation would show in different ways. But inside him it wouldn't measure any less.

Simon and David lifted Zac between them and took him inside. He was aware enough to keep his arms around their shoulders, but his legs were limp. He blinked once when Simon set him in the living room chair.

"Upright?" David said.

"It's strange." Simon tucked a needless pillow next to Zac. "He can keep his balance and such. He'll hold a cup of water if you give it to him, but if you want him to drink it, you have to put it to his lips your-self."

"Can he hear us?"

"He's never told me anything about what it's like. If he even remembers it." Simon patted Zac's shoulder the way one would pat a dog's head, then walked away, defensiveness in his posture. He didn't want David staring at Zac. "You'd think by now I could predict these things, but they still catch me off guard every time."

"He's gotten no relief all these years?"

Simon looked back at Zac sitting motionless and blank. "It's his story, not mine."

"He told me Moira was with him through the worst of it. After the First War."

Simon tilted his head and appraised David anew. "Huh. Well, yes, she was. Fiercely determined, too, that there had to be something to cure him."

She entered the room with a set to her mouth that hinted she'd heard everything, but the firmness dissolved as she met Simon's eyes. "Would you . . . until . . . I just can't right now."

"Don't go far."

"I promise."

They hugged each other, and Moira stood on tiptoe and pressed a kiss to his cheek. She met David's eyes as if she would say something, ducked her head, and left the room.

Simon wandered over to sit on the couch, leaned his head back, and shut his eyes.

"Ought she be alone?" David said.

Simon sighed. "Better not to argue with her about a short distance. Might prevent the longer."

The aftermath. Theirs to weather now. David sat at the other end of the couch and lowered his face to his hands. And prayed. But the words came between chasms of something he couldn't call *grief;* he hadn't known Colm well enough to claim that word for him. These others had. They had loved the man. Their sorrow oozed alongside their betrayal and confusion, fresh and raw, filling every space in the house. David was no counselor, but he could recognize an emotional triage situation. Zac's distress was only the most visible.

All right then. Yes, he was remembering the saber hilt's hardness against his palm and fingers, the resistance and give of its lowering, the sound as it struck through to dirt. But those things could be processed later. These others needed someone apart, someone who could see straight.

His purpose for now.

He got up.

A single tear squeezed from Simon's eye and dripped down his temple into his hair as he sat with his head back. Zac hadn't moved.

Triage. What did a man need when the damage sustained wasn't in his body?

Instincts stirred, long unused. David went to the kitchen. He got two cans of chicken rice soup from the pantry and set them warming in a pot on the stove. Coffee? No. He found a bar of dark chocolate and chopped it fine. No milk chocolate in the house, but a bitter version would suffice. Milk and half-and-half from the fridge, sugar and vanilla extract from a cupboard — ach, that bottle was dusty — and David began a concoction he hadn't bothered with since Ginny. A concoction she always said was his greatest kitchen skill.

The soup was warm first. David left it on low while he brought the milk and half-and-half just below simmering, removed the pan from the burner, added the chocolate and watched it resist a moment before melting. He added the rest of the ingredients, whisked it, and poured three mugs. He ladled three bowls of soup. He would eat later. No sound stirred from any other room. He might have been alone in the house.

Ladies first. David took a bowl, spoon, and mug into the library, where the light bled around the cracked door. Moira sat in the chair, head down, arms around her knees. She looked up when he entered. Her eyes were nearly swollen shut, her face a mess of new tears, her hair sweaty. David set the bowl and mug on a shelf and leaned down to her.

"Think you could eat?"

"I'd prefer not to," she said.

"You feel sick?"

She considered the question. "I guess I don't."

"Come then. Try a few bites."

She sat up and took the bowl, spooned a testing mouthful of broth and then another that included a bit of chicken. From there, she finished the soup, slowly, eyes closed. David traded her the soup for the chocolate, which was no longer steaming but still hot. As she sipped it a tear fell.

"Thank you, David." She wrapped her hands around the mug. "Did Simon eat?"

"I'm about to offer him some. Will you join us?"

A crinkle formed between her eyes. "I don't know if I can do that."

David squeezed her shoulder. She sipped the chocolate, and another tear fell.

"I keep getting this . . . pain." She pressed her palm to the center of her chest. "Here. And these thoughts. That he isn't dead. That wherever he is now, he tricked us into sending him there."

"Moira."

She leaned into his arm, too tired to know she was doing it. "I can't face it, David. I'm going to have to, but I can't."

"No more facing things tonight. Just be here with us."

"I . . . I'll try."

David wrapped a supporting arm around her and walked with her to the kitchen. He set her empty bowl in the sink and picked up the other two and their spoons. The steam had wafted away, but the bowls warmed his hands.

Moira picked up another mug. "If anything will bring Zac back to us sooner, sugar will. But don't expect him to take the soup now."

"Then the soup's for me," David said.

Simon accepted the food with quiet thanks. While he and David ate, Moira bent to eye level with Zac.

"Zac." Her voice was quiet, gentle. "This isn't a microwave imitation; it's the real thing. Can you smell it?"

He gave no sign of hearing her. His only

movement was the rise and fall of his chest.

"You should try some. The chocolate's not too sweet, and David didn't even scald the milk."

No response.

"Moira," Simon said quietly. "It'll be hours yet."

"Once he came back in forty minutes."

"Once."

"I just want to try it. If he doesn't take any, I'll let him be."

Simon sighed and sipped his own chocolate. "Can't hurt him."

"Exactly," she said and raised the mug to Zac's lips. She tipped it carefully, one hand cupping the back of his head, though he didn't need the support. A deliberate touch for the sake of contact.

After a few seconds, his Adam's apple dipped. His breathing deepened. He swallowed again.

Moira took the mug from his lips and brushed her fingers through his hair. "That's it, Zachary, that's it."

He blinked.

"Yes, that's it."

Zac's fingers curled at his side. Another blink, and he met her eyes.

"Zac, are you here?"

His gaze roamed the room and settled first

on David then on Simon. He didn't look for someone else to be there. He didn't jolt as if seeing them all without Colm had reminded him what happened tonight. He seemed to be absorbing the sight of each of them, as if he'd lived fifty solitary years in one catatonic hour.

Moira brought the mug to his lips again. This time he drank immediately. He took the mug from her and drained it, parched from whatever desert he'd been lost in. He lowered it with steady hands.

"What's the time?" he asked all of them.

"About ten," David said.

"At night?" He looked toward the windows and frowned at their darkness.

"You were gone only an hour," Moira said.

He looked down at the mug between his hands, and red stained his cheeks.

Simon sipped his chocolate and raised his mug to Zac. "Good stuff, huh?"

"Seriously impressive." When he tried to smirk, a wrinkle formed between his eyes.

After a little while, Zac ate some soup, and tension eased from Moira's face. Nothing more was said about his spell of silence. Or about anything else, for a time.

David had provided for their physical needs as best he could, and each of them seemed stronger than before. Warm food could fortify the soul as well as the body. They had shelter and safety here; all they needed now was sleep. Healing wouldn't begin without it.

It wasn't exactly a vigil, but as long as they sat up, he would sit with them. They asked him for stories of himself and told some of their own, none of which included Colm, until Simon interrupted a sleepy lull by standing and stretching and turning to all of them.

"For a short time we were five. Now we're four again."

"Yes," Moira said, and Zac nodded.

"Only we could stop him. So we did. And we rest with that choice. And speaking of rest." Simon pinned them all with a look almost fatherly. "If I'm tired, I know the rest of you are. Time we gave David his house back."

David nearly said it wasn't necessary, but maybe it was, for all of them.

A night alone, a long sleep. Yes. He saw his guests to the door. Shuffling footsteps, hushed good nights, and then the door was shut and the rental car's taillights were disappearing down the street.

David folded onto the floor and sat with his back against the door.

He got up and went into the back bedroom.

He stood in the tiny closet and looked around. What was he seeking? A message from Colm, scratched with a fingernail into the paint on the wall? David shook his head and put away the sheets and other storage items he'd dragged from the closet. Screwed the lightbulb back into the ceiling fixture. He fetched a screwdriver and returned the bathroom doorknob to its rightful place. Ten minutes, and the jail cell was a closet again.

He went to his own room and showered away the sweat and dirt of grave digging. He pulled on flannel pants and went to bed. Alone in the dark, the choice remained as clear as it had been, but faces drifted before him now — imaginary, conjecture, a brunette woman with pink lipstick on her way to a job interview, a balding man with a paunch and twin grandkids on the way, a dark-haired twentysomething college student engaged to be married to the girl he'd known since elementary school. Maybe Colm's victims had looked like them.

No more victims. David pulled the bedcovers up to his chin and tried to sleep.

Sitting up in bed. Cold sweat. Heart pounding. Lungs squeezing shut. David clutched the sheet in both hands and fought for breath. A nightmare. A dark, violent nightmare, not a memory — well, not anything now, he couldn't even recall the —

Tiana. Colm and Tiana, his last victim, her blood —

"Lord." He kicked the sheets away and staggered out of bed, dropped to his knees. "She's all right? She's all right."

His heart took long minutes to stop racing. He looked at the bedside clock. Not even midnight yet. He'd fallen asleep less than twenty minutes ago. This might prove to be a long night.

Wait. . . . He lifted his head to listen. Now that his breathing had quieted, a buzzing noise found him from another room. He padded out to the hall and followed the sound. His phone, vibrating, incoming call.

Tiana. His pulse tripped. The dream images flashed. "What's wrong?"

"David, thank God."

"What?"

"It's Jayde. If there's any way you can possibly come." Unshed tears drew her voice tight.

He shuffled the phone from one ear to the other as he dressed. "If she's in danger, you need to call the police."

408

"Chris locked her out of the house. He's in there right now and won't let her in. He took her car keys."

"Is it her car?"

"Legally? I don't know. He sold it to her or something, about a year ago. I'm going to pick her up, and I'd rather not go there alone."

"Absolutely not."

She gave a strained laugh. "Chivalry lives. When she called me, she asked if I was with you."

David held the phone between his ear and shoulder and tied his shoes. "If she wants me to commit assault and battery on that bully, she's picked a good night for it."

Tiana was quiet long enough for him to regret the words. He locked the house, got in his Jeep, and headed southeast.

"You're home?" he said.

"Yeah."

"All right. I'm on my way."

"Thank you." A quiet sniff. "I'll let you drive now."

"No." The word came too fast. "That is, I'd like to talk."

"What about?"

"I've got no topic in mind, only hearing your voice."

"You realize how unhelpful that is."

409

"It's all I have at the moment."

She was quiet, then, "I prayed for you today. Almost constantly."

"I apologize for the radio silence."

"I hope you'll let me listen, but I know you might not be able to."

Let her listen. No demand, only a precious offer. "Tiana."

"Hmm?"

"Nothing. That is . . . thank you, and I hope to be free to talk about it. In the meantime, your prayers are coveted."

"You don't have to covet them if I'm already giving them."

The chuckle filled him, a salve on the day's open blisters. "You know Jayde likely asked about me hoping I *wasn't* with you."

"When I said I was calling you, she said okay."

Well, but what else could she say under the circumstances?

Tiana sighed. "You don't know what you've already done for Jayde. You didn't fire her when you had the right to. You would have tossed Chris out on his rear that day if she'd let you. I've heard you ask for her opinion and put it into practice when you think she has a good idea — making the front counter more efficient or inviting or whatever. Do you think Chris has ever done that? And she's only worked for you a few days."

"None of that should be unusual." And tonight the same old story made him feel wearier than it normally did. David flexed his fingers on the wheel.

"She's been with Chris for three years. She puts up a confident front when she's at work, but that's not the real Jayde. I know I'm talking behind her back, but I have to at this point. She is terrified, David, and not of him. She'll go back to Chris before she'll quit school, and right now, financially, those are her two options."

High time a third option presented itself, then. David forced his tired mind into a higher gear than the speed of sludge. He didn't have a solution by the time he parked in the visitor lot of Tiana's apartment building. She was waiting for him in the carport.

She rolled down the car window as he approached, and he leaned in. "You want to drive?"

"I want her to recognize my car. Get in, Valiant Hero."

He chuckled and obliged her. He tilted his head back but kept his eyes open, watching the traffic out the windshield.

Dirt raining into the grave, onto the tarp. Clinking shovels and rustling trees.

"David."

He jolted awake.

"We'll be there in about two minutes." Tiana gave him a quick smile as she drove.

He scrubbed his palms over his warming cheeks. "I am so sorry."

"And I'm sorry for dragging you out of bed. There, now we're even."

He blinked his dry eyes a few times, sat up straight, and peered at the passing surroundings. Wait, where were they? Farther south than he'd thought.

"How long was I sleeping?"

"Well, you got quiet about an hour and a half ago."

"Tiana."

"Hmm?"

"Jayde drives ninety minutes to work?"

"I thought you knew that."

He shook his head. Chris the moron aside, he wouldn't want Tiana driving around this area alone at night. She parked at an apartment building that did nothing to relax him, then texted Jayde. They waited, but the foyer doors didn't open.

"She should be outside by now," Tiana said.

"Might he have taken her phone?"

"She called me after he locked her out."

That didn't mean Chris hadn't stormed

out after the call and stolen phone as well as car keys. David motioned Tiana to stay in the car and got out, scanned the area. At least the floodlights worked. The parking lot needed repaving, but so did plenty of parking lots — and roads — in Michigan. The immediate area was quiet, no troublemakers that might try to harass Tiana. He nodded to her without leaning down to expose his back.

Deep breath. This wasn't a battlefield. Aye, okay.

"Come on," he said, and Tiana nodded. He took her hand and held it to his side as they approached the doors. "How'll we . . . ?"

Tiana tugged on the door, and it opened.

"You can just walk in?"

"Yeah." She grimaced as they stepped inside. "This is not the best place to — oh."

Chris had crowded Jayde into a corner of the foyer. Her back wasn't literally against the wall, but close enough.

"And another thing," Chris said, "stop calling your girlfriends every time we have a little fight. It's nobody's business but ours, and you've got no right —"

"Hey, Chris," Tiana said.

He turned, saw them both. "What is this?"

"Um, you left her stranded in the foyer,

you loser. I came to pick her up."

"Get out," Chris said and turned his back on them with an egoist's confidence.

Touching him first would be a mistake. The kind that could end up with police on the scene and battery charges. David crushed the desire to crush the man's face and stepped up beside him instead.

"Jayde?" The way this night ended was up to her.

TWENTY-FIVE

Jayde blinked at him, eyelids smeared with leftover makeup remover. She was wearing a baggy nightshirt with a unicorn on the front and cotton pajama pants covered in running text.

"You came," she said.

Aye. The word nearly came out, the result of too much unfiltered conversation lately and five hours' sleep in the last two days. He nodded instead.

"Okay." Jayde drew herself up straighter and picked up a little black purse that had been dropped in the corner. "Let's go."

"What?" Chris still stood in her way, but now she stepped around him. "Baby, you can't just do this. We'll work it out."

"Good night, Chris." Jayde walked to Tiana like a woman stepping out of the rubble of an earthquake, each footstep surer as the ground held. Both of them started for the doors.

"I said no."

As Chris moved to block Jayde, David blocked Chris. He spoke to the women without breaking eye contact with the man who had frozen in front of him.

"Go to the car."

"Going," Tiana said.

Behind him the doors opened. Shut.

"Meddling moron," Chris said.

David took one step toward him. "Blustering coward."

Chris's fists balled.

"You're not a stupid person, or you'd have called me an obscene name instead of an accurate one. I'm meddling indeed."

"I'll take you apart."

"If you try, I'll break your arm, Chris. That's the only warning you get."

Chris took a step toward him but then went still. He swallowed hard. "And now you'll warn me to stay away from her? She's my woman."

"As you lock her out of your home and crowd her into corners, you're not her man."

"So you are warning me." Chris crossed his arms.

David mimicked the gesture. If posturing was what the man responded to, so be it. "I'm guessing Jayde will be setting her own

416

boundaries in the future without help from me."

Chris's glare maintained bravado for a few seconds. Then he ducked David's gaze and growled at the floor. "Get out."

"Whose name is on the title of her car?"

He looked up, startled into the truth. "Hers."

"Then go get me the keys."

"Not a chance in —"

"Now."

It was indeed a chance, that Chris's courage would be even scanter than he'd shown so far. David couldn't force his way into the apartment, and if he let Chris retreat, the man might stay inside and lock the door. Chris disappeared, and David ground his teeth while he waited, sure that was the end of it. But no, Chris came back. He shoved a set of keys at David — keys bearing a bronze key chain engraved with the words *I Read Dead People*.

"Now get out."

The demand held even less power the second time. David left Chris with arms still folded, staring at his own feet.

Jayde sat in the passenger seat of Tiana's car. David lifted the keys as he approached, and she burst out of the car to grab them.

"Thank you." Tears filled her eyes, but she

blinked them away. "I didn't know what I'd do."

"Would you like to ride with Tiana?"

"Well . . . I'd rather drive. If that's okay."

"It's your car, Jayde."

She smiled. "Yeah, it is."

As Tiana drove north, Jayde following, David fought a wave of fatigue. Might be a good thing he wasn't behind the wheel. "Where to now?" he said to stay awake.

"My place."

"You're set up for a guest?" Tiana's descriptions of her apartment had always sounded more like a studio.

"I own an air mattress. She can have my bed until something else . . ." The shrug admitted more than she realized. She and Jayde had no other plan. "We'll have to get her some clothes, but for tomorrow at work she can wear some of mine. She'll just have to roll the pant legs under."

"What about a hotel?"

"Definitely not in the budget."

"Hmm."

She glanced at him. "David."

"Would she consider it an overstep to offer?"

"I guess you'll have to ask her."

But she knew Jayde better. "If you think

she'd feel affronted in some way, please say so."

"I . . ." She shook her head. "I think even if she turns you down, she'll be touched by the offer."

Fine, but *touched* didn't accomplish anything practical. He sighed. "Does she have no one but you?"

Tiana didn't answer. He glanced over. Her mouth had turned down.

"I mean that a fresh start will be easier, the more support she has."

"Honestly? I think we'll be doing well if she accepts help from me. There's some things in her family . . . make it hard to be interdependent, you know? Sometimes she thinks alone is easier."

"We'll have to persuade her otherwise."

"Should I start calling you *pot* and Jayde *kettle*?"

"Tiana."

"Don't you 'Tiana' me all Scottish and — and —"

She was mad? How had that happened? "Perhaps we should discuss —"

"You need to be in church."

Wait, that's what this was about?

"For the longest time I assumed you were. Then about six months ago, something you

419

said gave it away. I figured it wasn't my place."

"And it is now?"

"Do you want to date me or not?"

He scrubbed a hand over his face. "Don't make this about that."

"I don't want to." She signaled for a turn.

"It isn't a thing I can do. Surely you see why."

"No, I don't."

"I might have to lie to the federal government and the corner grocer about who I am, but I won't lie to fellow believers."

"And your solution is to keep away forever?"

He sighed.

"David, you can't honestly think God wants you to live this way."

"It's part of . . . what I am."

"I don't know what that means." Her voice was gentler now, but she wasn't going to back off. Not Tiana.

"We were human, but it's been a long time since then."

The memory of the voice was so clear, Colm might have been in the back seat, leaning forward to speak his piece. David shook his head. He wasn't Colm. He would never be Colm.

She must have taken his head shake as a

refusal to explain. She reached across the gear shift and set her hand on his arm. "You need to be in church."

"For five years? Seven? By ten, they start to notice themselves looking older."

All the things Tiana had helped him see, helped him feel again, but this was different. He'd been wrong about some things, but he wasn't wrong about this.

"They?" she whispered.

"Mortals." He didn't mean to bite the word.

"Surely five or seven years is better than nothing."

"It isn't."

"Not just to serve others. To be challenged by good teaching, to be supported and kept accountable. Everyone needs that."

She wasn't listening. She'd said she would listen. His face grew hot as he pulled his arm away from her, and Tiana put her hand on the wheel again.

"You need them. And they need you."

"That can't matter."

"It does matter."

"Not any longer."

The words were snapping between them, sharp and metallic, and someone was about to be wounded because she wouldn't leave it alone. Tiana looked from the road to him.

"You think God doesn't care that you've isolated yourself from His church? I promise you He does."

"Then you tell me how to do it."

She threw her hands up, grazing one finger along the ceiling — at a red light, thank the fates. "What does that even mean? You do church the way anyone else does church."

"Tell me how to bear it."

Words he hadn't meant to say. His eyes burned, but he would not succumb to emotion in front of her, not twice in a single week. No. He pinched hard between his eyes and ducked his head, turned his face away from her.

"David," she said. Quietly this time. Gentle again. "How to bear what?"

"The leaving."

She touched his arm. He kept his face hidden. Had to.

"Okay," she said, "I get it. But you know you're not the only person who has to move away from people. Think about military families and . . . and . . . well, anybody whose job moves around a lot. They have to start over all the time, just like you."

"I know." Ach, he wasn't after her pity or her comfort. "I know that."

Tiana drove for a while. Soon they'd be at

her place, and then this discussion could end.

Not soon enough. "This is why you're not in church. It has nothing to do with deception, not really."

"I . . . I don't know." He'd thought it had. "Perhaps what Jesus said to Peter, about John — perhaps it's true of me. Perhaps I'm to remain until He comes for all the saints."

"If John were still here, would he be isolating himself from the church?"

"I . . ." He swallowed around a hard lump, petrified tears. They would not fall today. "Perhaps I'm supposed to continue bearing it. But I can't."

She set her hand on his. "I'm not saying there's an easy fix, or you just need to toughen up and deal. Or anything like that."

He ducked his head.

"But the church is supposed to help you bear it, David. And there are burdens on them that you could be helping to bear too. And when it's time to leave, He'll carry you through the leaving."

He closed his eyes. A single tear fell. He kept his hands at his sides, let it slide down his cheek unseen.

She sighed. "I'm sorry. We're both worn out. This could have waited."

"Well, it had to be said sometime."

"It did."

Right then, she'd said it. He would mull it another time, when exhaustion didn't push emotion so close to the surface.

They both let the conversation stall as Tiana drove the last few minutes. They had to stop at her place for clothes, whether Jayde accepted his offer or not. He saw the women inside and stood at the threshold.

His mental image of Tiana's place had been near enough — bedroom, bathroom, tiny kitchen, and an open living room with a dining table in one corner. It was a spruce little place, hardwood floor and a wide window over the kitchen sink, but it was too small for two people. The women would be taking turns and stepping over each other endlessly.

Jayde set her purse on the table and turned with hands on hips. At work that was her get-it-done pose. "Are the spare sheets clean?"

"Yeah," Tiana said. "But before we start rearranging the place, you should hear David out."

One eyebrow made a fine arc as Jayde turned to him. "About what?"

His spread hands encompassed the whole apartment. "This is fine for overnight."

"But?"

424

"But would you prefer a hotel room for a few days while you get a plan together?"

She blinked. "In a perfect world, sure."

"Then I'd like to put you up at the Best Western, if you're agreeable."

Jayde crossed the living room slowly, approaching him with a wisp of suspicion he'd never seen in her before. "Why would you do that?"

He shrugged. "You need a place to stay."

"What's the catch?"

"There isn't one."

"You let me keep my job, you get my car keys back, and now you want to gift me a hotel room?"

He pulled out one of the dining table's two chairs and dropped into it. "I let you keep your job because you're excellent at it. I got your car keys back without much trouble; the man was easily backed down."

"And a hotel room in Harbor Vale is only a hundred dollars a night." Jayde bit the words. "No big deal."

"Exactly," he said.

The irritation in the lines of her face morphed into confusion.

"The fact is, I'm wealthier than the average person. Your accepting my offer wouldn't be putting me out in any way."

"And is that also why you paid us that day

425

the store was closed?" A hint of skepticism lingered in Jayde's voice.

"Again, I wasn't put out by it."

"When you say wealthier than the average person, you're understating your case."

"A bit."

"Are you a mob boss incognito or something?"

She wasn't kidding, but a chuckle escaped him. "No criminal enterprises. Money passed down, that's all. Invested well over a good deal of time."

"The bookstore doesn't make your living."

"The bookstore is a hobby."

Now she gaped at him. "That's . . ." She swung her gaze to Tiana. "This isn't news to you."

Tiana shook her head.

Jayde looked from one of them to the other, pulled her purse to her side, drew herself up straight, and faced David squarely. "I want a copy of the receipt so I can pay you back."

He would never trample her dignity by telling her it wasn't necessary. He nodded instead.

"And . . . thank you."

"It's my pleasure, Jayde."

"I think you're telling the truth," she said.

"He always does," Tiana said.

Jayde turned to her, and the drawn-up posture caved a little. "Ti, would you mind . . . it's not exactly convenient, but for tonight, it would be nice . . ."

Tiana crossed the wood floor in three strides and grabbed her in a hug that swallowed Jayde's petite frame. "I was standing here hoping you'd ask. But I didn't want to be pushy if you wanted space."

"You and your space." Jayde's laugh was the kind that put off tears.

David waited while they packed. From the bedroom they talked in hushed voices that sometimes caught with emotion. He'd thought of financial and physical needs, but that Jayde might need companionship on a night like this never entered his head. He hoped Tiana hadn't felt bulldozed by what he'd thought was help. Well, if she had, she'd say so. He smiled at that.

As he ruminated, he wandered the living room's perimeter. The walls were painted red ochre, radiating warmth. On the wall above the sofa hung a canvas oil painting, an expressionist rendering of an agave plant in arresting shades of blue that contrasted a yellow desert background. Bold strokes, bright colors. On the opposite wall, to one side of the window, hung a pale resin plaque carved with words:

My soul has grown deep like the rivers.
                              LANGSTON HUGHES

David crossed the room and traced his thumb over the lines of the letters.

Feet scuffed at the edge of the room. He looked up. Tiana stood with a gray duffel bag slung over her shoulder.

"I've not been in your home before," he said.

She smiled.

He didn't have words for how right this space was, how easily he envisioned her in it, curled on the couch reading or watching a movie. And how dear to him that image made the room. Perhaps there would be a day to say it all.

The women rode together in Jayde's car, following David to the Best Western, where he booked a room for a week. The three of them went up together to the second floor, David carrying their bags. Jayde relinquished hers with a tolerant smile and eye roll, but Tiana looked purely amused.

Less than half an hour later, warmth spread through his chest as he walked outside to his Jeep. Jayde had taken bigger steps tonight than she realized. She was safe here, and she knew it. He hoped her resolve for independence would last. He would do everything he could to help her, but from now on he'd be more careful to consider all the angles and — well, all the people.

Habit caused him to scan the lot as he unlocked the vehicle. He froze.

Moira. No one could miss her if they looked in her direction. She was lying on her back, on the roof of a car he didn't recognize, squat and dark blue. Her arms were spread out to the heavens, and her hair spilled over the roof, lifting and falling in the breeze. Her boots hung down over the windshield.

He jogged across the lot, half expecting her to be dead. A broken heart or a screaming conscience might do what age couldn't.

She lifted her head at his approach, startled, but didn't move. His pulse settled back down to normal.

"Are you drunk?" he said.

"Wouldn't that be lovely?" She let her head fall back to the car roof.

"Whose car?"

"They left it unlocked. I've decided to hot-wire it."

If she was kidding, she had a great dead-pan face. "You know how to hot-wire a car?"

"Don't you?"

"I could figure it out if I had some time to tinker. But that's not what you mean."

"I could be driving this vehicle in under a minute."

"Impressive."

She sat up, legs still dangling over the roof onto the windshield. She hunched her shoulders against the cold. "I have no idea how to hot-wire a car, David."

He laid one hand on the roof. "Good?"

"I didn't want to be a skilled liar. I tried to separate us — the real me from the lying me. I tried to think of her as Defense Moira."

"Did it work?"

Tears sprang to her eyes but didn't fall. "Too well."

He couldn't find the right thing to say.

"And that's why I have to go."

"You think they want you to? Zac and Simon?"

She drew up her knees and set her chin on them. "This is the end of us. We can never be whole again."

"You don't know that."

"Simon and I will hash it out. He'll do some shouting. He'll say I've done something unforgivable, and then he'll forgive me."

"And Zac?"

She wrapped her arms around her legs, and her tears overflowed. "Zac."

He thought to stand beside her, respect her space, but since he'd met her she had known precisely when to offer him a hug. His turn to offer one. He circled her with his arms, bent knees and all. She rested her head on his forearm, and his sleeve moistened.

"He was the closest. So I had to push him away the most often, the most . . . harshly. Finally, one day I went too far, and now he's the one keeping safe distances. And he'll keep doing it the rest of our lives, because holes in Zac . . . they just can't seem to heal. And, David, I knew that. Every time I tore into him, I knew that and I had to do it anyway."

He didn't know Zac well enough to contradict her. He didn't know how to help. He stood still and let her tears soak his sleeve.

"And it was all for nothing," she said at last. She squeezed his shoulder and sat up, stretched her legs, and slid down from the car roof.

"Can I convince you to stay?" At least that, if he could do nothing else.

"You don't need to. This is right. My going."

"It isn't."

She bent and picked up her carry-on bag, which she'd set beside a wheel. She looked

431

past David to his Jeep. "Want to tell me what you're doing at a hotel at three in the morning?"

"Assisting a friend."

A furrow formed between her eyes.

"No, someone else."

"I see. Well, you can make your tally two." She almost smiled.

"I don't think so."

A pucker of hurt crossed her face.

David set his hand on her shoulder. "That is, I don't think I've helped you."

Moira looked down at his hand, lifted her own to grasp it, and met his eyes. "Not any shortcoming of yours, I promise."

"Stay."

She did smile this time. "No, David."

She hugged him and held on a long moment, and he hugged her back, cupping her head and drawing it to his chest, feeling in the tightness of her arms around him her desperation not to be alone. A need she was running from.

"Give them a chance to forgive you," he said.

"I can't."

"Will we know where you are?"

"Maybe in a few years." Tears dampened his shirt.

"Please don't go. You're needed." And

needing.

"Oh, I'm really not. Not anymore." She gave David a last hard squeeze and then let go to look up at him. "But will they have you?"

"What do you mean?"

"You could disown all of us at this point, and no one would blame you. If my choices and Colm's are going to cost Zac and Simon a family member, I should know that."

Ach, Moira. "To add to your atonement list?"

She took a step back.

"If they want to stay in contact," he said, "I'll be here."

"Thank you." Her head bowed.

She threw her carry-on over her shoulder and jogged off toward the street. She hit the sidewalk and made a right angle and kept going. She might go anywhere. Become anyone. She might wander the world alone for a decade before she could stop hearing Colm's voice over her shoulder. He closed his eyes and prayed protection and comfort for her, that she would find the forgiveness she needed most.

His shoulders sagged. A nearby car door opened and shut, an engine started, and David trudged back to his Jeep.

He got behind the wheel and sat for a moment. Driving five miles home seemed a daunting task. He sighed and slid the key into the ignition.

"Don't."

David jolted, alert now, too late. Had he left the vehicle unlocked? He had. In the rearview mirror a man met his eyes from the back seat. Dark brown eyes, hair as black as David's, buzzed short. A nose that might have been broken once. He draped his right arm over the passenger seat, in his hand a Colt revolver.

Engraved, even the barrel. Ivory grip showing around the crook of his thumb. That gun belonged in a museum. And this kid looked barely into his twenties.

"Any movement at all, I'll shoot you in the head, and you can explain your survival to the cops. Doubt the others would get to you before some mortal did."

Twenty-Six

The tension in the vehicle was charged like the air before a thunderstorm. David set his hands on the wheel and kept eye contact in the mirror.

"Who are you?"

"A friend to Sean and Holly — or did you learn their names before you killed them?"

"I don't know what you're talking about."

"I saw you go into that park, and I saw you come out."

With a body and without a body.

"Why the saber? Did you decide thirty hours was too long?"

David's pulse rushed in his ears. Dread tingled down his arms, into his fingers. He cleared his throat, and the man's fingers tightened on the gun.

"Tell me who you are. Please, from the beginning."

"This isn't what I came for. I came to speak to Zachary Wilson, to ask — but I was right. My people didn't die natural deaths. You killed them, and you should pay for it." He didn't raise his voice, could have been recounting the plot of a movie that had put him to sleep.

David risked turning his head to see the man face-to-face. The gun hand jerked, raised to guard between them. David forced his gaze up from the dark barrel mouth. This gun, unlike the last he'd faced, was loaded. And this man would use it with both experience and inclination.

"We've not harmed you," David said. "We've believed we were the only ones."

The gun did not lower.

"How did they die, your people?"

The man stared without expression for a long moment. "Age."

"Age?"

"Shriveled skin, gray hair, old age. In a day. Dead the day after that."

The words hung in the crisp quiet. David shuddered. "How?"

"You tell me."

"I am telling you. I don't know."

Maybe they'd been found in their beds, or maybe they suffered while this man could do nothing but look on. No wonder he wanted David's blood, but they might have a common enemy somehow. Or the serum

436

did have an expiration date.

"All right," David said. "The others are here, inside, which you must know if you've been watching us. Come and let's sort this out."

"A private room, three against one. Not a chance."

He'd seen Moira leave. He'd let her. A good indication he wasn't after immediate bloody retribution.

"Neutral ground, then," David said. "The lobby. Even at this hour, someone will be behind a desk. A witness."

The man sat a long moment, studying David. He motioned with the gun. "Get out."

David obeyed and he followed, the revolver lowered to his side. He nodded David toward the hotel entrance and froze. David followed his gaze to . . .

Zac. Less than fifty feet away, trudging over the sidewalk to the right of the entrance, up and down in front of the same few rooms. No anxious energy or controlled agility in his motion, only a doggedness probably bred from insomnia.

Zac looked up. Tilted his head toward David, questions tugging his mouth, weary and washed-out under the hotel's security flood-lights.

David shook his head, but Zac approached anyway.

"Zachary Wilson," the man said and raised the gun.

Zac stood still. Didn't speak. Probably experiencing déjà vu worse than David's.

The man turned to David while keeping the gun on Zac. "I'm going. Come after my people, and I'll expose yours. Those are my terms."

"You said you had something to ask of Zac. You found us because of him."

He nodded.

The shift in the wind, the plunge to the earth. Zac's misplaced foot had kicked so many dominoes.

"Ask it, then," David said.

"Not now." He stepped back, the gun still pointed at Zac.

He wouldn't fire it out here. That Colt would echo off the buildings like a cannon. David matched him step for step, hands still raised, not allowing the man to widen the distance.

"Don't come after me," he said.

"You need to listen. We're no threat to you."

"I could shoot him. But you'll chase me anyway."

To get answers, to solve this puzzle, to

prevent danger to all of them — aye, he would pursue him.

"Yeah," the man said as if David had spoken. He pivoted, knees bending, and didn't seem to aim before he pulled the trigger.

The boom of the shot hit David at the same time something punched him in the head. He was flat on his back, blacktop under him and black sky above, ears ringing, the stars pushing closer to his face then receding. He blinked. He tried to think. Fire licked a line along the right side of his skull. Zac was cursing.

Blue eyes and a frown blocked the stars. "Get up."

"Go," David said. He tried to get an elbow under him and flopped back to the asphalt. "Get him."

Zac grabbed him under both arms and hauled him upright, and the world pitched and spun. David's stomach turned. He swallowed hard as Zac threw one of his arms across his shoulders and tried to run toward the ground-level rooms he'd been pacing in front of. David's feet tangled.

"Zac, you have to get him."

Zac growled invectives as he fished his room key from his jeans pocket and waved it in front of the door lock. The light changed from red to green, both too bright for David's throbbing head. Or maybe that was the floodlight. Or maybe that was the bullet graze.

Zac pushed the door open and hauled David inside and dumped him onto the bed. He turned the dead bolt and rushed to the bathroom, came back with a white towel and shoved it at David.

"Here."

David pressed the terry cloth to the gash in his head and squinted as the throb spread through his skull. He drew a breath that sounded weak and ragged. "We have to get him."

"He's probably lying in wait to put one in my gut."

"We have to —"

"If he's still out there, he's setting an ambush in case I follow. Otherwise he's long gone."

They had to get him. David breathed again, but the room wasn't righting itself. Concession: he wasn't going after anyone. But Zac could. "Go —"

"David, seriously. Shut up."

Three sharp knocks came at the door. Zac peered through the blinds, keeping his body to one side of the window, then flipped the latch and opened the door. Simon strode in, clad in sweatpants and T-shirt, and shut it.

"Did you hear — ?" He scowled either at David or at the bloodstained towel.

"Ah, where to start." Zac motioned to David. "Some guy with a Billy-the-Kid gun . . . David, he had a message? For me?"

David blinked the stars away. His head hurt; did that count as a message?

"He's been shot?" Simon strode farther into the room.

"Grazed." Zac moved into David's vision and pulled the towel away from the wound. "Ouch. Not deep, though."

Think. Focus. The room remained fuzzy but stopped spinning. Another deep breath, and he could assess the damage. *Ouch* summed it up fairly well.

"He's part of a group; he didn't say how many."

"A gang of gun-wielding outlaws?" Zac leaned one hip against the wall.

"He didn't specify."

"They never do."

"Well, don't explain anything," Simon said. "Stand there yammering nonsense instead."

David closed his eyes, and focusing came more easily. "He's like us."

"What?" Zac seemed to shout the word,

but that was probably just David's head aching.

"His group — they're all like us. But two have died — recently, I guess. He came here to confirm Zac's status as one of them, and I'm guessing do a bit of recon. He knows about Colm — that is, he knows we killed him — and if he thinks we're threatening his people, he'll expose us to the authorities."

A shudder ran over the room.

"Did you happen to mention he's wrong about us?" Simon said.

"He didn't believe me." David opened his eyes and gestured to his head. "Obviously."

"Anyway, he might not be wrong." Zac's words were quiet.

"What . . . ?" Simon shuffled to the closest bed and sank onto it. "Colm?"

"Well, among us, he's the best suspect."

"He considered us superior. If he came across others, he'd embrace them as equals."

"Do we know that? Do we know anything about him really?"

"Something's not right, though," David said. "These others died of old age. How could Colm do that?"

Simon dropped back onto the mattress to stare at the ceiling. "Whether he did it or not, this guy's out there thinking we're

442

responsible for the deaths of his friends."

"I told Zac not to let him go."

That brought Zac's gaze from a bare corner of the room back to them. "I decided letting the hotel staff find you dazed on the ground was more of a risk."

Simon peeked through the closed blinds. "Nobody out there. No cops, no gawkers."

David's hand was warming as the gash bled through the towel. Head wounds. Inconvenient. He tried to think what else needed saying as spots edged into his vision. Simon went into the bathroom and returned with a clean towel, which he pressed against the saturated one.

"Any shock?"

David blinked. "Ah."

"Yeah." He marched back to his room and this time emerged with a red plastic sewing kit. "Suture thread in here."

Another blink.

"Comes from a hundred years of patching each other up. Be prepared for the other guy too, not just yourself."

A new way of thought, and not a bad way.

"Usually it's Zac, of course. Tempting the serum. Falling off things."

"I don't fall off things. As a rule."

"He thought he could walk across this open barn joist one time —"

"One time, sixty years ago."

Any other night, Simon might have continued the tale. Zac might have continued the swagger and the protest. But the comfort of an old story seemed to rub both of them like splintered wood over the palm of a hand. Perhaps Colm had been there that day. Zac crossed to the window and peered out the blinds. On rubber legs, David followed Simon to the bathroom.

David stripped off his shirt, though blood already soaked the crew collar, and knelt in the bathtub. Blood dripped steadily from his head. Simon sat on the tub's edge, threaded a hooked needle, and drew from his kit a squeeze bottle with a fine tip. Wound irrigation. The final item was a razor.

"I'll keep my hair, thank you," David said.

"Only around the —"

"If you can't do it invisibly, then don't do it."

"You're so vain?"

David's mouth twitched despite the shiver that took hold of him. "I don't want questions from customers, and I have a store to run come Monday."

"I leave it like this, you'll keep bleeding."

He huffed. Why couldn't the serum kick in now? "Indolent little beasties."

"We are a spoiled lot."

The next few minutes made David's eyes water as Simon cleaned and stitched. The topical anesthetic couldn't touch the ache that filled his head. When the work was finished, his legs were like a newborn foal's. Simon kept his hand under David's arm as they moved back to Zac's room, and David sat on the edge of the bed.

"I have Tylenol. Be right back." Simon closed his med kit and took it with him.

Zac was rummaging through his carry-on. In moments he came out with a Snickers bar, Starburst and Jolly Ranchers in varying flavors, and a fun-sized packet of original M&M's.

"Here." He thrust his brimming cupped hands toward David. "Blood sugar boost."

David took the M&M's and managed to pull the bag open.

"Far cry from homemade hot chocolate." Zac tossed the rest onto the bed.

"Thank you."

"Yep."

"We need a plan of action," David said as he munched from the bag. "I don't see how we'll track him, but we've got to try."

Simon came back with two white tablets.

"David wants to track the gunfighter," Zac said as David swallowed the pills dry.

"All the handicaps are ours," Simon said.

"He knows us; he can find us."

"Maybe he will again." Zac perched on the other bed and drew up his legs to sit cross-legged, hands on knees. "And be ready to hear us out next time."

Or to start a war.

Simon frowned. "Should we wake Moira? Seems she should be part of this conversation."

The adrenaline of the last few minutes ebbed as the earlier pieces of this night flooded in. Not only her shoes slapping the concrete as she ran. All of it. Jayde and that miscreant boyfriend. The sound of shovels on dirt, of steel brandished to end a life. He had never lived a longer night than this one. He was sure of that now. He lifted his head as Simon's hand found the door handle.

"Moira is gone."

Neither Zac nor Simon's face showed surprise. Neither asked why she'd left. They sat in silence, absorbing, accepting.

"I tried to dissuade her," David said.

"No one could have," Simon said.

"We ought to bring her back. She ought not be alone, and . . ." And if the things she believed about each of them were true, then Simon at least should agree with David.

But he was shaking his head. "She would see it as a cage."

446

"Not this time." Not the Moira who had cried on his shirt, who had hugged him goodbye. They knew her better, but they might be too raw tonight to understand her.

Simon sighed. "You won't find her until she wants you to. Believe me."

Zac was quiet. After a minute he reached over and took an M&M from the half-empty bag.

TWENTY-SEVEN

What David hoped to accomplish today wasn't something to be done over the phone. Then again, as long as it had been since Blaire Famosa laid eyes on him, maybe a phone call would have come across better. She might think he was here in person to make a *no* more difficult. A thought that hadn't occurred to him until he was a mile away from Blaire's Blooming Books.

He parallel parked a few cars down from her storefront. The place was blooming indeed today thanks to an announcement written on red poster board in the window, in a calligraphy hand that could have been a computer font.

FIRE SALE! MARKED PAPERBACKS $.50! MARKED HARDCOVERS $1.00!

He could hardly have chosen a worse day to show up unannounced. He grimaced as he fed the parking meter, half due to timing and half to the lingering throb along the side of his head. The night's sleep had not convinced his body to heal itself — an absurd thought, as if the serum were aware, but its selective process did make him wonder. He held the door for a family with a stroller, exchanged smiles and nods, and stood in the vestibule.

The building's units were deeper than they appeared from the street, and Blaire had made the sunlit front quarter a reading area furnished with rugs braided in colors of the earth, a burnt-orange leather sofa, brick-red chairs, and a fancy coffee machine. Tiana would like the bold color scheme — a new piece of knowledge David savored.

Warmth seeped from every corner of the store, but today David's eyes strayed from enjoyment of the atmosphere to search for the owner. Ah, behind the counter. That could be a good sign for him.

He waited about ten minutes for a lull in customers coming and going. He made himself a coffee, adding a liberal dose of French vanilla creamer and ignoring the sugar. Only bad coffee needed sugar. He stirred it, took a corner seat, and sipped. Blaire knew mediocre coffee was a worse offering to one's patrons than no coffee. He smiled while he watched her in her element, eyes shining, abundant black hair pulled into a high ponytail that bobbed with every move of her head. Her bright blue graphic tee read NEVER ENOUGH BOOKS. David's lips turned up. Blaire could have been a practicing paralegal to this day, wearing skirts and jackets to work instead, but at thirty she'd chased a dream, and eleven years later here she was.

She and Jayde had much to bond them, if only he wasn't too late.

When the last customer of the moment filed out the door, Blaire finally looked farther than five feet in front of her, and their eyes met.

A slow smile lit her face. "David Galloway."

He stood as she stepped out from behind the counter. "Blaire Famosa."

"So great to see you." She shook his hand and then clasped it between hers, and the smile grew. "It's been at least a year, hasn't it?"

"At least." He toasted her with his paper cup. "Good coffee."

She gave a low laugh, a husky sound he'd forgotten. "I'm sure you didn't drive two hours south for my coffee."

"I should have planned better. You might

not have time for conversation today."

Proving it, another group bustled into the store, college kids with wrapped pastries from the bakery next door.

"I can see the counter from here," Blaire said. She didn't sit, but neither did she look put out by his presence, and she didn't believe in dissembling. "How have you been, David? I mean, I know your store's doing well up there, but how are you?"

"I'm well," he said, and yes, it was true, though the last month had wrung him out in almost every way possible. "You?"

Her smile faltered. "We said goodbye to Dad a few months ago. That wasn't easy."

The words stilled his breath a moment. Only once he'd met Blaire's father, in this very place, but the man had been forthright and distinguished, virtues reflected in his daughter. David could still feel the leathery grasp of the man's hand and the gentle warmth of his smile as his cataract-whitened eyes looked past everyone in the store.

"So you're Blaire's competition in the book-selling business."

"An illness?" David's own voice brought him back to the present, hushed.

"Unexpected," Blaire said. "Just a kidney infection. We thought he'd be home from the hospital in a few days."

"I'm sorry."

He should have known before now. He'd withdrawn more completely than he'd realized, adding bricks and mortar to the defenses inside, fearing to hurt again while those around him, closer to their graves with every breath, continued to hurt. *Lord, forgive me.*

"Thank you," Blaire said. She studied him a moment, maybe curious about the depth of his reaction. "Four months later, it's still hard, but I'm doing well otherwise. Dad would be proud of how well the store's done recently."

David nodded. "He would."

"So is this more than just an idle visit? You weren't in the area?"

"I wasn't."

"You've made me curious."

She was drawn away as several customers came to the counter at once — always the way of it — but she returned to him as soon as she was able.

"First," David said, "it looks as if you've not replaced your assistant yet."

"I did."

He exhaled hard and hoped she didn't notice. His plan wasn't going to work?

"Twice. Let both of them go. The first couldn't do simple math, including drive time. Was late by at least ten minutes every single day. The second was stealing books from me. Had access to the till but ignored the cash and smuggled out antique books instead, either for the thrill of the crime or because she thought the cash would be missed faster. She was wrong about that."

David gave her a slow nod. "I see."

"Are you scheming something?"

"I'm no schemer, Blaire."

She gave a laugh. "I guess not. Well, come out with it already."

"I have an assistant for you."

"Oh?" Her eyebrows lifted with a hint of hope.

"She's going to school in Mt. Pleasant and working for me in Harbor Vale."

"Wow. That's dedication — either to you or the school or both."

He left Chris out of it, of course, only told Blaire about Jayde's geographical challenge and her need for permanent housing. The woman's sharp eyes pinned him halfway through a story with obvious gaps, but she didn't pry.

"If you're vouching for her, that's good enough for me," Blaire said when he finished. "She could start immediately?"

He sighed. He'd miss Jayde's work ethic. "You're fifty miles closer to her school. It makes more sense for her to work for you."

"And I might have an apartment for her too."

"Indeed?"

She cocked an eyebrow at him the way she always had when a less-than-current word slipped out of his mouth. Ah, more than a professional contact, Blaire was. A friend, one he'd missed without knowing it. A smile tugged his mouth.

"It's an over-the-garage apartment, owned by the mother of a friend of mine. She's still competent to live alone, but her kids are concerned. What if she falls . . . you know. The board would be free, and Jayde would have no caretaker duties as such, but she'd be living with an elderly woman."

"I'll ask her about it," he said.

"Have you talked to her about my hiring her?"

He shrugged. "I figured that was pointless if you'd already hired someone else."

"Well, I'll interview her, as much for her sake as mine. She might decide I'd be an intolerable boss."

David laughed. "Unlikely."

They talked another twenty minutes and were interrupted by customers three times. At that point, David said he'd let her get back to her fire sale. He tossed his empty cup in the trash and turned to find Blaire still standing there, watching him. He held his hand out to her.

"Blaire. It was good to see you."

She shook his hand. "Maybe we could stay in touch this time."

"I'll do better at that."

"I hope so." She squeezed his hand and let go. "I'll wait to hear from Jayde."

"Thank you."

"If she works out, I'll owe you a dozen favors."

David went out to his Jeep and pulled away from the curb, and something loosened in his chest that he hadn't known was coiled tight. It was only one step, contacting Blaire. Only one more step to act on Jayde's behalf. Yet each felt as though he'd triumphed over himself. The enormity of such small actions proved how far he still had to go.

"I'll do it." The brogue cloaked his words, now that he was alone. "Father, in Your kindness, teach me how to be part of them again."

David merged onto the highway and headed home for more sleep.

Twenty-Eight

Tiana was on break when police officer Jacob Greene and his wee girls came into the store Monday afternoon. The girls scampered off to the children's section the moment their father gave them permission to leave his side, but per his custom, Jacob lingered at the front for small talk. At the moment no one needed ringing up. David stepped from behind the counter, and they stood at an angle that allowed both of them to face the doors and make glancing eye contact when the conversation called for it. Habits of vigilance: no getting rid of them.

"I saw the news, the body found behind Appleseed," David said.

Jacob nodded.

"I don't suppose you can tell me much."

"Not much."

"Is there anything at all to go on? I'm not asking what that might be — only, is the perpetrator likely to be caught?"

"Keep your eyes open. Make sure your employees are careful when they leave after dark."

Answer enough. They didn't know anything. Well, what could they know with the killer buried in the park preserve? If Colm had left fingerprints, they might match a cold case from fifty years ago, but that would only baffle the investigators more. The only danger in this scenario seemed to be the unknown gunman who may or may not want vengeance on them all.

Jacob sighed. "Honestly, David, sometimes we never know why a man is killed. In a town like this, a tourist like the victim, it should be obvious. A confrontation on the street, an idiot mugger that went too far, something. Or if death came with him, we should be able to trace it back to where he came from."

"But sometimes you can't," David said.

"Sometimes we can't."

"It's got to be frustrating."

"Yeah." Jacob ran his hand over his crew cut. "There's a celebrity-of-the-minute in town, a professional daredevil by the name of Zachary Wilson, and this is an odd place for him to turn up. We looked for a connection, but not even that gave us anything."

A finger of caution touched David's spine

between his shoulders. "Well, I can put that one to rest for you, anyway. Zac's a friend."

"Visiting you?"

"I think he wanted to sightsee the Great Lakes, but he's stuck around to catch up."

"Good to know."

"As far as the rest of it goes, I'll watch out for anything unsettling."

"I'd appreciate it. Sometimes an alert civilian is exactly what we need."

They continued to chat until Jacob's girls came to the front with armloads, and he gave a mock groan.

"Please, Daddy? All these." The youngest hefted her stack of five picture books.

"You wouldn't make us put *books* back, would you, Dad?" The older girl, about nine, grinned as she showed him and David her finds — *The Sign of the Beaver, The Black Stallion Mystery,* a few Nancy Drew books, a beaten copy of *Misty of Chincoteague* with the original cover illustration by Wesley Dennis, and the hardcover edition of *The Red Pony.* Also illustrated by Wesley Dennis, looking innocuous in its slipcase. No reason Tiana would not have shelved it in the children's section, given the back cover called it the children's edition. "Ah, Dad . . ."

David waited for Jacob's eye contact.

"Have you read much Steinbeck?"

Jacob's mouth twitched. "I shut off the *Grapes of Wrath* movie. Was bored."

"Well . . ." David motioned to the book at the top of the girl's stack.

"But I had to read *Of Mice and Men* in high school," Jacob said, picking up *The Red Pony.* "I guess this is just as bleak?"

"A young horse-loving reader will end up with a nightmare or two."

"I've read almost all the books by Marguerite Henry," the girl said. "And Black Gold dies. So does the Godolphin Arabian, but not until he's lived a full life."

"Elise." Jacob set the book behind the counter on a discard stack. "I trust Mr. Galloway's judgment where books are concerned. He's read more books than I have."

Elise, that was her name. She'd been in David's store dozens of times. He had to start paying attention to people again.

"Just tell me, does the red pony die?" Elise shifted the weight of the books in her arms.

"Do you really want me to tell you?" David said.

She nodded hard. "Please."

"He does."

"Is it a true story?" Her eyes were wide, unblinking, waiting for the knowledge that no one in the room could grant her but David.

"It's not."

"Then why would the writer kill the horse? If he didn't have to?"

"That's a fair question, Elise. Why do you think?"

Her lips pursed. She looked down at the cover of *Misty* then back up at David. "I'm not sure. I have to think about it."

Warmth filled his chest. He gave her a firm nod. "An excellent answer. If you have ideas, let me know next time you come."

"Okay."

The rest of the books were purchased in short order. Jacob parted ways with a nod and a half smile. Two high cries of "Thanks, Mr. Galloway!" accompanied them out of the store.

He turned at the sense of a presence behind him. Not a customer — Tiana. Her smile was broader than the circumstance called for.

"What?" he said.

"You're not a bad teacher, Mr. Galloway."

He chuckled.

She crossed the wood floor of the vestibule, and by the time she reached him, her smile had fallen away. She studied his face, and whatever she found there brought the

460

smile back, but it was a softer version.

"There's possibility in your eyes now. When you look at me."

A month ago — a week ago — there'd been none, he knew. He tried to speak around the tightness in his throat.

"It's been a terrible week," she said. "But I'm grateful for this piece of it."

"Tiana, I . . ."

Her face crinkled. To be the cause of that confusion, possibly hurt . . . a knot formed in his stomach. But he had to be as honest as she'd told Jayde he was.

"I'm . . ." He took her hand, and when she gave it a squeeze, he could go on. "You're right, it's there. The new . . . thing, between us."

"But?" she whispered.

She already knew. He held her gaze. He would tell her in the words he'd avoided, when they talked of this before. "But I'm going to foul it up. Not because you aren't worth it, but because . . ."

Speak the words. Aye, all right.

"It's a fearsome thing." He cleared his throat. "No, I'll say it out. It makes me afraid."

"Do you mean the idea that we . . . someday?"

"Not someday. Not an idea. The thing

461

that's already" — he thumped his fist on his chest — "here. For you."

"Thing, huh?" Her smile was gentle.

"The . . . possibility. Your word is a good one."

"It's okay, David."

"I want it to be, only —"

"I don't mean you don't have to be scared. I mean it's okay that you're scared. You have every right to be."

He closed his eyes. She saw so much.

"Are you ready to try anyway?" she said quietly.

Am I? There was only one answer he wanted to give. "I'm ready."

He bent his head, and Tiana tipped hers up. Their lips met, sweet and slow. Her palm was soft on the two-day stubble of his cheek. As David deepened the kiss, her quiet sound of satisfaction stirred embers into fire. He drew back.

"Tiana." His voice was rough.

He wanted to sweep her into his arms, feel the curves of her body against him. Women were works of art, every one of them, but especially the woman standing in front of him now with her hand curved in the crook between his neck and shoulder and her cheek pressed to his chest, practically inviting him to carry her to the break room, demonstrate how thorough a kiss could be, and then . . .

He stepped back and walked around to stand behind the counter. Tiana's brow furrowed, and he put up a hand as she moved to follow him.

"A customer could walk in," he said.

"Let's hope not." She gave him a crooked smile that fed the heat between them.

"No, love," he said. "We ought to hope we're flooded with a dozen customers, immediately."

Reluctant caution surfaced in her eyes. "You're right."

They stood with the counter and uncertainty between them until he spread his hands on the laminate surface and cleared his throat.

"Tiana, I . . ."

John Russell had been loved at least once, perhaps twice. But he'd taken this new name to help him build new walls. David Galloway was never supposed to be loved.

Her mouth turned down at his pause. Such vulnerability in her eyes.

"I don't want to wrong you. Or cause you hurt."

The bell above the door jangled, making both of them jolt. A man walked in, nodded to them, and meandered back to the books.

"All I'm asking is that you don't give up," she said. "We're going to hurt each other. But we're going to keep trying. Okay?"

David nodded, his heart brimming over with more than he could say.

Love? Will You truly give me love again? A bird long asleep in his soul opened its eyes and gave a quiet trill. Perhaps in time, it could relearn to sing.

TWENTY-NINE

This time, when he walked out to his Jeep, his instincts weren't blunted by two nearly sleepless nights. He lifted his hand in a *good night* to Tiana, didn't move until her car had disappeared down the street.

He wasn't unarmed tonight, not after being shot in the head, but maybe he wouldn't need to defend himself. He got into his vehicle without being ambushed by a gunslinger or anyone else.

He sat for a moment with the phone in his hand. He didn't need help exactly, but perhaps he did need another perspective.

He scrolled through his contacts, his thumb freezing for a moment when it ran over Colm's name, and selected his two recipients for a new group text. Then he sent it: WE NEED TO TALK. CONFERENCE CALL?

Simon responded a minute later. NOW? PLEASE.

Nothing came from either of them for nearly ten minutes, long enough for David to reach home. He was unlocking the door when his phone pinged in his pocket. This time Simon's text came only to him.

ANYTHING FROM ZAC?

No, David texted back.

Almost immediately a call lit his phone.

"Hey," David said.

"He's not going to respond."

"Or he didn't see the messages yet."

"Or that. But he's . . . look, it's just a hunch. But I've known him since before there were automobiles, so it's a strong hunch. Anyway, I take it this is about our fellow longevite."

"It is."

"And you have thoughts?"

"Mostly I have concern. We need to find him. Where are you now?"

"Home."

"Florida?"

His grunt must be an affirmative. "Look, we don't even know the man's name."

"No, but I think he drove here, which narrows the search radius considerably."

"Hmm."

While Simon mulled, David settled into the stuffed chair in the library and ran the tips of his fingers over the hair that covered the stitches.

"He wouldn't have gotten that gun through TSA," Simon said at last. "Even checked luggage, if he was crossing state lines. And with ammo — forget it."

"Exactly."

"And if there are others, if he's acted in their stead . . ." Simon huffed. "There can't be many of them. Look how few we are."

"But we need to know." David stared across the room at the stately rows of books on their shelves. "How many and how they came to be."

"And what they mean to do about us."

"I thought perhaps with your background . . ."

"I'd need something to go on, David. Anything. A name, a city, a trail of some kind."

"What about the gun?"

Another moment of quiet and then Simon said, "It's an artifact. Anyway, you glimpsed it for a few seconds while under duress."

"If I saw it again, I'd recognize it. And it might have a history."

"You mean registered?"

"I mean historical."

"Not sure how that would help us."

Silence wrapped around David as a path failed to emerge from their words. Wasn't he supposed to do something about this? Identify the man, pursue him, deal with whatever threat he presented?

Only show me the path, Lord, and I'll step forward.

"I don't think we'll encounter him again unless he initiates it," Simon said.

"You could be right."

"You saying you want to be included if I come up with something?"

"Who called whom here?"

Simon huffed. "Right. Well . . . I'll keep you looped in, then."

"Thank you."

"If we get a lead on him — yeah, I was a cop, but my colleagues and contacts are retired or dead now. And it's not as if I could go to them wearing a face that hasn't changed in fifty years. Fifty? Forty?" Simon grunted. "It blurs sometimes."

"It does," David said.

The quiet now held a weight that had been missing before. Perhaps because Simon had been veiling it. David stretched his legs in front of him and settled back in the chair. Perhaps this conversation was the path God had set before him. For tonight, anyway.

468

THIRTY

He sat in his Jeep in the parking lot for ten minutes before finding the courage to get out. By then it was 5:55 p.m., and he had five minutes before church started. He marched up the walkway like a soldier to a drill, steps crisp, arms snapped to his sides, eyes trained ahead of him, shoulders back. It was the only way he'd make it through the door.

The L-shaped information desk was manned by a woman about fifty years old. Five stacks of paper lined the desk in front of her, and more brochures were spread to the side. Programs, opportunities, ways to invest one's time and talents in other people. David's feet slowed.

I can't. A sudden image of himself — dragged by the collar, kicking and flailing, and the hand dragging him was God's.

Not right. But the feeling didn't ebb. He stopped ten feet from the desk and shut his eyes one quick second.

Aye, Lord, it's been forty-three years. You see I've come back home tonight.

"Good evening," the woman said with a smile. "Can I help you find a class?"

"First I'll have to pick one, I suppose." The voice that came out was American and calm. Pleasant, even.

"Are you visiting?"

He nodded.

"Our fall electives are in progress, but you're welcome to jump into any one of them." She chose a sheet of paper and nudged it across the desk to him. "You can read over the options, and I'll direct you to the right room."

"Thank you."

"Sure thing."

No one else came to the desk while he scanned each choice. He glanced up once to find the woman studiously not watching him and had to smile.

"Where's Romans?" he said. Good topic to measure the church's teaching, though its status as Tiana's home church was the surest recommendation he could ask for.

He was directed down a hallway, made a right, and found room 441 down another hallway. Fewer than twenty people sat at the round tables fringed with folding chairs. His breath constricted. Too few of them to blend in. He took a seat at the back of the room.

His phone buzzed against his thigh. He pulled it out as a few more people filtered in and sat, one or two at his table, offering him a smile or a nod.

A text from Tiana. COFFEE DATE?

He texted her back. I'M AT CHURCH.

WHICH?

YOURS.

I DON'T USUALLY GO WEDNESDAYS, BUT I WOULD HAVE.

Would have been natural to ask her. He tapped his finger on his knee, choosing words, before replying. I DON'T KNOW IF THIS MAKES SENSE, BUT IT HAS TO BE ME AND GOD TONIGHT.

The man to David's left turned from another conversation to half squint at David. "You're visiting?"

David nodded.

He thrust out a long-boned artist's hand and shook David's. "Larry Scott." He motioned to the woman beside him, blond and glowing, heavily pregnant. "My wife, Karen."

"David Galloway."

"Good to have you. Hey, everybody, meet David."

Waves, grins, nods, and a few hellos. From

there the class came to order and began taking prayer requests as David's phone buzzed. He glanced down. Tiana again.

I'M PRAYING FOR YOU. AND I'M PROUD OF YOU. Followed by a blue heart.

He swallowed hard against the lump in his throat.

The prayer requests continued, human banalities and crises and triumphs. A man had twisted his ankle running a 5K. A young woman had last week lost her third baby to miscarriage. An older woman had been present when a long-prayed-for uncle professed himself a new follower of Christ. There was laughter at the story of a child's lost tooth. Tears at the story of a niece enslaved by drug addiction and prostitution. Elements of each one's story, individual notes in a divinely composed sonata.

Their lives were sacred. So would be their deaths.

Colm, the evil in what you did. They were not yours to take.

David listened to them, watched them kid and comfort one another. Friendship. Filling the room like a fragrance.

His chest stayed tight the full hour and a half. The teacher, a rail-thin and bespectacled man around forty years old, elucidated the text with skill and then served as a facilitator. Various people commented and asked questions.

Not until the group was filing out of the room in twos and threes did David's shoulders relax. He looked down at his hands in his lap. They were clenching.

A few people greeted him on their way out. He stood and mingled a bit, told them he lived in the area and was searching for a church, and every last one of them said they hoped to see him again. The sincerity soaked into him, but in a few minutes, he had to retreat. Too many people.

So he had a bit of reacclimating to do. An expected result of four decades of abstaining from human relationships.

The hall held only people coming and going, no one lingering. David took a moment to stand in the relative quiet, back to the wall, and roll tension from his shoulders and neck. Larry and Karen Scott were two of the last to exit the room.

"Oh, hey, David." Larry shook his hand again. "Will we see you next week?"

Everyone else had worded it as a hope, not a question. "Possibly."

"I'll take that." Larry grinned.

"What did you think of Al's teaching?" Karen said.

Not a typical question for a visitor. For all

they knew, David would take the opportunity to criticize. But they seemed curious. Open.

"He's knowledgeable," David said, "and skilled at drawing people into the study."

"Feel free to chime in next time," Larry said. "You only said two words, and they were your name."

Karen nudged him with her elbow, not attempting to be subtle.

Larry chuckled, but his face reddened. "Not that there's anything wrong with listening."

"That's where I prefer to start," David said.

They made small talk another minute, looked ready to move away, but Karen turned back. "David, you know Christ, don't you?"

It wasn't a question but a confirmation. "I do."

"I hope you won't see this as prying, but I'd like to pray for you."

Larry's expression sobered, and he seemed to measure David more carefully based on his wife's words.

Casual. Surface. Keep it there. *Lord, when I asked for help, I didn't mean . . .*

"If you like," he said. Surely she meant later.

But Karen and Larry motioned David to the corner near a fire exit door. He went with them and stood with his back to the corner. Prayer with Tiana was one thing. Strangers, something else altogether. A wall inside him quaked. He had meant to take this one step at a time.

He cooled his expression, drew his shoulders back, posting his KEEP OUT signs. But Karen put her hand on David's left shoulder, and Larry planted his on David's right, as if David had no signs, no walls. When they bowed their heads, he did the same.

"Dear Father," Karen said, "thank You for bringing David to church tonight. Please be his comfort and his peace, and please brighten his path as he seeks to honor You. And I pray You'll bring him back for more fellowship next week. In Jesus' name, amen."

Her words were arrows and ointment in equal measure. He lifted his head, and Larry dropped his hand to his side, but Karen kept hers on David.

"How did you . . . ?" David's voice came out hoarse.

"You seem like you could use some peace," Karen said. "That's all. And everyone can use some fellowship."

His KEEP OUT signs were falling to the

ground. Cracks formed in the walls, but he needed those signs, needed those walls.

"Is there anything specific we can pray for you this week?"

So many things, if he could but share them. If he didn't have to pretend to be so young.

"Thank you, but that will suffice."

Karen smiled, not the least put off. "Okay."

"Maybe we'll see you next week," Larry said.

They turned to go, but when David cleared his throat, they turned back.

"If you . . ." *Finish the sentence, you bumbler.* "If you want to pray for me in those terms again, I would appreciate it."

A deeper glow suffused Karen's cheeks as her smile grew. "There's plenty more where that came from."

They left David standing in the corner, where he remained until the hallway emptied, despite a few long glances in his direction. Then he shadowed the waves of departing people, keeping a few feet behind them until they passed the church sanctuary. There he stopped.

He faced the broad oak doors, shut now. He listened for choir practice or any other sound behind them, but there was only silence. He looked one way then another, tugged open one of the doors, and slipped inside.

He was alone. The lights were set low. Burgundy carpet, oak and red-upholstered pews, the aisle sloping down to the front platform and the orchestra pit. Ah, glory, an orchestra at morning worship. To the far right of the stage sat a grand piano — cover closed, shiny and black and beckoning him as the blank canvas beckoned the painter.

David strode down the center aisle, veered right, and stood beside the piano. He rested his hand on its cool side, stroked the length of its curve. He walked all the way around it, scanned the auditorium again, but no one had entered after him. He slid onto the wood bench and looked down at the keys, hands resting at his sides. His first piano had been a simple upright, the keys real ivory. He lifted his hands and poised them, lowered them, with his right thumb played the G two octaves above middle C, then with his left the F two octaves below it. The instrument was tuned perfectly.

Forty-three years since he'd entered God's house, and forty-three years since he'd touched a piano. He flexed his fingers. He stumbled on his first run over the B minor scale. He didn't stumble on his second.

Muscle memory — young muscles, young memory, forever. He might be the only musician alive for whom playing his instrument was like riding a bike.

He played a quiet trilling arrangement of "Loch Lomond" while tears rolled down his face. He wiped them away, composed himself, and began again, and the music poured out of him. Hymns. Concertos. Modern praise choruses. Classic rock ballads. Melodies gushed out of him, each one so strong he couldn't stop or pause as he blended Chopin into Scott Joplin into Elton John. He played and played and played. His soul bathed in song, sipped it like wine, gulped it like water.

The fervor of his fingers became a conscious thing again as he was picking out a soft jazz arrangement of "You Are My Hiding Place." He faded it to pianissimo and stilled his hands on a minor chord that left the melody open. He looked out across the pews.

No longer alone. The lights from the stage obscured the woman's face. David stood up, stepped away from the bench.

"My apologies. I . . ." His face grew hot. He had no right to this instrument. He strode up the aisle to her. "I didn't mean to disturb anyone."

It was Karen Scott.

"I'm sorry," he said. "I'll go."

"Wait. Please." She stood and stepped into the aisle to look up at him. "Larry's waiting for me in the café. I told him I wouldn't leave until you finished playing."

"What time is it?"

"Nine forty."

Church had ended more than two hours ago. David shook his head. "I — I had no idea. I'm sorry."

"Please stop apologizing, David. I've been playing here for the last six years. I was raised in this church and taught by our old pianist, who toured professionally, and I collect solo piano music, and . . ." She shook her head. "It's not your technique — I mean, don't get me wrong, your technique is like nothing I've ever heard before. You just played classical and ragtime and jazz and — and I don't know how many other styles — all equally well."

"I've been playing a long time."

"All your life, I would think."

"Essentially, yes."

"But it's not that. It's the spirit of the songs. It's like . . . like every song is a person, and you're introducing us to him or her, personalities and moods. . . ." She passed her hand over her belly as tears filled her eyes. "Sorry. Hormones. But saying you have a gift is not saying enough."

He ought to respond. Thank her, at least. But the music was still there between them, notes he hadn't thought anyone else was hearing, some of them raw and open. Had she heard that? He looked down at the carpet. All this was too much for one night.

"I'm so glad you snuck in here," Karen said. "And that I was walking by."

He tried to nod, but he wasn't glad. He didn't know what he was.

"They've been looking for a replacement for me. I'm stepping down when the baby comes, at least for a year. If you decide to make us your church, maybe pray about it, see if it fits into your life right now."

"All right." No other polite reply.

"Anyway, Larry's texted me twice. I told him to stuff it, but I should go now."

To this, he could nod.

Her hand settled on his shoulder. "And I want you to know I'm going to pray hard for you this week."

"Thank you."

A squeeze of his shoulder before her hand withdrew. "Good night."

"Good night."

She trundled out into the hall, and David followed her. Larry was sitting on one of the stools at the coffee bar, chatting with a man David hadn't seen in their class. Karen turned to wave as she headed over to them.

David stood alone in the vestibule, turned a full circle. A few voices drifted from down another hall, likely the direction of the offices. Maybe Karen had been the only one privy to his concert.

He sank down on a sofa along the wall near the front doors. Bowed his head. Sat that way a long time while the music continued to reverberate inside him.

THIRTY-ONE

By mid-Thursday, in the moments between helping customers and answering phone calls, David had filled Tiana in on the main details of church last night. He left out Karen Scott's suggestion that he play piano for them. He'd share that part when he'd sorted out what he thought of it.

From noon till six, certainty grew. He checked a few stores for their hours and found one open until eight. While he and Tiana locked up, David asked if she had plans. As far as he knew, her Thursdays were usually free. This one was too.

"I want to go into Traverse City," he said. "For some shopping, followed by dinner."

"Shopping?" Tiana arched one eyebrow. "What do *you* shop for?"

"Would you like to find out?"

She rolled her eyes. "You're terrible at being mysterious."

David got her coat and held it for her.

"You're hoping feigned indifference will con the details out of me. It won't work, love."

She gave him that one-sided smile. "Let's go shopping."

On the drive she guessed a few times, always wrong. Then she shifted in her seat and looked away from the passing landscape, to him.

"When did you hear from them last?"

"I talked to Simon Monday," he said, the words sitting on him with a weight that wasn't new. "He's back in Florida. Nothing from Moira. Or Zac."

"It's only been a few days."

"I know it." From Moira, he didn't expect to hear anything in the next weeks and months. From Zac . . .

"Has Zac left for Denver yet?"

David signaled for a turn and shrugged. "Not that he's said. I think he's just wandering northern Michigan."

Alone. Or perhaps he had departed, after all, but surely he'd let David know. David had texted him Monday and got no response. He was choosing to respect Zac's space, but Zac didn't seem the solitary type even in crisis. Especially in crisis.

"Let's ask him." Tiana seemed to read his thoughts. "If he is leaving, we should tell him goodbye. I might never meet him again."

"Unlikely," David said as he pulled into the parking lot.

"What do you mean?"

"As long as we belong together, and as long as I belong with them . . . your crossing paths in the future would seem inevitable."

She smiled. "I would love that."

"I'll try texting him again."

"I'd love that too."

He thumbed out ARE YOU STILL IN TOWN? and hit SEND. "Now, are you ready for the destination reveal?"

She looked out the window. "A music store?"

"Follow me."

The store was what he'd expected, having viewed pictures of the interior online. Mostly stringed instruments, only a small selection of wind. Three other customers in the store right now, two guys browsing the guitars and a girl strumming ukuleles and chatting with a sales assistant. At the back — there they were. Black-and-white keys that would soon belong to him.

"Okay, help me out here," Tiana said as she, too, stared at the pianos.

"I'm here to make a purchase."

Her mouth opened in an O.

He strode to the back, and Tiana followed him. She grabbed on to his arm, staring up at him while matching his stride.

"For your house?"

He chuckled. "No room for it at the store."

"Oh, David. A piano."

He motioned her to a baby grand. "Would you like to try it out?"

Tiana looked around the store, eyes landing on each customer, each sales assistant. "I guess that's what they're out here for, isn't it? For serious shoppers."

"And so we are."

She spun toward him, rose on tiptoes, kissed his mouth, and turned back to the piano before he could react. She sat and hesitated not a moment before pounding both hands onto the keys in a block C chord, not too loud for the environment but not unnoticeable either. And of all the things she began to play . . .

"Television theme songs?" he said when she launched into the third one of her impromptu medley.

"Nothing more fun," she said without missing a note. "But I can try something else."

"Whatever you like."

One of the sales reps on the other side of

the store kept pausing his stock work to angle a look in their direction. If no one approached them soon, David would go to one of them. For now he watched Tiana play the original *Star Trek* theme with a flair he'd never considered the melody to have. When she threw a trill into a measure in the most absurd place possible, he laughed and sat beside her.

"We owe ourselves a duet."

"What do we both know?" she said, glancing at the customers. She seemed to relax when she saw they were ignoring her.

David brought his lips close to her ear. "If it was written in the last hundred years, I've probably heard it."

"Hmm," she said, with mischief that sent his pulse into overdrive.

If she turned her head an inch, their lips would meet. In public. He straightened on the bench and settled his hands on the lower octaves, while Tiana moved hers an octave higher.

"Well," she said, "one of my favorite pop songs is 'I Will Always Love You,' the Whitney version. I taught it to myself."

"Go on. I'll add the flourishes."

"You really think this will work? I don't want to crash and burn in the middle of a music store."

"Trust me," he said.

Tiana touched the keys with a care her TV tunes hadn't called for. He kept his hands still for the first verse, soaking up the song the way she heard it, the way she recreated it. The tenderness in each ritardando, the longing in each crescendo. When she finished the song, she looked up at him.

"You didn't play."

"There was nothing to add." And oh, he wanted to kiss her.

A smile blossomed. "Thanks. But we should play something together."

"Go ahead, choose another."

"Do you know 'Beauty and the Beast'?"

He laughed.

"You told me to choose," she said with perfect deadpan.

"Oh, go on then, the right hand starts."

They stumbled a few times and laughed at each other, but Tiana had a solid sense of timing, and by the final chorus, they were both secure in what the other would play next. David let the sweetness of the melody flow from his fingers until the last few measures, which were Tiana's to play.

As the final notes faded and she lifted her foot from the pedal, the store associate who'd been eyeing them approached at last.

"Nice. Anything I can help you with?"

"I'd like to purchase this piano," David said.

The young man's eyebrows shot up into his shaggy brown hair. "Really?"

"It's not spoken for, is it?"

"Oh, no, it's just most people who come in and play a piano for a few minutes walk back out."

As he followed the kid to make his purchase, David's phone vibrated. Zac, returning his text.

NEARBY. TRAVERSE CITY.

David's mouth tugged. He thumbed in a response as he walked behind the kid. FINE COINCIDENCE. TIANA AND I ARE AT TRADEWINDS MUSIC CENTER.

He'd signed the paperwork and his payment was processing when Zac's next text came through.

WHAT YOU DOING THERE?

BUYING A PIANO.

HA.

NO JOKE.

THIS I HAVE TO SEE.

COME ON OVER.

Purchase complete, delivery date set, they could have left, but the store didn't close for another forty minutes, and given they "sounded good," the associate gave them hearty permission to keep playing.

488

"Now you," Tiana said after they attempted "Time after Time" with markedly worse results than their last duet. She stood up from the bench and grinned. "Play me something old."

"You asked for it."

He played "As Time Goes By." He let the chorus lilt then found himself embellishing in a jazzier style than the original. When he swiveled to sit outward on the bench, Tiana was staring at him.

"David," she said quietly.

"Yes?"

"I had no idea."

A warm pleasure filled his chest at the admiration on her face, but he couldn't have her thinking he was some virtuoso, regardless of what Karen Scott had said. "Keep in mind how many years I've had to hone the skill, and it's a mite less impressive."

"No, it isn't. You can be taught to hit the right keys. You can't be taught musicianship."

Indeed, a musician he was. He'd denied it for too long, told himself owning an instrument would be a waste with only the turtle to hear his music. Let himself retreat from the piano as he retreated from people.

At the front of the store, the door opened. Zac.

He was unchanged on the surface — smirk, jaunty stride, mussed hair in the twentysomething-white-guy celebrity style. No one who knew him from a distance would see any difference. But shadows lurked under his eyes, and Tiana's quick frown at David must mean she noticed them too.

Zac stared down at David seated at the piano. "No kidding."

"I play."

"Let's hope so, since you're buying the thing."

"Bought. And paid for. Being delivered this weekend."

Zac gave a slow nod. "Okay then. Hi, Tiana."

"Hi, Zac." Her smile was open, kind. "How've you been?"

"Oh, you know." He shrugged. "So what're you still doing here, if you bought it?"

"Playing it," Tiana said.

"Okay, so play me something."

"Like what?"

"Something old."

Tiana's same request, but Zac wouldn't mean 1940s old.

"Nothing specific in mind?" David said.

Zac leaned one hip into the piano's broad

curving side and ran his thumb along the propped cover. "Play 'Shenandoah.' "

Without waiting for Tiana to sit beside him, David fingered the opening bars. As he played, Zac bowed his head, bracing one elbow and forearm along the top of the piano. He nodded, more to himself than to them, and as David repeated the verse, Zac began to sing.

"O Shenandoah, I love your daughter. Away, you rolling river. I'll take her 'cross yon rolling water. Ah-ha, I'm bound away, 'cross the wide Missouri."

His voice was low tenor. Quiet, aimed at the floor, yet held a controlled power. As he sang the last line, he nearly choked up. David let the note linger. When it faded, Zac looked up.

"You sang the lyrics a little different." Tiana's voice was hushed in the wake of the song's melancholy.

"There aren't any official lyrics," Zac said. "It's one of those folk songs that kept changing." He looked at David. "Now play 'Hard Times.' "

"Ah," David said. "Remember the hard-tack version?"

Zac smirked. "Sure, but that's not the one I want to sing."

"No one wants to sing that version ever again."

"Fact."

"It's more of a fiddler's tune, I think."

"Your skill will make do." Zac took a step back from the piano, spine straight again, and a light had returned to his eyes that had been missing when he walked in. "Come on, and then they'll probably kick us out. Store's closing in seven minutes."

"Thanks. I'd have annoyed them."

"I would have stepped in if needed." Tiana smiled.

The rest of the customers had long since left, and the employees were beginning the closing process. David called to the kid who had sold him the piano.

"Any objections to a final number?"

"Nah, you guys sound good," the kid called back.

"I can't believe how long we've been here," Tiana said.

"It's a music store. I'm sure they get this all the time." Zac shrugged.

Perhaps they did. David closed his eyes a moment, hummed the tune, and began to play. It was a block-chord kind of song, and Zac's voice gained a richness as he allowed himself more volume.

"Let us pause in life's pleasures and count

its many tears, while we all sup sorrow with the poor. There's a song that will linger forever in our ears, oh! Hard times come again no more." He seemed to choke again at the rest between the verse and chorus, but David continued to play, and Zac didn't miss a word or a note. " 'Tis the song, the sigh of the weary: hard times, hard times, come again no more. Many days you have lingered around my cabin door, oh! Hard times, come again no more."

When the last note faded, David stood and nodded to the two employees closing up.

"I've never heard that song before," Tiana said as she, David, and Zac left the store.

"Stephen Foster," Zac said.

"As in 'Camptown Races'?"

"Hey, not bad." He grinned at her. "Same guy."

"I wouldn't have guessed they were the same composer at all. And by the way, Zac, did you have dinner?"

He followed them toward the Jeep. "Ah, no, actually. You guys?"

"We had a piano to buy first, and then we just kept on playing." Tiana grinned. "And now I'm starving. Join us?"

"I could do that."

They left Zac's car and drove less than a

block to a bar and grill that was mostly empty. They ordered every available appetizer — chicken wings, fried mac 'n' cheese, stuffed potato skins, fried mushrooms, pot stickers.

"This is the most heart-stopping meal I've ever eaten," Tiana said as she dipped a breaded mushroom into the ranch sauce.

"Don't make a habit of it," Zac said. "David wants to keep you around."

Tiana laughed, and maybe someday mortality would be a topic David could jest about too. Not yet, though.

"How does that work?" She snagged a chicken wing from David's plate, although the basket still held several. "Your blood organisms magically break down cholesterol forever?"

Zac shrugged. "We don't know."

"Really?"

"And that's not the only example. We call it the serum, I guess because *potion* sounds more like a witch's brew." A smirk crossed his face as he stabbed a pot sticker with his fork. "But how it works is often a mystery."

They had moved on to sharing a giant brownie sundae when Tiana said, "I think you guys know there's an elephant in the room."

David turned to look at her. She was staring at her spoon. "I suppose there is."

She looked at David a moment then at Zac, who set down his spoon and held her gaze. "I know one of you died this week. The one who left that man dead behind Appleseed. And you had to be the ones . . . to do it."

Zac swallowed, muscles straining in his jaw.

"That has to be . . . horrible."

Zac's nod was stiff.

"And Moira would be here right now if she were still in town."

"She'll come back," he said, but the words were hoarse, faint amid the drone of the restaurant.

Tiana looked from him to David as if realizing for the first time she might have somehow broken a code of conduct. "I just wanted to say, Zac . . . I'm sorry. For what you've had to go through this week."

"Thanks," Zac said.

"I'm sorry if I shouldn't have mentioned it."

"No. Really, Tiana. Thank you."

She took another bite of sundae. "I guess we should change the subject now."

At first no one did. Then Zac picked his spoon back up and dug into the hard corner of the brownie. "Hey, Tiana."

"Yeah?"

"Chicken or fish?"

Ice cream dripped from her spoon as she hesitated with it halfway to her mouth. "Um, what?"

He rolled his eyes. "You've never played This or That?"

"Oh!" She hurried to put the spoon into her mouth then licked it. "Chicken. Um . . . country or rap?"

"Eighties country or earlier, nineties rap and no later," Zac said. "So I guess my choice is country, since it has more than one decade of quality. David, dog or cat?"

An easy one. "Neither."

"That answer doesn't count," Tiana said.

"I don't want to own a dog or a cat."

"Turtle wasn't one of the options. Especially when you haven't named her."

David smiled. "Who says I haven't named her?"

"You, the last time I asked." Tiana nudged his spoon out of the way to capture the last bite with fudge sauce. "Did you change your mind?"

As he sat in their booth eating far less than a third of dessert, it came to him, as if his pet had always had this name and he'd never bothered before to ask her what it was. "I simply hadn't found it yet."

"Wait, and now you have?"

"Oh, the suspense," Zac said.

"I'm going to call her Adagio."

Tiana giggled, a sound David had never heard before. "That. Is. Awesome."

"That is unoriginal." The smirk was back. "Everyone names turtles 'Slowpoke,' you just found a more pretentious word."

"Shut up, Zac. I adore it."

"Well, if the girlfriend adores it, then . . ."

She reached over the table and shoved his shoulder. "Shut *up,* Zac Wilson."

"Stop waylaying my quest for personal information." He fake rubbed the shoulder. "So far all I've learned is that Tiana likes chicken and David sucks at this game."

They played a ruleless, laughter-filled version until nothing but a melted vanilla puddle remained on the plate in front of them.

Half an hour later, they'd returned to the music store for Zac's car. They got out of the Jeep and walked with Zac to the rental. He jingled the keys in his left hand as he stood beside the car.

"Well, I'll see you," Zac said. "Though I don't know when."

Would there be a longevite Thanksgiving with only four of them — or three, if Moira was still keeping away? The family was

497

fractured. As Colm predicted.

"When are you flying back?" Tiana said.

"I have a ticket for tomorrow afternoon, boarding at two."

"Do you think you'll ever come back here?"

Zac raked his fingers through his hair. "I think so."

"Whenever, wherever, I hope I get to see you again."

"So do I." He smiled, but it lasted only a moment. "David, thank you for everything."

David held out his hand, and Zac shook it. "I'm glad you came to Harbor Vale."

"Are you?" The shadows under Zac's eyes seemed to darken, to leach the color from his face. "Yeah, I guess the alternative is worse."

Something pricked in David's soul. He turned to Tiana. "Are you wanting to get home?"

She shrugged.

"I was thinking . . ." He had to make it sound casual. Like something he wanted to do for his own sake. "Well, if you've never been to the dunes at night, it's a fine sight. Would be a memorable send-off to our evening."

"Do you have blankets for when we start shivering in the lake wind?" She propped her hand on her hip. "Because that's unavoidable in October."

"Enough blankets in the Jeep to sit on and wrap up in."

She gave him the crooked smile, but then she sighed. "To be honest, I'm wiped out. And I don't understand why you two aren't."

"Sleep is overrated," Zac said.

"That's crazy talk."

"Well, maybe next time I'm in town. We can say our farewells here."

No. That prick in David's heart was more like an actual word.

"I'm going out to climb a dune," David said, "and I'd welcome company."

The quick arch of Zac's eyebrows wasn't part of his mask. He studied David, seeming to search for any insincerity, and then he nodded. "I'll be up for a while, anyway."

Tiana rolled her eyes. "Take me back to my car and go conquer the dunes, boys."

Zac grinned. "You know it."

In David's soul, a mission felt accomplished. He didn't know why it mattered whether Zac returned to his hotel now or in a few hours. He only knew it did.

THIRTY-TWO

Zac followed David to the first public lot past state park property — property that was, of course, gated for the night. They parked and met at the front of the Jeep, and Zac gestured at their surroundings.

"Can we get to the beach from here?"

"It's not so much a beach as a lot of sand piled up, with some grass at the bottom. The water's distant. It's about half a mile to walk."

"Cool."

They trekked a winding path down to the water and had to walk another quarter mile to an area of beach backed by dunes, none of them as grand as those in the park but still a challenging climb. They left their shoes at the base of one and started up with a blanket each. Tiana's presence would have required at least three more — a sitting blanket, a lap-draping blanket, a wrap blanket. She'd told him once about her enjoyment of sunset gazing and her list of necessities.

They'd have to do that soon.

Dune climbing wasn't an exercise anyone in poor physical shape should attempt. The cold sand squished and caved underfoot, forcing a digging in of the toes to keep from sliding backward. David's thigh muscles felt the work immediately, and his increased heart rate brought a throb to the healing gash along the side of his head.

Halfway up, Zac strayed to their right. Now he stood still, facing the water, the mostly empty parking lot at their backs.

David came up beside him and let his pulse settle, his head ease.

"You can't see the horizon," Zac said after a moment. "Or the lake. You can't see much of anything."

"No, not without a moon."

Zac shivered and rubbed his arms as the wind kicked up. "It's really dark out there."

"At night it's about the climbing experience, not the view."

"Right."

They continued on. David half expected Zac to cartwheel his way to the top, but he let David set the pace. When the throb in his head forced him to rest for a minute, Zac dropped to sit beside him in the sand.

"Go on, I'll join you presently." David gestured toward the top.

"Nah."

David sighed and pressed one hand to his head.

Zac dangled his hands between his knees. "Guess you're hoping not to see that guy again."

"Unlike you?"

"I wonder what they're like."

"My headache doesn't much care."

"Hmm."

"What?"

Zac shrugged. "You might find out whether you care to or not."

"Why would he have anything more to do with us?"

"Curiosity maybe. Or revenge."

"You think his people are being killed? By someone other than Colm?"

"Don't you?"

"The serum can't last forever."

"I might be wrong. It's just . . . something in my gut."

"I told Simon to keep me informed if he finds a way to identify them."

Zac grinned. "See, you're curious too."

When they reached the top ten minutes later, Zac sprawled on his back on one of the blankets, arms open to the stars, wind ruffling his hair. David spread his blanket and sat, knees up, arms propped on them. Far out where he knew the water to be, he might have seen the light of a boat. The wind was stronger up here, rustling the remaining dry leaves of the cottonwoods.

The energy of the trek eased away like a sigh. The night settled over them with a chilled benevolence. After a while David settled back on his elbows and tilted his head toward the inky void above. It had to be near midnight by now.

Zac got up and sat close enough for a conversation, but neither of them spoke for a long time. Maybe Zac had nothing to say. But David did.

"You need to know something. About Moira."

Zac's head swiveled toward him. "What about Moira?"

"When she left, she told me why."

"What did she say?"

"I asked her to stay and have it out with both of you. Deal with it, with what she's done. She told me Simon will forgive her, in time."

Zac's stare drilled into him. "Yeah, and?"

"You won't. You'll keep her at a distance. She said it's her fault, that she created the distance as protection for you and Simon."

Zac made a choking sound. "Protection."

"She said the distance won't be bridged now. I think that's why she left."

Slowly, Zac shook his head, then turned to stare out at the lake. "I'm supposed to — to accept her silence about the death of innocents because it was for my sake?"

David sat and waited for Zac to break the silence this time. He waited for long minutes.

"I can't," Zac said.

"She knew you wouldn't."

"David, I *can't*. They could have lived."

"Aye, they could."

"He's ruined us."

Maybe he should hold his peace now, but, "Moira said the same."

Zac drew a ragged breath. "I can't even think about him without wanting to bring him back to life so I can be the one to kill him. I've never hated a man before."

David blinked as the wind made his eyes water. He waited, though he didn't know for what.

"All the years he was killing, all the years he was terrorizing her, I was calling him my brother. My best friend." Zac lowered his forehead to his knees.

David gripped his shoulder. Zac shook with emotion as David kept his hand on him and prayed. And then he knew what to say.

"You have to mourn it, Zac."

"I will not mourn that man!"

"No, not Colm. You have to mourn what's been done to you. To all of you. Mourn for the damage inside Moira. Mourn what you believed you had. It's a hard loss. Don't deny yourself that grief."

"God," Zac said.

"He's here."

A keening, long but quiet, and then the only sound was the work to collect himself, to even his rough breathing and stop the sobs. David held on to his shoulder. Zac fell silent, at times motionless and at times shaking. Time passed.

When he lifted his head, he seemed calm, though his eyes were exhausted. David withdrew his hand. He prayed that some shard had worked its way out of a wound, that Zac would be able to heal now though he was bleeding still. He also prayed that Zac would bend his knee before God had to wrench his hip.

"We should head back."

"Aye."

But neither of them moved.

"What's in Denver?" David said at last.

Zac cocked his head at the change in topic. Shrugged. "The Rocky Mountains, skiing, natural beauty, a decent hockey team, diabolical winters . . ."

"Michigan has several of those covered, you know."

He studied David a long moment. "I guess it does."

"You have people here, in addition to diabolical winters. You can hole up if you need. And if Moira doesn't return and you decide to go after her, I'll help as I can."

Zac stood and walked away, ten yards or so across the sand. He faced the invisible horizon. He bent and planted his hands in the sand and slowly pulled his body up into a handstand. A long minute passed, easy tension in his muscles as he held himself still and then lowered his feet back to the ground and straightened up.

He walked back to David and sat in the sand, knees up, arms draped across them.

Awhile later he sighed. "Yeah, okay."

David nodded. "Good."

Shoulder to shoulder, they looked out on the night.

DISCUSSION QUESTIONS

1. This book is a collision of Christianity in the real world with a fantasy story, but *what if* there were "longevites" living today, unknown to us? In what ways might their existence fit into God's plan for humanity? As a "normal" human, do you ever ask God questions about His purposes similar to those David asks?

2. Zac, David, Simon, and Moira have no way of predicting their life span. How would this uncertainty affect your daily life, human relationships, and relationship with God?

3. Which of the books referenced in this story are you most familiar with (*The Picture of Dorian Gray, The Red Pony,* etc.)? Do the themes of these titles intersect at all with the themes of *No Less Days*? Is David this book's Dorian Gray,

or might someone else be?

4. Choosing a book's point-of-view character can be a challenge for an author. How does David's perspective shape this story? Is he always a reliable narrator? What might the story have been if told from another character's perspective?

5. Did your opinion of any of the characters change as you (and David) got to know them? Did any of them surprise you?

6. In the bookstore the night Colm is found out, when Tiana confronts David with scripture, he sees his error and confesses it. Have you been in Tiana's place, speaking truth to someone who needs it? Have you been in David's place, needing to hear truth from someone who cares enough not to back down? What past choices led David to this place?

7. When David asks Zac *why* he can't surrender to God, Zac says he doesn't know, and David doesn't believe him. Do you believe Zac? From what you know of him, why do you think he might be wrestling with God?

8. Were you familiar with the Langston Hughes poem that the quote on Tiana's wall is taken from? What do you think this quote means to Tiana? What does it mean to you?

9. Colm speaks several times about his motives for taking mortal lives, and other characters sometimes challenge his explanations. Is he consistent? Does he tell the truth about himself at any point in the book? If not, is he lying only to the others or to himself as well?

10. The longevites decide that Colm's death is the only way to protect mortals and bring about justice. Do you agree with their decision? If not, what would you have done?

11. Do you think reconciliation is possible between Zac and Moira? If so, what will it take to bring them to that point?

12. Discuss the significance of the book's title.

ACKNOWLEDGMENTS

If you took part in the creation of this book, you probably know who you are. Some of you helped unearth the bones; some helped them grow flesh; all were vital to the process, and now is my chance to say public thanks to . . .

My brainstormers and/or first readers, for friendships I cherish and also for your individual expertise: Serena Chase (Team Zac enthusiasm), Jocelyn Floyd (meteoric plotting), Kristen Heitzmann (the agelessness dichotomy), Jess Keller (Team Simon enthusiasm), Melodie Lange (romantic analysis), Emily Stevens (philosophical excavation), Andrea Taft and Charity Tinnin (all the things; you two never quit).

My agent, Jessica Kirkland, for believing in this book and in me.

My editor, Linda Hang, for lessons in style

and for making David's story the shiniest version of itself.

My lovely new house, Barbour, for saying yes, for wrapping my "kids" in a splendid design, and for all-around greatness.

My family, for love, memories, group texts both serious and silly, and togetherness. By the time this book is out, we'll have met my own first nephew!

My Creator and Father, Fount of every blessing; my Savior in whose hand I reside forever; the Spirit who nudges and pokes when I am prone to wander. Lord of every good gift, thank You for giving me stories. Thank You for David's story, and may the words of my pen be pleasing in Your sight.

ABOUT THE AUTHOR

As a child, **Amanda G. Stevens** disparaged *Mary Poppins* and *Stuart Little* because they could never happen. Now she writes speculative fiction. She is the author of the Haven Seekers series, and her debut *Seek and Hide* was a 2015 INSPY Award finalist. She lives in Michigan and loves trade paperbacks, folk music, the Golden Era of Hollywood, and white cheddar popcorn.